GOLD BOYS

GOLD BOYS
HIGH SCHOOL IGNITION

RUBY WICKED

TATE PUBLISHING
AND ENTERPRISES, LLC

Published by Tate Publishing & Enterprises, LLC
127 E. Trade Center Terrace | Mustang, Oklahoma 73064 USA
1.888.361.9473 | www.tatepublishing.com

Tate Publishing is committed to excellence in the publishing industry. The company reflects the philosophy established by the founders, based on Psalm 68:11,

"The Lord gave the word and great was the company of those who published it."

Book design copyright © 2016 by Tate Publishing, LLC. All rights reserved.
Cover design by Joshua Rafols
Interior design by Shieldon Alcasid

Published in the United States of America

ISBN: 978-1-68270-942-9
Fiction / Thrillers / Psychological
16.02.05

Respectfully, I give praise to my Heavenly Father,
all my children, grandchildren, and family members.
I would like to especially acknowledge
my oldest daughter and her husband
for their direct contributions to a few scenes.
For my true friends, thank you for your inspiration.

A day for toil, an hour for sport,
but for a *friend* is life too short.

—Ralph Waldo Emerson

So-Cal Times Movie Review

It has been a whirlwind of events for this up-and-coming new star. We found him about to receive an accolade he deserves, but it wouldn't compare to discovering just how meaningful a best friend can be. Life is dull without humor. So if you missed the opening ceremony, let me cap it for you briefly.

The Annual Movie Awards ceremony was taking place, and the host was about to announce the next category.

"Okay, let's see...Where are we? Yes...Best actor in a leading role...And my mother said a monkey could host this show. Hah!"

He turned to see what the audience was looking at. "What?" A little monkey walked up to him with an envelope and gave a thumbs-up.

"Really, Mom? You had to go there?"

The monkey jumped up into his arms and tried to feel around in his jacket.

"*Whoa*, what do you think you're doing, little anthropoid! I don't have any bananas on me."

The monkey finally pulled one out and grinned ear to ear.

"Really, you found one. Okay, Mom...

"Listen, little fella...If you're *so* smart, I wanna see you read the contents of the envelope out loud."

The monkey grabbed the card and playfully pretended to read while a narrator behind the stage said, "The nominees for best actor in a leading role are..."

The host snatched the card back and said, "I knew you couldn't! Hey, wait just a minute, you're a monkey. Why did you give me a thumbs-up?"

The monkey placed his hands on his hips and moved his lips in sync to the announcer. "Because I've seen all those movies."

The host glared at him, and the monkey handed him a paper to read, "We…just…love…your…mother."

The host turned his head and cast his voice to the announcer behind the stage, "Let's give John a *big* round of applause for all his monkey business! Oh, by the way, that's my lovely mother." He pointed to the second row. "How much did you pay him to pull that off?"

His mom answered, "The monkey? Or John?" The audience laughed out loud.

"And the award goes to…Garrett Pierce for *Constant Judgment*."

Just who is *Garrett Pierce* anyway?

He is an extremely handsome teenager with dark-brown hair—almost black. His green eyes are stunning against a golden, flawless complexion; standing 6′2″, and weighing approximately 185 lbs as varsity quarterback. A humble personality and sense of humor made him well liked; in summary, *stuck-up* does not apply to this 3.8 GPA.

Garrett is commonly referred to as G on campus. From kindergarten through eighth grade, he attended a private school but transferred to the public school, Excalibur High, in Southern California, due to their national football ranking. There was no way to foretell acting would blaze his future, and at age four, Garrett contracted with So-Cal Talent, a very distinguished agency. Commercials, still photo ads, videos, and small parts in several movies were his agenda, until landing the lead role in the movie *Constant Judgment*, where he played Taylor Smith—the youngest lawyer in history. The aforementioned accolade was about to light upon the viewers.

As the camera followed Garrett rising to the announcement, we saw him kiss his little brother on the forehead and embrace his mother for several seconds. He gave a high-five slap and a hug to his best friend, and then headed down the aisle slowly.

At that point, most of the people in the audience, as well as the viewers, knew about his tragic experience, and they began applauding as he neared the podium. Garrett walked down the aisle poised. He was happy yet extremely preoccupied; in fact, with each step, the crowd's adulation seemed to dissipate in his mind.

His head stayed downward until he gazed at the presenters to receive the award. With the statuette in hand, he turned toward the audience with a bashful smile and then glared downward again as he inoffensively delayed his words. For seconds, there was silence; au courant tears began to flow from the corners of each eye as they waited. The audience rose to their feet out of respect, anticipating his every word.

Subsequent Saga

Those streams of sorrow began a year and some earlier at his father's funeral. Garrett's dad lay close by in a bronze casket lined by a white glimmering tranquility that symbolized one of his favorite songs, "Nights in White Satin" by the Moody Blues. He played this masterpiece over and over—the one and only time he ever broke up with Barbara while dating. Thommason Edgar Pierce was a corporate lawyer and head partner in the firm Pierce, Goldstein, & Corcoran before a freak car accident ended his life. Barbara, G's mother, began the eulogy—her speech was slightly choppy.

"There aren't enough words...to illustrate...my beautiful husband." She looked at the closed casket with extreme sadness.

"Thom was our life, and I'm not sure how to move forward. When you marry someone exceptional, you realize how wonderful love can be, and I was gifted with twenty incredible years. He is a reminder to all of us that life is fragile.

"He's in heaven now…and we will see each other again one day. That is the comfort I hold on to." She wiped her eyes. "My son is so much like Thom. I was truly blessed twice, and as I look into Garrett's eyes, I'll always be able to feel the presence of a man who made life so complete.

"Thom's kindness flourished in many ways, especially engaging in charity organizations that benefited children. Thank you, everyone…for the love you have shown. Your donations to the PGC Kidz Camp were greatly appreciated by him, and with your help, it blossomed rapidly and will continue in his honor. I'll leave you with our favorite motto from the great American author Zig Ziglar: 'When you put faith, hope, and laughter together, you can raise positive kids in a negative world.'"

Mr. Lowell, Barb's father, escorted her from the podium, and the pastor concluded the funeral. It was so full; some had to view it from another room on a large screen. A sharply dressed gentleman stood alone near the exit at the back wall in the chapel. His arms were crossed. He made no sounds nor showed any emotions, except for a half smile as he left the room. Perhaps he was an old friend of Thom's. He left as quietly as he appeared.

At the burial site, beautiful music played while the pastor conducted the final message. When the casket was lowered into the ground, Garrett could not restrain his emotions and ran to it. He cried uncontrollably, and Barb wept for two.

For the next few days, they did not leave their home. One late afternoon, Barbara was sitting on a piano stool holding the calendar which had a symbol on the date of their upcoming family vacation. She put it down gently and began to play soft musical notes, but as she continued, they became erratic; keys were strummed violently, over and over, until her head plopped down on the keyboard. "I miss you so much…You can't be gone, baby. You just can't!"

Her son heard the vandalized sound and entered the room. He watched his mother in silence and then turned to focus on the family portrait taken six months earlier. Softly speaking, he said," I love you, Mom…He's still with us in spirit…always." Garrett walked over to the picture and stared for several seconds, fixated on his dad's smile, and then turned to her and gulped in tremendous agony before walking away.

Shortly thereafter, the phone rang, and on the other line was a familiar sweet voice, Barb's best friend Linda. "Hi, sweetie, I'm coming over and bringing some of my homemade chocolate chip cookies."

Barb replied, "Thank you…I need you right now."

Linda arrived thirty minutes later, and they hugged for quite some time while grievous tears burst from Barbara's eye. Linda and her husband were very good friends of the Pierces, so she recounted "good old times" as much as possible, and they found moments to laugh about funny memories. They called Garrett into the kitchen, and though he didn't stay long, he politely thanked her and willfully took a small plate of cookies to his room.

Linda smiled, "Garrett's such a remarkable kid. He really is a reflection of how well you two raised him."

Barbara suddenly remembered that Garrett had a game on Friday night and invited Linda to go. They continued chatting for a while and decided to ride together that night.

Phantasm

The first quarter of the football game was in process, and Garrett had not been playing well. The coach was concerned but for therapeutic reasons, kept him in the first quarter anyway. Garrett had constantly been glancing at the bleachers, when all of a sudden, the distraught quarterback stopped citing the play in mid-sentence. He stood up, looked over at his mother, and hallucinated. The teammates were judicious and looked at each other perplexed.

He perceived a mocked figure of Thom and abandoned the huddle, running toward the sideline and yelling, "Dad! Dad! You made it!" The coach called for a time-out, and the referee stopped the play. Coach then ran to restrain Garrett.

Barb made her way down to hold him. "Oh, sweetheart!"

Garrett looked up frantic as the image of his father disappeared. He began screaming, "No! No! Dad, No! Please no!" They assisted him off the field. The home team fans were aware of his recent loss, and the crowd had a mixed reaction as the atmosphere of the game turned somber.

There was one *kid* captivated by the sadness as he clutched the fencing. He peered inquisitively at Garrett and felt extremely sorry for him, shedding a tear. The irony of this connection? A pain he knew too well—the absence of a parent, though his were still alive.

This kid was the same age and always wanted to play football, but the conditions of his homelife would not allow it. Despite misfortune, he loved sports and was quite the trivia buff, even collecting memorabilia when possible. He would not meet G until they had a class together and unbeknownst to him, would be a favorable and life-changing event. This kid was Scholls Parker.

Egg Donor

Scholls's mother was an alcoholic who's unaffectionate and frequently belittled him. She was gone a lot at night, while his father worked the third shift in a plant; consequently, her job and playtime revolved at the bars. People had seen her with other men, and she frequently came home at the light of day. This was Tina Parker.

She's fairly nice looking, but a gaunt appearance dulled her existing beauty. With one *blurt* of censure, she could change Scholls's face to alabaster. It wasn't in her stars to have a child, and she made it known he was a mistake. Why care? Her family didn't love her and even sent her away to an aunt when she was only seven years old. Her uncle heedlessly introduced her to alcohol by age twelve. Before Tina's drinking became customary, she was an above-average student. Those desires went far and beyond a young girl's dream: a model and married to the perfect man. Hell, she wanted to become an astronaut.

Her lack of trust in men heightened at age eighteen. A professional-looking businessman approached the Hamilton family in a restaurant, contending Tina had the right look for modeling. He explained an agency needed new talent and left a card. Aunt Stella wasn't having this. She just knew it was a hoax; however, Tina found the card later that evening and called the man the following Monday.

He was interested all right. He wanted her to pose nude and audition "privately" on his couch. Easy money was tempting, but no funds were given as she abandoned the offer. Repeatedly, Tina was let down by men who seemed to love her; sadly, it was sex without ties. She was left with low self-esteem and an uncompleted education. Her psyche grew cold, and her heart grew calloused.

By the time she was twenty-two, she had treaded through five relationships, one miscarriage, and one arrest for DUI. Eventually, she met Harry Parker. He was the first man who offered to help her without requiring advances; although cautious, she decided this must be a real relationship and bit the bullet of matrimony.

His brutish personality wouldn't emerge until finances were strained, which escalated her alcoholism and increased his rage. When Scholls was conceived, she mourned the thought of losing her freedom. They never got ahead financially, and it seemed life was to remain destitute.

Instead of comforting and latching on to the baby, she did the exact opposite. What a gaffe. Scholls kept her tied down and linked to a man who was extremely moody. She had become hateful herself and hell-bent to ride out the situation for as long as possible.

The best side benefit she received from waitressing was exposure to men she could be with. Maybe one day, a pot of gold would be at the end, and using them was her way to ride the rainbow of justice. She ultimately became what she despised.

Sperm Donor

Harry Parker's a well-built man and tall at 6'4". It was mentioned he had qualified for a football scholarship in high school, but with no encouragement from his family, he lacked fortitude and barely graduated. Like so many people, the legacy of his parents went full circle. He could be physically abusive, as well as emotionally.

Harry and Tina progressed recklessly via alcohol. Their initial feelings of attraction and instantaneous love were hidden by irresolvable learned behavior. Surprisingly, Harry came from a family whose parents were still together. Their appearance of normalcy was actually a facade. Pictures on the wall were only images of a camera that captured a family who posed for show. His father was abusive, hitting the kids and his mother. He was one of six boys and very inexperienced with estrogen-driven challenges.

Tina was his true love, and the first few months of marriage were great. After the pregnancy, money was tight, and the homespun tsunami began; in conclusion, it seemed as though both parents resented Scholls's birth.

Familial Warmth

There was one uncle, Harry's oldest brother, who escaped the *genetic cesspool of losers*. Indeed, he was an honorable man. General Randolph Parker previously served in the Air Force and was currently a behavioral scientist for the FBI. He contacted Scholls by phone or e-mail and tried to fly in to see him at least twice during the year. Randolph Parker was right over six feet tall and had a distinguished appearance. He dressed dapper and on almost all occasions wore a hat, sometimes a beret, but favoring the style of early FBI agents. His life did not conform to having a wife or children. Excessive travel for the Air Force left him with only a love interest from time to time, and as usual, long-distance affairs rarely last. Scholls was his concern since Harry's parental skills were pathetic.

"Ahhh-spicious" Kid

Scholls lived in a trailer that bordered the zone, allowing him to attend the better school district. In fact, he had lived the majority of his life in a trailer and spent the vast proportion of his nights by himself. Magnified by poverty, he became quite the loner but managed to get out and do scrap jobs for money.

Never forgetting that game from last year, he revisited the memorable cries G made for his father and painstakingly shared this football kid's anguish.

Would he even grieve like that should his own mom or dad die? The thought crossed his mind but was not conclusive. In fact, he just might feel a sense of confliction. Would this be wrong? Scholls didn't understand the feeling of indifference. He just— simply did *not* know.

His appearance was grungy, and his dirty-blond hair was greasy and tousled more than halfway down his neck. The eyeglasses he wore were crooked and broken, thanks to Harry Parker's temper. Their rims bordered unkempt thick eyebrows, and underneath them lay secluded blue eyes. His clothes were not stylish by any means and a target for kids to scoff at.

Students at this school were from upper-middle-class money to varied wealth, so he stood out like a sore thumb just on appearance alone. It was common to hear things like, "Hey, does your momma shop at the thrift store?" or "Did you get dropped off at the wrong school?"

Poor Scholls, he was tarnished by his mother and classmates with limitless occurences. This kid was a warrior in the battle of flatulent people. He was incredibly smart, a straight-A student, and despite many obstacles, possessed an insatiable desire for success. He never missed school because filtering out the crap on campus was better than being home. He thrived on knowledge.

CHAPTER 1

Une Nouvelle Vie (A New Life)

THINGS HAD CHANGED in the Pierce family. Both Garrett and Barbara struggled to deal with the absence of Thom while continuing to carry on with relatively busy schedules.

Barbara decided to go back to work, teaching at a private institution for autistic children. This was a demanding job that filled personal aspirations since her little brother had the illness. She loved her siblings and always wanted a brother or sister for Garrett, but a difficult pregnancy ruled out a second birthing.

She created programs involving musical performances for the students at least twice a week. The kids seemed so relaxed and calm during the sessions, and sometimes Garrett would show up to visit them, pleasing his mother beyond words.

This school had a doctor who specialized in neurology. Barb and Dr. Peter Berg would meet and connect where the kids were concerned. While the months passed, she began to feel guilty; the physical attraction was catching up to the mental attraction. What would people think? Her husband had passed away just over a year. She confided in her friend Linda, who subdued the uneasiness by explaining that when it came to renewing your life, feelings of guilt implicitly accompany a longing for new companionship.

In fact, after the Pierces married, this subject came up. One afternoon, a TV story came on about the wife of a young couple who died after only three years of marriage. They both agreed that moving on was natural and necessary should it ever happen to them—moreover, at a youthful age. So many emotions had bombarded her mind, but she was *most* distraught about how Garrett would feel. If he objected to her *moving on*, then she would just abandon feelings toward the good doctor.

One of the main things the teacher and doctor shared in common was their unforeseen position of sole parenting. Peter's spouse claimed she fell out of love and was detached from being— even—a mother. She pleaded with him for a divorce and signed over the rights of the child. It left him devastated. How could she do this?

Leaving him was one issue, but totally wiping out the concern of her child was incomprehensible. There was little choice in the matter, and he suspected adultery; in brief, pretty confident her abandonment was due to another man. It paralleled with his biological father who took off when Peter was two. His mother, Ursula, never said anything except that he was a loser and she never wanted to speak about him again. They were never married; however, she did marry his stepdad Charles.

Each decision that was made gave new direction, producing a positive or negative reaction. Barb moved on, and it scared her.

"G" Course

Now seventeen years old, Garrett was still heavily involved with acting and modeling. Last year, he got a call from So-Cal Talent Agency that would change his life even more.

A new movie was in the works, and they needed a character to play a teenage boy who becomes the youngest lawyer in history.

Garrett didn't hesitate, and it took a total of three auditions to land the part. Of course, this meant he would have to miss school and complete on-site studies with a tutor, since most of it was filmed in California and Connecticut. When he did return to school, everyone was keyed up to find out how the movie was coming along. He, on the other hand, was excited to see the girl he missed the most. Her name was Tally, and Garrett met her on the very first day he entered the public school district.

With his urbane looks, girls didn't have a problem at all, often referring to him as G Q. Guys took to him at a slower pace. G and Tally had several classes together over the years, which created a foundation of friendship with uncharted love.

She was a very cute girl, though not in the traditional, polished way. Her brown hair was a bit uncommon, her figure was not an hour glass, and she was quite quirky. Garrett found her to be incredibly kind and funny; that was what he compounded as most desirable.

"Impromp-two"

Fate paired Scholls Parker and Garrett Pierce together in biology, and though normally the shy one, it was Scholls who decided to break the ice first.

"Hi, it's Garrett, right? I'm Scholls."

G looked at him kind of confused and answered, "You mean, pronounced like the footpads?"

"Yeah, but I'm about ten years away from the doctor part!"

G let out a quick laugh. Mr. Walker raised his eyebrows at them, and they both quietly snickered again and then exchanged phone numbers for communication on their assigned project. By mutual comments about the football team, they discovered sports were high on their list of commonalities.

Several minutes later, Garrett got up to sharpen his pencil, and a kid named Brandon stopped him. "Bro, I'm sorry you got stuck with that weirdo. You can switch and partner with me!"

G replied, "That's not gonna be necessary, dude, 'cuz I like him. He's funny, and I can tell he's smart. I don't want to change partners. If you say anything crappy to him, I might have one less friend." Brandon looked frozen.

Garrett went back to his seat and said, "Our assignment is what—*animal regeneration?*" He looked at Scholls and sent him a text: "WTF is that?"

If anyone got caught using a cell phone without permission, they could be suspended from school, so G remembered and lipped for him to explain. Scholls heard his phone vibrate, looked at the message cautiously, and then started smirking.

He whispered, "Don't worry, dude, I know what to do. We need a planarian flatworm."

G gave him a look of bewilderment, and the two began to formulate their experiment on paper. It's mind-boggling when the most popular kid in school liked just about the most unpopular kid in school, and this had classmates instantly puzzled. Eventually, they overlooked the imbalance and apprehensively started accepting the inevitable.

The bell rang, and class was out. Garrett immediately invited Scholls to come over to his house. The project deadline was a little more than two weeks away, plus he wanted to get to know him better. They had a natural flow with words, as if they had known each other for years, not fifty minutes. Garrett also had some baseball cards he wanted to give Scholls, so he sent him another text as they left the room and headed to different classes.

"Hey, can you get to my house around four thirty?"

Scholls came back to let G know the phone belonged to his dad and only used during school to communicate with his parents. He awkwardly tried to fabricate a story. Garrett just couldn't meet his mom and dad; beyond that, he's also ashamed his home was a trailer. Garrett came from money. How can he subject him to the poverty and chaotic lifestyle he lives? This guy's filmed a movie. He's a movie star.

G picked up the vibe and offered to come get him instead. Reluctantly, Scholls agreed and then began to explain the probable conditions. If his mom was there, she would be sarcastic, or possibly drunk. If his father woke up in a bad mood, he would not be pleasant. Scholls dissuaded G picking him up at 1726 Barker St. #2 by saying he would walk to the corner of Lancaster and Hollister.

"Okay, I will be in a black Hummer. See you at four thirty."

Wow, a black Hummer. He went home to find his mother Tina in a fair mood.

"What in the hell are you doing? Don't forget to make your father something to eat...and get it ready before he wakes up."

"Look, Mom, I can't tonight. I have a school project I need to work on, and my friend is coming to get me in a while."

"Bullshit! I'm going to leave soon, and someone has to feed the bear, and it damn sure isn't going to be me."

"C'mon, I don't ever get to go places, and this time, it's really important. I'm tired of always cooking. For once, I am not going to be the chef on command. I'm not getting dinner ready."

"You cocky little bastard! I have plans, and if your father wakes up to find us both gone and no dinner, he'll start his shit. Is that what you want?"

Something inside of Scholls weakened; his spirit was gone and his energy diminished. He pulled out hotdogs and began to cook them on the stove. Forever willing to avoid confrontation, he started drowning out her voice so the inner rage would stifle and he would remain obedient. He couldn't wait for her to leave. He reasoned under his breath, "Just perform the task at hand, she will get dressed and go, and then you can slip out and meet G as planned."

"Scholls! Get out here! The damn car won't start. It's the battery again!"

He walked outside, and sure enough, the car wouldn't start. Scholls said under his breath, "What the...?"

"Mom, I have an idea. Can I text my friend Garrett to see if he can help us? We are working on a project for biology, and he's picking me up down the road at four thirty. We won't have to wake up Dad."

"Oh really? So the kid must have his own vehicle. Spoiled with money, no doubt! Why isn't he picking you up here?

"Look, it was easier to give him directions from cross streets. Using the dumpsters as landmarks isn't impressive."

"So what makes you think he will just come here and help you? That rich little bastard."

"Because that's how he is. Really cool and down-to-earth."

"Okay, I will finish dinner since you came through with a plan."

Scholls knew his mom was not being nice. She was just helping to get what she wanted. Yet, for a brief minute, it did sound symbiotic. He had some good times with her as a youth, specifically when Tina read books to him, pushed him on the swing, and played hide-and-seek. What made her so hateful now? He'd grown accustomed to it. Time was a factor; eighteen would come soon enough. He sent G a text to ask for help.

Within minutes was a yes response, saying, "I'm on my way." How nice to know someone cared unconditionally. Scholls headed down to the intersection with deep thoughts. His heart was beating fast, and for a moment, he thought about just taking off with G and leaving his mother to deal with her own crap. But the house would be a living bombshell later, so he conjured up the nerve as Garrett unlocked the door.

"Hey, dude, I just want to prepare you for what you are about to see. It's not gonna be pretty. I live in a dump, and my parents can be real assholes. I almost called it off 'cuz I'm so embarrassed."

"Listen, I know things are rough for you, so don't sweat it! Your parents might actually like me. Anyway, you're *just ten years* away from the doctor part." They both snickered.

Garrett drove up and was greatly saddened as the eye-popping homestead encased his heart. He would *never* let Scholls see it. As they parked, voices were coming from inside the trailer.

"Crap, they're fighting. Wait here, dude. Let me see what's going on."

Garrett decided to walk up and made his presence after a few moments. G felt he might kill them with kindness. Most of the yelling had stopped, and when Scholls saw G at the doorway, he nervously invited him in.

"This is my mother, Tina, and my dad, Harry."

"Nice to meet both of you. I'm Garrett Pierce."

Tina said, "Bet you thought you got lost or something." Tina began to laugh. "This must be a far cry from your side of town. You're GPS probably went off. *Warning!* Income levels in this area...too low...Turn around."

Garrett winked at Scholls and didn't entertain her sarcasm by politely answering with a different expectation. "So your car needs a jump? I have cables in my truck. Let's go have a look."

Scholls' dad was pissed off after waking up early and stepped outside to see what was wrong. G explained it was not a problem, and they both jumped the car from his Hummer. Tina plopped into it before she had to deal with Harry and drove off, blowing a kiss toward the boys.

Scholls motioned his hand to Garrett. "C'mon, man, let's go. See ya, Dad."

In twenty minutes, they arrived at 11 Huntingdon Cove. It was palatial and immaculate, with a pool, tennis courts, and enough land to play football. No neighbors anywhere, just a whole area on the slope of a hill that overlooked the beautiful coastline. Right out of a magazine. Scholls had never even been near a home like this. Maybe driving by, but never in person. Inside, it smelled of lilac, Barb's favorite scent. She was not there at the time and would be home around 7:00 p.m.

"Hey, Scholls, let's get some food before we get started. Are you hungry? There's this little place down the road called Hombres...a Mexican food joint. You do like Mexican food, right?"

Of course, he did, but it was the money *he* didn't really have to spend—because what he earned went for summer funds. Garrett assured him it would be okay and he would pick up the tab. This weighed heavy on Scholls because he did not take advantage of people and pledged to pay it back soon. Hombres was a nice quiet place, perfect for strategizing the project and learning more about each other.

"So…you gotta fill me in on this animal regeneration thing. It sounds complicated, and it sucks we got stuck with this assignment?"

"Dude, we got lucky 'cuz this is super easy and really interesting. Have you read about stem cell research? Well, we'll get to see it in action. The planarian flatworm is capable of regenerating its own body…even after being cut multiple times."

"What! You're messing with me?"

Scholls shook his head and began to educate Garrett. "We need a Petri dish, a marker to identify our dish with our initials, the time and dates of the experiment, some DETAIN solution which helps to sustain the process, spring water, a small art paint brush, and a scalpel to cut them. We probably don't need to cut them up multiple times, but at least four or five worms differently. We'll figure it out. Then we put them in a dark area where they will begin to grow back their body parts and multiply…heads, tails, et cetera!"

"Man, *no way*! You're kidding me?"

"Yes way. I'm not bullshitting you, dude. They even retain their old memory when you cut off their head, and it grows back."

"Awesome. Never heard of this. Now I can't wait to do it. I can even borrow a scalpel from my mom's boyfriend. Well, actually, her fiancé. The wedding is in eight days."

"Garrett, can I ask you a question, and if I'm out of line, will you just tell me to shut up and mind my own business? How ya doing since your father passed away?"

"It's hard, especially when I played a lawyer in the movie. But I applied mimic acting based on his techniques, and this made me feel better. It really felt like he was there helping me."

"That's cool."

"Anyway, it's not just the aching you feel but also dealing with the pain your mother has to go through. Man, she wouldn't stop crying every day for months. I never thought I would ever have to learn to live without a father. That's stuff you hear about and don't process until it finally happens to you. My dad was always there to support me in anything I did. He was so caring with people. They always joke about how lawyers are conniving and dirty and that they just want money. My dad really enjoyed helping people. I'm a lot like him. I always want to help people who are less fortunate."

"I know that's right. Look at me. I'm about as less fortunate as they come, dude."

G rolled his eyes playfully.

"I miss him when I need advice, like…advice about football. He was at my practice games as well as real ones. I thank the Higher Being for my life. Do you believe in God? Myself…I'm not sure if the title is correct, but I know we have to be stupid not to know there is something so powerful it can create life."

"For sure…I do know that I have a guardian angel out there, a Higher Being. Call it spiritual, or whatever, but it exists. We don't go to church or anything. I just read the Bible occasionally. I watch shows. They've been able to create sperm or eggs from existing skin cells…but *not* from scratch! Mostly, I take into accountability how bad it could really be. I'm poor with effed-up parents, but I could be a cannibal on an island or born severely deformed."

"No lie! Makes you put things into perspective. But, yes, I miss him dearly. Mom's new guy is okay, but I'm not sure I want him around full-time. Sometimes he acts weird."

"Like how, dude?"

"It's just this feeling I get with him. He seems to like me, but I catch him staring at me, and it's almost eerie. The cool thing about him is his son. I like that little guy. He's kinda like my shadow. His name is Casey. He's eight. I'm trying to teach him to catch a football. It's so damn funny when he runs out and turns around and the ball hits him in the head 'cuz he puts his arms up and then suddenly moves them away. I use the Nerf balls so he doesn't get hurt. I think he's more the computer nerd type." They laughed.

"How did your mom meet him?"

"Good question. Still don't know if I can pinpoint the exact moment. He's a doctor at the facility where my mom works. She started talking to him on the phone, even asking me if it was okay. I told her I never expected her to be alone the rest of her life, but secretly I wanted her to be. *Maybe* 'cuz I'm nervous about any more changes. Either way, I gave her my approval. They dated, and now they are getting married. *Maybe* it's a little fast, but I'm not in their shoes. *Maybe* she sensed the same comfort level I did with you. Who knows?"

Scholls commented, "Wow, a doctor. That's cool. I'm glad for your mom. My parents really don't need to be together. They seem unhappy with each other, and all they do is put the other one down. It sucks. Love is complicated. I hope I have better chances. Hell, using them as a template should help quite a bit. You gotta girlfriend?"

"Nah, but I guess there's one chick I really like. I hesitate to get too involved with anyone. Between football and acting, my time is limited."

"Who is it? Anyone at school?"

"Yeah, it's Tally Martin. Do you know who she is?"

"I'm pretty sure I do. Does she hang around with this blond-headed chick named Tabitha? They usually sit together in the student lounge."

"Yep, that's her. She's not a knockout like Elena Duggins or Allison Steinbeck, but she is a whole hell of a lot nicer! And she thinks my jokes are funny. I'm comfortable talking to her. I don't feel like I have to skate around her words *like totally*—Ha! Some of these chicks are ridiculous. All that bod with no brains or personality. What a waste!"

"You ain't lying. At least you have choices, G. Bods, brains, airheads, etc. No one talks to me. I barely get any glances unless they are checking out my super fly outfit for the day!"

"Man, you crazy, Scholls! Hey, not trying to embarrass you or anything, but I believe I have some clothes that will fit you."

"Dude, really? I wasn't trying to get you to fix up my threads."

"Nah, I know that. I just have too many frickin' clothes. We're about the same height. When we get back, Ill check out my closet and see if you want any of my stuff."

"Man, I feel funny. We've only known each other a few hours… Well, at least formally…and I'm already your charity case."

"It's not like that at all. I just have tons of clothes. So why not give them to a friend. We give plenty of things to real charities. By the way, are you gonna go to the homecoming dance?"

"Unlike Cinderella, I'm a peasant *all* night. I haven't even given it a thought. I do see they nominated you for king, so you got my vote, Garrett. But yeah, I wouldn't even know how to get there, have anything to wear, or for the most part, a girl to take. Hell, I can't even dance well. In junior high, I went to one and pretty much was ignored. So dances are not high on my list. But thanks for asking."

"I just might have a plan for that. My wardrobe stylist is outrageous. He makes me laugh all the time. I can ask him to help get you ready."

"C'mon, really, G? That's way too much. One thing I need you to realize is that I am not an opportunist. I know your story, and I'm not going to use you for clothes or girls or anything. Shortly after your dad passed away, you were playing a football game, and I was at the fence watching you. Dude, I felt sorry for you. It was pretty messed up 'cuz you ran toward the bleachers and thought you saw your dad. I wanted to get to know you, but we were from two different worlds. People were talking about your situation, and I felt a connection I couldn't explain. And now here we are, becoming friends. I know I can't offer much except my friendship. Just know I don't expect anything from you. I saw you on campus many times and thought you were cool, not at all like most the other athletes. You *always* seemed cool and even said hi to me when we passed in the halls. So I need to hear that you know where I stand and what I am saying."

"Dude, knowing you cared for me when you saw me hallucinate is something that just touched my heart. I'm a good judge of character, and that's why we connected so fast. I could have a friend for years and never mesh on the same mental level as we did in just one day. Please never feel like you are my charity case. I just want to give you some clothes and have Randy, my wardrobe stylist, lend a hand. When it comes to style, he's got a great eye. We have become close since filming the movie. He loves challenges. Just kidding, man!

"Seriously though, I want to hang out with someone I can laugh and joke with. Sure, I have lots of friends on campus, but no one I hang out with socially on a routine basis. There's something about us that just clicks…like finding that piece of a puzzle you need! I'm taking Tally, and she may know a girl who can be your date. We will borrow wardrobe clothes from the set. That's one of the perks in acting."

"Let me get back with you on the whole homecoming thing. It's a month away, and I have some odd jobs lined up. I can earn some money by then. Maybe I should meet this Randy one day, I mean, if I decide to go through with it. Now, let's get back to the project. We got this made!"

"Oh yeah, so I can't believe they can just grow back their whole body parts after being cut off. How do you know about this shit, Scholls?"

"Let's see. Me, home 90 percent of the time, if I'm not at school, mow yards, clean garages, and read. You, filmed a movie, play quarterback in football, do charity work with your mother, model, golf on the weekends, and do miscellaneous activities with family or friends. *So...you still wondering why I have time to know this stuff?"* G just looked at Scholls with a slight smile. "Now, the better question is, how much can we get accomplished in two weeks? Actually, we should see initial results in just minutes. These creatures reproduce fast. I think we should document with pictures in stages and also set up for video."

"Sounds good to me. You need to be the lead in this project. This is your niche."

They finished their food and headed back to Garrett's place. He went through his stuff and found a few shirts and shorts to give Scholls. When his mom arrived, G walked out of his room alone and greeted Barb with a big hug. He wanted to borrow a scalpel from Peter.

Barb's eyes rose as she asked, "What are you planning to do with it?"

"We have a project in biology, and we need it to cut up our... uh? Hey, Scholls, what's that thing we're cutting up?"

Scholls came out of the bedroom and said, "Planarian flatworm."

"Oh, hey, Mom. Sorry...This is my friend Scholls."

Barb reached to shake his hand. "It's very nice to meet you. Are you new at Excalibur High?"

"Uh...no, ma'am, we have a class together, and well, now, we're paired up for this experiment."

"Yeah, Mom. Hit it off immediately. It's amazing how easily we just talk and laugh. He loves sports like me. So can you ask Peter for me? Pretty please, with sugar on top?"

Barb replied, "Absolutely. In fact, in about thirty minutes, we can all go to dinner."

"Well, actually, we already ate. And we are working on our project. Is Casey coming?"

"Of course, he lives with Peter. You do know his mother left them? He's going to be your legalized brother through adoption."

"For some reason I didn't know his mom did that. Maybe you told me early on. Why did she go?"

"Let's keep this subject for another time. I'm sure you and Scholls—am I saying it right?" He nodded yes. "Have other things to talk about, and I need to change. It was great to meet you, and I will cook dinner one evening very soon and have Garrett invite you."

"Sounds great! It was nice to meet you, Mrs. Pierce. Bye."

Garrett thought about what she told him and said, "Man, I like that little guy so much. His mother sucks."

"How old do you think he was when his mom left?"

"I'm guessing he was real young, 'cuz Peter never mentions her, and come to think of it, he never even speaks of a name. I really don't get into deep conversations. Like I told you earlier, there is just something about him that doesn't seem right. Hell, if I told my mom that, she would think I was just judging him prematurely or think I was jealous. Which I'm not, but then again, I am a *mama's boy*. Ha."

"You're funny, *mama's boy*. Now let's get back to the worms!"

It's about 7:30 p.m., and suddenly, they felt the bed move. Casey ran into G's room and jumped on the bed.

"Hey, little guy, what's up?"

Garrett introduced Casey to Scholls. He continued to jump, and they played with him for a few minutes.

Scholls asked Casey, "You wanna see what we're doin'?"

Casey answered, "Yeah."

"Okay…Look at this picture. You see those tiny little worms?"

"Uh huh."

"We will cut them into pieces, and they will grow back together in about a week or so."

"Wow, that's cool! But wait…Will they feel it?"

G said, "Good question. I suppose they might. Tell you what, I will ask one of them and get back to you on that." He chuckled.

"You're funny, Garrett. I like you being my big brother. My dad says that he will make sure you are taken care of."

"Did he now? Huh?" He looked at Scholls and raised his eyebrows to give him a look of uncertainty. Garrett told Casey he needed to speak to his father, and they walked into the living room where Barb and Peter were sitting. After the introductions, they began talking about the experiment, and Barb mentioned the scalpel. Naturally, Peter offered to get one the next day from the hospital. At 8:50 p.m., the boys wrapped things up for the night.

G told Scholls, "Man, did you hear that earlier? *He will make sure I am taken care of?* What the hell does that mean?"

"Dude, I think he means he is going to take care of you in a good way…like he cares for you. He's gotta know you miss your father and maybe he's trying to help fill the void."

"Well, I don't need him to fill the void. He just needs to be good to my mother, and her happiness is all I care about. I'm going to college after this year. Hell, I might even pursue more acting jobs. I don't know."

"Is there anything he's done in particular that makes you think he is weird?"

"Well, it's the way I catch him looking at me sometimes."

"What do you mean? Maybe he just studies you 'cuz he doesn't know you. How long does he look at you?"

"Just a few seconds, but it's creepy. He stares right through me. Does that make sense?"

"Could? When you guys talk, is he nice? What kind of things does he talk about?"

"Different stuff. Mainly about my mom and random chitchat. We haven't really had many one-on-one encounters."

"Dude, it sounds like he cares. After all, he is the odd man out. He knows you and your mom are close and definitely needs to establish a bond, so what a better way to do it than through your mother."

"I guess you're right. I can't think of one bad thing he has done. I suppose my mom is happy, and maybe just the mere thought of someone in my dad's shoes makes me pessimistic. He did offer to help me choose colleges. And he does seem to take real good care of Casey. I guess my mind is still foggy when it comes to the whole marriage thing. The wedding is next week."

"Well, dude, just relax and make the best of it. Your mom deserves to have someone love her, and he's never gonna take the place of your dad. From the stuff you told me at the restaurant, your father was terrific. I could only dream of what that would be like. Mine is combative and a loose cannon. Let the chips fall. Give it time." Deep inside, Scholls stored this information but on the surface appeared to be unconcerned.

Garrett surmised, "I guess you're right. Don't really have a choice 'cuz life goes on whether we like it or not. Hey, man, you'll know what it's gonna be like when you have your own kids. You're a good person who's driven. I'll know 'cuz our friendship *isn't* going to fade after high school. I see us old and gray and going to the race tracks!"

"Yeah, I can too! Okay, we need to go after school tomorrow and get the stuff for our project. I think I have a Petri dish in my room. We'll buy the rest of the things."

"Cool, but tomorrow and Wednesday I have practice for football. We have an away game this Thursday night. I finish around 6:30 p.m. So I will be at your house around seven."

"That'll work."

G dropped him off and smiled about his new friend. Scholls felt relieved. His dad was gone and his mom was out at the bar working. She wouldn't come in 'til early morning, and he could just get up and head to school as usual. He pondered about how much they had in common; it's as if two people of the same womb were separated and placed in different socioeconomic environments. He was grateful for their merge in class.

CHAPTER 2

Lurching Links

ALL THE GUYS gathered around Coach Johnson. The away game on Thursday night was against St. Clair High. Such a great team—they had always been a huge challenge in the district. Those guys looked like they ate steroids for candy. As the coach went over the plays, G began to feel a bit dizzy. He had been having some blurriness with his eyes as well. He knelt down.

"What are you doing, Pierce, praying for us?" They all laughed.

G got up and said, "No, coach, I was just dizzy for a minute. I'm good." They broke apart and started practice.

Garrett threw the ball far. This was one of his greatest abilities as a quarterback. When he was small, his dad challenged him to throw the ball through a homemade target with a circle cut out. Each week, Garrett would have to master throwing it inside the circle five consecutive times before he could move it out—five feet farther. Thom called it five-for-five. This helped him to be accurate and have the strength to throw far. G always admired the old-schoolers in football. He really liked Roger Staubach, John Elway, and Joe Montana.

Toward the end of practice, Garrett staggered. He shook it off and thought maybe he might be worn-out or possibly getting a virus. At home, he took some medicine, changed, and then headed over to Scholls's place. G inquired, "Hey, where do we buy these worms?"

Of course, Scholls already had the info, and he told G, "Well, dude, we need to drive about forty minutes or so to the Wiggle Worm Farm."

"C'mon? It's really called the Wiggle Worm Farm?"

"No lie. That's what they call it. They sell biological supplies. The guy on the phone said they are cheap in price and easy to breed if we want to go into that business. LOL. They sell all kinds of worms, so our options are wide open. I'd like to buy a few red worms and place them in my parents' bed." "Now that would be hilarious. You need to be close with a vid cam so you can put it on YouTube."

"Now you're thinkin'. We could pull the ultimate prank on people with our worms."

"I knew there was another reason I gravitated so quickly to you...'cuz you're incredibly funny and have distorted humor like me. It's nice to know we have a backup plan should our careers tank."

"Yeah, you could star in your next movie about the youngest worm farmer ever to succeed. A story on how this child who was institutionalized, developed a friendship with Willy the Worm, and they conquered their fears. Willy's...never to be eaten or used for bait. Yours, to protect the innocent from harm...playing now at your nearest theatre."

"Okay, only if you are the movie director. And you have a beautiful costar for me that isn't a worm...maybe a girl who speaks French in my ear and makes me proud of the worm farmer I am."

"It's all good. I can see the money rolling in now." They laughed. "Back to reality, I will give you some gas money and buy the supplies. I saved money from mowing yards. I also have the money for the food you bought me at Hombres. Just didn't have it on me at the time."

"I told you it was on me, bro. As for the gas, I fill up weekly from the initial funds they paid me for my part in the film. You can buy the worms if you like."

"So where's the wedding being held?"

"At the Gran Palazzo De Cote."

"I don't know where that is. I bet it's gonna be the bomb. The name even sounds like it."

"Scholls, did you grow up in California?"

"Nah, we came here from Arizona when I was eleven. I grew up in Phoenix. My dad got a job with GWP, and here we are. He has steady work, but he doesn't have a high school diploma, so I'm guessing he won't be climbing too many rungs up the ladder."

Garrett was still having some slight dizziness while he and Scholls were talking. He didn't want to make a big deal of it 'cuz he had vertigo before, and it was from his environmental allergies.

"Rube-hicks" Cube

G said, "Don't sweat it. Not everyone in my family has a higher education. I have cousins in Texas that get drunk all the time. They work scab jobs, and hunting is their life! Sometimes when they hunt, it is out of season and illegal, but that never stops them. They just jump in there four-wheeler and ride around drinking till it's time to get to the deer stand. And the stories they tell are effing hilarious. Same ones you're gonna hear over and over. By midnight, the doe is now an eight-point buck. By 3:00 a.m., that buck now has twelve. Those campsite parties can be a combination of sophisticated hunters, hillbillies, and outsiders. There's even an occasional lease lizard."

"What's a lease lizard?"

"Well, let me put this gently…an unglorified, wavering female who solicits romance for the night on someone's deer lease."

"Damn, there's hope for me yet!" They both started laughing.

"My cousins rarely leave a radius of twenty miles, unless they are in need of hunting supplies or alcohol. Most of them hang around their friends from childhood. It was a trip to meet them when we went to a family reunion. Why lie? I mean, it was a funeral, which they dubbed as a family reunion." They both smirked. "And that's not all. They live in a trailer you can barely see as you drive up. I mean, their yard is something else. Topped with mounds of empty beer cans and the weeds are so high. I'll let you vision it."

"You're just making that up, dude. Really worse than my place?"

"Hey, your trailer may need repairs due to its age, but your yard is pretty clean. Theirs…hhhmmm. Inside, you'll need to keep a straight face, 'cuz hoarders is putting it lightly! I asked my uncle why he collected so much stuff, and he said, 'Your aunt goes to all those garage sales, and if I try to throw anything away, I might as well go deaf, 'cuz I'm gonna hear backlash for months.' Funny thing, my dad didn't blink an eye. He prepared us for it. But, bro, something like that really has no impact until you see it."

"So it's your dad's side of the family?"

"Yep, and he had not seen them for years. The kids have redneck rhythm."

"Redneck rhythm. You funny, G."

"Heck, sometimes I think they have it easy. I mean, I feel sorry for them in lots of ways, but they don't really give a damn too much what people think. I kind of admire that about them, but it's a double-edged sword. For instance, my cousin Bubba shot his gun off into the ceiling of their mobile home, and no one even got mad. He said he was cleaning his gun, and they just went outside, got a board and some duct tape, patched it up, and laughed all night."

"Did he really do it accidently?"

"I'm not sure. Bubba has random tantrums. He gets drunk and no telling what he thought."

"What! He's allowed to drink and get drunk as a teen?"

"Uh huh. Sure is. They started giving him beer when he was a small kid. I guess they figure it's better he drinks with them instead of sneaking out to drink." He shook his head side to side. "Redneck cousins! Gotta love 'em."

"Wow, it sure would be crazy hanging with them for a day or two. So what else has he done?"

"Supposedly he throws a fit when he doesn't get his way. He's spoiled. Once, he shot holes in his father's deer stand because he was grounded from hunting. That's like taking away a *cell phone* for you and me. Instead of being punished, they laughed, let him hunt again, and ended up calling it 'holy territory.' They think it's funny. If you or I were to do that, we would definitely be in trouble."

"Yeah, you see my glasses. They're broken for a reason."

Punchy Chit-chat

G said, "You know, I was going to ask you about that but didn't want you to think I was prying. What happened to them?"

"One wound-up Harry Parker backhanded me for leaving the lights on all night. He's usually home around eight in the morning, and it was a weekend, and I was so tired I fell asleep and didn't turn them off…or the TV in the living room. He fights with Mom all the time about money. Anyway, he woke me up and began yelling at me. I could smell alcohol on him. That usually means he has been recently fighting with my mom. For some reason, I started to defend myself for being—excuse me—normal and capable of not being perfect.

"He took it as me being a smart-ass and *wham!* My glasses flew off my face, and I felt his knuckles hit my eye. I patched them up with superglue, 'cuz I can't see things well without them. They're a bit crooked, but good enough."

"Man, Scholls, I had no idea. It's hard for me to hear this. How often does he hit you?"

"It varies…once or twice a year. I stopped counting when I was younger. This past year has been lots better. Something really bad has to happen before the volcano erupts. As long as they stay on their schedules, I don't have to see them much. When I need papers signed, I sign them. I filled out the original registration paperwork, and the school thinks my writing is their signature. That way I don't ever have to worry about them forgetting."

"Bro, that's pretty damn clever!"

"Works for me!"

"Seriously, man, I'm not even use to the idea he can just up and hit you. If that happens again, get a hold of me somehow. You can stay at my house. I just don't want him to hurt you."

"Thanks, I appreciate that. I look at it like this, G. I only have the rest of our senior year, and I am bound to be gone. My uncle works for the FBI but retired from the Air Force as a general, and he's pledged many times to help me succeed. I'm going to take him up on it, if I have to. He's the oldest brother on my dad's side. I hardly know my other uncles. Oddly, I do love my dad. I think he harbors resentment about my mother's affairs. It's strange to love someone and intermittingly hate them at times… really strange. The older I get, the harder it gets for him to hit me. No one is truly close in our family. I don't even know most of my relatives. Now our friendship…we seem like brothers who were split apart at a young age and reconnected."

"Yeah, that does seem strange…with your dad and all. I believe you and I were meant to meet. So my long-lost bro, how much farther does the GPS say we have 'til the worm farm?"

"Approximately three miles."

As they pulled up, G's mother called, "Are you guys there yet?"

He explained they just arrived and should be back in about an hour and a half.

Barb asked Garrett, "Honey, do you feel better now?" Scholls overheard as G described what he felt like that day.

This store was fascinating, to say the least. Scholls found a clerk and asked, "Hey, mister, do you know where the planarian flatworms are?"

He guided them to the worms and went over all the precautions. Generally, they liked liver and egg yolks. He studied Garrett's face and said nothing, though his eyes did the talking. Just wearing a hat wasn't going to be an effective solution for privacy as the movie was slowly climbing the ladder in ratings. It wasn't long before they purchased all supplies and headed back.

Peter brought the scalpel to the house; finally, their project would get underway. Because it was getting late and Garrett had been to practice that day, G dropped Scholls off on the way home.

The next morning at school, they made plans to get together that Friday night. Garrett eagerly asked Scholls to spend the weekend. It had been years since anyone invited him to spend the night, and he felt elated about their mutual friendship. Garrett didn't just like him in school, but he genuinely liked him. Why was this so hard to believe?

Quasi Compassion

The football game ended in a loss for Excalibur High. Garrett was upset after throwing an interception in the second half that caused them to miss a much-needed touchdown. In the fourth quarter, he was hit hard and knocked back. The athletic director and staff ran onto the field. He didn't move for several seconds; Coach Johnson removed him from the game. His eyes were dancing a bit, and he was sluggish. They notified Barb, and she came to pick him up.

"Oh, Peter, honey, I need you to see Garrett as soon as possible. He got hit in the game and was hurt. They suspect it could be a concussion."

Dr. Peter Berg replied, "Sure, sweetheart, bring him to me, and we will head to the hospital. Lay his seat back about forty degrees."

Dr. Berg had direct connections to the ER of the hospital where he did his residency and currently still treats patients. His poise and mannerisms were admired by everyone. Ten minutes before they arrived, he set up a private room for the star's examination. Normally they would go through triage, but Dr. Berg informed the ER admittance to bring him back ASAP, and he would have

Barb do all the necessary paperwork when he examined his soon-to-be stepson. Garrett was escorted to the room, and Peter said, "Son, I hear you took quite a blow. How are you feeling now?"

"My head hurts…like a bad headache, and I'm still a bit weak."

He examined him using the Glasgow Coma score and had the nurse call the phlebotomist to draw his blood. She left the vials so Dr. Berg could take them to the lab. No one questioned him on anything because this was his family.

He explained to Barb that he would hold off on scheduling a CT. However, if Garrett's headache did not go away or he showed signs of fine motor skill impairment, reduced vision, speech problems, significant drowsiness, or difficulty in awakening, he would scan his head tomorrow afternoon. Then Barb and Peter stepped into the hall.

"Honey, what would a CT of his head show?"

Peter replied, "If the symptoms I mentioned occur, he could have an intracranial injury."

"Oh god, no, I'm scared."

Peter held her tightly. "Baby, he's gonna be fine. If I thought it was serious right now, believe me, I'd order the CT immediately. He needs to miss school tomorrow. Let him rest and check on him every couple of hours through the night. Ask him how his head is when he wakes up. We will fill Garrett in on the symptoms as well. I gave him some acetaminophen for his headache."

Dr. Berg loved this woman to the point of obsession. He hated sharing her love with Garrett. For now, he would have to.

"Honey, can't you give him something stronger?"

"It's best to use OTC medications for now. I need to see if his symptoms are still present. We need to limit his use because there are studies that show excessive analgesic use with concussions can exacerbate, or increase the severity of, chronic posttraumatic headaches in adolescents."

"It's just that Garrett has been a bit blurry eyed for a while, and I want to make sure he is fine."

"Sweetheart, he's my stepson now, and I won't let anything happen to him. His Glasgow score was thirteen, and that is pretty good results. I'm gonna check everything in his blood to make sure there is not an underlying issue. I love you, babe, and your son is in the best of care now."

"I love you too. I'm so thankful you are in my life."

They kissed sweetly. Garrett waited for their return and cut up with the nurse. She studied his face intensely, and his eyes were a dead giveaway. "Aren't you the actor in that movie *Constant Judgment?*"

"Okay, I am, but please don't say anything."

Nurse Martha said, "Absolutely, you are Dr. Berg's son, and your visit is confidential. I would be violating HIPAA laws. Would you sign my stethoscope? This thing's fifty years old, and I treasure it. I'm so excited. I just saw the movie this past weekend."

"I'd be happy to. What's your name?"

"Martha."

"Okay, how's this? For Martha, my caring nurse, Garrett Pierce." He dated it. "You can tell people you met me at a charity event for the hospital." He winked.

"That's wonderful. Thank you so much! I hope to see you in more movies."

Peter and Barbara came back in to educate Garrett of all the possible latent symptoms. He didn't want to miss school on Friday but needed their podiatrist to check his foot that was sprained. By all accounts, he insisted on going through with his weekend plans that included Scholls.

Barb promised, "If all is well, you can still have your friend over."

While heading home, G thought about the game. *Why did Tally have to see it?* His feelings were rapidly changing for this girl. It would be even more awkward facing her after what happened because he took the team to a loss and that's embarrassing. Oh, then there's homecoming. Is he going to blow that game as well? Due to the circumstances, he *wouldn't* be in their math class tomorrow and needed Tally to ask someone if they would go to the dance with his friend.

Excalibur was missing the most popular student, leaving Scholls to discover what happened through gossip. He decided to use the phone. Garrett didn't answer, so he left a detailed message, and when G finally woke up, he sent a response to Scholls, expecting him as planned—5:00 p.m. Then G called Tally, and she picked up the phone.

He said, "Hi, how's it going? Got a minute?"

"Hi, Garrett, yes. How are you doing today?"

"I really screwed up the game last night…from what I heard. I don't exactly remember the hit and fall. The band on the other hand played awesome new tunes. I'm doing much better."

"Why, thank you, Mr. Pierce. Just don't be hard on yourself. I was terribly worried about you and would have called last night, but I knew it was best to wait until today. You must have ESP. I was about to call you. Thank you for putting my mind at ease."

"My soon-to-be stepfather is a doctor, and he examined me. My headache went away and I feel better today. I won't let the school down next time. You'll be at the homecoming game, right?"

"Yes, Garrett, the band usually shows up for every game."

"Oh, yeah, duh, you're right. Great! Don't forget to give me a wave in the stands. I mean…uh…if you get the chance."

"No problem, you're the cutest quarterback on the team."

"Hey, I was wondering, can you do me a huge favor? Will you ask one of your friends to be Scholls's date for the homecoming dance?"

"Who?"

"Scholls…from our school."

"You mean Scholls Peterson or Parker or something? The kid who is shy and kind of a loner?"

"Yeah, him. We've recently began hanging out, and he's cool. He may be a loner, but that's because a lot of people treat him crappy, so he just doesn't associate with too many kids. I found out we're like soul brothers."

"Huh, interesting...Okay, I guess I could start asking girls I know. I can't promise anything, but I will give my best effort."

"Good. Thank you so much. Just let me know if you have any luck."

They talked a bit more and hung up. Garrett dialed up Randy next.

"Hey, Randy, it's me, Garrett. I need a favor and hope you can pull it off."

CHAPTER 3

Dandy Randy

HE's JUST ABOUT the best wardrobe stylist in Hollywood. This gay African American was one fashion guru. He'd make you try on outfits until he got the "click." He made this clicking noise with his tongue—*click, click, click*—three times in a row. When you heard that, you need not to try on anything else. He'd look you up, down, around, and back again, and of course, no one questioned his techniques or finished products. After all, he'd earned that much respect.

Most people didn't know he was a teacher in his twenties who taught science and math. He was considered to be the best-dressed teacher in his district.

Frequently, he would go to the studio with his partner, who was an actor on the nighttime drama *Desperado*. He volunteered to help piece together outfits, and the casting director loved them. Soon, they asked him to be an assistant stylist on the set. The pay scale was $8,000 more a year than his teaching gig, so leaving was a no-brainer.

His humor was icing on the cake. Quick witty comments are his specialty, and if he liked you, you were a target. If he didn't, you just didn't exist. He ignored people who annoyed him. Within five years, Randy managed to impress the right people, which led to his transition as lead stylist, frequently requested for television or movies; his salary was now top level.

Randy replied, "Sure, Garrett, what you got?"

"I have this friend who is challenged, and he needs to be, well, made over."

"Huh, mentally challenged?"

"Oh, sorry, I just mean he is economically challenged."

"So you need *super smooth* to fix up a white kid that was born on the other side of the tracks? I didn't think your school could take anyone who wasn't driving a sports car or luxury SUV. Child, please, what's his real story?"

G laughed. "The story is, he lives just on the border of our school district in a trailer park. His parents aren't supportive, but he has managed to be an honor roll student, and he's my biology partner. We've only known each other a few days, but we connected super fast. People treat him like shit, and I want to take him under my wing 'cuz he is one of a kind. I guess I want him to do things he probably never would get to do while he is young. He needs help in the *swag* department. Can you fix him up for our homecoming dance?"

"You never cease to amaze me, Garrett. When is it?"

"A few weeks from now."

"Well, if you want me to work miracles, I need to meet this Po'thing? Bring him tomorrow if you can. I'll meet you boys at the studio dressing room. How big is he, roughly?"

"He's about my build, thinner than me, and nearly the same height."

"What color hair does he have?"

"Good question, I think its blond, but it is greasy and it looks brown, but then again, it looks more blond sometimes, but then again…"

"So he's a chameleon dragon? Okay, what about his eyes?"

"Uh…I'm not sure…blue, maybe brown?"

"Now, see, honey, if you *weren't* straight, you'd know. One more detail, is he pale or tan?"

"Huh, he's sort of tan…not really pale…definitely not pasty white."

"Okay, I will get some ideas going, and see you guys tomorrow around noon. Ciao, baby!"

Garrett can't wait to see what Randy will do. Feeling confident, Scholls had potential behind his broken glasses and messy hair. He still wasn't sure if his friend would have a date for the dance. G did have one ace up his sleeve. If Tally has no luck, he would just have to pay someone to be his date. Yeah, that's what he's going to do. The furthest thought from his mind was that Scholls was too nerdy. He really wanted him to go, and not as a third wheel. No one had to know. He'd find a girl from the movie set or maybe one from the gym.

It doesn't matter—whoever she is will be cute and nice. His friend deserved to experience what every senior should; few classmates ever gave Scholls a chance. Garrett wished he had met him sooner because this guy was going to be his best friend. G picked up Scholls at 5:00 p.m. like clockwork.

Peter appeared very concerned about his condition and told Garrett he can resume football in a couple of days. They worked on their experiment till 10:00 p.m., and before they shut their eyes, G let Scholls in on his plan with Randy.

"Oh, by the way, tomorrow we are going to the major film studio that produced the movie I was in."

"Really? You don't have to do all this."

"I'm gonna tour you around, but there's one catch."

Scholls thought for a second and said, "Let me guess…Randy. Apparently you are set on me going to homecoming. I doubt I can get a date unless we call up one of the lease lizards." He chuckled.

"You're going date or not. It's our homecoming. Nothing you can say will change my mind. Seriously, it's gonna be fun, and we will look back at this for years to remember."

"A'ight, I give in. I'll look at it positive and make the best of it."

"Done deal, nite."

"Nite, G."

Saturday Sorcery

It's nearly noon, and they arrived on the studio grounds where Garrett filmed the drama *Constant Judgment*. Scholl's felt extremely honored to be there.

As they got to the gate, the guard said to Garrett, "Son, I need an ID from your passenger. You can pick it up on the way out."

Scholls did not have a driver's license but was able to pull out his student ID card. They drove to lot C where Randy was at.

Garrett asked Scholls, "Dude, you don't have your driver's license yet?"

"No, my parents won't take me to get one 'cuz they don't want to have to pay for insurance. I've been studying the manual, so I can take the written test one day."

"Hey, no sweat, when I get a chance, I will teach you to drive. I mean, shit, at least get your license. That is something everyone needs."

"Ya think? Actually, I have driven a bit. My uncle in the FBI came down a couple of months ago, and we went to this remote area so I could practice. He's cool. You would like him. He was a general in the Air Force, and now he does behavioral profiling for the FBI."

"Really, that's 360! A real FBI agent. I'd love to meet him one day."

"Well, you just might get the chance to soon. He usually visits every Christmas. We stay in a hotel, and I usually swim if he gets one with an indoor pool. If not, I go to the hot tub. The fighting between my parents makes him sick."

"Sounds like a plan. We're staying here for the holidays."

They entered the dressing room and found Randy. He took one look at Scholls and said, "G, a challenge? He's a hot mess." Randy went up to Scholls and said, "I guess you know who I am, and if you don't, honey, you will by the time we get through."

"Uh, yes, sir, I do. Garrett told me you could really fix me up."

"Uh huh, and did he tell you I don't play? You'll be like my canvas. I create artwork. I'm going to have to do some things you might not agree with. Are you willing to let me do my thing 100 percent?"

Scholls cut his eyes at Garrett. G just smiled and nodded his head yes. Then Scholls cut his eyes back to Randy and said, "Yes, sir, no prob."

Randy told G that it was going to take two sessions. Today will just be about the wardrobe. Randy studied him for a minute and then said, "Come with me." They headed over to a lounge, and both boys sat down. G loved this 'cuz he got to just relax and watch. He stretched back into the chaise and placed his hands behind his head. In a few minutes, Randy returned with some shirts and pants. He told Scholls to go behind the curtain and put on the first combination.

When Scholls stepped out, G started laughing because he had a scared look on his face. He'd never worn such a bold-colored shirt.

The pants were tapered at the bottom, and he wasn't a fan of that at all. Randy put his fingers under his chin and said, "Potential."

Scholls cut his eyes at Garrett with every outfit he tried on. G kept on grinning. The look on Scholls's face was hilarious.

"Listen, Schollie, you want swag? You got to act swag. Now let me see you walk with game." Scholls took off strutting. Both Garrett and Randy busted out laughing. Randy said, "You trying to be a rooster at a chicken farm? Stop moving your head when you walk. Just kick a smooth stride extending your leg out a bit with your shoulders upright, and be confident."

He started off, and they both began to fall on each other laughing harder. "What are you doing, Schollie? I said a bit, meaning a few inches, not a foot! Mercy, your shoulders are slouched."

Poor Scholls, he truly did need *help* in every sense of the word. After they continued practicing his walk, Randy said, "Okay, I think we found the right outfit, including jacket. The next time I see you, we are going to groom you from the face up. Oh, let me see your hands and feet."

Randy let out a shriek, "Someone get me a *genie*! Child, do you see what I see? Please, next visit, I'm going to have Karen here to shampoo, cut, and highlight. Little Phoung will do those feet, hands…and your unibrow!"

They left the studio grounds and headed back to G's house. Garrett really wanted Scholls to go to the wedding as well. With this thought, he said, "Hey, *Schollie*, do you think you can make Mom's wedding?"

"Yeah, he really likes to pick on me. The name Scholls is bad enough, and now I'm *Schollie*?"

"Told ya, man, he likes you. He would have been quiet if not."

"Well, about the wedding. I would be crashing it. Your mom probably wouldn't appreciate me coming at the last minute. Besides, I still look like crap, remember?" He laughed.

"Look, okay, think about the wedding part if you want, but at least come to the reception afterward. You can borrow my suit for the wedding. The reception is gonna have a comedian and a magician."

"And your mom won't care?"

"Dude, she's my mom, and she won't. I want you to meet some of my other family members. I can't explain why I bonded with you so fast. And I don't really care why. It just happened, and I'm glad it did. If you say no, I will understand. But you can't, so it's a done deal!"

G nodded his head yes—firmly. "Garrett, you're a trip. I'm glad it did too."

"So when we get back, you can try on a suit I wore last year. It's blue. Hell, just wash your hair that morning, and you will be good to go. Can you see up close without your glasses?"

"No, I have astigmatism…and only have one pair."

"Damn, you will just have to go as is. If anyone asks, they broke that morning, and we fixed them temporarily. I've kind of made a pact with God about white lies. In general, I don't lie. But a white lie is fine when you are protecting someone's feelings."

"So how many can *you* tell in one event?"

"Hadn't really thought that far ahead, but I'm sure as long as it keeps from hurting someone, probably a good two or three is okay."

"*Whew*, that should cover my glasses and any questions about my family." They both laughed.

"So, dude, can you believe my movie is out already. Seems like we just filmed it. I haven't even seen it on the big screen."

"Why not?"

"I don't know. Didn't even go to the screening. Which my agent was upset about."

"Let's go see it tonight. If you want to borrow some of my clothes, they will never know it's you. LOL."

"Yeah, I already avoid going in public, 'cuz it's been out for a week now, and some people have recognized me. The paparazzi are starting to piss me off. They have cameras outside at the school parking lot. Our principal, Mr. Wheeler, was interviewed, and then he talked with my mom and she told him I could do one interview at school and that was it. They are relentless. I think it's because the movie is already being cited as a potential nominee. And they even mention I might be up for best actor."

"What? That's awesome, dude. Okay, we *are* going to see the movie tonight. This time, it's my turn to transform you. Let's ride over to my place 'cuz I have enough crappy clothes and baseball caps to disguise you. Even some jacked-up shoes if they fit." He chuckled.

"I guess we can. It's gonna be kinda cool dressing incognito."

"Ha, you may change your mind once you see yourself. It's gonna be badass to know people are watching you on the screen, and they don't even know you are in the theater."

"Smooth! I just hope I don't hear someone say I suck...or the movie sucks."

"Dude, from the reviews, I hardly think they will find it in bad taste. My opinion, you know the girls are gonna go crazy over you...like they did about Leonardo DiCaprio in the movie *Titanic*. You can't even walk down the hall without some girl drooling."

"Bro, you're too funny. When Randy gets through with you, we will have the same problem."

"Yeah, but when they see me get on the bus, their salivary glands will dry up like the Mojave Desert."

"Scholls, you really are too damn funny! Okay, I will transform later. Right now we need to start this project."

CHAPTER 4

Let the Worms and Squirms Begin

THEY SORTED OUT all their stuff and began an outline of what they would do and how it happened. Fortunately, G had a really good microscope his father bought him in tenth grade. This was one of the things they needed when they cut up the planaria. Since they were starting the regeneration process outside of class, the dishes would have to put it in a dark place. Garrett decided he would put them in shoe boxes on the top shelf of his closet.

G asked Scholls, "So, mastermind, what's the plan?"

"Well, we definitely need to show a comparison of a standard worm versus a regenerated one. So we need to save two and look at them under the microscope."

"How in the world do we get it to stay still?"

"They usually have a gliding motion but can move faster if stimulated. So first, we do a *squeeze test*. We need to put a ring of jelly on a cover slip and place the worm in the center of a drop of spring water. The planarian is approximately a half inch long. Then press the second cover slip onto the first one and gently squeeze the worm until it is flat. Now we will be able to flip it over to see both the dorsal and ventral side."

"Man, you are so knowledgeable. How old were you when you studied this, two?" He chuckled.

"Actually, I was in the fifth grade and read a book on Thomas Hunt Morgan. He was an embryologist in the late 1800s and did a whole series of tests on them. He cut up the worm a massive amount of times…over 290, and they all regenerated. They are also hermaphrodites."

"A what?"

"That means they have female and male organs."

"Oh hey, we studied people like that in our human growth and development class, but continue."

"Yes, and they can also go through an asexual reproduction that is genetically identical. In mitosis, chromosomes in one nucleus are separated into two identical sets of chromosomes within their own nuclei."

"Okay, that went straight over my head, but keep going."

"Now, when we go to cut them, let's say, their head, the cells in the tail area self-destruct and provide energy to survive. Essentially, they feed off themselves. They have a special set of stem cells that are embryonic-like. Overtime, the tail will shrink to make the exact proportion of the planarian's head. Once the head is whole again, it will begin to feed on itself and grow back to the original size. So you see, no matter how you cut it, the worm will recreate itself until it is whole again."

"*Wow*, dude, this is really interesting. Now I know you're capable of being any doctor you want."

"Okay, so when we place it under the microscope and cut it, we need to get the video cam ready, 'cuz within about ten minutes, the wound closes by muscular contraction."

"Oh yeah, let's make sure the sound is on. Remember, I need to ask the worm if he felt any pain for little guy Casey. Dude, you know what we should do? Make two videos and have one of them for the project and one to show Casey. We'll have the worm squeak out, 'Hey, man, that hurt. Watch what you are doing!' Now, let's hear your best version of the worm."

Scholls let out a moan, "Ahhggg…Couldn't you have cut me from my best side?"

They both started laughing. Then Garrett said in his high voice, "Ooouuch…Are you stupid or something? That's a sharp instrument!"

Then Scholls said, "Does this Petri dish make me look fat? Okay, sounds like a plan, but we're gonna have to stop clownin' and make one more childproof. I can't wait to see what Casey does. This should be fun!"

"Yeah, sure, but let's keep our other version for class. Okay, Scholls, then what happens?"

"After another twenty minutes or so from the initial muscular contraction which closes the wound, the epithelial cells heal over the wound. Once this happens, the blastema cells or neoblast cells form, and the process of regeneration begins. Usually within eight to nine days, the entire worm has regenerated to its full size."

"Man, that's so awesome. Is that what happens when a starfish grows back a missing limb?"

"Yep, same process. Just takes longer."

"Too bad humans can't do that."

"Actually, we do, when we cut ourselves and new skin grows back. Unfortunately, our systems are way more complex, and this is still an ongoing research for humans."

"You were right all along. We did get lucky with this subject. And me even luckier getting you as my partner."

"Garrett, what can I say? We make a ridiculous team." They slapped high-five and decided to create an original shake.

The boys began setting up all the items they will need to document the experiment. Garrett's tripod allowed them to film their opening comments together and introduce their project. It had to be filmed on several takes, because they kept making mistakes with their speech, which caused them to bust up laughing uncontrollably. Call it the bloopers and blunders, "Take 27 and Counting" episode.

Finally, they filmed the actual process. Garrett decided he will be the cameraman and let Scholls do the cutting. This mime artist's desire was to become a doctor specializing in stem cell research, so dialogue will be important.

In a few minutes, the camera was aimed on the worm whose head was cut off. This worm has to be placed in the dark because it is *negatively phototaxic*—moves and grows away from light. They zoomed in on the worm and documented what it looked like ten minutes later. All the regimented steps were repeatedly captured every ten minutes over an hour period of photographic documentation. S and G cut up more worms in different ways and placed each one in their own personalized Petri dish.

They had to do each procedure twice in the beginning so they could make Casey's taping. It will be interesting to see if he gravitates toward knowing more, or if he will *not* follow in his father's footsteps and think it is gross.

Riches to Rags

Due to the extreme fascination of the project, they forget about G's movie. Scholls impulsively remembered they were trying to make the show at 9:15 p.m. "It's about seven thirty. Let's call it a wrap." They cautiously placed the dishes in the shoe boxes and upon their return, would resume filming and photography.

At Scholls's place, his dad was still asleep, and Tina was not there. "Thank God for small miracles, Mom's gone and Dad's asleep. Shhh, let's see what we can do for you, young man."

Garrett took in all the surroundings. He noticed there was not one picture of the Parker family on any walls. He thought, *I suppose his parents must have some love for him. They do provide what they can and could have given him up for adoption.* The award he'd receive in an *internal* ceremony was *lead actor* for hiding sorrow about Scholls's upbringing.

"Dude, take a look at this. I've worn this shirt for five years. The holes are perfect. What do ya think? And these shorts are not too bad. They are larger than I normally wear. My mom's friend gave them to me. Anyway, I have a thirty-inch waist. What are you, 'bout thirty-two, thirty-four?"

"Pretty damn good guess. I am thirty-two-, thirty-three-inch waist. What size shoes do you wear? "

"Size 13."

"Well, I wear a twelve, so it won't be too bad. Give me the oldest pair you have. I don't want to ruin any of your good ones."

"No sweat, 'cuz I only have one good pair. Look down. The other pair has multiple grass stains and dirt from when I mow lawns or clean up garages."

"Okay, those will work. Let me try 'em on."

"Now all we need is a cap and some glasses for your face. You have a distinctive look, and people, girls for sure, will recognize you."

"I thought you only had one pair of glasses?"

"I do, but my dad has lots of readers lying around. You might just get a bit blurry eyed before we get inside the theater and sit down. At the movie, you can pull them down. Hell, if we sit at the very top, then you can take them off. Yeah, that's where we'll go, so get dressed, and I will find them. We need to leave soon so we can get the seats we want. We can eat a burger on the way." They managed to go before waking up his dad. The readers made a huge difference.

Coy Burger

Soon, they pulled into Schultz's Burger and ordered hamburger baskets. It's a mom-and-pop drive-up-style place. G rolled down the window, and a girl walked up to take the order. She's taller than most girls, wearing glasses, had brown hair, and was thin.

Kipper said, "Hello, welcome to Schultz's. Can I take your order?"

G replied, "We'll have a couple number 1 combos."

"Okay, with fries or onion rings?"

G looked at Scholls and asked him what he preferred. "I'll take fries. Oh, and I'd like Coca-Cola for my drink."

Garrett said, "Yeah, I'll have fries and Coke as well."

"Is this going to be here or to-go?"

"To-go please"

"Will that be all?"

"Yes, ma'am!"

She totaled up the ticket and told them it will be $20.76. This time, Scholls pulled out his wallet and gave Garrett twelve dollars. As she left to place the order, G noticed Scholls watching her walk away and how many times he looked to see where she was over the next fifteen minutes.

"Dude, I believe you think she's *choice*."

"Huh? Well, she was all right. I don't know her or anything."

"Just all right?" He coughed "BS." "That's not what your face told me. Want me to ask her what her name is?"

"Not really."

"What if I told her you were single and available?"

"*Negative.* She'd never be interested in me."

"Dude, I think you're wrong. When I was ordering, I caught her looking at you several times. She even seemed a bit embarrassed that I caught her."

"Now you're delusional."

"And stop putting yourself down so much. You don't look that bad. I mean, yeah, your hair is different. I mean, kind of messy, and your glasses are broken, but what the hell, you are a pretty good-looking guy under all that."

"Are you serious, dude? You crack me up. You know damn good and well I look jacked-up. My clothes are…*not* stylish, and I think it's pretty obvious I need new glasses. So that spells out I'm either poor or not too interested in grooming myself. Now let's see, which one do you think she would say?" He chuckled.

"Neither one. I saw the gleam in her eye when she looked at you. Some people aren't caught up in fashion."

"And you're not?"

"Don't be lame. Of course I am! But I know hormones aren't stopped by clothes. Anyway, I plan on expanding your wardrobe from mine."

"Man, I told you, I'm not about to take a bunch of gifts from you."

"I know what you said, but I know the difference between someone who uses me and someone who doesn't. Take for instance that guy Brad Fleming. You know him?"

"Yeah, who doesn't?"

"Well, I avoid him like the plague. He was constantly coming over and wanting me to introduce him to people on the set. He even asked to spend the night without being invited. I let him, and all he did was go through my things while continually asking if he could go on the set when I was filming the movie. He's conceited. Well, he is good-looking, not that I'm into rating guys' looks, but I'm not blind. Now his personality…can we say *boring*, anyone?" He yawned. "He's also up for homecoming king. Hopefully he wins. I kinda want to just relax and not be in the limelight. Enough of me. So when it comes to you, I know what a good guy you are. It'll make me feel happy to give you clothes. You're *not* a charity case. I do *not* think you are using me. Besides, my mom even mentioned that she wanted to sort through my stuff and give you first dibs. So you don't want to hurt her feelings now, do you?" G cocked his head to the side with a puppy dog look.

"If that's the case, no, I wouldn't." In his peripheral sight, he saw the girl approaching the Hummer. "Oh, crap, she's coming!"

"Ha, you look scared."

"Shit, don't you dare tell her I'm single and interested."

"Okay, okay, just chill."

"Hi, here are your drinks." She handed them to G. "And here's your food." She smiled at Scholls.

Garrett handed her twenty-five dollars and told her to keep the change.

"Oh, hey, my friend Scholls, over here, was wondering what your name is?" Scholls almost choked because he had just gulped some soda from his straw. His eyes got huge, and he looked at Garrett like a deer in headlights.

60

"Thanks for the tip." She stepped up on the side rail and said, "Hi, my name is Kipper."

Scholls was excited but pretended to be calm. All of a sudden, he started hiccupping. *Hiccup.* "Uh, hi…it's nice to meet you." *Hiccup.* "I'm Scholls." *Hiccup.*

"Hey, I thought I was the only one around here with a different name. It's nice to meet you, Scholls."

"Likewise." *Hiccup.*

"Well, I hope to see you guys around some time. Oh, and by the way, Scholls, you need to increase your carbon dioxide level, and those hiccups will go away. Just breathe in and out fast for several seconds into a bag so you are breathing the carbon dioxide you exhale and not new air. They should go away. You can use the bag the food came in. Good night."

Scholls's jaw dropped, and he continued to hiccup a bit before saying, "I can't believe you just dogged me." *Hiccup.*

As Garrett laughed, he apologized, "Man, I'm sorry. I knew you wouldn't ask and I knew you wanted to know. Sometimes you just have to intervene when you know what's best." Still laughing, he said, "You're not mad at me, are you?"

"Let's just get to the movie. I'll deal with you later. Maybe we should let everyone know who you are. Hhhmmm, it's crossing my mind now, but I'm not vindictive and she just made me melt with her intelligence. Did you hear how smart she sounds? Now that's a girl who could study with me anytime."

Garrett's clock started ticking. If Tally had no luck, then he would come back and see if Kipper can go. He's going to have to do it on the sly. They arrived at the theater and bought tickets.

Notable Nerds

Fortunately, they were there early enough to buy another drink and candy. Climbing fast, they sat all the way to the very top and far right. Garrett's costume had been successful and not one person noticed him. He just may have to keep these items for future exhibitions.

There it was, *Constant Judgment* across the screen. Garrett let out a burst of air; he's excited and nervous at the same time. It lasted just over two hours and twenty minutes, and the entire movie was riveting. Scholls was noticeably proud his friend did an excellent job. During one segment of the movie, they heard a couple girls talking about how sexy Garrett was when he came into the storyline. The youngest Taylor Smith was a child played by a kid named Alexander Ross. The youthful one was played by a kid named Michael Peterson. Garrett enters the movie at age fifteen, which encompassed the vast majority of the picture.

When it was over, the credits rolled slowly, and G's name appeared first. It was at this very moment he felt a confirmation; equally important, he *did* enjoy seeing the movie. They waited until most of the people had left the area, and while exiting outside of the theater, they heard someone say, "If that doesn't get a nomination, I'm going to be floored."

"I couldn't agree more, G. That was a really, really a good movie. I hope you don't get bruises when I kept hitting your knee every time I felt excited you were up there acting away. It was so cool! There's no reason you guys shouldn't get a nomination. Hell, sometimes I don't understand how they pick certain movies. Mostly, I'm in sync with the picks. We will just wait and see."

"Yeah, time will tell. I'm not gonna be too anxious until I hear from my agent. For now, I'm just regular old Garrett Pierce—graduating high school soon, transforming my friend for homecoming, finishing our project, and accepting my new life with a little brother and stepfather."

As soon as they returned, the two passionately raced into the closet and checked on the worms. The obvious changes were documented with new photos, and amazingly, the project had gone relatively smooth. It sparked such an interest in Garrett that he picked at Scholls's brain to discover what age he wanted to become a doctor.

All their activities had made them restless, so they decided to play a video game. It's now almost 1:00 a.m. They chose Need for Speed Rivals, and G jokingly said, "You don't need a license for this." One thing was for sure, both boys were very competitive and fed off each other's energy. After an hour or so, they called it quits.

G asked, "You tired?"

"Nah, but I could use a snack about now."

"Me, too. Let's go into my kitchen and get some chips and sodas."

CHAPTER 5

G's 101 on the 411

WHEN THEY WERE finished eating, Scholls told G, "I need to brush my teeth." Garrett had a perfect smile. His teeth were straight and very white. S. Parker's teeth were pretty straight for not having braces but dingy. G remembered he has some whitening strips in the drawer and explained how to use them.

Scholls asked, "Is that why your teeth look so white?"

"Yep, and my gums pink! My hygienist will know if I don't floss routinely. For a while, my gums bled pretty easy. So I need to do that first. Do you floss?"

"I do routinely. Ever since I researched oral bacteria. I don't go to the dentist because my parents stopped taking me these past few years. I've never had a cavity that I know of."

"Wow, I had a couple fillings when I was younger, and the shot makes me cringe. It hurt like hell. They were like, 'Okay, Garrett, were gonna put this little mask over your nose, and it's gonna make you a little bit sleepy.' Sleepy, my ass, it made me dizzy, and then they had the nerve to tell me to hold still. Really? All I saw was two giant heads with giant eyes, glasses, masks, and four hands with a drill coming at me...inches from my face! Let's just say, you are lucky, bro."

"Let me see one of your fillings."

Garrett opened up his mouth and pointed to a lower molar. When Scholls looked inside, he was confused. He could not even see the filling.

"They use white-colored materials now, and they blend very well." Scholls had read about it and was intrigued. He told G,

"When I start working in college, I'll just have to make an appointment to get my teeth looked at, and pray nothing is bad. They need to be cleaned for sure."

"How long has it been?"

"Probably four years, I'm guessing."

"Yeah, that's a good idea. Even Einstein was adamant about his teeth. I can't remember exactly what he said, but it was to his son."

"I'm impressed, G! In 1915, he wrote a letter to his son Hans. Wait, let me look it up here on my phone so you can hear what he wrote. Of course, the letter was written in German, and some documented interpretations are different. Okay, here's the part about the teeth. Einstein to Adu: 'Brush your teeth every day, and if a tooth is not quite all right, go to the dentist immediately. I also do the same and very happy now to have kept enough healthy teeth. This is very important, as you will realize too yourself later on.' "They're starting to find out that oral bacteria have an effect with some *systemic* issues. If Einstein was in this time period, it's likely he would have also instructed them to clean well under the gum lines."

"Systemic. What does that mean?"

"It means affecting the entire body."

"How?"

"Some studies have shown the more complex bacteria from periodontal disease, or gum disease, are associated with diabetes, heart disease, and even able to permeate some tissues of other organs. For instance, it goes both ways with diabetes. The association has been extensively studied for decades. Both diseases have a major inflammatory component, which plays an obvious role in their existence. If you have diabetes, then you are more predisposed to getting periodontal disease with substandard dental hygiene/or care…because people with diabetes are more susceptible to contracting infections if the blood sugar level is not under control. "Likewise, gum disease can increase your blood sugar level, which increases your chances for diabetic complications."

"This is interesting. I have a question. What is the normal blood sugar level supposed to be?"

"Well, hopefully I can explain it in lay terms with unavoidable medical terminology. Basically, your blood sugar level is determined by a unit that measures the concentration of a substance in a specific amount of fluid…milligrams per deciliter. Normal levels when you have not eaten in eight hours should be around 80 to 120 mg/dl and less than 140 mg/dl…two hours after you eat. Patients that have moderate to advanced periodontitis, or gum disease, will *often* have a *higher* blood glucose, or sugar, level in their blood test.

"The A1C blood sugar chart is also used, and it ranges from 4.0 to 15. If your range is 5.7 to 6.4, then you are in a zone that can be indicating prediabetes. Once you hit 6.5, you are now officially a diabetic and will be asked to do one or more of the following: change your diet, begin exercising, take medicines, or possibly need to have insulin administered daily.

"So it is important for you to know your level and see if it changes throughout the course of your life. Our body is interlocking in many ways, so taking care of yourself early on will lower your chances of living a substandard life with complications. If your gums are swollen, red, bleed, or sensitive with or without trauma, then there is inflammation present. Inflammation is the body's *attempt for self-protection* by removing harmful stimuli, and harmful stimuli would include damaged cells, pathogens, or irritants.

"Now three things happen before and during inflammation. First, small branches of arteries, or arterioles, dilate, or expand, and supply blood through capillaries, the weblike network that connects arteries and veins, allowing blood to pass through to the damaged or invaded region, resulting in more blood flow.

"Second, the capillaries become more permeable, or able to pass through, and exchange the oxygen rich blood from arteries allowing the gases into the tissue. Then the capillaries pass the waste-like products from the tissue, like carbon dioxide, to the veins for transport to the heart.

"Third, microphages and macrophages, or white blood cells, migrate out of the capillaries and small venules, veins that go to capillaries, and move into spaces between the cells. They have the ability to ingest or destroy microorganisms or foreign material."

"Dude, you just absolutely blow me away with your knowledge."

"Thanks. Now are you starting to get the drift that *nerds* are smart because they stay in and read? Their brains aren't overloaded with social experience, and that's why they retain a whole lot more!" He chuckled.

Garrett laughed out loud for several seconds. "Okay, continue. I'm so interested in this stuff. I mean, we briefly studied this in school, but somehow you are making this way more understandable."

"Hey, what time is it?"

"About 2:00 a.m."

"You tired yet?"

"No, man, besides, we need to photograph our worms again."

"Yeah, you're right. Get the camera, G."

They talked into the vid cam and gave a time line on the project. G zoomed into the worms and Scholls said, "I think we should name them after the Seven Dwarfs."

"Except the eight one. We cut its head off. We'll call it Anne, who married King Henry VIII."

"Why?"

"He had five children but only one girl named Mary survived. He wanted to divorce his wife Catherine of Aragon, who was Catholic. When the pope would not grant it, he cut ties with the Catholic Church and declared himself head of the Church of England. He then marries Anne Boleyn, whom he loved and was convinced she would bear a male heir. She had a girl, and when she failed to give him a son, he had her head cut off. Incidentally, the girl she had became what most people refer to as England's greatest Monarch—Elizabeth I."

"Whoa, you're even a history buff. Damn, Scholls." He shook his head in astonishment. "Oh! I forgot about the one we left whole and squeezed."

"Hmmm. I know, let's call him SqueezeBob. LOL. So we have Anne, SqueezeBob, Bashful, Sneezy, Dopey, Grumpy, Happy, Sleepy, and Doc. Now that we've done that. Heigh-ho, heigh-ho, it's off to bed they go! I want to finish hearing about the systemic stuff. Hell, I play a genius in my movie. You, on the other hand, truly are one."

Systematic

Scholls said, "That's nice of you to say, but actually, I have never been tested, so I can't really say I am. I've always been told how smart I am. I just want to do research and help people. Like computers, stem cells are the next revolution. They already use it now, but people are scared because they associate it with cloning humans."

"Really?"

"There's always gonna be fear of the unknown. Like anything else, if it's used properly, only good can come from it. It's such an expensive area in medicine requiring very complex equipment. There won't be any Mary Shelley's *Frankenstein* or television's *X-Files* in common households. The FDA has what they call the GMP, or good manufacturing practice, which ensures that a cell has to be grown in identical, repeatable conditions. This means each batch of stem cells has the *same equivalent* properties for treatment."

"That's only fair."

"Exactly, and as far as religious aspects go, I think it's agreed that God gave us all free will. What we choose to do with it is on us. People instinctively know right from wrong unless they are mentally impaired. It's applied to all decisions in life. We have the ability to save lives through technology. Remember, we were created with a brain! So we use it! For example, a special committee called the AVC, or the Bureau of Arms Control, Verification, and Compliance, is in effect. They advance national and international security through effectively verifiable data, negotiations, and implementation that diligently monitors the US and other foreign countries to comply with *all* arms control.

"Henceforth, the NPT, or the Treaty on the Nonproliferation of Nuclear Weapons, binds everyone to an agreement for *peaceful* nuclear technology. They want to prevent the spread of mass weapons of destruction, promote cooperation with tranquil uses of nuclear energy, and to further the goal of military disarmament for offensive or defensive use in wars.

"My point is, we can have a similar type of committee on controlling the use of stem cells. If we limit its use for fighting and curing blood diseases, heart damage, infertility, rejection of organ transplants, growth of human tissue to restore disfigured skin or body parts, curing neurological disorders, arthritis, and so much more, what's the problem?

"The fact is, *scientists* are often portrayed as evil in this area. You know, G, *they are real people.* Many have children and loved ones who have been affected by all kinds of health misfortunes. Certainly no different than one of us wanting to help our own family member or friend. Being a humanitarian, isn't that one of the greatest gifts of all?"

"Wow, Scholls, you're gonna make a hell of a doctor some day, and I have the privilege of knowing you."

"Yep, you're stuck with me from now on. But, you know, I am just as in awe of you and your acting. Not to mention how nice and genuine you really are to people, and I have the privilege of knowing you."

"Hey, it's 3:45 a.m., and I'm not even tired, are you?"

"Not really, I stay up a lot at night when my parents are gone at work. I usually get about six hours of sleep. Besides, this is special, and we have Sunday. Oops, I mean today, so we can sleep in. I don't have to be home until this evening, or whenever you decide to take me home." He chuckled.

"Around 8:00 p.m. is good. Casey will be here at 4:00 p.m., and I really want us to show him the video. It should be hilarious. Mom has invited you for Sunday dinner at six, so this works out perfect."

"Thanks, G."

Filming the worms had been interesting. Now, they could just do it twice a day until they completely regenerated. Garrett and Scholls needed to ride together on the day of the presentation. They wrapped up the project for now, and Garrett pursued Scholls to *continue* with the systemic health information.

Open Wide

Scholls replied, "One of the biggest interests is with heart disease. Gum disease is a chronic inflammation of the tissue around the teeth. So, G, the inflammation can be reacting to what stimuli?"

"It's gotta be bacteria, right?"

"You are correct! Now, we do know that chronic inflammation can last for months to years as a result from persistent bacteria… in addition to viral infections, overreactive immune system reactions, and persistent foreign bodies.

"The outcome will be fibrosis, or thick and scarred connective tissue, and/or necrosis, the death of tissue or cells. Basically, your immune system is always dealing with an ongoing infection, and this can't be good.

"It's known that elevated white blood cells are inflammatory markers. And they are linked to having a higher risk for coronary heart disease. As of 2016, heart disease is still the number one killer in the USA. In 1953, the federal government founded a cabinet level department called the US Department of Health and Human Services. They recently reported approximately

2,200 people die from cardiovascular disease *each* day. So do you know what *cardiovascular* means?"

"It deals with the heart?"

"You are correct. It also deals with the vessels, which is the *vascular* part. Okay, so that means that nearly eight hundred thousand American people die from it each year. That's nearly one out of three deaths. It could be you or me, but let's take care of ourselves and let someone else be the statistics. LOL."

"Whoa, I didn't realize that."

"Now, among the *oral bacteria* is one little guy called *Fusobacterium nucleatum.* I'm gonna refer to it as Fus Nuc for fun 'cuz it's such a long name to repeat. It can adhere to a wide range of gram-positive and gram-negative plaque organisms. Now Fus Nuc is capable of opening up tiny little *doors* in *blood vessels.* That means it allows itself and other substances to permeate, or pass through, inside the vessel. Bacteria can now enter the bloodstream. Human infections of the head, chest, lungs, liver, and abdomen have also been associated with Fus Nuc invasion. You can learn even more from nih.org, scientificamerican.com, medicalnewstoday.com, *Journal of Periodontology, The Journal of Neuroscience*, and many other sources.

"This is a huge concern because once they get in the bloodstream, they can travel anywhere in the body. It can bypass other cellular barriers, such as the blood-brain barrier that has precise control over substances that enter or leave the brain. Now the barrier is composed of capillary endothelial cells that restrict the diffusion of microscopic organisms, for example, bacteria. Fus Nuc alters the endothelial integrity. It's also been proven to pass through the placental barrier of mother and fetus."

"Keep going, man. I might have to change my major." He chuckled.

"So Fus Nuc can potentially let in a quite an invasion. Now this is where our defense comes in. The body has to recognize the invaders. The invaders are *antigens,* or foreign substances or microorganisms. This is going to get a bit deep, but I'll simplify it for you. Since an antigen is foreign, our immune system recognizes this immediately. Lymphocytes are white blood cells, or WBC. Red *bone marrow* is the tissue inside our bones, mostly flat bones in adults. It makes red blood cells, or RBC, which include stem cells, platelets, and B cell lymphocytes. The *thymus*, located between the lungs and upper part of our chest, makes the T cell lymphocytes. You with me?"

"Yep."

"So now, helper T cells, or CD4, scan the areas and have receptors that recognize the antigen molecule is different. They send out their own type of *Paul Revere*, and this activates the B cells to form a protein to latch on to the antigen. This specifically identifies the antigen and matures the B cell as the antibody, which replicates over and over, also kicking in the reaction for the killer T cells, or CD8, to destroy them by phagocytosis. We also have NK lymphocytes that do just that. They naturally kill invaders without being activated. The microbes are engulfed, Pac-Man-like, and destroyed by either using oxygen based chemicals that tear or burst the antigen, or by digestive enzymes that break it down.

"When it is completely finished, the suppressor T cell inactivates the lymphocytes to return to normal, or calling off the troops. Now this happens with each type of microbe or foreign obstacle we get, so my thoughts are simple. The less I give my body to cause inflammation, especially *chronic*, the healthier I am.

"There are conditions like pericarditis, the inflammation of the sac-like lining that surrounds your heart, or myocarditis, which is an infection of the heart muscle that is damaged. Documentation shows that viruses, staphylococcal and streptococcal bacteria, and fungi can cause or contribute to them.

"You've heard of CPR, right? Well, there is an acute phase protein that is called CRP, or C-reactive protein, so don't mix up the two. Anyway, it is agreed upon by medical experts that this is a predictable risk factor for CVD, or cardiovascular disease, and other ischemia, a shortage of blood supply to tissues.

"Chronic periodontal infection contributes to systemic inflammation by elevated CRP levels, IL-6 interleukin cytokines, and fibrinogen, the coagulation factors in blood. You can also go to the American Heart Association Web site, my.americanheart. org/statements, and read more about inflammation. So no one is saying gum disease is the direct *sole* cause of these conditions, but in my opinion, there is certainly enough evidence to show it's linked. You're gonna need a healthy immune system to fight it off, and this is one of the only diseases you can control by direct hands-on efforts, except for abnormal immune deficiency periodontitis.

"Everything is progressive until our body has an overload. Then we either feel or see the disease manifest. Now we know the mouth flora contains over five hundred-plus species of bacteria, many are streptococcal in nature. Also, it can harbor fungus, like *Candida albicans*. The anatomic proximity, or nearness, of the gum tissue to the bloodstream can facilitate bacteremia, which is bacteria in the bloodstream. It is so important to remove microbes from your mouth, preventing decay, abscesses, or periodontal disease. My logic tells me there isn't a sign in the body that tells microbes, 'No trespassing. This is the heart!'"

"Okay, maybe I will be a dentist. LOL."

"Wow, G, it's almost 5:00 a.m. Guess we should go to sleep. Nite, G."

"Instead of having visions of Diane Lane in my head, I'm going to have dreams of the lymphatic system. Ha. Good night, Scholls."

"Why her? She's a lot older than you."

"Because she is sexy, and I really like her acting. Who do *you* think is hot for an older actress?"

"Definitely Kate Beckinsale, but for a classic beauty in their *era*, hands down, Elizabeth Taylor."

"I agree on them for sure."

"What about ones our age?"

"Well, probably Georgie Henley or Ariel Winter."

"Good picks. For me, I like Dakota Fanning, or maybe her sister Elle."

"Okay, pick one and we will talk in a few hours. Good night, Scholls."

"Good night, G Boy."

CHAPTER 6

"Tri-Oh-logics"

THE BOYS DIDN'T wake up until almost two thirty in the afternoon. Barb knew they had stayed up late because she passed by Garrett's room, so she asked them not to eat a huge lunch because dinner was just a few hours away.

They filmed the worms, worked on their project, and ate a sandwich. Scholls called and spoke to his mom. Of course, she was fine with him returning at eight. She wouldn't be there anyway.

He knew his dad would be waking up about the time he arrived.

Schultz's Burgers crossed his mind, and he wanted to ask Garrett if they could stop there to get his dad food. He did have an ulterior motive—Kipper. Something about her, especially her conspicuous intelligence, made his heart skip a beat.

Kipper was pretty in an unflashy way. It's like she didn't even care his glasses were broken. Most of the time, people looked at him and then focused on the frames. Was Garrett right? Did she like him? If he got the chance to see her again, he would ask for her number.

Or should he? Damn, his parents would freak if he used their phone to court a girl. Good thing they rarely look at the phone bill's breakdown. He's watched his dad pay it plenty of times. Perhaps, if he did not go over the limit of *minute use*, they wouldn't know a thing. Oh, it all sucked: no phone; no license; no car; no decent clothes; no decent home; no decent parents; and no damn money.

"All right, shit! Stop right there! Am I crazy or something?" The situation was solved. He would *not* try to get her number.

75

He's not going to ask G to go there. One day, this stuff wouldn't matter. The sound of Dr. Scholls Parker had a nice ring to it, and all the inequalities would be gone.

The video they made for Casey was done, and in just a little while, he would get to see it. Garrett and Scholls showed it to Barb first. She thought it was funny, clever, and in good taste. Afterward, Scholls followed her to an area where she had a box of clothes sorted out from G's belongings. He looked at Garrett with a shy smirk, and G looked back with an "I told you so" look. They went into the room, and of course, she picked out each item and placed them up against his body to make sure they fit.

Barb said, "By the way, Scholls, if any of the pants are too big in the waist. I mean, really loose, let me know and I will have our housekeeper, Juanita, take them up an inch or two. In fact, please go and try them on so you can leave anything that needs adjusting."

"Yes, ma'am. I really appreciate this."

Garrett explained to his mother that Scholls felt as though he was a charity case. With that said, Barbara decided to talk more with her son's newfound friend, easing his mind and giving him a personal invitation to the wedding next weekend.

While they waited for him to come back, Barb asked Garrett about his feelings again. Even though it had been a year since Thom died, she had recurrent thoughts that her son might not be happy about the marriage.

Barb started, "Honey, I know we have talked about this several times and I don't want to keep rehashing it, but I need to know if you are truly okay with the wedding. It's only a week away, and we have the rehearsal dinner in a few days."

"Mom, I need to know if you *really* love him. It's hard for me to understand how your love for Dad can be replaced."

"Oh, sweetie, it can never be replaced. Please don't think like that. Your father is forever in my heart." She held G's hands in both of hers. "I could never have known we'd be sitting here talking about this. I always dreamed one day we'd be watching our grandchildren play in a big yard. My heart was so empty when Daddy died. When you fall in love one day, you will be able to understand that the need for this kind of emotion is not something you can easily avoid. I didn't plan on meeting Peter. Honey, I will always love your father. *No one* can take that away. My love for Peter is just an extension of life. He knows and understands my feelings. You and Casey are what matters the most.

This wedding would be postponed if you told me you weren't ready. I mean it. I love you, Garrett. When you gave me your blessing to date Peter, I was relieved. I was lonely. Your dad is a hard act to follow. There are things about Peter that will never add up to Daddy. Just give him a chance to join our family. I know you are fond of Casey. He's definitely crazy about his big brother!"

G thinks, *That was so profound.* Her happiness did matter, and he had been selfishly aloof at times. For sure, Peter was attentive with the whole concussion thing, and it did sway his opinion in a more positive light.

Garrett responds, "This is hard, I'm not gonna lie…and realizing life has no set blueprint puts me at center stage with it. I'm giving you my blessing and our relationship will never change. I love you, Mom. I really do. I doubt I will ever call Peter Dad, but I will call Casey my little brother."

"Honey, thank you. I needed to be sure."

Fifteen minutes later, Scholls returned and handed Barb three pairs that needed tailoring. He thanked her repeatedly, and then she told him, "Son, you are more than welcome."

Garrett looked at his mother, without a sound, and lipped to her to invite him to the wedding.

"Listen, I would really like it if you could come to my wedding next weekend. If you have plans, we understand."

"Garrett did mention it to me. I just don't want to impose on you guys."

"Oh, silly, I'd love to have you there. We are having a smaller one with only limited family and a few friends. Both Peter and I had big weddings before, and we want it more confined. In fact, Garrett wasn't even going to invite anyone before he met you. Just get use to us, because we are your new extended family."

Squirmy Wit

Just before 4:00 p.m., Casey and Peter arrived. Everyone chitchated for a while, and the boys left to G's room. Casey eagerly sat down to watch the video. They explained the project, and his face brightened up as it started. Garrett and Scholls had done their introductions and talked into the camera as if they were talking directly to Casey.

Casey exclaimed, "Hey, you guys are talking to me!"

The worms replied, "Yep, just listen and see what happens next."

All of a sudden, the Petri dish zoomed in on Anne.

It appeared as if the worm was talking to Casey.

In a squeaky voice, the worm spoke, "Hey, little guy, you're name is Casey, right?

He looked at G and Scholls with widened eyes and said, "Now she's talking to me!"

"Well, go ahead and answer her."

They calculated the video with appropriate amounts of lapsed time in between questions. Then Casey said, "Hi, Ms. Worm, I am Casey. How did you know my name?"

Anne answered, "We heard Garrett and Scholls talking about you. How old are you?"

"I'm eight. Well, almost eight and a half."

"Do you know when my head is going to grow back all the way?"

"Awww, it's okay, Ms. Worm, you will have your head real soon. Did it hurt when it got cut off?"

"I definitely felt something. Casey, did you help them cut me up? I guess I needed a new head."

"No, Ms. Worm, I could never do that. Did you see Garrett and Scholls do it? Their teacher gave them this project. That darned ol' school made them do it."

"Gosh, I'm not sure, my glasses fell off, and I couldn't see. Now I don't have my glasses."

Casey gave them a dirty look. He folded his arms and squinted his eyes. Garrett sent Scholls a text: "LMAO."

Casey said, "Okay, when you grow back together, I will get you and save you. I don't want you to feel sad or cry ever again."

He looked at Garrett and Scholls to ask if he could take Anne and the whole worm gang with him. They paused the video and explained he could take them after the project was finished at school.

Anne said, "Oh, thank you, Casey. You are so nice. Can I be your new friend?"

Casey replied, "Yep, and all your other friends can come with me too."

"Yippie! Well, Casey, we need to go to sleep right now. When it's over, come get us. Bye, my friend."

"Awww, Ms. Worm, I will. Sweet dreams, Ms. Worm and friends. See you soon. Bye"

The video ended, and Casey was frustrated. He told the boys, "I don't ever want cut up anyone or anything that is real."

They got their answer. He *was* going to be a computer nerd. The boys watched cartoons with him, and they passed the time until dinner.

CHAPTER 7

A Hard Dish to Swallow

PETER ASKED EVERYONE to bow their heads for dinner as he said the grace. As he was praying, Scholls scrutinized him. All along he felt there was more to Dr. Berg than meets the eye. He just didn't want to feed into Garrett's uneasiness. Keeping his friend free of stress was important. He decided to use a sublime approach and got some answers. Scholls was smart, and Peter knew it.

They began eating. Casey told his dad about the worms and asked if he could keep them. "Son, you may keep them as long as you like."

Casey lit up. The one thing nobody doubted was Peter's affection for his son. In the midst of dinner, Scholls inquired about Peter's background. Berg's voice got lower and monotone with each question.

Scholls asked, "Sir, where did you grow up?"

"In Baltimore, Maryland."

"Are your parents still there?"

"No, they are both deceased. I had a stepfather. My real father abandoned us when I wasn't yet three. I never knew where he went or why. He could walk by me today, and I would not recognize him."

"I'm sorry, sir, to hear that. What about any brothers or sisters?"

"No, I was an only child."

"Oh, just like Garrett and me."

"Yes, just like you guys." Peter looked away from them in a trancelike state. With a slow and controlled voice, he said,

"Unfortunately, my stepfather drank frequently and smoked like a chimney. They determined he must have fallen asleep in the living room. The cigarette caught his recliner on fire, and the house went into full blaze. I lost both of them."

"Oh my god, I'm terribly sorry. That's horrific. You had to be strong."

"Yes, it was terrible. I suppose I was saved for a reason in life. A couple months before that, I lost Paul, my best friend, to leukemia. I would have traded my life for his. We grew up together. I became angry and very depressed after he died. He was the *only* one I trusted and confided in, so when they died, I was sent to live with my mom's sister in DC.

"You two remind me of my friendship with Paul. We were... very close. Both of us vowed to be in the medical field, so on his behalf, I'm fulfilling his dreams every day. Cherish what you have."

The rest of the dinner was peculiar because he did not speak again for three or four minutes and excused himself to take an emergency call. Covertly, Dr. Berg loathed their friendship; simultaneously, it was a *double digs* sharing Barbara's affection with the accomplished child and witnessing the boys materializing their extraordinary friendship.

They finished eating and went back into G's room. Garrett voiced sympathy, "Dude, I didn't know he lost his family when he was a teenager. It's pretty sad about his friend."

"Yeah, I wonder which type of leukemia his friend had. That's one of the first uses for stem cells."

Scholls got his backpack, and they left. The thought of his family dying in a fire and his best friend dying of leukemia was weighing heavy on their minds.

G said, "Hey, Scholls, this guy has been through a lot. No wonder he is so protective of his son. The only thing that struck me odd was that he *only* trusted and confided in his friend. He barely mentioned his family. Plus, it makes me nervous. He's got so much bad luck."

"Look at me, my parents are not people I trust and confide in. I've shared more of my thoughts with you than I have ever shared with them in my teen years. We just don't talk much. I can understand it. Now the bad luck part…it does make you think. But he didn't cause any of the stuff." Scholls filed that.

"Let's hope his luck has changed. I'm sorry, bro. It struck a cord in me. Then again, he is a doctor and has a great kid, so he must also have some good luck, well, skills, for sure, being a doctor. Maybe that's why he seems weirded out. I'm not use to vying for attention from Mom."

"Yeah, give it time."

"I suppose. Did you notice how hollow he looked as he told us?"

"If it makes you feel any better, I did notice he was sort of in a daze."

"Yeah, he disconnected…kind of out of body. What's the word?"

"Metaphysical."

"Yeah, exactly."

"What's your gut instinct telling you?"

"That he's lost. I know that feeling well, unfortunately."

"Sorry, G."

"Thanks."

"Are you still a bit jealous of him, mama's boy?" He laughed.

"I guess a little bit if I'm being truthful. Peter is now part of my mom's center, and I guess it's a little crowded at times."

"Man, G, you crack me up, but I like your style. Time is of the essence." Scholls silently summed up Berg's incident as ominous.

"Purr-fect" p.m.

They arrived at the Parker residence, and Scholls went inside to take the plate of food Barb sent with him, relinquishing it to his father. He wrote a note on the plate and left it on the stove. Exhausted, he headed off to sleep, yet one mischievous cat wanted to play.

"Hey there, Bandit. How's my precious little kitty doing?"

This cat was special. She was gray with green eyes and very affectionate. One day when Scholls was mowing a lawn, the cat came up to the side of the yard and just stared until he finished. The noise of the lawn mower did not even scare the kitty.

Scholls asked the owners if they knew whose cat it was—and to no avail. They asked him to take it, and surprisingly, Tina allowed him to keep it. The one thing he made sure of was putting Bandit in his room whenever either one of his parents was in a bad mood. In no way shape or form would he ever want his cat to be kicked or hurt by them.

"So what's my Bandit been up to? It looks like you ate your food while I was gone. I'm going to get you some more. C'mon, Bandi, let's get you some good stuff."

At one point, Scholls thought he might want to be a veterinarian.

He loved animals; however, when stem cells hit his ear drum, it trumped that plan. The furry kitty loved to sit on his chest and nuzzle. Whenever Scholls was upset or sick, she would not leave his side.

In a baby voice, he said, "So, Bandi, it's been a great week, and now we have a good friend named Garrett. He's got a cool family, and ours is, well, you know, *not*. Now your master is going to research stem cells, so you have to hang on for at least thirteen more years. Okay there, little Bandi? And by then, I might be able to prolong any conditions that should arise. Okay there? Make me this promise, will you? Good! You're my buddy, and I love you."

He began to get sleepy with random thoughts. It was so much fun when Casey watched the video and talked with the *supposed* worm. He thought about Garrett and how fast they became *so* close. The wedding should be fun. The homecoming dance made him nervous. The last thought he had was about Kipper. She just kept creeping up in his mind from time to time. Oh well, it was a lost cause. He finally fell asleep.

Unveiling Truisms

In mid-week, they rehearsed for the wedding, and since it was a small one, it took less than an hour. After the rehearsal dinner, G called Randy. "Hi, Randy, do you think we can do the transformation on Saturday before homecoming? I have a game on Friday night, and the dance is Saturday night."

Randy answered, "G monster, I checked with your school about homecoming. See you two in ten days."

"Thanks so much, Randy, I really appreciate everything you are doing and have done for me in the past. You're my go-to guy on style. It's not just that. I really care for you. You have become a close friend of mine."

"Garrett, we're cool like that, and I thank you. Besides, your friend Schollie is a neat kid who needs our help. Hell, he might be operating on me one day, and I damn sure don't want him remembering I was an ass, waking up afterward to discover he used those stem cells…and now I have three eyes!"

Laughing, G replied, "How could he be angry with you making him into the sophisticatedly dressed surgeon he will be?"

"You mentioned his parents weren't supportive. What did you mean by that exactly?"

"They are both complicated beings who he describes as resentful people. His mother is an alcoholic who puts him down, and his father is mean at times, punching them, and frequently exploding in anger."

"Damn, G, he turned out pretty good for all that. Have you witnessed any of it?"

"I haven't known him very long, but I did see his mother belittle him the first day I met her. Scholls is good-hearted. He must get his DNA from other family members."

"Nonetheless, the poor child will look fabulous when I get finished with him. He's gonna be like a bottle of Domaine de la Romanée-Conti grand cru."

"What's that?"

"A rare burgundy wine that in 1780, the Archbishop of Paris declared '*velvet and satin in bottles.*'"

"Nice."

"You two will definitely be the dynamic duo. Is he gonna have a date?"

"Funny you ask, I'm working on it right now. A friend of mine named Tally is asking some girls at school, and there's this one chick Scholls and I met recently."

"What's her story?"

"She's tall, probably about 5'11" or so, and she looks cute and all. She served us our take out burgers the other day. I could tell he was interested in her."

"Make sure she has brains, 'cuz Schollie is sharp. I picked that up immediately."

"Funny you say that too, 'cuz she told him how to fix his hiccups *scientifically* before we left, and he really perked up then." He chuckled.

"Perfecto, 'cuz I like him and I can relate to being an *outcast*. It's hard for a gay teenager to tell people. You feel so ashamed for being different. I suppose his poverty parallels the way I felt, and believe me, you are judged by everyone. But it's all good now."

"So you were in your teens when you knew you were gay?"

"Absolutely, I knew in grade school. As a kid, you aren't sure how or why you don't like the girls all that much. You go along with everyone out of peer group pressure. As you figure it out, a cloud rests over your head. You wonder who knows and who will treat you cruel when they find out. So you just keep it in, and one day, you find someone who feels the same. Thankfully, it is more accepted now. My partner, Victor, is still scared to let his parents know we are together. He disassociates himself from them to avoid conflict. They are devout Christians and against same-sex relationships. It might be what breaks us up one day.

"On the flip side, my parents have totally accepted me and Victor. I really had no clue as to what they would do. I just decided to tell them and my sister. I figured, 'Adios if they didn't like it.' Not everyone has a lifestyle change. It can be genetically induced. Either way, a person shouldn't inflict cruelty on people just because they don't agree with it."

"Yeah, like Scholls and I talked about. They have hermaphrodites. That happens during the formation of the fetus. There will always be irregularities in cell development and hormonal imbalances. Anyways, it's none of my business who you like or want to be with and if you truly believe that the Lord is the *only* one who can judge, then *stop* judging! As an adult, live your life and worry about your own actions when you stand before our Maker."

"You go, G! See you soon. Ciao, baby!

Vows on the Sunset

The Gran Palazzo De Cote was beautiful. That wedding was planned before dusk so they could see the sun setting in the background of the ceremony, which embellished the perennial aristocracy of the *Harmonie Jardin*; its array of many different flowers was breathtaking. Their theme was "Cherish the love we have every day."

Barb's parents, her sister Donna, her brother Phillip, Garrett, Scholls, her nieces and nephews, Linda's husband Rick, and close friends sat on the bride's side. Casey was the ring bearer, and Barb's niece Lilly was the flower girl. Due to the intimacy of the wedding, she had no bridesmaids and chose Linda for her matron of honor. They have been best friends since second grade.

On the groom's side, there were only eleven people. It wasn't strange; after all, his immediate family had perished. His best man, Jonathon, was a friend from undergrad. Seated were his aunt and uncle that cared for him after the tragedy, their daughter Marie, her kids Brandon and Brandi—twins, and a couple colleagues from where Peter attended medical school.

The reception was held in the Cour Petit Rassemblement. A few more friends from both sides attended this part. The comedian and magician were both fantastic, and the three-man band played soft rock.

Scholls and Garrett were having a blast. In an effort to wind down, they walked outside and got some air. Unexpectedly, G became dizzy.

G said, "Hey, I need to sit down for a minute."

SP replied, "Sure, man, let's sit over here. What's goin' on?"

"I'm dizzy again."

"I wonder if it's residual from the concussion. Can I get you anything?"

"No, I'll be fine. I just need a couple minutes."

"Dude, you don't look fine right now. I'm gonna get your stepdad to come over here."

"No, I will be okay. My mom will get hyper, and it's going to ruin their wedding."

"Eff the wedding. Your mom would want to know her son is sick."

"Please, dude, chill. I promise I will tell her after homecoming. They won't let me play, and I'm not jeopardizing the game again."

"All right, Garrett, but I want you to tell them afterward, or I will. This is not normal. You've had blurry eyes and dizziness a few times already in a short period. How long has this happened?"

"Probably six or seven times within the last two months. I've been eating right and exercising. I take vitamins and drink protein shakes. I'm trying to gain more muscle mass."

"Muscle mass…My skinny ass could use some. I might have to work out with you. Seriously though, when's the last time you had your blood work done?"

"The sports physical this summer, 'cuz it's required for football camp, and just the other day, a lady came in to draw my blood after my concussion."

"Do you remember your glucose level?"

"Not sure, I think my levels were normal. Unless the new lab work shows me different. Peter is getting the results back soon."

"Yeah, that's right, I remember you showing me the report. Promise me you won't just blow it off or forget to let your mom know. You realize I'm a doctor in progress, so I can't let you slide. Ha!"

"Bro, you don't forget much. Looks like I'm surrounded by doctors now. I promise. Give me a couple more minutes. You can go back inside, and I'll catch up with ya."

"Dude, we can sit here as long as it takes. I'm not going anywhere!"

Several more minutes went by, and he felt better despite the weakness but able to continue throughout the night. Even though Barb and Peter just got married, they put their honeymoon on hold. Their schedules would allow more time in late November or early December, and then the plan is to spend two weeks in Europe. They would stay the rest of the weekend at the resort.

When he heard his mom say "I do," it solidified that life at 11 Huntingdon Cove would be very different. Peter did offer to buy a brand-new house for the family, but Barb rejected his offer early on, making it clear she wanted to remain there. She mindfully pointed out that Garrett was in his senior year and his life had already been disrupted enough; furthermore, it had not even been two years from the time it was built. It sort of took Peter by surprise. The master bedroom she shared with Thom was sentimental, and they made it into a small shrine on behalf of Garrett and his father's memory.

The other side of the home had a west wing, appropriately shouldering where the new master bedroom would be. If Peter had conveyed problems with this, then the marriage would not have moved forward. Barb explained that she loved Peter; however, they needed the comfort of memorializing Thom.

Peter accepted this and was fine. At least that's what she believed. Inside he was tormented by the ghost of Mr. Pierce.

He remembered the words she spoke at the funeral. "I was truly blessed twice." It took him back to the feeling he had when his mother gave all her attention to Charles, his stepfather. Peter was whacked hard repeatedly and punished in altering fashions, namely, deprivation of food and isolation in the basement. He learned to hold his bladder all too well and mentally deflect pain from types of heat.

Charles burned him with hot matches, hot wax, and a cigar once where it did not show. When Peter was seven, his stepdad pushed him down the stairs and broke his leg. He could say nothing out of fear. Anyway, his mother, Ursula, turned a blind eye when it came to the abuse, and there was plenty of it. It's undetermined if she would suffer any abuse as the result of protecting him, but regardless of this, she never bothered to leave or take her son to a better environment. This clearly spelled out that she was a shitty, irresponsible mother who remained sexually entwined with such a monster. He met his best friend shortly after getting his leg cast. Their initial contact came when Paul, a neighboring kid, helped him up after Peter maneuvered the crutches improperly and fell to the ground. The only thing that surpassed Peter's pain was Paul's suffering from leukemia. He treasured his friend, and when that boy died, so did Peter's soul.

The next several years would formulate a doctor with hidden emotional disturbances. There can be a fine line between brilliance and insanity; Peter Berg was straddling that proverbial fence. An advanced degree wouldn't protect someone from developing a psychiatric illness. He wore a white coat with a black lining.

CHAPTER 8

Dr. Spy Berg

P ETER WAS THE mysterious well-dressed man in the back of the chapel at Thom's funeral. Unbeknownst to Barb, Peter knew who she was well before that.

He's quite the distinguished doctor, obtaining his MD and PhD in neurological medicine. Some of the kids he studied and cared for were at the autism school, and Barb might not have spotted him earlier because he did majority of his work on the top floor. It had a walkway connection to the university where he was also a faculty member, and it also connected to the gateways of the medical center.

Pangs of emotion filled his heart when he first saw Barbara. He mumbled, "Femme exquise." At that time, Thom was still alive. Barb was a volunteer with high interest in teaching there; her music was just what the kids needed, and he loved watching her perform.

When Dr. Berg wanted something, he got it, but this would not be easy as she was married with a family. One day, Garrett came with her to the facility, and he wasn't sure who the teen was. In months to follow, his feelings for her grew incessantly, and if she did not come in for a while, the delays maddened him. Dr. Berg hired a private detective, and Steffan recited the findings in an orderly manner:

"She has been married for almost twenty years and has one son. Her husband is an attorney in corporate law. He partners and owns the firm. They employ nearly sixty lawyers. Their home is near an inlet and was recently built. Her parents are well-to-do.

Her father is a CPA with prominent clientele. They also have investments and bought commercial realty for thirty-five years.

"She has a master's degree in special education. Her best friend is a childhood schoolmate. Her family relocated to the west coast when she was five. She likes to hike and plays tennis on occasion. They do not belong to any country clubs. They have a few family gatherings each year and mostly with her family. Her son is an actor and was recently cast for a movie being made called *Constant Judgment*. He plays quarterback at Excalibur High School. I have all the specific names and addresses listed on a separate page."

Dr. Berg said, "Thank you, Steffan. I will let you know if I need any further information." *So that* was *her son the other day. Huh, she is happily married…no chance of her divorcing that man. I just have to be with her! No one has ever made me feel so excited. Even my own wife, who I loved, did not expound these kinds of emotions.*

He was impatiently patient—what an oxymoron. She had applied to teach at the facility, and he made sure she got the job. Thom had passed away by then. In accordance, Dr. Berg initiated the plan that consummated his variations of fluttered pulsation.

Totally smitten, he finally approached her. Mrs. Pierce's voice drove him deeper into obsession. She was very attractive and professional, and those lips of hers were targets for his pupils. He fantasized about kissing them in the lab, and Barb had no idea he was harboring such a mental composition.

Barb said, "Oh, it's nice to meet you, Dr. Berg."

Peter replied, "Yes, Barbara, I am pleased you have joined our staff."

"Do you work directly with specific children?"

"Yes, I have several kids whom I have treated and studied."

"I am happy to be here and hope to make a difference in their lives. Autism cases have increased considerably in the past two decades. Well, you would already know that." She giggled. "My little brother is autistic and is now thirty-four years old."

"I'd love to meet him one day. We need more people like you who understand just how much they need social interaction. You play the piano so beautifully. I'm excited to be working with you." How excited? She had no idea. "Please seek my help with the children for any reason."

"Why, thank you, Dr. Berg."

Peter sighed. *Rien pour vous, mon amour.* Anything for you, my love.

Barb walked away unsure of its meaning and too nervous to ask.

This was the beginning of their story. Now, Garrett was the only thing in Peter's way. The doctor's perfect outcome would be a family of *trios* (three).

CHAPTER 9

Which? Hunt

After the wedding, G drove back to the house, and they played with Casey until Juanita put him to bed. Garrett realized he will now see his little brother every day, and things would surely be different. Only thing was, it's probable he will leave the house after graduating. He decided to make the dauntless effort and accept the change, feeling less conflicted with Peter and increasing adoration for Casey. The boys calmed down from the night.

Scholls asked, "Hey, Garrett, how are you feeling?"

G replied, "Tired a bit. That's all."

"You up for playing a video game?"

"Sure, I can handle kicking your butt again." He chuckled.

"Oh yeah, I think I have the hang of it now. You're on, dude."

They began to play and talked about homecoming. Garrett still had not heard from Tally, and the dance was only one week away with no confirmation of a date for his friend. The next day, they woke up before noon, and Scholls must go home to do chores. G took him back and said, "I had so much fun this weekend. Thanks for being a part of it."

"G, I should be thanking you. This was the most fun I have ever had with anyone. Please thank your mom for me. I will see you in school on Monday. Don't forget to take more photos of the worms. I'll wrap up the written portion of our experiment. See ya."

"Will do. Later, bro."

Garrett dialed Tally's number.

She answered, "Hello?"

"Hey, Tally, how are you doing?"

"Hi, Garrett, what are you doing calling me on a Saturday?"

"Oh, it's okay, isn't it?"

"Sure, you've never called me on a weekend before. It just threw me off for a second. Is there something up?"

"Well, it's about that favor I asked of you. Did anyone bite?"

"I've been meaning to talk with you. So far, no luck. I tried three girls, and they all seem to think he's pretty, well, not my words, *disgusting*. I tried to get a hold of this one friend of mine in another city, but she already had plans with her family that weekend."

"Man, that's totally messed up. I can see them saying he might be too poor or a bit nerdy, but…Who'd you ask?"

"First I tried Mary Ellen Gatsby. She said, 'Oh hell no!' and took her fingers and mocked like she was going to put them down her throat to vomit…and walked off."

"Wow! Really? Okay, who else?"

"Then I asked Priscilla Smith…which was a long, improbable shot, I know, but I did anyway, thinking she might have a soft side to her. Everybody knows her high standards, so it's logical they would think she was being helpful."

<hr />

Priscilla looked at Tally and said in her valley girl voice, "Are you crazy or something? Like…do I look like I am desperate? Yeah, I mean, Roger Jennings and I broke up, but come on, like, look at that guy. He's like…totally disgusting. I would never go anywhere with him."

Tally said, "Okay, I'm sorry…It's just that Garrett and I are going to the dance and he is bringing Scholls. We wanted a date for him so he doesn't feel awkward."

"What? You're effing kidding me, right? G is his friend *and* your friend? Like, you're joking, right?"

"No, you heard right!"

"Not to be rude or anything, but you're not G's type. Is he doing all this for charity or something?"

Tally got pissed and said, "Charity? Now you crossed the line with me you stuck-up, overdramatic, academically mediocre, prebotoxed, wannabe Barbie. Sorry you just can't stand the thought of Garrett Pierce having such plebeians in his inner circle."

"A-play-beh-eh-uh-ian? Whatever!" She rolled her eyes.

"Oh, that's right, blondie. You made a C minus in world history. Frown lines are causing your face to wrinkle, and like, you *totally* pronounced it wrong!"

—•—•—◆◉◆—•—•—

Garrett started laughing so hard and said, "That's effing funny. You really said all that to her? Academically mediocre, prebotoxed, wannabe Barbie."

"Damn skippy…and I felt like saying something even worse, but I let it slide after that. Her brain was overloaded at that point. Ha!"

"LOL. I'm impressed. You didn't take any shit off her. She is so conceited. I can't stand chicks like her. Thank God I have more sense than physical influences. So who was the last candidate?"

"So I went into the library, right, and talked with Annie Wilson. I thought for sure she might do it. Turns out, she thinks he is even too nerdy for her."

"What? That's jacked up. Isn't she shy and a loner herself?"

"I thought so too. Go figure. Anyway, she was the least insulting but made it clear he did not do anything for her."

"Whoa! I can't figure girls out at times. You did your best and I appreciate it. Oh hey, I meant to ask you sooner, would you like a standard corsage or wrist corsage?"

"I guess I would prefer a wrist one."

"Perfect, we'll go over our plans for homecoming tomorrow. I have some work cut out to find Scholls a date. I will call you then."

Take One for the Kipper

Before going home, he drove over to Schultz's Burger hoping to find Kipper. This time, a short, stocky girl with multicolored hair came to the window.

Carhop Bianca asked, "Hey, cutie, you ready to order?"

"Hi, I'm gonna have a grilled chicken sandwich, except no cheese or mayo…add mustard and pickles…and a large ice tea."

"Okay, that's a grilled chicken…minus mayo and cheese…plus mustard and pickles…with lettuce and tomato. Okay, now do you want the bun toasted or plain?"

"I guess toasted."

"Does that complete your order?"

"Yes, but I was wondering if you could tell me whether Kipper was working today?"

She looked around and pointed over to another area. G asked the girl, "What's your name?"

"I'm Bianca. And yours is?"

"I'm Garrett."

"Do you know Kipper? Are you two an item?"

"No, actually, I just met her the other day. It's my friend who digs her. I came by to ask her a question. Can you tell Kipper to come to my vehicle when she gets a chance?"

"It's kind of against the owner's rules. We are not supposed to socialize too much with customers while we are on the clock. Our place is known for fast service, but I'll let her know and tell them you are her cousin if they ask." She winked at Garrett and left to place the order.

"Hey, Kipper, there's this super, I mean, *suuuuper*fine dude in a black Hummer that wants to talk with you. His face looks so familiar. Just can't pinpoint it yet. Anyway, I told him our rules. See him over there?"

Kipper looked and got excited. "Yeah, I met those guys recently. Remember I told you about the guy I liked that had hiccups?"

"Yeah, I do, but there's only one person today. Was it the driver?"

"No, he sat on the passenger side. His glasses were broken, but I could see pure handsome right through them."

"Damn, girl, 'cuz this guy doesn't have glasses, and I can see pure sexiness right through his window. I told him I would send you his way. Remember, he's your cousin." She winked twice. "So take the order to him when it's ready, but I still get the tip if he leaves one."

"Of course, I'll tip you myself if he doesn't."

"Don't forget to fill me in on the details. Inquiring girls need to know."

When the food was ready, Bianca handed it to Kipper. She wondered what Garrett was going to say. He rolled down the tinted window and she gave him the food. "How's it going? Garrett, right?"

"Yes, ma'am. Listen, Kipper, the reason I wanted to talk is on my friend's behalf. He has no idea I am here and would kill me if he knew I was doing this."

"Go ahead, I'm listening."

"We go to Excalibur High. Our homecoming dance is next Saturday night. It's a long story, but I am taking a date, and Scholl's does not have one. I kind of made him go to this thing. I don't want him to feel like a tagalong, so is there any way you could go and be his date? I know this is really strange to ask since you hardly even know us. I'd pay you if I have to."

"Oh boy, my parents require me to introduce them to anyone I go on a date with. They want names, numbers, and destinations. I'm not sure how I would pull this one off. My dress alone would be a huge red flag. And I think I'm scheduled to work Saturday night till midnight. Has Scholls mentioned me at all, you know, since we met?"

"Well, we talked about you, and he couldn't stop smiling. He really loved your advice about the hiccups and definitely likes you a lot. I think he feels like he might not have a chance because his family doesn't have much money."

"I kinda figured that, but I don't care. My family isn't rich, and we're not poor. There was just something about him that made me *melt*…'cuz I was immediately attracted to him. I don't mean to imply I couldn't be attracted to you, 'cuz you're pretty hot. I guess it's the pheromones. So if I get this straight, you are going to surprise him on homecoming eve?"

"Have to. If I tell him before, he may try to back out. I really want him to go to the dance 'cuz he rarely goes places. I'm even having someone help get him ready for it. They are going to fix his hair and clothes. By the way, he said the same thing after we left. You made him *melt*."

"You are a really good friend. Let me think about how to make this happen 'cuz I *do* want to go. Here's my phone number. Let me get yours. But I need to ask you for stuff…and your license plate info. My father is a cop, and he's taught me to check people out. I hope you don't mind because it's not safe for women these days. You look harmless. It's just I need to get my mother on board and skate around my father. If she checks and it's fine, then she might go along with it. Sorry, but that's the only way I can do this."

"Hey, I fully understand. It's no problem. Here's my name, number, date of birth, and license plate info. If you need more, just let me know. I can even bring my mother by if I have to. What nights do you work this week?"

"I will be here Tuesday and Wednesday till 10:00 p.m. We close earlier through the week. I'll call you by Monday night. Bringing your mother will help. I will get my mom to meet her after the 'clearance' issue. Ha."

"Hey, Kipper, thanks a lot. If you can't, don't worry. It is a last-minute request and highly unusual. I would understand, bye."

The whole idea of this was funny but nerve-racking. Coincidently enough, it was par for the course. Their friendship had blossomed in such a fast pace it made sense. G made a call to Randy for some advice. "Hey, Randy, me again."

"What's up, my nominee? The buzz is you guys will be up for awards. Has your agent told you?"

"Yeah, he called to let me know how much money it grossed the first day and week."

"Top of the charts, my friend. So what you got?"

"We need to fix Schollie's glasses. Do you have any suggestions?"

"I do…but it will be hard to get him a new prescription before this Saturday. If he is farsighted, we can use a pair of readers."

"No, man, he's not. It's more complicated."

"Okay, I can work my magic and find a pair of frames and have an optician set his lenses. I would need them by no later than Friday at 4:00 p.m."

"Damn, Scholls doesn't have a car, and I have a game that night. He needs his glasses for school during the day."

"Well, let me find out if my friend can help Saturday morning. While he is getting his locks cut and highlighted, you can take them over to the eye store. We'll fix him up. Don't fret, my man. Now, how was the wedding?"

"It went better than I expected. I just tried to be positive, and it was fine. Scholls even went and we had a blast."

"How did he look? I'm scared to ask."

"He washed his hair, and I loaned him a blue suit…still had the broken glasses. His hair was sort of frizzy, and it had electricity in it. He just didn't seem to care, but it was noticeable. There's a pic we took at the reception, and it is really sticking up. He's like, 'That'll work,' when he saw it. Ha."

"Po' thing, he just doesn't have a clue. I like his nonchalant attitude. He's probably gonna faint when he sees how handsome he really is. Get your video on your phone ready when we unveil Schollie. By the way, Victor and I took our friends to see the movie, and they loved it."

"Thanks, man, I had this awesome stylist who made me look fabulous! LOL. And the whole cast and crew did a fantastic job. James is a great director. I'd work with him any chance I could."

"Let's talk again Thursday. Be at the studio by noon on Saturday. Ciao, baby!"

There's a lot to do by next weekend. His main focus was on the date. He headed back home to take more photos of the worms.

Casey wrestled with Garrett for a few minutes, while Juanita fixed them dinner. They watched TV afterward, and out of the blue, G received a series of texts from Kipper. She told him about her routine before, during, and after work. They discussed a probable time line for events to fall into place. He smiled like the cat that ate the canary. Casey fell asleep, and G put him to bed. Barb and Peter would be home tomorrow.

On Sunday morning, Garrett was working out at the gym and had been nauseated in two ways: First, people coming up to him frequently. Damn, this was only the beginning. It never occurred to him he was famous. Maybe short lived for now—who knows—but there is a price to pay for losing your autonomy. Second, his stomach was irritated all morning.

One of the things he considered was vamping up the home gym. It needed more equipment, and the new income could do the trick. This muscle mass increase was becoming a pain. Would Tally even notice or care? Plus, he had received a script to audition for an athlete in another movie.

What about furthering his education? In the back of his mind, college was not going to be abandoned. Mr. Pierce spent many hours talking with him about it. Sustaining paternal admonition was important.

Peter had suggested applying at schools toward the east. Thom, on the other hand, wanted Garrett closer. During the previous summer, he attended a couple combine and showcase camps that the scouts attended. He just wasn't convinced to play ball anymore—the loss of his father was immense. Thom's death eroded G's future athletic goals, though he loved and respected the sport.

Where would Tally go? Heck, he didn't even know what she wanted to major in. There's so much stuff to find out. He couldn't wait to meet her parents formally. They had seen each other over the past three years at school functions, yet for some reason, his feelings for this girl were no longer platonic.

CHAPTER 10

Vial and Vile

BARB AND PETER returned from the resort around 1:00 p.m. Casey jumped into his dad's arms, and Garrett hugged his mother. They reminisced about the wedding and reception for thirty minutes. G would not reveal any of his sickliness.

Barbara spoke about her concerns with Garrett alone in another room, even though she texted him many times during the weekend. Peter was quite annoyed by the distraction on their wedding night.

Barb said, "Sweetheart, you wouldn't keep any symptoms from me, would you?"

G answered, "Mom, please, I will let you know if anything happens. Look at me, I'm doing great. Silly." Good thing he wasn't Pinocchio, or his nose would have grown two inches.

Playfully, he picked her up by the waist and whirled her around. She started laughing and pleaded, "Okay, okay, put me down. I'm just being a mother."

Peter heard the commotion and hurriedly walked into the den.

"What's going on in here? Is everything all right?"

Barb answered, "Yes, dear, Garrett and I were just having some fun."

Peter nodded. "Oh, I wasn't sure because I heard you shout out."

"Garrett's so strong. I forget he's growing up." She pinched him on his cheek and said in a baby voice, "But he's still my little boy and always will be."

Laughter filled the air, but Peter was jealous inside. He whispered, "Her little boy doesn't have long in this household."

Garrett had been meaning to ask his stepfather about the lab results of his blood. "Dr. Berg, I mean, Peter, did you get the results back for my blood work?"

Peter replied, "Oh yes, everything is somewhat normal at this point. I was going to tell you tonight."

Barb said, "Sweetheart, that's great news."

Garrett and Peter turned to her and replied the *same thing* at the *exact same moment*, "Yes, it is!"

Both of them were referred to as *sweetheart*, so it wasn't clear who she had addressed it to.

Barb said, "Well, Dr. Berg, you're my sweetheart as well, and I also want to thank you for the great news." He was so pissed but kept a smile on his face.

Those vials of blood the phlebotomist drew at the hospital were taken to the lab by Dr. Berg. He already knew Garrett was type O because he looked at his lab report from the sports physical. He switched Garrett's vials with his own blood and then destroyed the sports document. The new report showed the results of his blood as type A positive. He would get plenty of vials through medical supplies and pay with cash. Dr. Berg was ill. His traumatic events from youth had created personality disorders; he was a sociopath with psychopathic tendencies, though they were somewhat alike. When Berg's best friend died, he was cast into emotional turbulence, and Peter became a master of disguise.

He hated his mother for allowing years of abuse from Charles. So one night, he decided to finally get rid of the two people who hurt him most. During Paul's final stages of leukemia, his stepfather popped off with statements he could not forgive. Years of pain and agony surfaced into a ball of rage, and he wanted them gone forever.

Peter was fifteen then. He'd been crying all afternoon when his stepdad came in and started laughing, referring to him as a pansy. Peter couldn't stop. Paul was dying. He needed to get back to the hospital and was focused on doing just that; nonetheless,

Charles, his stepdad, demanded the *whining* stop and jerked him by the collar. For the first time ever, he pushed Charles back into the wall and screamed, "You son of a bitch, keep your hands off me. One day, I'm gonna kill you!"

Charles backhanded him hard and then cocked his fist to warn. "Don't you ever touch me again or I'll bust up your face permanently. You're a weak, pathetic kid. He's going to die anyway. He had no chance. It costs us taxpayers out the ass to keep these experimental cases going so they can be guinea pigs."

"That's *not* fair! His mother put him in the study so he *could* have a chance."

"Believe that all you want, kid. The federal government provides these programs, and they blend in under all that bureaucratic bullshit. Your friend was always terminal, and they knew it. So you better suck it up. Like I said, he's better off dying young. Now get your ass in there and do your chores."

"What about his mother? Maybe she wants to be with her son as long as she can in this lifetime. Maybe her pain will soften if she does all that she possibly can for him! She loves him. What's wrong with you?"

"Oh hell, she should have prepared herself for the inevitable. It's sad, but that's how the ball bounces. We're all gonna die."

"You know, Charles, you *are* a real asshole and probably the cruelest man I will ever know. You act like he's nothing!"

This struck a nerve with him. "I suggest you get the hell in there now, or you're gonna find your face on the end of my foot in two seconds. Oh, and don't think you're getting another ride back to the hospital today. You can go tomorrow."

"No! I have to go back. He's not doing well. His mother called earlier, and they don't expect him to make it much longer. I have to go back!"

Charles walked out and went to the living room to watch TV. Peter dropped to his knees and prayed to the Lord for Paul. He also chanted a message to his friend. "Hold on, buddy. I'm gonna be there soon. Please don't die before I get there. I'm on my way. I love you."

He finished the laundry and tried to find a way to sneak out. In the meantime, he was worried sick because Paul's mother had not called. He picked up the portable phone and went into his room to call the hospital. The nurse cannot give him details, so he begged her to recall who he was; she whispered, "Please come right away," and hung up. Peter was scared; he had to get there, and when Charles finally dozed off, he ran to the bus stop.

The nurses let him pass even though he was underage. Paul's aunt Rita instructed them to do so, if he arrived at anytime, stating he was "family."

As he approached the room, Francis, Paul's mother, was speaking in a sweet, low voice. "Baby, you're with the Lord now. No more pain for you, darling. No more needles to hurt you. No more medicines to make you sick. Just love all around you. Mommy is here with you. I'm always gonna be here. You're so precious. I'm gonna miss you, my sweet angel. Soon, when it's my time to go, I will see you again my darling." She stroked his cheeks and kissed him.

Peter walked over with tears streaming down his cheeks. Francis reached for his hand and placed him next to her son's side.

"He loved you. My baby held on longer than expected, and I think it's because he heard me talking to you on the phone earlier. When I said your name, he knew you were with him in spirit. I went to find a nurse to bring more blankets. He was shaking badly, but my angel slipped away in that brief moment. We both missed his final breath. He didn't want either one of us to see it. That's how loving my son is."

She cried even harder and told Peter he could say his good-byes privately. Staring at his friend's face with intensified sorrow, he held Paul's hand. He could hardly speak because his throat was tense; his heart was broken:

"Hey, bud, it's me…your best friend. I'm sorry! I'm sorry I got here late. I really am…Please forgive me." He broke down even more. "I'm gonna miss you so much. Who am I gonna talk to now?" He laid his head on Paul's chest. "I love you. I really do. You're my only friend. Oh God, why?" He laid his head on his heart. "I'm always here if you wanna talk. Can you send me a message. Please send me one. I'll never be the same now."

A strange note saying Purple-100-Final was written in his friend's writing. No one knew its meaning except Peter. He picked up the paper and put it in his pocket and then let out the most agonizing sound this hospital staff had ever heard from such a young person. It was a long, gradually increasing, combination of moaning and crying, which caused them to release tears of empathy. He knelt to the floor weeping and heard nothing but "Moonlight Sonata," his favorite classical piece by Beethoven. They removed Peter from the room, and Francis went back to her son until he was taken away. Rita gave this young man a ride home; his challenge of going inside unnoticed had potential repercussions waiting. Any faith bearing was gone, and he abruptly began spiritual discord with God. All he wanted to do was curl up in his bed and die himself.

The next few weeks were mortal agony with insurmountable loneliness for Peter. He began taking out anger on anything, even kicking the neighbor's dog, causing it to whimper for several seconds. This channeling of pain was the precursor of eminent doom. Infuriation set in, and he was apathetic; his schoolwork suffered, and he became academically uncooperative. The counselor interceded because all the teachers reported his above-average grades had declined rapidly, and while speaking to Peter, it was evident there was an acute problem.

She referred them to a therapist for evaluation. Ursula and Charles would not take him, for fear he would spill the beans about his homelife and get them in trouble. So Peter got worse. He no longer cared about his immediate world, except Francis, and they would visit the grave sight weekly.

After years of a malign environment and three months of swift psychological derangement, it was time for his parents' demise.

The last place he saw his stepdad, when his best friend was dying, was in his *recliner*. He always fell asleep there every night. So that is where he decided he would be when he dies.

He talked out loud in a slow, low, grisly voice, "You bastard… you no-good, thoughtless piece of shit. Because of you, I missed being with my friend when he needed me most. Your life… will end…the same place you were…at the time of my friend's death…*your recliner*. As for my mother, she will be…in *her bed*… where she treasures copulating with you!"

Earlier that day, he got into the stash of sleeping pills, crushed several up into fine powder, and put them into *their* food and drinks. While he was adding an additional dose of muscle relaxer to his mother's sauce, a sarcastic voice surfaced. "Now, then, Mother, since you like me to cook all the time, I thought I would make your favorite. Ahhh, yes, spaghetti. We'll call it your last meal of ill refutes. That's what death-row inmates get. It's only appropriate. The little pharmaceutical concoction is also for your back pain. I wouldn't want you leaving this world in any discomfort, would I? No, absolutely not. I'm far more attentive to you than you ever were for me when your effing husband…beat me…burned me…starved me…and broke my leg! Remember that, Mother? You called me clumsy so the doctors wouldn't suspect a thing. You always could lie well. Darn!" He looked at his watch. "We just don't have enough time to go over all the inflictions. Sleep well, Ursula…for you will now reap the benefits of the child you molded to kill."

There would be no chances of them waking up. By 8:15 p.m., both were in a deep medicinal stupor. They never replaced any batteries in the smoke detectors, and this lack of preparedness would be to his advantage. He checked on his mother first, and there she was, out cold *in bed* with a book in her hand. Out of curiosity, he walked over and looked at the *fictional* title.

"Hhhmm? *Gates of Hell*. You know, Mother, you always said you wanted to be in a movie." Happily, he blurted, "Guess what?

You're starring in this one! You finally got the part you deserved after years and years of method acting. Way to go!" He gave her two thumbs-up and headed to Charles.

He put a well-lit cigarette into his stepdad's fingers and waited heinously across the room until it burned down enough to drop into the ugly yellow-and-brown plaid material. He helped flames engulf the chair by lighting the area where the whiskey had spilled from the glass his stepdad had in his other hand. "Oops!"

He crossed his arms and spoke in a whispery voice, "You shouldn't fall asleep with a cigarette in one hand and alcohol in the other. It's a bad combination. And you don't listen well either, underestimating me all along. I warned you this day would come…after you mocked me while I wept in agony for my friend's life. Une fin Naturelle! Quite *a natural ending*."

Everybody knew his stepdad smoked and drank heavy. In the prior year, he parked his car crooked along the curb in front of their house and passed out drunk, causing his cigarette to fall into the interior. A blaze caught the neighbor's eye. In Olympic speed, he ran over, busted the window, and put out the fire with Charles's jacket. It was documented on the police and insurance report.

As the house was burning, he vocalized an epitaph to Charles, "RIP. Rest in **P**eace. *Au Contraire.* For you two, it means, RIP, 'Rot in **P**urgatory.'"

He waved slowly and said in a low controlled manner, "Good-bye…"

Peter always jogged at night, and neighbors knew this as well. He dug a hole and hid a small gym bag in some bushes a few blocks away, taking only a *few* sentimental items. One of them was Paul's favorite book, *The Wonderful Wizard of Oz* by L. Frank Baum. He believed he'd retrieve the bag later.

The police ruled the catastrophe an accident while fire officials cleared it from foul play. As he's driven to the station to await his aunt and uncle from DC, memories of Paul diffused every crevice of his heart.

CHAPTER 11

007 Homecoming Heaven

GARRETT LEFT THE room to call Tally and gave her the good news about his blood work. He wanted to text Scholls but knew the rules, so he'd tell him tomorrow in school. G dialed her number. "I hope she answers...Please answer, please answer—" The phone rang three times.

Tally answered, "Hello, Garrett."

"How did you know it was me?"

"This time, I looked at the caller ID before I answered. Ha!"

"Oh yeah, that's right." He's so nervous when he heard her voice. "Do you have a moment to go over the details about homecoming?"

"Sure."

"By the way, the picture of your dress you e-mailed me was beautiful. We are going to look great together. My tux has a bow tie. I'll send you a pic when we hang up. At first, the guys on the team were gonna wear their leather jackets. I voted *no* on that, and fortunately, so did most of the guys."

"I'm pretty sure you are going to get homecoming king. So I'm just gonna seethe at the queen."

"Don't worry about that, Tally. If I do, it's only show for the ceremony. You're gonna be the real queen on my arm."

"Garrett, that's sweet. I was just kidding."

"Oh yeah. Of course. So I'm going to pick you up around seven. After I visit with your parents and we take pictures, we will drive and pick up Scholls at another location. My friend Randy is going to bring him out, and we need to have our vid ready when he does."

"Vid as in *video*? For?"

"Randy is going to make him over in a big way. So we need to capture the expression on Scholls's face when he checks out his new image in the mirror. This should be hilarious."

"I can't wait. Let's make sure we take a group pho at some point."

"LOL. Group pho. I like it! There may be a secondary shock phase to my plan. If all goes well, we will leave and drive to this burger place where Scholls and I had lunch the other day. He fell in love with the girl who took our order. Since the prima donnas at Excalibur High think they are too good, I found someone who is worthy of my friend."

"I do not understand how she jumped on board for this if you just met her."

"I had to play 007 and go behind his back to ask her this favor. She needs to get approval from her mother, and if all goes well, we will pick her up at the burger place where she will be waiting. Her father is a policeman, and she has to do this on the sly. My mother will vouch for us, and I'm going to take my mom to meet hers if she can."

"That's a lot of work. You really do like him, don't you?"

"Yep, I have been blessed all my life, and it pleases me to give back to others who don't have it so good. I met my best friend for life. It only took me forty-eight hours to figure it out. Now I have eighty years to prove it to him."

"Garrett, you're a special person with a big heart. Forget all the movie star stuff. You are one hell of a guy. I got teary eyed from what you just said."

"Why, thank you, Ms. Martin." She laughed. "You just reminded me of something. Speaking of movie star stuff, we need to outsmart the paparazzi, so I'm taking a different vehicle that belongs to my father. I wanted a part of him with me for this. It has very dark-tinted windows. They will be expecting me in my Hummer, so we have permission to park in the back area of the school and go through the kitchen and work our way to the dance. The school has banned them from the property. We will go home just before midnight."

"I'm down with all this. I will definitely never forget my homecoming. There won't be one dull moment!"

"If Kipper, the girl we met, comes through as his date, she will go to work as usual. Her father always stops by in his police car around 7:15 p.m., orders a soda, and sits doing paperwork for about twenty minutes. Once he leaves, her mother will bring the dress and shoes. I'll bring the corsage, which my mom will buy on their behalf. She will get ready inside and meet us before 8:00 .m. Hopefully, everything will go smoothly, and we will be at the dance before 8:30 p.m. We will get back about twenty minutes after midnight, and her mother will be there waiting to let her change before taking her home. She has a license to drive but for safety her father insists she be dropped off and picked up from work. Kipper has some side work she does after closing and usually does not leave until 12:30 p.m. We just need everyone's guardian angels in sync."

"Okay, 007, I like the plan. So Scholls has no idea she will be his date?"

"Nope, I told him we might have someone lined up, but not to worry 'cuz there's no reason we can't have a great time with just the three of us. Of course, I'm gonna say we couldn't get anyone toward the end of the week. Now…you'll be the driver, and I will tell him we need to sit in the back to avoid being noticed. It's pretty sneaky, and I can't wait to see him freeze up when she gets into the car. I will keep Scholls occupied, and you will pull to the back area of Schultz's Burger…That way, Kipper can creep up and get into the car."

"So I'm like one of the Bond girls?"

"Oh yeah, baby, you're gonna be like Honey Rider for this episode."

"Honey Rider." She laughed. "What a play on words, Garrett."

They both laughed and then talked extensively about the dance until they halfheartedly hung up.

"Good night, Bond."

"Good night, Honey."

Just before he dozed, a wishful forthcoming popped in his head. *I just might want to say that for the rest of my life.*

Dental Bonding

Scholls and G met up early before classes to talk about the project, but another idea was brewing in an altruistic fashion from the all-American kid. The transformation, the girl, the glasses, the dance, and now, the teeth were part of his total undertaking. Garrett updated Scholls he was going to set up an appointment on Thursday at 5:00 p.m. in the interest of cleaning his teeth. He had his mom call Dr. Melicia Tjoa to explain the special circumstances. She had two offices called BRSH Dental, with no *u*. The primary one is located in Houston and secondary in Southern California. He loved her personality and the whole staff. Garrett also wanted another cleaning before the dance.

"Okay, now you want to pay for my cleaning? I can't let you do this. Enough is enough. Dude, I'm so appreciative for everything that has happened, but it has to stop."

"Oh, c'mon, man, you need to have it done. Please, I want you to look the best you can be. That's all. If you feel better, I'll let you pay me back. I'm gonna have mine cleaned at the same time."

"That's a given. I have an idea. My father does get benefits from his job. Let me find out if we have dental insurance. If not, then it's gonna have to wait. Besides, who's gonna see my toofers anyway. It's not like I have a date. Chill, G, I will get it done one day." Garrett held back his smile. If his friend only knew what was transpiring.

"All right, but the offer still stands. Can you find out tonight? I can give them your information so they can start the verification.

You'll need to fill out a health history and a patient information sheet, plus questions concerning your teeth. There's one catch. Your mom will have to make the initial appointment with you. Do you think that is even possible?"

"Man, G. Ha! A *catch* is becoming a pattern with you. Yeah, there is a microscopic chance her motherly instincts will kick in. She actually could, 'cuz she doesn't have to be to the bar until 7:00 p.m. Just likes to leave early before my dad wakes up. I will ask the Wicked Witch of the Westward Trailer Park if she has time to portray herself as my mother. This should go over like Sasquatch at a bald convention."

"Damn, Scholls, you crazy. It's gonna be that awkward?" He kept laughing.

Scholls stayed focused on G, moving his head up and down, lips pressed together. Garrett couldn't stop laughing. "Let's put it this way, Sasquatch at least has a reason for feeling awkward."

"Call me tonight if possible. I know you can't use the phone much. Talk with your mom about the dental appointment and ask her if you have insurance. Find out if she is game and explain she must be there initially because you are not eighteen years old. Or you just might have to negotiate like my *other* cousin from Texas—Simpleton Simon."

They spontaneously acted out a scene for fun.

Scholls began, " Y'all take trade-ins for your teef work?"

Garrett talked in a female voice. "Excuse me, sir, what do you mean by trade-ins exactly?"

"Deer, hogs, alligators, opossum…"

"Well, sir, we don't. Is there any way you can come up with some money?"

"Hell yeah-ya. I play Bingo every Saturday, and I usually win!"

"Okay, sir, we will be here when you get that money. Would you like to make an appointment?"

"Hell yeah-ya. Put me down for next Sunday morning before I go drink up all my profits."

"Oh, sir, we aren't open on Sundays."

"What? Most good ol' stores are."

"Sir, we aren't a store. We are a dental office."

"Damn, y'all city slicker's options are like a redneck in a round room try-na find a corner. I'm just gonna go over to Uncle Barney's and borrow a pair of pliers and pull out that rotten one myself."

"Sir, that's not a wise idea."

"Darlin', who said anything about me being wise? Say, ya sound mighty pretty over the tel-e-phone. What's your name? I gotta big ol' truck we can go muddin' in. What time ya get off work?"

"Sir, I am married, and this is inappropriate. Now do you want an appointment or not?"

"Nah, looks like y'all folks won't do nuttin'. Pretty set in y'all's ways. City slickers are more a pain in my ass than what's in my mouth!"

They both busted out laughing. "You know, Scholls, we find humor in so many ways, dude. I've never had this much fun with anyone. We just flow. I think you're frickin' hilarious and smarter than hell. You've become my best friend, and I hope it's mutual. Time didn't define us, but it's gonna strengthen us."

At that very moment, Scholls Parker was inducted into the "hall of best friends." Other than his uncle Randolph, he couldn't think of anyone more uplifting. Garrett will be his best friend. He remembers the words from Wilbur, in E. B. White's book *Charlotte's Web*:

> "Why did you do all this for me?" he asked. "I don't deserve it. I've never done anything for you."
>
> "You have been my friend," replied Charlotte. "That in itself is a tremendous thing."

The seed had been planted, and he would nurture it for the rest of their lives. He decided to make his own personal manifesto: "It was by way of fate I met my friend. Though hurriedly in pace, it shall by all accounts remain steadfast."

Mums the Word

Kipper had given her mother, Kelly, all the information on Garrett. Her mom was mischievous and understood life needed a little mystery and fun; coincidently, to meet Karl Manning, Kipper's father, she pulled something similar. Being a pseudo detective was right up her alley, and having your spouse in law enforcement gave you direct contacts to detailed information one might usually have to pay for. She called her close friend, Susie, a bailiff, at the courthouse and gave the name and license plate info Kipper obtained. Within a few hours, Kelly was pleased to learn all was kosher, but Susie *did* cast another educational tidbit her way.

Susie said, "You might want to sit down on this one. That kid, Garrett, is the main actor in the movie that's out called *Constant Judgment.*"

Kelly Manning replied, "No way. Are you kidding me! Are you bullshitting me?"

"Nope, he is, and his family is as normal as pumpkin pie."

"Whoa, I am shocked and excited all in one. I don't think Kipper knows who he is. For sure it would have been mentioned! A teenager doesn't forget stuff like that. I'm not going to say anything to her, and if she does find out, we will keep it under wraps. Put it this way, I want this kid to feel comfortable. There's humble pie as well, because he never told my daughter."

"Good luck, Inspector. We'll go to lunch when it's over and have a good laugh! I can't wait to hear how you pull this off. Karl will explode if he finds out. Have you got a plan if he does?"

"Yeah, it's called 'night of the seductresses' remorse.' A little music, wine, food, sexy lingerie with sexy talk…and my slate is wiped clean, girlfriend!"

"Ha, ha. Now that's power of persuasiveness right there."

"Susie, thanks a million! Call you soon."

When Kipper got home from school, Kelly shared the completed investigation, and everything checked out positive. They went over the protocol for homecoming night. Kelly reassured Kipper there's plan A—smooth success, or plan B—rocky success, but it would happen regardless of the chain of events.

Last year, her daughter wore a beautiful dress to her own homecoming at Windmont High, and she could use it for this dance. Garrett would bring his mother to meet hers at Schultz's Burger this Wednesday night, because on Tuesday eves, Kelly had labs for nursing school. Kipper called Garrett with the good news and confirmed 8:30 p.m. for the mothers to meet. All was moving forward, and soon, Scholls would actually get to be with the girl who made him blush.

Insured Plans

Back at 1726 Barker St. #2, Scholl's mother was her usual self. "You want to know what?"

Scholls replied, "If Dad has dental insurance."

"Yes, we have it. And this is because?"

"I'd like to go and get my teeth examined and cleaned."

"Yeah, well, I'd like to go get a bunch of those fake teeth Hollywood superstars have. We don't have the money for you to just be all 'proper' and everything. It's that rich kid, isn't it? He's putting all this into your feeble brain."

Scholl's thought, *There's nothing feeble here but your parenting skills! If you knew your own kid, you would know he's on target to be the valedictorian, Ms. Clueless!* "I disagree. My brain is not wimpy. Garrett has a family dentist and has gone to great lengths to see we get an appointment. On the initial visit, I must have a legal guardian present to become a new patient since I'm not eighteen years old."

"Wait, so you want to use up extra money for unnecessary things and want me to go to this office and sign a bunch of paperwork?"

"I hardly think a dental appointment is unnecessary."

"Okay, do you have a toothache?"

"No."

"Then what's the urgency?"

"Oh, I don't know…Maybe I want to make sure my teeth are in good condition so I don't experience one. Plus, look at them. They are dirty. I can see stains on the front teeth."

"Boy, Scholls, you were fine until that kid showed up in the picture."

"He's not the enemy, Mom. He's my best friend and treats me better than any other kid I've known."

Tina laughed hysterically. "You really think he cares. He's rich. He's probably just doing some humanitarian crap for God knows what. When school is out, you'll be history."

"By the way, it's not going to cost us anything for the initial visit. That is, if Dad's insurance can be accepted at their office. Can I please check?"

"If that's the case, I guess so. I'm not gonna wake him for this shit. Go get Dad's wallet and pull out the insurance cards. If they take it, then I will go up there with you, but I'm just going to make my appearance and leave. You can fill out the paperwork, and I'll act like I signed it." It was déjà vu. *I already do that for school.* "I'm not going to hang around while they try to find everything under the sun. Get the basic stuff *only!*"

Though thanking her for this would be weird, Scholls said, "Thanks, Mom, it's this Thursday at 5:00 p.m. We need to be there about fifteen minutes earlier."

"Damn, I usually meet up with some friends for dinner on Thursdays before I go into work. I guess I can be late. Let me know for sure if you are going."

"Yes, Mom, I will."

Tina walked over to Scholls as if she wanted to hug him. Unable to show affection, she just responded, "Okay, then," and walked off. He witnessed his mother in a vulnerable moment—a sober moment. How come she can't even hug him?

He was cognizant about his friendship with Garrett. Misery loves company, and Tina never had a best friend she can recall. Thus and so, she was wrong about G.

Scholls opened the wallet and pulled out two cards, took a picture of them with his cell phone, and then sent them to Garrett, along with his birth date and father's Social Security number. Then he erased the info and went into his bedroom to pick up Bandit.

"Hi, little girl, I love you. What did you do all day…sleep? Good kitty, you need your rest. Remember, you have to hold on at least thirteen more years. Let's call Garrett and see if he got my information." Bandit sat on his chest and nuzzled his chin.

The phone rang. "Hey, Scholls, how's it going?"

"Dude, I can't believe it. My mother will go up there Thursday if the insurance is okay."

"Really? Awesome! I'm gonna shoot this to my mom's phone, and she will take care of it for us. I'll know by tomorrow eve. If they don't, you're just gonna have to pay me back. *You* are getting your teeth cleaned!"

"G, my intuition tells me the insurance will be fine. Okay, see you in school tomorrow. Thank your mom for me, and you know you have a surgeon for life. I'm gonna owe you for so many favors it's ridiculous."

"Dude, you don't owe me jack. See you tomorrow in class. I'm still filming the worms. Did you get the pics I sent of pics of Anne?"

"Yep, they were kick-ass. Later."

"Later."

On Tuesday after school, G was at practice but only able to watch. Coach Johnson was a firm believer in vitamins and read vitamin B12 injections help swollen tendons. Garrett's injury during the St. Clair game prompted him to recommend them, and he contacted Barb and Peter for their take on it. Peter insisted he start as soon as possible and purchased the vial and syringes.

There would be about six injections over a month's time, which allowed the liver to store a good supply. Thereafter, he would need an additional shot every two to three months.

The day after the injury, he had been examined by their podiatrist and got a corticosteroid shot which alleviated the pain right away. Garrett's left foot was wrapped with an ace bandage, and he had to sit on the sidelines in practice, but there was no way he would forfeit playing the homecoming game. He would get his first injection soon.

Barb relayed the insurance information to Garrett when he got home. The dental plan was active, and Scholl's could go see Dr. Tjoa. She made their appointments simultaneously on Thursday at 5:00 p.m. G sent Scholls a text to let him know. Hopefully, Harry and Tina would understand that some texts were important.

Dr. Berg now had a new vessel to cause Garrett symptoms. Just a few weeks ago, he began adding a medication to Garrett's protein mix, and this one in particular was used for Parkinson's disease. He would grind up the tablets in a fine powder, like he did for his mom and stepdad's special day, and place a certain amount into the protein powder that Garrett used. The medication had side effects for a person with the disease, let alone without.

His undergrad was a premedical track for biochemistry majors with plenty of pharmacology. He bought the same brand of mix and switched out the canisters, so his exposure was not daily. As previously mentioned, Garrett's vindicated expiration would be relatively similar to his parents; likewise, he would die in a way that was a fluke. The biggest difference would be that Garrett would not die in one big blaze of glory; rather, his would be an underlying health issue that went array.

The vitamin B12 injections would give him the ability to increase G's level of insulin. Too much insulin causes the cells in the bloodstream to absorb more glucose and the liver to produce less glucose, making it dangerously low. Hypoglycemia has many symptoms, including blurred vision, light-headedness, headaches, weakness, seizures, and unconsciousness. Severe hypoglycemia can cause comas and death. His symptoms would be similar, and at any given time, he could control Garrett's final path. Of course, he thought it was rather fun changing the methods with different chemicals. He was like the puppet master of fate.

The other half of "truly blessed twice" had to go. Barbara would need him even more than ever if her beloved son passed. And Scholls, why should he benefit from having a lifelong friend? If Peter couldn't have Paul, then logically, Garrett would be the missing piece of the puzzle, thus *killing* two **gold**-birds with one stone. When duty called, the appropriate action would be used, and this time, he would be sitting at a funeral consoling his spouse.

Berg said, "Hey, babe, can you call Garrett in here so I can administer his B12 injection?"

Several minutes later, G came into the kitchen to receive the first shot. His trust in Peter had escalated, and he no longer felt eerie about him.

CHAPTER 12

A? B? We'll See

IT WAS WEDNESDAY around 8:30 p.m., and Garrett took his mother to meet Kipper and Kelly. They pulled up to order a soda. Bianca waved to G and approached the Hummer.

Bianca said, "Hey, Garrett, her mom is right there in the silver Tahoe. Kipper has all of us on scout duty for your arrival. Ha."

"Hey, Bianca, it's nice to see you again. This is my mother, Barbara." G's mom waved to her and said hello.

"Hi, ma'am, it's nice to meet you. I can see where Garrett got his looks."

Barb replied, "His father is responsible, believe me."

Kipper walked up and introduced herself to Barbara. They got out of the Hummer, and Kelly got out of the Tahoe. After all the introductions, Kelly and Barb conversed easily. They both thought the plan was incredulous and quite frankly, couldn't wait to do it.

Bianca brought their drinks, and G handed her a $5 bill and waved off the change. Barb told Kelly, "You're gonna love his friend, one of the nicest kids you'll ever meet. His parents work in the evening, so I thought I would vouch for Scholls."

"Well, it certainly is a different name. Kipper sure thinks he is cute. We ran a check on him as well, and there wasn't one issue. I hope you didn't find it too offensive when we did background checks on everyone. My husband is a police officer. To make this happen, I had to do my homework as a protective mother and obedient wife. LOL."

"None taken at all. More parents should do this."

"Strangely, he doesn't have a driver's license. I thought all kids couldn't wait to get one. Kipper does, but her father insists on her being driven to and from work for safety reasons. We allow her to use the car in the day."

Garrett answered, "Yes, ma'am, he will soon. His parents have some particular rules." He felt the need to wrap up the inquiry to avoid discussing the financial reasons for its absenteeism.

Everybody went over the plans A and B. Barbara let Kelly know she was volunteering at the homecoming dance and was also given permission to bring a few students from the autism school. The parents signed field trip slips, and some would be chaperones. Excalibur High was known for community interaction with different organizations.

Kelly announced plan A. "Okay, so I will meet you guys here on Saturday night between 7:30 and 8:00 p.m. I will have to park across the street so Karl doesn't see the Tahoe. Once he is gone, I will bring her the clothes and help Kipper get ready. We have permission from her boss. Please try to send me a text for the ETA. We usually get home around 12:30 to 12:45 a.m., and her father gets home around 11:15 to 11:30 p.m. He stays up to make sure we get in safe. He will be communicating with me frequently. She can jump in the back and change. This ought to be a hoot!"

Kelly whispered in Barbs ear about her eve of seduction if they got caught.

Garrett asked, "So what's plan B?"

Kelly explained plan B. "Karl finding out. I'll throw down the gauntlet of tears with a whole lotta begging." The moms giggled while the kids were confused. "I will check in with you Saturday morning. It was nice to meet you two."

Barb replied, "Thanks, Kelly. It was a pleasure to meet both of you. I will be waiting for your call."

Kelly drove off in disbelief. Not one word was ever mentioned about his status as a movie star. Kipper still didn't know either.

The movie had been out a couple of weeks, and it wouldn't be long before everyone will figure it out. She modestly embraced the fact they would have pictures of him. "Wow, now that is quite a story to tell my family and friends…when the time is right."

Gleaming, Teaming, High Jinks

On Thursday, Coach Johnson called the team together to review films. His style was to eliminate physical contact the day before a game and respectfully remind them of the wrongdoings, while praising their accomplishments for balance.

When they dressed out in uniform, they played a different theme song and voted on it before each game. A jam box and a CD set the mood; it pumped them up and heightened the camaraderie. In addition, he picked a veteran of war who died in action and gave their background, and everyone prayed in honor. His philosophy was not only to develop a great team but to develop their appreciation for others.

At 3:30 p.m., G's practice was over, and the boys headed to BRSH Dental. Tina would drive herself to the office so she could leave as soon as possible. Garrett was about a month earlier than normal for his cleaning but wanted to share the experience with Scholls firsthand.

G asked, "So, dude, you ready?"

Scholls replied, "Guess so. I just hope Mrs. Parker doesn't conveniently dis the appointment. She promised me and I'm banking she won't eff this up."

"Good question. I'll call her right now."

Her phone rang, and Tina answered, "Hello, Scholls."

"Hey, Mom, are you having any trouble finding the place?"

"Nope, I'm parking right now. How close are you?"

"We're about five minutes out."

"I'm just going to sit here in the car and listen to music. I am parked more to the left."

"Okay, see you in a few."

They turned into the lot and parked close to Tina's car. Scholls walked to the front with his mother and checked in, while Garrett was quickly pulled to the side by a couple of the girls. They talked about his movie and asked to take a few selfies with him. As planned, Scholls filled out the papers, and Tina said, "Am I good? Can I leave? You'll explain to them I have to be at work. Won't you, honey?"

Talk about a jaw dropper. *Honey? Where did that come from? I guess she needs to act like my mother for show.* Hearing all the endearments that G and his mother frequently exchange was nice, and dolefully, he wished his mom's were real. Garrett told her it was fine to go, and when Scholls looked up, all he could see was the door closing. He took the papers to the front and waited with G to go back.

Garrett prepped Scholls on what to expect for the visit. "When Dr. Tjoa greets you, she will smile real big and shake your hand. 'Hi, I'm Melicia Tjoa, nice to meet you!' Before she comes, you'll get a whole crap load of x-rays. They use digital sensors now, and some of the x-rays are hard, but you'll get through it. Since our appointments are scheduled at the same time, she will do your exam, cleaning, and fluoride treatment." G would pay for the fluoride without letting him know, because his policy didn't cover anyone older than fourteen. "I'm gonna be in the next room with Hilda, the hygienist. You nervous?"

"Put it this way...fear of the unknown. How do you pronounce her name again?"

"Like 'trois' in French. Don't worry, dude, everyone is friendly."

"It's my *teefers* I'm worried about." They recalled the skit they did and laughed.

"You're gonna be fine."

"Shit, I'm embarrassed to open my mouth. They're pretty dirty."

"That's what we're here for. You don't ever take your clean car to get it washed, do you?"

"What car?"

"Oh shit, I'm sorry, man. It was an analogy. Ha!"

"Forgiven, but give me at least six years and I *will* take my clean car to get it washed in celebration of the fact I finally have one." They laughed together.

"I bet you're gonna love the way they look after she finishes, and they feel so smooth after the polish."

"I hope I don't have any cavities, because if I do, my mom already enlightened me I would have to pay the portion of the bill the insurance didn't cover."

"Scholls, I hope you don't either. Oh hey, they're walking out to get us. This is my friend Scholls. He hasn't been to the dentist in a few years, so give him the royal treatment."

"What's your name? Scholls? We'll treat you like you are Garrett's brother. I'm J-9. Just follow me and I'm going to take x-rays on you first."

Figuratively speaking, they were brothers.

Scholls lipped to Garrett, "J...9?"

G lipped back, "It stands for Jeanine"

"'Kay, cool."

The digital sensor was bulky all right, and he gagged a few times when it was placed near the back. They also had a wand-like camera that took pictures of your mouth and teeth. He was really interested in the appearance of the office; it was chicly sophisticated with chandeliers in *all* the rooms. The whole experience went well, and now he understood why G loved his dentist. When he looked in the mirror to see his clean teeth, he shouted out, "Oh my god, they are so much better. Thank you. I can't believe how good they look."

Dr Tjoa replied, "You're welcome. You had a great checkup and no cavities. We will see you again in six months."

Garrett and Dr. Tjoa smiled at him, and they said their good-byes. All three of them posed for a pic on her phone. They left the building, and Garrett said, "See, it went just fine."

"Yeah, I have to admit. I was nervous. You seemed like you were having fun in the next room. I kept hearing you guys laughing."

"Hilda always cuts up with me, and it makes being here fun."

He was proud of his clean teeth and relieved to be self-conscious of them when he talked to people. Timidly, he asked Garrett if they could go to Schultz's Burger and get a soda. Thirty minutes would be up by the time they got there, and it was important to him that he followed the fluoride rules. Garrett was agreeable because the key reason for that request was Kipper, and soon, Scholls would be closer to her than he ever imagined; moreover, the whole scheme made him laugh out when he was parking.

"What's so funny, G?"

"Ah, nothing…I was thinking about something Hilda said during the cleaning." He used one of his white lies.

"Oh, 'cuz I thought for a minute you were laughing at me because of Kipper. Is it that obvious I like her?"

"Please, we could have gone to the local gas station for a soda."

"Yeah, I'm busted. I did make an excuse to see if she was here tonight. Like a mirage, I can see her but I can't touch her. Hopefully we can be good friends. If not, the burgers they make here are pretty damn tasty."

"True that. What do you want to drink?"

"A shot of whiskey, but if they don't have that, I'll take Coke."

"You funny, but maybe we can go visit my cousins in Texas and fulfill that wish of yours."

"Do you drink, Garrett?"

"Not really. I've tasted champagne before when we celebrated my parents' twentieth anniversary. Moderation is cool if I decide to indulge in the future. What about you?"

"Same here, I think I had a beer my mom gave to me around age seven. She was laughing when I drank it. Another time I tasted some wine with my uncle. I'm never gonna be a big drinker, and my take on alcohol is liberal. Mom's alcoholism is the best deterrent I know for overindulgence. Dude, here she comes. She's angelic…Okay, okay, I mean, a hottie!" G nodded at Scholls's updated description.

Kipped asked, "Hey, guys, what's up?"

Scholls's head was downward at first, so she winked at Garrett before he looked up. They both had smirks on their face and were forced to contain themselves. Garrett started the conversation.

"We were in the area and thought we would stop in for a Coke."

Scholls rolled his eyes.

Kipper asked, "Okay, what sizes?"

"Two mediums. You want anything else, Scholls?"

"That'll work."

"Oh, hey, Scholls, did those hiccups go away with my remedy?"

"Yes, they did. Your advice was effective. Thank you kindly."

G looked over at Scholls and lipped, "Effective? Thank… you…kindly?"

Scholls shrugged his shoulders and made a gesture of uncertainty.

He followed it up by talking nervously nonstop, "I didn't think you would be here tonight, for some reason I thought you said you usually didn't work on Thursdays unless you wanted to make extra money, which coincidentally you did mention you were trying to buy a new purse which makes sense you would be here…and it's good to see you."

G looked over again and lipped, "It's…good…to…see…you?" He then rolled his eyes.

"Scholls, you have a great memory. In fact, I'm working tonight because I have something special happening Saturday night, and I'm making up some hours."

His heart was just hit with a verbal dagger. *Something special?* Her dating anyone made him squeamish. *Was there a boyfriend? I don't know her enough to ask and frankly, don't have any money or transportation, so what the hell was I thinking anyway?*

Kipper and Garrett had a hard time maintaining normal composure, and she left to keep from laughing.

"Be right back with your drinks."

"Dude, please, you sounded like you came right out of a Ted Turner classic movie. Could you have been anymore old-fashioned?"

"Sorry, she makes me nervous. Bro, what should I have said?"

"Try letting Kipper know that her advice was *thoughtful and clever*. Tell her she has a *pretty smile*. Compliment her hair. Let her know it's *great* to see her. Chicks love to be complimented. It sounded like you were talking with an old professor or something."

"Okay, okay, I effed up, but I think she has a boyfriend. She has something planned Saturday night, and it's messing with my head."

"Here come our drinks. I will find out more. Just sit there and look like the future MENSA member you're gonna be."

"Here you go. These are on the house tonight, boys."

G said, "Why?"

"Because I comped them. I get complimentary sodas every day, and I'm giving you mine."

"We can't let you pay. Here, take this $5 bill and keep the change."

She let it drop to the ground. "Nope, it's my treat."

She picked it up and threw it back into the Hummer. That little act of feistiness made her even more appealing. Garrett winked his left eye at Kipper so Scholls couldn't see him and said, "So, Kipper, where are you going Saturday night? It's cool if you don't wanna say."

"Oh, I have a date with someone. He's really nice. Look, I don't mean to cut this short. We can't BS any longer 'cuz the manager is on us big time tonight. Some people have been slacking off. It was nice to see you guys again. Good night." They waved and told her the same.

"I knew it, bro. Fantastically effed-up fate!"

"You're gonna cop out that easy? Maybe she won't like the guy."

"With my luck, she will."

"You're right. She probably will 'cuz I believe Kipper seems to have her head on her shoulders. Don't sweat it, man. There will be another girl that will come along."

"Somehow your words don't make me feel better, dude."

"By the way, I jack up my words sometimes when I talk with Tally. She makes me nervous too."

They drove away with the radio on, and G wanted to laugh again so bad he turned up the radio louder. He started singing "Jealous" by Nick Jonas. Scholls cut him off and said, "Really?"

G finished the lyrics in a high-pitched tone and then sang his own words, "Could you be more jealous?"

Garrett bantered back and forth with Scholls until he dropped him off. Tomorrow was the homecoming football game against Raleigh High Tigers and Excalibur's mascot King Arthur and the Knights of the Round Table. The band played a rendition of Darth Vader's theme song "The Imperial March" by John L. Williams.

"Hey, bro, you coming to the game?"

"Duh, my best friend is the quarterback. I'll see ya tomorrow. By the way, we need to get all the stuff done on our project. Since we have the dance Saturday night, let's finish it Sunday. I wish I could stay Sunday night too, but I have to tend to Bandit and make sure my parents don't need me for anything. Thanks for taking me by Schultz's. Later, dude."

"No prob. Later."

So far, Garrett had not had any symptoms and what a relief. If so, he would definitely need to fib to his mom and his coach; no way on earth was he missing the game. The sidelines would be depressing, and this was senior year. G had no idea if he wanted to pursue college football even though he had been scouted and approached. It was the indecisiveness between acting and football; he loved them both. Fact of the matter was, college quarterbacks couldn't come and go, before or during the season, so if he was filming, it would not work. There was still time to think about his future, and he wasn't leaning more toward one or the other. Mr. Pierce taught him that haste *does* make waste. Four blocks away from Scholls's place, Garrett pulled off to the side and began talking to his father.

"Damn, I miss you, Dad! Everything's changed, but you know the only reason it has. Mom's good. She still cries for you, I can tell. You were a hell of a man, and I was lucky to have been your son. I'm taking the Benz to the dance. I need to be in it. I need your spirit with me in that car 'cuz you already know there's something sneaky happening. If only you could have met Scholls. He's so smart it's unbelievable…and funny as hell. He would have made you laugh, and I believe would have spent a lot of time talking to you. His parents suck, Dad. He's such a good person it's hard to believe the neglect he gets from them. He'll never know what it is like to have an awesome dad like you." He hung his head sadly, asking, "Do you have any advice for the game? I really screwed up the last one. I can hear you saying, 'Go out there and enjoy it like you did when you were young…when it was fun. Keep your throwing game dominant and slide to avoid being injured. Always watch the peripheral zones when passing.' Damn good advice, and I do it each game, except last week. I wasn't focused and ended up getting a mild concussion. This is an important game. Two scouts have talked with me. Don't worry, haste makes waste. I listen to you, Pops. I haven't abandoned college either. I'll talk with you soon. Watch as I rub my left shoulder on the opening play. It's for you. Love you, Dad."

There's one more person to talk to—Randy, and he drove away, dialing his number. Scholls needed to be at the studio no later than 1:00 p.m. to get the makeover. And while that was happening, Garrett would take his glasses and have Randy's friend set them in new frames. He would bring the glasses back after he got Tally and returned to pick up his BF. Due to time restraints, the couples would not be able to stop and eat at a nice restaurant. G had that taken care of that as well. All four of them would eat the combo's from Kipper's job, and the food would be ordered via text to Kipper before their arrival. Bianca had promised to handle this and bring it to the Benz before they left.

Scholls couldn't see well without his glasses, and this turned out to be a blessing. Garrett wanted Randy to wait and give him his glasses at the last minute while they prepared the vid and captured the unveiling of wonder boy.

Randy would also have his camera for photo shots and wanted *Schollie* to strike poses for his portfolio. Along with his eye for fashion was his eye for photography. By working with many clients, he could tell if they loved the camera and the camera loved them. Not everyone was photogenic, and without a doubt, he was certain of Scholls's synergy.

Garrett also wanted to capture his expression when Kipper got into the car. Due to the circumstances, he'd let Scholls know they needed to make a pit stop at Schultz's Burgers for "food to-go." It's assumed he will be bummed out when they drive up because of Kipper's alleged date with the *mysterious* guy, who just happens to be the last person he would think about—*himself.* If they pull it off, their homecoming will be outrageous. Scholls will be unrecognizable, and no one will know Kipper since she goes to another school. G might play them off to be his friends, or cousins, or who knows? One thing for sure, when those unwilling ladies found out it was Scholls, they would be eating crow burgers.

Championship Wisdom and Woe

"Touchdown, touchdown, touchdown, boys. You make the touchdowns, we make the noise!" The pep rally at Excalibur High began at noon. They announced the homecoming court, and all the nominees took a bow. Garrett looked at the band and Tally winked at him, and then he looked around the gym for

Scholls. Where the hell was his best friend? Finally, he spotted him coming into the pep rally late. After Scholls settled on the side of the bleachers, they connected eyes and G nodded his head upward, receiving a thumbs-up in return.

This year, the crowning would be announced differently. Two of the candidates from the football team were up for king—quarterback Garrett and running back Collin Janakowski. Before the game, they would parade the court along with the parents. The homecoming queen would be announced during halftime at the game. The homecoming king would be announced at the dance. Coach Johnson and the administration felt it would be a distraction for the two key players and wanted their attention focused on the game.

That evening, the game was underway and they had a terrific opening. Their home team passage onto the field had a medieval tent with images of the shields. Their primary colors were gold and maroon, with secondary colors white, black, and gray. Twelve knights, six on each side, bordered the path from the tent. The theme song commanded attention as King Arthur appeared from the tent on his white horse, maroon cloak, and the Excalibur sword in hand. All the players emerged and followed directly behind the mascot.

Coach Johnson and the other coaches were last to appear. The band did a terrific job, and just as expected, Tally waved to her date. Then, the music stopped abruptly. With a hidden microphone, King Arthur declared an altered statement from George Lucas's *Star Wars'* Darth Vader. "You may dispense with the pleasantries, Tigers. We are here to put you back on schedule…defeated!" Then he turned the horse around facing the players and raised his sword. The home crowd went crazy, and there was uproar of exuberance. The opposing fans booed, but it's not loud enough to matter.

The referee tossed the coin, and they would kick off the first quarter. Garrett wondered if Scholls had made it to the game. He saw Tally and said to himself, "I can't eff this up." As promised, he rubbed his left shoulder before attempting his initial play. He felt an inner rush of encouragement from his father that electrified his energy.

Scholls was still trying to find a ride because his mother promised she would take him and was not at home. He completely missed the first half and hoped he didn't miss the entire game. Out of the blue yonder, Tina pulled up. She entered the trailer to find Scholls with his arms crossed. He could smell alcohol on her and knew not to push the incident too far.

Tina inquired, "Why the hell are you standing there with your arms folded?"

"Oh, I don't know, I guess it's because a *certain* someone promised me a ride to the homecoming football game. It started an hour ago."

"Huh, so I'm late. You're lucky I even came home. Get your damn self into the car, and I'll drop you off. You have a ride home, right? 'Cuz you know we will both be at work?"

"Not really, but I'll work it out. Let's go."

"What's so effing important? I never made it to a lot of my high school shit."

"For one, it's my senior year, and two, Garrett is the quarterback, and three, I would like to see my friends."

"Hell, what friends? That kid and who else? They won't be there for you in the future. Mark my words. The world is full of promises for the fainthearted. It's a lesson you will learn soon enough."

He questioned her words silently, "*This is coming from a woman who created her own path of destruction?*" He got into the car and gave directions to the field side. "Bye, Mom, thanks for the ride." Tina reached in her purse and pulled out a five-dollar bill. "Here, get a drink or candy...or whatever the hell you kids eat at games." He was confused at her attempt of generosity but took the money.

Scholls already purchased the game ticket in school, and now, all he needed was a place to sit; however, the bleachers were full, and he must go all the way to the top. It was halftime, and they were calling out the names. Sure enough, Chelsea Bloomingdale won as queen of homecoming. Scholls felt this was pretty accurate as she had the full package—smart, athletic, friendly, and not at all like her opponents. But even her beauty could not divert his stargazing about Kipper. Tomorrow night, she would be with a guy and possibly starting a relationship. What a blow to his heart—and thwarter of his hormones.

"Thirty-four…Blue 80…set hut," Garrett took the snap and threw it for a touchdown pass to Collin. It was a beautiful sixty-two-yard bomb that tied them with Raleigh High late in the third quarter. All he could think about was winning the game. He had no symptoms and his foot felt fine; he kept the wide receivers and running backs busy. In the fourth quarter, he was close to being sacked and ran for eight yards to get a first down—sliding as his father instructed him. The best play of the game came down to the final twenty seconds. Garrett took the snap and tossed it to the tailback, Quade, who handed the ball to the wide receiver, Jason, coming on a reverse. Garrett worked his way up the sideline toward the end zone wide open, and Jason hit him in stride for a thirty-yard spiral as G's cleats crossed the goal line to win. Everyone was crazy happy. He found his mother and Casey and brought them on the field. Although the school was heavily protected with law enforcement, the paparazzi snuck someone in as a student and took several photos. That guy was arrested and escorted off the property by a policeman, when a coach noticed unfamiliarity and just *a bit too old* for a student.

Scholls found Garrett, and they clasped hands in their special handshake sequence they created. G asked, "Who brought you, dude? I didn't see you at all. Thought you didn't make it."

"My mom, late as usual. I had to go all the way on top and stand. Your popularity has the place packed wall to wall like sardines."

"Did you see the last play? It was radical! We executed it perfectly."

"Sure did, man. It was awesome. In fact, I got here by the second half, and you guys were solid."

"Thanks, man, is she picking you up?"

"No, I was hoping I could bum a ride with someone."

"Hey, there's no bumming a ride. Give me about thirty minutes to celebrate with the team and meet me and Tally at the Hum then. Coach wanted us to answer questions and take photos."

Several people met up at Rooskie's Place. It's a local restaurant with quite a large outside area of tables. The whole team and family members went there to eat, including the cheerleaders and some of the band members. Priscilla Smith kept staring at them. When her eyes locked with Tally, she quickly turned away and acted aloof. Those brain cells were rattled enough from jumping in the game, but everyone had their place and Tally held no animosity toward her.

It had been a heck of a day and night. The three left, and Garrett dropped Tally off to her car. He walked over, helped her load the trumpet into the backseat, and then hugged her good-bye. In a turn about fair play affection, she kissed him on the cheek. His heart was pounding, and he beamed ear to ear for several minutes.

"You guys look good together."

"It's so strange to me, 'cuz all of a sudden, I'm crazy about her."

"Love knows no boundaries, G. Remember the great words we read of Mahatma Gandhi? *Where there is love, there is life.* So be aware of its power. We also read about the great sixteenth-century philosopher Lao Tzu. '*Love is of all passions the strongest, for it attacks simultaneously the head, the heart, and the senses.*' So bottom line, dude, we are screwed…in a good way. The two best words you're ever gonna learn are 'Yes, dear.'"

"Scholls, you kill me! You have an incredible memory."

"I might, not sure, just know some things don't leave my cranium."

"Bro, tomorrow's gonna be action packed, so get ready. I'll be here about noon to get you."

"Dude, I'm trying to imagine what's up Randy's sleeve. To tell you the truth, G, I'm nervous."

"Get your big boy boxers on and deal. Later. See you tomorrow noon."

"Okay, later.

G returned home late to find his stepfather and mother sitting on the sofa. Casey was exhausted from being up at the game and went straight to bed. Peter acted happy. "Hey, son, I heard you played very well and got the winning touchdown. Congratulations are in order. I would have been there if I had not been needed at the hospital. It was a rough evening, and my patient came close to dying."

"I understand. The patient is lucky to have you. No apology needed. We may go to state, and I'll let you know as soon as we do. Thank you for letting Casey go. He had tons of fun, and I let him take photos with a couple of the players."

"Not a problem, keep me posted. To celebrate your victory, I'm thinking about taking all of us to this exclusive restaurant where the chef is a personal friend of mine. Have you heard of Le Palais Enchante? The food is magnificent, and the view is gorgeous. In fact, your mother and I went there when we first dated. Their ingenuity is panoramic with the finest of flavors in all California."

"No, I haven't, but it sounds awesome. Would you mind if I took along my friend Scholls?"

Vexation arose in him, but he skillfully camouflaged it with an act of kindness and replied, "Certainly not, he's more than welcome to join us. Let's plan on next Saturday night at 7:00 p.m." All those years of abuse trained him to adapt spontaneously and appear to be calm, when in fact he was deeply enraged.

It's not clear if he really understood the depth of love between a woman and a man because many children from abusive parents demonstrated impaired ability to regulate emotions.

What was certain was his attachment to Barbara. Psychopaths were highly skilled at hiding their real personalities and plans. He never expected to feel love like this, such as the story of Pygmalion, the Greek mythological sculptor, who was sickened by the Propoetide's prostitution and became disinterested in women. He then sculpted an ivory statue of his ideal woman and unexpectedly fell in love with it. He wished for a bride who was the living likeliness of his carving, so Aphrodite granted his wish, and when he kissed the statue, it came to life. Peter felt anguished with his emotions which uncovered a layer of profoundly deep affection for another person.

The only one he ever felt this way about was Paul. Barb and Peter's relationship was even more enigmatic, because it had a combination of intricacy and sex. Peter actually had a chance of normality, if he had sought help. Unfortunately, he was invidious in nature, and the action behind his thoughts would choose to guard *his* "statue" from all others. She was a possession within his obsession, and discerning love was difficult for him to do.

This boy had some nerve asking if his friend could go with them. It was unsettling. After all, he had not tampered with his mix or vitamins in several days, so in his mind, he had already done him a favor.

Seeing and hearing about the magnificent friendship between Scholls and Garrett was difficult and fluxed even more feelings of anxiety and jealousy. One jolt was Barbara who doted on her precious son; that in itself was taunting enough. The other agitator was the deep admiration and happiness between the two **gold** boys.

He excused himself from the living room and went into the bathroom to vent. The mirror reflected his face of evil as he spoke to it.

"You were truly blessed twice. Sickens me, Barbara. I cringed during that eulogy as you spoke so eloquently about Thom and your precious little boy. How do you expect me to listen to all this crap?

"Even more sickening is that shrine you have for Mr. Pierce. Huh, he's so wonderful, yet he's so dead! Get that through your head, my little pretty. I'm alive, and we don't need constant reminders of him or G's accomplishments. Your son is a brat, so to speak, and he wears a veil of perfection. Ha! I see right through it, but no, you can't because he lives…and breaths…your very soul. I remember those words you spoke to me on our first date. I listened with contempt and smiled with false empathy.

"And you, my stepson, sicken me the most. You're an actor, an athlete, a model, and loved by all…except me. I loathe your gentle persona. You think I couldn't have been just as great as you if I hadn't been beaten and tormented? *Do you?* You'll never know what its like to rise above true iniquities. I can hear you now, 'Man, I'm starving. What's for dinner?' Try actually being deprived of food, you spoiled punk. Then come to me with your opinions on life, and I will listen. Your days are numbered, oh precious one. I think a little nausea is in order."

His dual personality challenged these statements, and he lashed out, "You have no idea what you are talking about! Leave me alone! I am in control here!"

Peter got his composure and went back to the living room to find Garrett and Barbara engaged in a conversation. He interrupted them by saying, "I'm sorry about that. My stomach isn't well at the moment. Where were we?"

Barb questioned him about his stomach and went to get him some over-the-counter medicine, and they left to go to bed. It had been a long night, and everyone seemed exhausted. G headed to his father's room and talked with his dad again.

"We did it, Dad. I could feel you with me during the whole game. Our next project is the dance. This should be fun. Got any advice for me? We'll talk soon. Good night, Pops."

CHAPTER 13

See, Almost B, and Revelry

S ATURDAY WAS FINALLY here, and Garrett woke up tired but worked out. He took his vitamins, drank the protein mix, and still had two more days before he needed to take the B12 shot. He got nauseated again, and his vision blurred for a while. He felt light-headed and decided to lie back down because he damn sure wasn't going to miss the dance. He looked at his phone to find a text from Randy: "Call me PLZ...before you get here!" G called to find out what was so important. Turned out, he was just finalizing the plans for the day and confirming the ETA, or estimated time of arrival.

He sent Scholls a text asking him to call as soon as possible to discuss everything and then laid back down, but soon thereafter, the phone rang, with Scholls on the other line. He called Randy back and told him they should be there by 12:15 or no later than 12:30 p.m. Garrett tried to lie down again, but Casey came to his room to play. G showed him the worms and confirmed after Monday, he could take them to his room.

Garrett totally forgot he needed to practice with Scholls about their project, and using the other taped version would be very entertaining for the classmates. With Scholls at the reigns, G knew there was an A around the corner. This kid couldn't get a B unless he bought it on the television show *Wheel of Fortune*. He never got to rest, and it was time to pick up Schollie.

Scholls said, "Hey, dude, I brought the paper for the assignment. You got the pics and film ready? We need to practice it on Sunday when we get up."

"I was just thinking about that earlier this morning. It should be funny as hell in class. The best part is how they are going to react to your new look."

"Shit, I totally forgot about that. Let's hope Randy doesn't turn me into a total metrosexual vagrant. Remember, I'm only gonna be Cinderella for so long, and then it's back to the daily rendition of Pauper Boy."

G laughed. "A metro…sexual…vagrant?"

"A stylish bum. The ultimate oxymoron of fashion!"

G laughed harder. "Damn, Scholls, you're so effing funny!"

"Yeah, best part for me will be when we wrap up the project. I don't particularly want to stand there and be scrutinized by fellow classmates who dreaded my appearance daily…and will now show restitution by gazing steadily in amazement."

"Shit, Scholls, my ribs are killing me, dude. It's gonna flow. You'll see."

"Yeah, like molasses in a Minnesota January."

"Dude, were in Cali…so it should help. LOL."

"Viscosity is irrelevant. These kids work on numeric summaries, as in dollar bills. They'll be thinking, 'You can let the rat loose in the maze, but there's still a crap load of passages he needs to get through!'"

"Whatever, dude, you a-*maze* me."

"Really, G, that's all it took?"

They arrived at the studio grounds, and Scholls forked over his ID to the guard. Randy was there waiting with his entourage. He took a deep breath and said, "Do I have any say in the outcome?"

Randy scorned him quickly, "No!" and sidebarred a conversation with Garrett while Scholls took his glasses off. From this point on until they were finished, he wouldn't be able to see any of the transformation. Randy instructed G with all the what-to-dos on how to get to his friend's office and who to ask for when he handed over the glasses for repair. They would continue to communicate via text as the day progressed.

Garrett dropped them off, and Lance, the optometrist, let him know they would be ready in a couple of hours and to be back by 3:00 p.m. G called Tally to tell her he would swing by at 6:30 p.m. and formally meet her parents before they leave. Then he called Kipper to let her know they should be at Schultz's around 7:45 to 8:00 p.m.

So far, the plan was intact. The next step was getting the Benz and having it washed and waxed. He couldn't bring himself to get in the car after his dad died, but the groundskeeper maintained it, along with the other vehicle his dad owned—an Aston Martin V12 Zagato. This would have been the choice for the dance if it had enough room; instead, he would use it another time for a ride with Tally or Scholls.

As soon as the driver's side door opened, he began to break down. The last time they were actually together was in the Mercedes-Benz. Thom hung out with Garrett the preceding day and evening before his death, and they talked about anything and everything. This car would have had more protection then his company mid-size.

Remember the vacation Barb had circled on the calendar? One of the topics dealt with a trip to the Mayan ruins in Mexico and Belize. Their family vacations were always fun-filled, and seeing other cultures and historical sites was fascinating and educational. He hadn't taken into consideration the new family; nonetheless, at some crossing, the vacation would be carried out in honor of his father.

Since Tally would be driving them around, he stopped and bought one single red rose with a thank-you note so he could place it on the wheel. Romantic gestures were not strange to him as he watched his father and mother exchange them quite often.

The Benz was ready, and Garrett called his mom to make sure the corsages were, too. He felt fairly good but still had a bit of a blurred vision from time to time. What could this be? His blood work was fine but maybe he still had residual effects from the concussion. The problem with that theory was G experienced some of the symptoms prior to the game where he was injured. Was his eyesight going bad? Or was he having vertigo again? His allergies were the culprit before, and they might be again. G picked up the new pair from Lance.

Those pair of glasses were stylish and sophisticated, and would make *Schollie* appear way different even without his makeover. Still, Garrett couldn't wait to see what his best friend would look like in his new skin. Randy was going to play "Sharp Dressed Man" by ZZ Top, when he brought him out. The vids would capture the sound and the expressions on Scholls's face. It would be worth a lifetime of conversation.

Lance placed the old broken and glued rims in a box so G could give them back to Scholls. Hell, Garrett might borrow them to wear for future outings like he did at the theater. So far, no one had bothered him much since his public outings consisted of baseball caps and sunglasses.

Barb laid out Garrett's tux and bow tie. She put the corsages in the refrigerator so they would be well preserved for the dance. G checked on the worms and took a few more photos before he headed off to shower and shave. Randy shot another text: "Hey, Garrett, things are poppin' and *Schollie* seems to like all the attention, except for the pedicure. His feet are so damn ticklish. What's your ETA?"

G shot back, "7:15. How's my man looking?"

"Well, he was Schollie. Now, it's *holy moly* Schollie. You won't believe it till you see it. Ciao, baby!"

Just what was going on in lot C's wardrobe? The first feat, was his hands and feet; secondly, he got that unibrow mowed down and actually had a passage between his nose and forehead. His hair was more than halfway down his neck and sort of wavy, very thick, and brown with natural blond highlights. Randy decided to cut it shorter, fade the sides and back, and accentuate the blond with highlights, which now made it primarily blond with brown lowlights. All this preparation had showcased those vibrant baby-blue eyes—*a sea of sexy*. Looks like Kipper had seen this through her magic ball of pheromones.

Randy told him he could part it on either side or blow it back and set it with gel. Poor Schollie, even if he could see, Randy was like a pit bull and guarded him from any mirrors. He wanted to know what the suit was like, and though Randy wanted it to be a surprise, he did make him happy by revealing the colors. Scholls's biggest fear was the style of the pants, and he hesitantly asked, "Are the legs super tapered?"

Randy paused for a second and then said, "Sweet child of mine, you're not in skinny jeans. Yes, there's a taper with cuffs. Just chill while I finish. One hundred, remember?"

"Yes, sir."

Garrett was able to catch a few zzz's before he got ready and didn't wake up until 5:00 p.m. Barbara talked with him about the autism kids and wanted Garrett and Scholls to dance with a couple of the girls. Not surprisingly, he was more than willing to do so and quite confident Scholls would participate. She would meet him at the dance and make sure the paparazzi were under control. Linda, her best friend, would drive the Hum with Barb in the passenger seat. Hopefully, it would curve the attention toward them. Peter would stay home with Casey and take him out for food and fun.

Garrett's suit was burgundy with a gold lining, his bow tie was black with silver-and-gold threading, and his shirt was off-white. This all-American kid was gorgeous inside and out. He took pictures with the family and headed off to pick up Tally.

Her father greeted Garrett at the door and invited him in. They shook hands, and her mother gave him a quick hug. Tally was still putting the final touches for her appearance, so they visited and went over the rules for the evening. A few moments later, his school pal entered the room with unassertive beauty.

"You look gorgeous, Tally! That dress looks better in person."

"Why, thank you, Mr. Pierce. You are sweet. And may I say, stunning as well!" She winked at her mother.

Mr. and Mrs. Martin were aware of the diversion plan and walked the two out on the porch to say good-bye. Garrett escorted Tally to the driver's seat and her face lighted up as she saw the rose and card.

"OMG, thank you, Garrett. This is so thoughtful."

"You're welcome, Tally. I have the best girl, and she deserves the best night."

Tally got to the next block and suddenly stopped and put the car in park. She unlocked the back doors and got out, opened his side, and leaned in to kiss Garrett on the lips. She kissed him for five seconds and then said, "I've wanted to do that since ninth grade."

Garrett was in a stupefied state of passion, and he did not open his eyes but answered slowly, "Wow, your lips are soft. That was awesome."

Tally jumped back in the driver's seat and headed over to the studio. She checked her rearview mirror a couple of times, and G waved to her with his fingertips each glance. It was the best night. Tally, Scholls, his mother and the children, Randy, the team, and his father's spirit.

They pulled to the gate, and G rolled down the back window so the guard could see he was with her. He took Tally's license, and they headed over to the studio. Garrett helped Tally out of the Benz, and he gently kissed her cheek. Randy received the text that they had arrived and set up the music for his entry. Both phones were prepared for vids, and they worked their way back to the dressing area. ZZ Top's song was blasting, and the mood was set.

Randy led Scholls out, and he still did not have his glasses. Tally and Garrett were filming every step, and both of them looked at each other in astonishment with their mouths wide open. When he got to the full-length mirror, Randy got the glasses and put them on Scholls' face. "Now open your eyes." Schollie was in shock. He kept staring at himself and looked up and down several times.

He pinched his wrist and looked over to Garrett and said, "Dude, is this really me? Damn, I can't believe this."

They got closer and zoomed in on his face. Scholls showed his teeth with a big grin and said, "Randy, Garrett, and that damn genie he kept asking for did a hell of a job, and these glasses, they are the bomb! Do I get to keep them?"

Everybody was caught off guard, and they laughed at his reaction. Randy said, "Of course, it's on me. Now get over here and give me some swag for my portfolio, Schollio!

He took several poses for Randy, and the whole gang took pics on their phones.

"Listen, Cindefella, I cast a spell so you could refrain from pauperism after midnight. Enjoy yourselves and let me know how it went. Ciao, kiddos!"

Scholls high-fived G and then turned to Randy and hugged him before they left. Randy got choked up and looked like he was forming tears. His passion for style and compassion for life were one in the same, and he clearly understood how Garrett could have bonded so fast with this bright, witty kid.

G, Tally, and Scholls would talk nonstop about his transformation as they drove to Schultz's Burgers. He had no idea what was about to happen, and when they arrived, Garrett accidently blurted out, "Oh crap!"

Scholls gave him a confused look and said, "What's wrong, G?"

"Nothing, I just thought the paparazzi might have spotted us, but we're cool. Besides, there's some police officers if we do have any trouble."

Tally looked in the rearview mirror, and Garrett gave her that look that let her know something was off. She caught his drift and winked. To his surprise, Kipper's dad was still in the parking lot and talking with another officer parked beside him in the opposite direction. Damn, was plan A about to become plan B?

Bianca was on her game and had already talked with Kipper to keep her informed of Karl's whereabouts. He never did this. It's usually twenty minutes: hello to his daughter and quick paperwork. What was this other cop doing? Across the street sat Kelly in the Tahoe. G texted Kelly and said, "OMG, how long has he been there?"

Kelly replied, "About twenty-five minutes. And that's his friend he is talking with. Not sure but I will execute plan B if needed. How we doing on time?"

"We're okay for now. It's about seven forty."

"Okay. I'm gonna leave the Tahoe and sneak across the street and go into the back door to meet Kipper. I'll start getting her dressed, and hopefully he will wrap up things soon. Keep me posted."

Bianca came to the Benz and greeted them. Garrett introduced her to Scholls and Tally. She reiterated the order and left to get the food. Karl got out of his car and stopped Bianca. "Would you tell Kipper I need to ask her a question real quick before I leave?"

Bianca replied, "Yes, sir, I will go find her." Bianca was nervous because Kipper was in the process of makeup and wardrobe. She went to the back of the restaurant and let Kelly and Kipper know what Karl had asked her to do.

Kipper said, "Mom, I can't go out there now. You gotta do something, please."

"Hang tight, sweetheart. Mom is gonna fix this little problem quickly."

She sneaked back across the street, got into the Tahoe, and drove up as if she had to come there on an errand for Kipper. She parked next to the cop cars and got out. "Hi, Jim, can I speak to Karl real quick?"

He said hello, told Karl he'll finish the conversation later, and drove away. In a convincing voice, she said, "Hi, baby, perfect timing. Kipper called me to bring her something right away. Girl troubles."

Karl inquired, "Huh? I just saw her a few minutes ago. She was fine. What kind of trouble?"

"Baby, monthly female issues." She tilted her head to the side and opened her eyes wide. "I have to get in there quickly, hon."

"Oh…Okay, I guess she wouldn't want to come out. Tell her daddy says good-bye and I'll see both of you tonight." Kelly kissed him and whispered in his ear. After he pulled away, she went back to finish helping her get ready.

Scholls looked bummed out as G predicted, so he diverted his attention to the dance. "Dude, you ready to break some hearts at the dance?"

"Like mine is doing right now. Kipper on her date? Listen, I'm super appreciative of everything, and I won't let it spoil the night. Just wished she could have seen me tonight…instead of my broken-rimmed, shaggy-haired, unibrowed, limited-wardrobe-havin'-hobo-essent image."

"Dude, we'll swing by here next week and let her see the new you."

"Yeah, I guess she needs to see this premed masterpiece before her new guy swoons her into the high heavens."

Tally kept giggling, and Garrett did his best to keep from laughing too hard. Scholls sensitivity level was on an all-time high, and he had no idea that the girl of his dreams was minutes away from climbing in the car. Bianca brought the food; Garrett paid her $60.00 and winked at her to keep the change. Scholls was keen to his surroundings and notices four combo drinks and bags. "I believe we ordered too many burgers and Cokes."

"Oh yeah, I guess it got mixed up. Well, we'll just keep it for Casey."

"Good idea, G."

Garrett's phone lighted up with a text: "On my way."

Tally began talking to Scholls as he opened his bag of food and grabbed the burger. She looked at Garrett, and they saw Kipper just steps away from the door. When it opened, Scholls looked up and immediately stopped the bite he was about to take.

"Hi, guys!" He was so immobilized that her dress went unnoticed. She climbed in and said, "We ready to go?"

G couldn't contain himself any further, "Surprise, dude, *you* are her date. We fixed all this up behind your back."

They began cracking up, and Scholls was too gleamingly startled to say anything except, "Kipper…hi!"

"Well, hello, Scholls. I'm lovin' what I see."

Her opinion about the total change was limited in conversation, because she had been spellbound by his original looks and the new one did not impinge her existing libido. Tally caught the whole thing on vid.

They arrived at the school near 8:40 p.m. and drove directly to the back as instructed. Barb received Garrett's text, and she was waiting near the door of the cafeteria kitchen to let them in. They jumped out, and both boys grabbed the girls by the hand and ran in. When they got to the dance floor, Kipper asked them why they had to run in and go through the back. She still had no idea who G was, so Barbara pulled her off to the side and explained her son's recent status.

"OMG, I had no idea who he was. One of the girls at work said he looked familiar, and I blew it off. Gosh, I feel honored to be here with you guys."

Barb replied, "We are just normal people at a dance for homecoming. You don't need to feel honored about being his friend. I'm happy you saw that young man over there"—pointing to Scholls—"was a neat person and didn't judge him by his appearance."

"Yes, ma'am, I was smitten by him right away. Your son is undeniably also a great guy, and he didn't brag or say anything about his acting. I will make sure my family goes and sees his movie to support the film."

"Thank you, honey, he will appreciate that. Now go have fun with Mr. Debonair. Linda and I are going to get the kids situated, and maybe later you girls can join them for a dance or two."

"You got it!" She slid back over next to Scholls and walked around meeting their classmates via Garrett. People were definitely interested in knowing who this other couple was, and G politely introduced them as friends.

Mr. Wheeler hosted the ceremony and introduced Chelsea Bloomingdale as homecoming queen. She took the microphone and began prepping the crowd for the homecoming king candidates. Tally and Kipper whistled and gave extraloud ovations when Garrett's name was announced as the winner. He blew a kiss to his date and gave Scholls the okay signal.

After his acceptance speech, the first dance between king and queen was performed. Garrett didn't really want to do it, but tradition prevailed. As he danced, he smiled at Tally several times to make her feel comfortable. She wasn't thrilled about it because Chelsea was pretty, but confident enough to wait it out with a smile on her face. Fortunately, Chelsea's boyfriend cut in before it was over, and Garrett returned to Tally for the rest of the dance.

Scholls and Kipper were having loads of fun, and G said to himself, "I wonder what two brainiacs talk about?"

G asked, "Hey, Kipper, can I steal him from you for a bit? I want to talk to some of my teammates, and we'll bring back drinks for you ladies. Would you care for any snacks?"

The girls left to go help Barbara with the kids. Garrett and Scholls approached the punch bowl, and lo and behold, Priscilla Smith was standing there with a Cheshire cat smile and over complimentary demeanor. "Hi, Garrett, you're such a handsome homecoming king and super great actor. Don't forget to autograph my scarf when you get a minute. Like, too bad you are here with that girl Tally." She leaned into G's ear and said, "Oh, by the way, who's this fine specimen next to you? He's totally gorgeous. Is he a relative?"

"No, he's my friend."

Priscilla looked at Scholls. "Well, hey there, handsome. I'm Priscilla, and who might you be?"

"I'm Scholls. Scholls Parker."

Priscilla was taken aback and started giggling. "That's funny. You guys are like *totally* too funny? Scholls Parker. That's a good joke. Really, what's your name?"

"As you wish. It's *Scholls Marcel Parker.*"

Garrett intervened, "Yes, this is the guy you found 'totally disgusting' when my girlfriend considered you as his date."

She was startled.

"I...I...I...had no idea he was playing such a trick on everyone. I mean, like he's...I mean, you had all of us fooled. Is this for a reality show? I just turned him down because I thought he needed an average girl or something. Well...like...now that we have this all cleared up, would you like to dance?"

"I'm sorry. It's Priscilla, right? I'm here with a date, and she deserves my full attention. By the way, did you ever find out what that word meant?"

"What word?"

"Plebeian."

"No."

Looking at Garrett, Scholls said, "I rest my case."

Looking back at Priscilla, Scholls added, "Oh! And if you ever decide you want to broaden your vocabulary, here's another one you may want to learn—*meretricious!*"

They turned and finished getting the girls there stuff and headed back to his mother's area. G asked, "Bro, meretricious?"

"Deceptive, insincere, and gaudily alluring."

They toasted their cups together and worked their way through the crowd to find Kipper and Tally. Everyone was having a blast, and the kids from the autism school danced with the gang. Throughout the whole evening, Priscilla went around telling everyone about Scholls and people gawked in awe of his new look—crowding them for obvious reasons. On a more meaningful note, Barbara danced with her loving son before they had to leave, then escorted them back to the cafeteria door, and waited as they drove away.

Time was of the essence, and Kipper sent a text they should be at Schultz's around midnight where her mother was patiently awaiting their arrival. Karl called Kelly's phone, but she avoided answering it and let it ring through. She needed a few seconds to think of an excuse. Kipper sent her a text earlier explaining she messaged her father, telling him she was busy and to call mom. Kelly called Karl. "Hi, honey, what's up?"

"Can I speak to Kipper?"

"Hun, she can't get to the phone right this second because she is elbow deep in dishes and trying to finish so we can leave. I'll relay the message if you want me to."

"Huh, okay, ask her if there are any openings for wait staff. Jim's son is looking for work, and I told him we would find out ASAP."

"All right, sweetie, I'll have her give you a call in just a few minutes."

Kelly called Kipper and told her to call her father in five minutes.

Kipper called Karl. "Hey, Daddy, you needed to speak to me?"

"Yes, dear. Jim was wondering if Mr. Henry had any openings. In fact, can you put him on the phone for a minute, and I will ask him myself."

"Sure. Oh wait, Daddy. He went around back for something. I'll have him call you in a minute."

"You guys must be incredibly busy tonight. I can't seem to get anyone on the line. Have him call me. Thanks, sweetheart."

"Crap. Scholls, I need you to pretend you are my boss Mr. Henry. Can you deepen your voice a bit? My dad wants to talk to him directly about employing another kid."

"Yeah, I can fake it. What all do you think he will want to know?"

"His friend has a son who needs work. He'll probably ask you if you are hiring and what he needs to do. Just play it by ear, and if you get stumped, lip to me and I will lip back what you need to say. If it's too complicated, hang up and I will call him back and say the connection is poor. Oh…and keep it on speaker phone. Thanks."

In a deeper voice, Scholls talked to Karl. "Uh, hey there, Karl. Kipper said you had someone in mind for a job here?"

"Yes, Robert, another officer who's a good friend of mine has a son who is looking for part-time work in the evenings. Are you in need of anyone at this time?"

"Well, there may be a position opening up soon. Let me look at the staffing and get back to you in a day or two."

Kipper gave him a nod in agreement.

"That sounds good. Does he need to have previous experience in the food industry?"

Kipper lipped, "It depends."

"Well, Karl, it depends on his interview. I can tell right away if he will have what it takes to work here. I go by personality and give a few questions that help me determine if they are trainable."

"Good enough. I'll wait for your call. By the way, can you have Kipper bring me home one of those large chocolate malts of yours?"

Karl's brain was churning oddities.

"Sure, good night, Karl. Talk with you soon."

Kipper announced, "Oh no, we shut the ice cream machine down around eleven thirty, and I won't be able to make him one. Now what am I gonna do?"

Garrett spoke up and said, "It's a whole hell of a lot harder to lie than tell the truth. It just keeps getting more and more twisted. LOL."

Scholls replied, "We need one of your white lies about now, bro. Help us out."

Kipper said, "Okay, let's swing by Jack's drive-thru and order a large chocolate malt. Hopefully it won't be too different."

Scholls's logical mind was always working. "What about the cup? It will have a different logo."

Kipper blurted, "You're right. Okay, I will put it in a regular glass and say we were out of to-go cups."

Kelly received a text about the change, and they arrived at 12:15 p.m. Kipper jumped out of the car and opened the back door to give Scholls a kiss good night. She handed him a piece of paper with her phone number on it and then kissed his cheek.

"Call me, partner in crime. I had a blast." Then she turned to Garrett and said, "You're a cool guy, Garrett. Thank you so much for the invite, and it was great to hang out with everyone. Good night. Nice meeting you, Tally."

Still astonished by the kiss, Scholls watched her walk away and mimics a spin on, *"I'm melting...I'm melting."* Just like the wicked witch moaned when the water was poured on her in the 1939 movie *The Wizard of Oz.* She scurried to the back and found a glass to pour the malt in while Kelly drove. They sent a text to Karl. Kipper changed her clothes inside the vehicle, put her hair in a ponytail, and wiped off most of the makeup.

"Mother, did you know that Garrett is that actor in the movie *Constant Judgment.* His mother told me when we got to the dance. I had no idea until tonight."

Kelly replied, "Actually, I did. Susie told me when we were running background checks on everyone."

"He never said anything. He's so cool...and nice. I still can't believe it. My dreamboat is his best friend. I'm the luckiest girl in town!"

Mrs. Manning was feeling great about the accomplishment, yet guilty she had to use such furtive lengths to pull it off. It aroused her sensuality, and she decided Karl will reap the benefits after all.

Karl greeted the two, "Hey, girls."

"Hi, Daddy, I'm pooped. Going to bed. See you in the morning."

She hugged him good night and then ran up the stairs. Karl looked down at her feet and noticed she did not have any shoes or socks on. He started to ask Kipper about it, and simultaneously, Kelly realized his wheels were turning, so she quickly grabbed his butt and placed her arms around his neck.

She looked him directly in the eyes and said in a sultry voice, "Hey, babes, I'm not pooped at all. Let's put this malt in the freezer for another time and see what the rest of the night has in store."

The malt went into the freezer; she grabbed a bottle of wine, the opener, and two glasses. Kelly pulled him behind her to their bedroom. Karl was concerned about his shoeless daughter but was soon distracted by evidence of his facial expression and eagerness to follow his wife.

Tally's mom and dad indicated they would be up when she returned, and as promised, Garrett got her home by 1:00 a.m. They walked to the door, and her parents invited him in to say good night and briefly discussed the evening. He hugged her good-bye, and she whispered in his ear, "You're the best."

The mood inside the Benz was an electrifying mix of hormones and happiness. They kept recalling events from the evening and how lucky they were to be in the company of these girls. Garrett let out a deep sigh.

G asked, "Bro, you in love? 'Cuz I think I am."

"Put it this way, G. If love feels this good, I'm in like Flynn."

"Okay, Flynn. Let's get to the house and crash. Tomorrow we need to nail our presentation and unfortunately, get you home. Are you sure you can't spend the night?"

"Probably not, man. My parents like me to do laundry on Sundays. It's jacked up, but what can I do?"

CHAPTER 14

Perceptual Projects

WHEN THE BOYS woke up to start their day, it's already noon. Garrett's mom had cooked breakfast and left two separate plates for them to heat up. Peter, Casey, and Barbara were gone but left a note to let them know they will be back late afternoon. They ate the breakfast, took showers to get refreshed, and sent texts to their homecoming dates.

The biology class was first period, so tomorrow's assignment needed to be polished. While making Casey's special taping, they also filmed one for the classroom which was educational and funny. All that was left to do was organize the photos in the proper time line, showing the progression of each worm, and making sure all Petri dishes were labeled by name and dates with fully regenerated planarian. Scholls already completed the written hypothesis, observation, and deductive reasoning. Mr. Walker sensed their project would be fun and assigned them to break the ice and be the first presenters.

Scholls was edgy and concerned his new image might overshadow the seriousness of the project, and he wanted to wear his old glasses and ordinary clothing.

G opined, "Bro, forget it. Don't let them control you by their ignorance 'cuz that's what it is, and if they do know better, then its just plain stupidity!"

Scholls replied, "I can deal with stupidity. Have my whole life. It's just looking at them in a state of disbelief. It might eff up my words and the project."

"Problem solved. I will do the intro and be the main speaker. You will be the voice who explains each pic and the filming already has audio. We will conclude it together. Is that cool with you?"

"That'll work."

A few hours later, they wrapped up the project and headed to Scholls place. In the morning, Garrett would pick him up at 6:30 a.m. and head straight to the classroom to set up the exposition. He entered the trailer, and both his parents were home. Sunday was the only day he saw them together, and for that matter, more than any other day through the week.

Harry was on the couch watching TV, and when Scholls walked through the door, he sat up immediately and exclaimed, "What the hell happened to my kid? You look completely different."

He had forgotten that his parents did not know about Randy's canvas. Tina heard Harry's comment and ferociously surfaced from the bedroom. Clasping her mouth and laughing, she exclaimed, "OMG, your hair…it's so blond! And short! And your glasses…where'd you get the money for those? In fact, for the whole damn everything?"

Scholls replied, "Let's just say I was part of a generous group of people who wanted to help me look my best for homecoming."

Tina smirked. "Let me guess. The rich kid and his family… the righteous ones."

"Well, you would be correct, and righteous is a good start. I tried to get out of it because I couldn't pay them for what they did. Anyway, when I reach success in the future, I will return the kindness to them and anyone else who may need my help."

Harry said, "Help in the future, huh? Got it. And what about your good ol' parents who raised you the best they could?"

"I thank you and Mom for all I have and won't let you down."

He felt strange anxiety and answered to avoid any stress.

Tina tried to rile him with her comment. "So, Romeo, did you have a date for the homecoming? I take it you did all this for attention…and getting your teeth cleaned. Did it help?"

"Actually, I did have a date. Her name is Kipper, and she is really nice."

"Kip-per? You both have two different names. I know how I came up with yours, but how'd she get that one? Was this a one-time wonder or are you going to shame yourself and let us meet her one day?"

"I think she likes me, but it may be a bit premature to assume she will be my girlfriend. We exchanged numbers, and by the way, I was wondering if I could text or call her from time to time with the phone?"

His dad quickly replied, "Maybe…we can't let the minute usage get wild. It adds up, and we are already on a tight budget. Your mother does a good job of using most of it."

"Shit, excuse me for having any use of the phone. I'm done standing here listening to Mr. Cheap Ass. Why don't you cut out all the card games and online gambling. How 'bout that?"

"Listen, bitch, I'm not in the mood for your mouth, and I suggest you shut it immediately!"

Scholls interrupted, "Please, let's keep this civil. I didn't mean to start a war. I will get more jobs and get my own phone one day. I'll get started on the laundry. What do you two want for dinner?"

Unpredictably, it did stop the train wreck in its tracks. He went to his room to gather up any dirty clothes and picked up Bandit, his furry companion.

"Hey, sweets, I missed you. Thanks for being you, little one. You won't believe how much fun I had this weekend. Too bad you couldn't be there. Maybe next event. If I have to sneak you in my duffel bag, I will. Ha! I hope you can meet Kipper one day soon. I'm liking that girl. Heck, I'm *crazy* 'bout her. You and Kipper are neck in neck for my affections. Don't worry, little buds. There's room for two. She would love you, and I think she mentioned she had a cat as well. Gotta do the damn laundry, so consider yourself lucky you don't have thumbs. Otherwise, I would have you control the knobs on the machines. Just playin', my little *Felis catus*. That's your scientific species name. I'm gonna put you down for now, and we will talk again when I get ready for bed."

Animals were such a pleasant way to express love therapeutically. How can anyone hurt these precious gifts in life? He was fond of Albert Schweitzer, a physician, philosopher, theologian, and medical missionary, who won a Nobel Peace Prize in 1952 for his philosophy of "Reverence for Life." He wrote down his words and read the paragraph frequently.

> We must fight against the spirit of unconscious cruelty with which we treat the animals. Animals suffer as much as we do. True humanity does not allow us to impose such sufferings on them. It is our duty to make the whole world recognize it. Until we extend our circle of compassion to all living things, humanity will not find peace.

Scholls's perception of humanity was a driving force for use of stem cells in medicine. It would reduce animal testing, which could have a morbid outcome; meanwhile, animal testing was also used fundamentally in other areas of science. During the movie *Project X*, with Matthew Broderick and Helen Hunt, he cried about the inhumanity of chimps used in flight simulators for radiation exposure levels that could ultimately kill the testee.

It helped determine how long a pilot might survive in a nuclear exchange, known as the secondary strike scenario. It's a paradox that touched his heart because we needed the information to move forward in our world of technological expansion for safety; however, monkeys and chimpanzees were not a threat to society and had humanistic qualities. So in his mind, it would be much more sensible to send up a convicted mass murderer to study the effects on humans.

In the present moment, he had laundry to finish and dinner to make. The driving forces behind his chores were peace in the household and a son's diligence at Westward Trailer Park, USA.

Before Bandit, Scholls kept a diary, and now he had both. The year couldn't end soon enough for his homelife—and couldn't be slow enough for his friendship. What a contradiction of time.

On the other side of town, 5:15 a.m. awakened Garrett from a full night's rest, yet he still felt sluggish and weak. The proper thing to do was go get a full physical with his stepdad at the reigns, so he decided to talk with his mom and Peter this evening. The eye exam was also high on his list, and he would call Lance at lunch to schedule it. Both his mom and dad needed glasses to read, and logically, he might as well.

Scholls was on the front porch wearing a very similar style to Saturday night's hair, so it appeared Randy did his job and Scholls took it to heart. A khaki shirt and blue jeans from G's donation made his friend feel balanced. Garrett praised his hair and said he wouldn't need to worry about the kids at school because if there was any smack talking from them, he would put a halt to it.

Tally greeted them at the front of the building and helped carry stuff to the classroom. Scholls began setting it up and motioned for G to talk with his girl in private. It was hard to tell who was more excited from the smiles on their faces. That prompted him to send Kipper a text and say hello. The conclusion about the phone issue was inconclusive; he ran with a side of himself he wasn't accustom to defying—the laws of Parkerville.

Mr. Walker started the class by reassuring the students that *presentation* was important for the assignment, but he wanted it to be fun; in short, any gallant attempt would reflect in the grade. He started them at fifty and then added twenty-five for presentation, weak or strong, and then factors in the quality of preparation, founded hypothesis, variables, and accuracy of written documentation.

Garrett began, "How's everybody doin'? It's a privilege to present our project, 'Constant Planarian.'" Everyone started laughing because they knew he did a word play on the movie he starred in—*Constant Judgment*. "And this is me"—pointing to

Scholls—"before I became a brunette." He lightened the mood and took pressure off his best friend.

Without skipping a beat, both boys ran a smooth delivery. Just before it ended, Garrett turned around to gather the Petri dishes and suddenly felt dizzy, collapsing. Scholls got to him first, and Mr. Walker helped determine if they should call 911; however, in just a few seconds, G said, "Hey, guys, I'm all right," and made the effort to get up, assuring them he lost his balance. Mr. Walker allowed Scholls to walk him to the nurse's office. Another fib was honored.

The nurse called his mother. "Hello, may I speak to Mrs. Pierce?" Peter and Barb were still at home when they received the call, and Peter quickly corrected the caller, "It's Mrs. Berg now. Please make the appropriate changes, and this is Dr. Berg. To whom am I speaking?"

"Yes, sir, my name is Betty Ansell. I'm the nurse here at Excalibur High, and I apologize for calling her Mrs. Pierce. Your son has collapsed, and he probably shouldn't drive until his BP is better. We would like someone to pick him up as soon as possible."

"What were his vitals?"

"He had hypotension. His systolic was ninety, and diastolic was fifty-two. He looked pale initially."

"Yes, thank you, Betty. We will come right away. Tell Garrett to lie down until we get there. Can you give him some orange juice?"

"Yes, sir, we have some in the cafeteria. Will half pint be enough?"

"That's fine, thank you. Give us twenty minutes. Good-bye."

Barbara was really nervous, and she asked Peter to do a complete and thorough checkup on her son. Scholls told everything he witnessed during the incident, and they checked Garrett out of school.

Scholls said, "I'll call you later, G. Keep me posted."

"Later, Scholls, thanks."

Garrett went with them to his hospital, and Peter prompted Barbara to return to the school because it was going to be an all-day event. He gave her the car keys. They drew blood, ran an EKG, and scheduled a CT for his head. He was there several hours, and Peter kept Barbara informed of his findings as they occurred. The radiologist promised his friend he would read it immediately.

Dr. Berg borrowed a colleague's car and went eight blocks from the medical center where he still owned a condo. He got newly drawn blood from the refrigerator, as he anticipated something would happen. He increased the initial dosage of Parkinson's meds, and this caused the drop in blood pressure. There's Dr. Berg—Dr. Jekyll—the loving doctor, and the other, Mr. Hyde, though he needed no potion to turn evil; his mind had defective neurotransmitters.

He would imply that Garrett was apparently suffering from an allergic reaction to the soy that was in his protein mix. This was total trickery because Garrett had already seen an allergist when he had vertigo, and to properly diagnose food allergies, a skin test was given as well as blood work. He knew no one would question his findings, as a prominent neurologist wouldn't lie, would he?

Peter did conclude this was not the *only* thing he felt was responsible for all the symptoms. It would give him a smoke screen for future health endeavors, and he advised Garrett to immediately stop drinking the protein shakes. Peter suddenly realized he would have to end Garrett's symptoms for a bit; Barbara would never leave his side if he was ill, and Europe would be cancelled.

When Scholls left the office, second period had already started. He returned to biology and retrieved his backpack. Mr. Walker had already placed it on his desk. He asked about Garrett and then commended their project.

Scholls, in a nutshell, was brilliant, and onlookers reflected a genuine interest and respect for his intelligence, witnessing the precursor to an imminent doctor. Maybe these people would stop harassing him, and sadly, it took a physical makeover to convince them. Now it's fair to surmise that Garrett's popularity would have cannon bolted anything at anytime; nonetheless, the biology assignment was well deserving of an A.

The rest of the day, kids from Excalibur stared at, and commented on, Scholls's new look. He passed Priscilla in the hallway, and she smiled nonstop. How incredibly self-involved to think he would suddenly become her newest quest. That's what egotistical people do best—have unreasonable expectations of especially favorable treatment. She couldn't touch Kipper with, *like*, a total ten-foot pole.

Even though the day was pleasant for once, he kept his head low and eyes toward the floor. Their *interest* was uninteresting; their *attention* was uninteresting; their *smiles* were uninteresting. His heart was accustomed to forgiving, but jumping on this friendship wagon was like *going to hell in a handbasket*. Of course, this was figuratively speaking, as one theory behind that saying was used to reference the guillotine executions in the sixteenth century.

They collected the decapitated head and placed it in a handbasket, confirming the death of the wrongdoer and making their entrance into heaven impossible. The common faith of the Holy Roman Empire believed the gates of heaven would not open for anyone who did not have their whole body; in other words, they would go to hell. Scholls had no desire to befriend people who were not friendly before; despite that, he remained cordial. Years of misery divided by forty-eight hours of sudden acceptance equals friendly pretense.

Just before fifth period, Scholls called Garrett to find out if he was okay, and they talked about the testing and miscellaneous chitchat.

G asked, "Well, Schollie, what's our next venture? I was thinking about a double date with the girls. Sound good?"

"I'm game. Just need to prepare my funds. The money I have saved is for expenses this summer."

"Bro, we don't need any money to hang out. We can eat at my place and go to the beach right down the road."

"Sounds good and all. Thing is, G, I can't give this girl much, and I think it will end up hurting me emotionally when she gets tired of picnics…and dumps me."

"I understand your concern. I really do, man, but you might be undermining a good thing. Lots of people start out slow and work their way into long-term relationships."

"I can't deny you have a point. I'm just scared of getting hurt. I've never had a girlfriend, and I have never even made out with a girl before. Sure, I kissed a girl on the cheek in grade school, but she ran off. Honestly, what if I can't kiss right, dude?"

"Seriously, you never have?"

"Never."

"Well, I can tell you my first make-out session was pretty whacked, but I got through it. I kept hitting my tooth on her lip, and she actually said, 'Ouch, you cut me.'"

"That's messed up, but funny, wait a minute, what am I laughing about? Shit, if you did that, I might really screw up."

"It definitely takes practice. I got better at it, and it's awesome when two people have a connection. I forgot to tell you, after we left Tally's house. Dude, she pulled off on the side of the road and opened the back door on the Benz and kissed me! It was effing incredible, and she surprised me. I can't wait to kiss her first the next time."

"Sweet. Ha! I want to kiss Kipper so bad myself. Just scared I might end up slobbering on her or moving my tongue wrong. I hear girls in school talking about bad kissers, and they are brutal."

"Seriously? What do they say?"

"Oh, things like, 'His breath was kickin' my ass.' Then there was a comment about this dude whose tongue reminded her of a cow chewing cud, and let me not forget the worst, this one chick said a guy 'sucked up the floor of her mouth,' and she felt the tear under her tongue, so she pushed him off her. I was going to tell her that was the frenulum that tore, but I didn't want them to know I was eavesdropping."

"Damn, Dr. Diagnosis, they are brutal! Did they say any specific names?"

"To tell you the truth, I was behind them, and I heard some names, but no one I knew, and no, I didn't hear the name Garrett or G. LOL."

"Thank God for that. Ha! All right, here are some tips I can give you. Just make sure your breath is fresh, always have gum handy, and make sure your lips aren't too stiff. Oh, and go slow. If I were you, I'd tell Kipper you haven't kissed anyone before 'cuz she seems cool and probably would be flattered to be your first."

"Are you serious, dude? That's not gonna happen. That's frickin' embarrassing."

"Maybe so, but it might make things more forgiving if you do screw up."

"Ya think? I feel better now, dude. *Not!*"

"Sorry, man, just trying to help. LOL."

"No sweat, so are you gonna be in school tomorrow?"

"No, Peter told me to rest, and I'm gonna miss practice too."

"When's the next game?"

"This Friday, away game with San Monica High, and I want to play."

"I know you do, dude, but you need to make sure you feel fine. What else did your stepdad say?"

"He basically told me I could play if there were no other symptoms, and now that I'm allergic to soy, well, I can get a protein mix that doesn't have it, and I should be okay."

"Man, I read up on allergies to foods, and you did have the symptoms. It can even cause death. I just need to know when you started the protein drinks. Can you remember? 'Cuz it was before we started hanging out."

"Probably a month or more before. Why?"

"I'm keeping a log in my head about this stuff, trying to make sense of it all and making sure there is nothing else happening."

"Like what?"

"So you developed reactions soon after you started drinking it?"

"Pretty much that I can remember."

"Then there was the concussion on top of this."

"Uh huh, and your point?"

"Like I said, I am tracking it."

"Whatever makes you happy, dude."

"'Kay, I'll hit you up tomorrow, and I'll take notes for you in biology. Talk to you soon, G."

"Thanks, Scholls, later."

"Later."

CHAPTER 15

"Condo-Mental"

IN HINDSIGHT, PETER was glad he did not sell the condominium because it was undoubtedly the most convenient habitat for operation Garrettless. The perfect temperature for storing a vial of blood was 39.4 degrees, and his refrigerator was 40 degrees. He had all the supplies needed to concoct any method chosen for his marionette with transparent strings. The damn honeymoon delay altered plans to weaken his second son and definitely put a halt on moving forward until Mrs. Berg was comfortable with going away. He visited the condo at least twice a week for solitude.

There was little food or drinks in his condo, but he did have furniture and several mementos from Casey's childhood. That little procreated wonder was the only reason he was normal at all. His sickness was defined like the quote by Friedrich Nietzsche, a German philosopher in the 1800s who said, "Whoever fights monsters should see to it that in the process he does not become a monster. And if you gaze long enough into the abyss, the abyss will gaze back at you."

Dr. Berg had read Nietzsche's book *Beyond Good and Evil*, and he favored the eight-page tirade against women. He certainly saw the obvious distinctions in his mother, but Barbara was the balance. She reminded him of Francis, Paul's mother, and it grounded him.

Nietzsche also claimed, "There is always some madness in love. But there is also always some reason in madness."

He opened the fire safety box and found a picture Casey drew when he was almost seven. It depicted a family of three with body-like shapes of himself, his father, and the third one having an outline of an empty face, confirming that his son knew he had a mother who was gone. The moment of truth would wait until Casey was older to reveal her absence and why. After discovering this drawing, he exclaimed angrily, "Miserable bitch of a mother! Our son is beautiful, and you are the true substance of manipulation. I had literally and figuratively exonerated my past…the death of my wretched mother, worthless stepfather, and random acts of mishap. I was content…as content a man of annihilation could be…and your Medusa-like ways turned me to stone. It awakened my demons I fought so strongly to resist. This picture makes me vomit! I cannot bear to see my son's interpretation of a faceless mother. How could you walk out on this precious angel?"

Everybody, including Barbara, had no idea he was six years old when she left because Peter eluded the truth. His divorce to the ex was finalized just months before he laid eyes on Barbara. It catapulted his need to fill the void and stirred up a considerable amount of anxiety, which enticed him from being alone. Furthermore, he refused to accept friendships that mirrored his with Paul.

Thommason Pierce did not die from a fluke car accident as determined by the police. Dr. Berg wanted Barbara, and he paid someone to cause the accident. Once he got the information from the private detective, the street-savvy plan was set in motion. He recalled an emergency operation performed in the ER where he did his residency. The patient stated he would do "anything" if his arm was saved from amputation. Dr. Berg preserved it, and the man gave him a phone number to call in case he ever needed a favor of "any kind." He kept that number for years and cashed it in plus gave additional monies to seal the deal.

His own actions as a youth were vigilante vengeance; therefore, his psychotic mind had room to explore potentially justifiable outlets. With the proper help and medication, Dr. Berg would have been the promising individual he was born to be. He sought out to specialize in neurology; coincidently, the common genetic link to the five major psychiatric disorders; moreover, abnormal functioning of neurotransmitters—which he had. There was a dual personality disorder along with distortion. Verbalized sessions could be spawned toward another voice that reared its thoughts when anger kicked in. It had no name, though believed by the doctor to be the voice that opposed him and manifested when anyone threatened his inner circle.

He thought about the extent of evil he could really inflict, and quite frankly, he had no need to go as far as some of the world's most notorious monsters. Staying in the tertiary level *was* fine—first, father, second, husband, and *third*, sporadic evil. It was like an ace up his sleeve.

He uttered to opposition, "Why are you challenging me? It appears there is no cause for me to be as cruel as cruel can be. My sanctuary lies just beneath my love for Casey, and now Barbara. You annoy me. You have no right to call me evil. You want to talk evil? How about Genghis Khan? He avenged his father's murder by killing every male taller than three feet in the Tatar Army! He boiled chiefs alive and used survivors of enemies as human shields in war. He poured molten silver into the eyes and ears of people. My stepfather got off light. Wouldn't you say?

"Oh, let us recall the evils of Idi Amin, the butcher of Uganda. For starters, he cut off limbs and genitals of people and let them bleed to death. *You interrupt me?* Let me finish! He also flayed humans alive and made them eat their own flesh!

Now you say nothing?

"He ordered men to stand in a line…and starting with the first person, they would lie down, while the man directly behind them smashed their head in with a hammer. Then, the same man who killed the man in front of him would have to lie down, only to receive the same treatment he just gave. And you still think I'm evil? Let's not get into Hitler's genocides.

He felt challenged. "My friend, please."

I don't care what you think. "I'm finished with this conversation!"

As he calmed down, he held the poem his son wrote a few months ago to his chest. A huge smile spread from cheek to cheek, and he read it over and over.

> I love my daddy, and my daddy loves me.
> We are best friends.
> My daddy loves me, and I love my daddy."

The only reason he did not name his child after his best friend was because his ex wanted to name him after her grandfather. Either way, it's the embodiment of Paul that Casey has.

There was time to stew and construct the next act of infringement on his serendipitous stepchild. It was like a game of chess, and he was in check. Dr. Berg was displeased he had to wait but understood the outcome was merely on hold and acquitted himself from the change in plans.

A part of him briefly thought about accepting Garrett. He was fine with some of the moments, but with unannounced recollections as a youth, green waves of jealousy engulfed his childlike senses that burned in the memory of how his mother avoided him and nurtured his stepfather. That one section of his brain, the amygdala, was responsible for emotions of fear and aggression. Anything that triggered an emotion he experienced from physical or mental abuse would activate and override reasoning.

He kept reliving the part about Barbara's words that Garrett's eyes would remind her of how Thom made her life so complete. He had to get rid of those eyes.

He'd been gone for an hour and a half when suddenly, the hospital called to see where he was. The CT was completed, and Garrett was back in a room. Peter was so caught up with his son's picture that it completely removed him from reality and he forgot the original reason going to the condo. He took the vials of blood back to the hospital and returned the car keys to his colleague.

The CAT scan had not yet been read by the radiologist. Dr. Berg was too curious not to see it and headed over to review the findings, if any. Obviously, he was not anticipating much, as he was the sole cause of Garrett's troubles, less the concussion. He looked for any signs of arterial tears or swelling and found none. Later, it was confirmed that the CT was fine, and Peter called Barbara to let her know the good news. Garrett was passive to know he could play football again after several days of rest.

When two scouts from last year were at the homecoming game, they contacted Barbara and Garrett to schedule a dinner and talk about future collegiate plans with this young athlete. All he dreamt about from the time he was in third grade till last year was playing in the NFL, but when Thom passed away, the desire diminished, and he felt more of the urge to seek an education or pursue acting or directing.

Eye Doctor, Me Doctor?

The next day after school, Scholls anxiously sent G a text to say he would call around 4:00 p.m. It dawned on him that he *never really* had a problem with the limited phone use because he *never really* had anyone to frequently talk to. Finally, the bell rang at 3:10 p.m., and school was out. Scholls dialed G's number.

G answered, "Hey, Schollie, what's hanging?"

"Someone sounds like this guy I know named Randy. Nothing hanging but my neck if I go over the minute use. LOL."

"Okay, keep it short. What all did I miss in biology?"

"No notes, dude. Just finished all the presentations, and he gave us reading assignments which will result in a pop quiz on Friday. You got a pen ready?"

"Just a sec…Okay, shoot."

"Start reading pages 125 to 160, and he made reference to an online article that concerns marine biology as well. Do you still have the printout he gave us last week?"

"Yeah."

"On that sheet, there is a link for the marine biology information. When are you coming back to school?"

"Actually, I will be there on Thursday. I have an eye exam tomorrow with Lance. I may need glasses. Plus, Randy's friend can do a thorough eye exam."

"Huh, are you still having blurred vision?"

"No, but it's only been a couple of days, and I want to make sure I have 20/20 vision. By the way, we, you and I, were invited to go to dinner at some fancy shmancy place that Peter likes on Saturday night. It's a postcelebration dinner from Peter for my homecoming game. He felt bad he was not able to go."

"Hit ya later. I'll try to get a ride to your place on Wednesday eve."

"Forget it. I will come to you…and sweet talk your mom. See you around five on Wednesday."

"You're a trip, Garrett, later."

Missing school was not what G had intended and certainly not missing football practice, but his stepdad knows best, and he pledged to give Peter a chance and promised to carry it out.

The eye exam made him curious as to what he would actually be tested on. When he was dropped off at Dr. Lance Vogel's Eye Center, the front-office girl was so smitten with his entrance she hung up the telephone before her conversation was completed. It began ringing nonstop until Garrett signed in and told her the phone was going off. "Oh, crap, I totally forgot I had someone on the line. You're Garrett Pierce, the actor, right?" He winked and shook his head no to ward off any attention to his presence. She timidly picked up the clipboard and apologetically lipped to him "I'm sorry" and then gave him the new patient history forms to fill out. He put his sunglasses on and said, "No problem," and then sat down to fill out the information. It was difficult to see the words because the glasses he brought were very dark, so he lifted them up to see the lines and answered the questions at hand.

A couple people in the waiting area looked at him and studied him as if they recognized his face somewhere—probably in the media—and he turned his body away from them by crossing his leg. Lance was notified G was in the building and quickly summoned his administrative assistant to bring him back immediately.

This made an old lady very upset, and she blurted out, "Well, I have been sitting here for thirty minutes and now they take back that boy. You'd think he was a celebrity or something! I have an appointment, too."

Garrett and the assistant both looked at each other and smiled. He knew it was special treatment and decided to ask them to start her appointment first. Staying grounded was another lengthy conversation Thom had with him during that drive the day before his accident. They brought back the elderly woman.

He loved older people and enjoyed hearing their stories of life, especially the parts about how technology has changed. Upon occasion, he would take donations to a nursing home that was not far from the studio, and his favorite part was helping out the social activities department by calling out Bingo. Garrett's dry humor made people laugh, and he got such a thrill being able to shed some happiness in their life.

One of the residents named Lawrence Morris was genuinely liked by everyone and definitely challenging in more ways than one due to his fluctuating dementia. To give you an example of what he would do, they went to a Shriner's Circus, and before it started, he had to go use the restroom. One of the male chaperones took him in and had to use the restroom himself, but after he finished, he could not find Mr. Morris. This was confusing because he personally put him in the stall, shut the door, and not even a minute had lapsed. Lawrence had other plans, and he apparently tricked the guy and walked out before he could get noticed. After a couple minutes, he was located at the concession stand where he was ordering twenty hotdogs to go.

How can you really get mad at people who suffer from this? He was once a very productive man in life but may not have prepared his finances for retirement or medical mishaps. Garrett knew nursing homes were important in society, and it took special people to work there. Most cultures found it natural to take in their elderly parents and grandparents, and if necessary, he vowed to take care of Barbara until she left the earth.

It was fair to mention that many circumstances required expensive medicines, medical equipment, and around-the-clock care by professionals; thus, no one should be looked down upon if they were unable to care for their family in these situations. They might not be physically able to lift them for daily activities or stay home and care for their loved ones when the time comes. Quite understandable and he judged none, just wondered with sympathy about how and why some of the people were living there.

"Hey, Garrett, nice to see you again." Lance shook his hand and went over his health history. "I see you have experienced some blurriness and dizziness for several weeks. Can you tell me about this in time lines?"

Garrett discussed all the symptoms and the concussion in detail and told him the recent finding that he was allergic to soy. "We need to do a thorough exam which will include several tests."

"Dr. Vogel, I've been meaning to ask you what all is involved for testing my sight?"

"You can call me, Lance. First, I am going to ask you to follow my pen as I move it around. Okay, good. There are a series of tests we need to complete before I can substantiate my findings. Come with me and let me introduce you to Beth. She will be recording your manual visual field. I'll be back when it's over."

G greeted, "Hello, Beth."

"Hi, Garrett, just sit here and you are going to look into this screen while several small flashing lights appear. They will blink on and off. This won't take long."

He headed into another area and did the visual acuity exam, which included reading letters on a chart. He read with both eyes and then separately with each eye. This allowed them to determine how his pupils respond to depth perception. They also did other tests to determine his color vision, eye muscle movement, and peripheral vision.

G inquired, "Now what are we doing?"

Dr. Vogel answered, "I'm going to place a few drops of liquid in your eyes to dilate your pupils, and it's going to take about twenty minutes before we can proceed." Dr. Vogel explained he would measure the curvature of his cornea, the clear outer surface of the eye—keratometry, to determine if there was astigmatism. Next, he measured his eye pressure via tonometry, the pressure inside the eye, to determine if any glaucoma was present.

"What's astigmatism anyway? My best friend has it."

"Yes, I could tell by his lenses set in the new frames. This is a condition where the eye has two different focal points. For example, the eye, or retina, may be clearly focused in the horizontal plane of an image, but not in the vertical plane of that same image, resulting in blurred vision, which makes it difficult or impossible to see fine details."

"Huh, no wonder Scholls is so interested in medicine. I hope I'm not bothering you with my questions."

"Not at all, I like inquisitive patients. Just not one's who make me revisit my board exam. Ha!"

"No worries, Lance, I just have a couple more."

"Go ahead."

"You mentioned glaucoma. What exactly is that?"

"Glaucoma is often thought of as one eye disease, but it can be a result of different reasons and is irreversible optic nerve damage. Your eye contains fluids, and when they cannot drain properly, the buildup will increase the pressure and cause this damage. Or you may have normal pressure in the eye, and the nerve becomes damaged from improper blood supply to the nerve or a defective nerve. Fatty buildup in arteries, called atherosclerosis, can block blood flow. Retinal detachment or other parts of the eye can bulge and cause blockage of blood or decreased drainage of fluids. Trauma, heart disease, tumors, high blood pressure, diabetes, and hypothyroidism are all associated risk factors with this disease. Certain ethnical races have increased genetic predisposition, so for all these factors, eye exams are important because *it* is the leading cause of blindness that is *not* congenital, or with birth, in the USA."

"Glad I'm here, so what's next?"

"Garrett, I'm going to do indirect ophthalmoscopy, which gives me a very detailed 3D vision into the back of your eye and other areas."

Lastly, Garrett looked into a wheel of lenses that changed to check for the sharpest vision which would determine if he had nearsightedness, farsightedness, or astigmatism like Scholls.

After the examination, it was determined that he had experienced minor bleeding in his right eye, but it was healing fine and probably due to the concussion he suffered. His eye sight was 20/20, and at this time, he would not need any glasses. G purchased some of the biggest and ugliest frames with nonprescription lenses to add to his wardrobe for outings.

"Thank you for seeing me today. Hey, Doc, did you hear about Scholls's transformation? Between you and Randy, he was undeniably a 180. Here's a pic of him *before* that night."

Lance's eyes widened. "He's certainly interesting, and yeah, those glasses were in dire need of replacement. Glad I could help."

"Now, here's the vid. Look how stunned he is to realize his new look, and Randy is almost like a proud parent in the background."

"That's Scholls? Randy did an amazing job! Your friend looks shocked. Wow, that's 180 three times around!"

"Ha, for sure! I really appreciate what you guys did and won't forget it."

"It was my pleasure to help. Thank you for entrusting me as your eye doctor. I will call Randy later."

Barbara picked him up, and Garrett put his sunglasses on until the dilation effect was gone. He took a short nap until it was time to head over to Westward Trailer Park. Every time he pulled down the small road that led to 1726 Barker Street #2, he was reminded of how blessed he was. Their backgrounds didn't matter, and whatever came along henceforth was the continuation of destiny. What seemed ironic was this kid, in this trailer park, already knew what he wanted to do and how to get there. With all Garrett's advantages, an avenue of clarity was missing. Sure, he pondered careers in football, acting, and now a new intrigue in medicine; yet for all that, his future was not absolute, which left him in a quandary.

The continual buzz was that there motion picture was a top contender for an award and that G was also in competition for best male lead in a drama. It seemed surreal. He had not contemplated all the effects it would have on his life, and complicating matters was not appealing to him. At first, he felt honored to make that much money on his own, but he soon learned there was a great deal of work an actor has to do and the myth they had it so easy was false. Secondary issues were what bothered him the most, such as paparazzi, screaming fans, loss of privacy, new proposals, interviews with media of all sectors, and segregating his real life from his newfound fame. He was not opposed to just dropping the actor persona for an education first. After discussing it with his agent Wes, he decided not to pursue the role that required him to buff up for athleticism. This disappointed his agent, and he conveyed a possible way for him to balance both at the same time, but Garrett knew there were few examples of actors who were successful at this in their primetime. It wasn't that he didn't appreciate being famous, it's that he wasn't prepared for the sudden change. People began warning him he could lose opportunities in show business if he didn't jump on board, and that was okay with him. He liked maintaining a teenager's lifestyle without all the bells and whistles and wanted to ride out the current wave and make his decision post high school.

What he admired most were the athletes and stars that limit themselves to every camera angle not associated with their current project. "Get in where you fit in" didn't work for Garrett; it was more like, "Stay out and be way out." All he wanted to do was be a kid—laid-back, happy, laughing, and helpful to those who needed it. He pulled into Scholls's driveway and got out to knock on the door.

Tina was drinking a beer as she opened the door. "Oh, hey, it's you. Scholls will be back in a few minutes. He had to borrow something from a neighbor and is returning it. So how's the big life treating you?"

"You mean the fame?"

"What in the hell else do you think I mean? C'mon! Listen, I just have to get this off my chest. My son and you just don't seem like a match. I think its crap you want to lift his spirits now, but I doubt seriously you will be there for him later."

"I'm really sorry you feel this way, Mrs. Parker. He's the best friend I have ever had. We get along great and we have a lot in common."

"Shit. Please, now that sounds so ridiculous. Listen to yourself. It's only been a few weeks. Just what in the hell do you two have in common? Look where you live, how you dress, who you know."

"We both love sports, trivia, history, culture, have the same quirky sense of humor, and there's absolutely no pressure in being his friend. He's kind, funny, and the smartest person I know... seriously."

Tina laughed. "Really? He's the smartest person you know? Yeah, he makes good grades...always has, but that doesn't mean he is a genius. He reads all the time in his room, and I think he needs to get out and socialize with more than one person at a time. I have tons of friends and don't need a 'best friend' to make me happy."

"Mrs. Parker, I don't mean to be rude in saying this, but do you realize he's likely going to be the valedictorian for our school?"

"Huh? No, I didn't. He never talks to me about school. Maybe he is ashamed of me or his father to attend the ceremony."

"I bet he isn't and would be proud to have his parents see this accomplishment."

"You seem to know so much about my son. What makes you the expert on his inner thoughts?"

"We share our thoughts and feelings on many issues, and the short time we have known each other feels like a few years."

"And…"

"He feels saddened that his immediate family isn't that close."

"Listen, Mr. Big Shot Actor. Not every family is as tight-knit as you are with yours. It doesn't mean we aren't good people, and it certainly doesn't mean I don't love my kid! I didn't want a child, but I got him and we made it work. Maybe not to your standards, but we did. You think being on a low budget makes us less of a family? Or apparently, you and my son feel this way."

"No, please, Mrs. Parker, I only meant to express that he wishes that he could spend more time together with you guys."

"Well, our work schedules don't allow it. I'm not educated like your mother, and Harry isn't either. Our choices for employment are limited. Hell, I drink because I am bored in life. I wanted to be in college myself, but life didn't throw me that bone, so I stay with his father to make sure Scholls has a roof over his head and food in his mouth. Truth be told, when my son leaves, if and when he does, I will follow shortly afterward. I'm not happy and I'm damn sure my husband isn't either. We are far from the *Leave It to Beaver* clan."

"I know it must have been difficult for you, and I believe Scholls is such a great person because he did have parents who stuck it out and raised him with the best means they could. Look at the people who leave their children or lose them to foster care and won't fight to get them back. I'm happy I met him and appreciate talking with you today."

Tina wasn't expecting such a composed, politically correct answer, as she liked to rile her opponent for antagonistic default. Garrett would not dare reveal his true estimation of just how emotionally neglectful they were, and it wasn't his objective to be disrespectful to adults; once again, judging was a cranial interpretation better left unsaid—the Higher Power is in charge. He felt sorrow, the only negative factor he had concerning Scholls Parker.

Scholls appeared in perfect timing. "Hey, man, what's up? Sorry, I had to return a shovel to my neighbor."

"Your mom and I were just chatting about life in general. So much so that I forgot to ask you"—turning toward Tina—"Mrs. Parker, can Scholls go with my family Saturday night for a dinner that my stepdad planned? And possibly spend the night again?"

"I don't care. Knock yourselves out. I've got to start getting ready for work. Scholls, just be back on Sunday at a decent time so you can do your laundry and any schoolwork you need to finish."

"Thanks, Mom, someday I will take you for a special dinner. Just wait and see."

"Okay, kid."

Tina was hard-pressed to show much emotion toward Scholls, and G wrestled with why she couldn't. Garrett was experiencing an outlandish side of life, and at this fleeting moment, he pondered the idea to study human behavior in psychology. Maybe they'd both be doctors in different fields. This idea was brand-new, and it certainly put another log on the fire to stoke; all in all, he now had three types of careers to consider.

CHAPTER 16

"Eti-quotes"

THURSDAY WAS A welcome sight for Garrett. He was looking forward to seeing his friends and participating in football practice. Excalibur High was about to face San Monica High, and if they won, hello state championship for the Knights. Personally, G was not going to be devastated with a loss because his stats were acceptable for a scholarship and wouldn't make much more of a difference with the scouts. On behalf of the school, he wanted to defend last year's state title and give 100 percent. Coach Johnson spoke to him before practice starts.

"Hey, Garrett, I'm glad you are doing well. I heard the test results for the CT are negative. How do you feel about starting against San Monica?"

"It's whatever you feel is best. I know I have missed practice, so if you want to start Mark, it's cool."

"Let's see how you do today."

"Sure, coach, thanks."

He was a bit winded during warm-up and laps but managed fine during the scrimmage game. Coach J decided to start Garrett on Friday night's game. Pressure from more than football was heading his way. His agent called to let him know they are scheduling some interviews with the media and also had invitations to SAG events. It all seemed so easy before the movie.

G was dealing with a change in family, health, privacy, graduating, and now a newly begun grandstand with the reality of becoming a star. His simple life was amalgamated with so many things he wanted to do, had to do, and expected to do—a perplexing path less travelled. That evening, deep in thought, he decided to call his best friend with limited time to talk.

Scholls answered, "Hey, G, what's up?"

"Dude, I really need to talk to you. I'm starting to feel a lot of pressure with my life and need your help, or at least your words of wisdom."

"Sure, man, what's troubling you?"

"It's gonna take a few minutes to sort out the details. Why don't I swing by and we can sit on your porch and talk. Do you think your dad and mom will care?"

"Hell, they only care if it affects them. We can take a walk or drive. Sadly, I'm almost always in my room, and they don't even look…or say good-bye most of the time. So head over."

Something about Garrett's voice was different, and the tone was melancholic at best, so Scholls knew it was an issue that weighed heavily on his friend's shoulders. What could a kid who has it all be so distraught about? Thirty minutes later, he saw the black Hum and walked outside to greet him.

"Hey, G, let's take a short drive to this little spot I go to when I get a chance."

"Point the way."

A bit later, they arrived near the top of the mountain and pulled over at the lookout. Scholls guided G down a small path where they could sit on some large rocks. The view was a calming factor, and Garrett opened up to his friend:

"Scholls, thank you for not even hesitating to see me. That means a lot to me."

"Hey, I'm always gonna be here for you, and whatever I can do for you, it's done."

"This probably sounds so stupid…to be troubled by fame. The fact is, I had no idea what it meant. Modeling clothes and doing commercials do get me attention, but it's not as noticeable by everyone. Yeah, occasionally someone recognizes me if they happen to have seen my ad or commercial. Hell, I did most of my modeling when I was smaller and in my early teens.

"Now, I am being scouted for football, and with my pops gone, the drive to play in the NFL is, too. I love acting, don't get me wrong, and doing the movie was certainly a privilege, yet the aftermath of its effects is scary. I'm so effing stressed out, dude."

"Garrett, how are you feeling healthwise?"

"Pretty good for several days now."

"Okay, I want to talk to you about something later. Go ahead. What else is eating at you?"

"I have all these engagements for the industry, and our movie is a probable nomination in different categories, even best male lead in a drama. I'm nervous. Some of the other actors are well-known, and I don't feel comfortable accepting an award if it happens."

"Point noted, but, bro, each one of them had their initiation into the industry, and at one point, they were the new man out. Truth is, a movie needs to be strong in all aspects—story line, cast, crew, sound, costumes, visual effects, director, producer, location, spectators, etc., and if you do win, it's just a reflection of the compiled blood, sweat, and tears everyone put into it. You have a gift. Don't beat yourself up over this."

"Hell, I feel honored for sure. It's just the unexpected outcome. I went in naive. I just want to stay grounded and have the respect of my peers."

"Garrett, you will. You are one of the kindest people I know, and it's not phony, dude. I saw you for a few years before we ever met, and I knew you were a genuine person from your actions. Remember, actions will *always* speak louder than words. No one can take that from you. I sense your fear is that life will be more of a whirlwind than you are used to. Look at it from a new perspective. These are a few inspirational quotes I keep in my phone by famous people who summarized change." Another hidden folder from his parents.

John F. Kennedy, thirty-fifth president of the USA: "Change is the law of life and those who look only to the past or present are certain to miss the future."

Socrates, a Greek philosopher 469–399 BC: "Remember, no human condition is ever permanent. Then you will not be overjoyed in good fortune nor too scornful in misfortune."

James Baldwin, an African American writer, 1924–1987: "Not everything that is faced can be changed, but nothing can be changed until it is faced."

Olga Korbut, a 1970s Olympic gold medalist in gymnastics: "Don't be afraid if things seem difficult in the beginning. That's only the initial impression. The important thing is not to retreat; you have to master yourself."

"Dude, you're a damn good friend. Wait, that's damn good *best friend* to you."

"Thanks, man."

"Those were incredible, and those people certainly have notoriety. I like hanging with you. One of the best things that could ever happen to someone is having a best friend in life to share their deepest fears and thoughts. I'll always pay respect to the planarian flatworm, that's for sure! LOL."

"True that. It's like we have swapped roles for comfort. Usually I am asking for yours, and it is nice to know I can return the favor. That's what makes you so down-to-earth; you are not afraid to let your emotions show or tell someone what you think."

"By the way, on Saturday night, we need to dress the part. Not quite as extensive as homecoming, but a jacket and slacks would be good. I think there was a black pair of slacks in that bunch my mom gave you."

"Yeah, there was. I think you gave me the whole suit. Is it that fancy of a restaurant?"

"Yep, and we have reservations on the terrace with an incredible view. My stepdad is going all out and he knows the chef."

"Cool, are there any specific mannerisms I need to know at this shindig?"

"Bro, you're cool. Don't sweat it."

"No really. The silverware intimidates me. There's more than I'm use to on the table. Remember Julia Roberts in the movie *Pretty Woman*? I can relate to that scene, so you need to be Richard Gere and help me. Seriously, dude."

"All right." G laughed. "It's complicated, but I will break it down like you did for me with the *systemic* stuff. Here it goes.

"First, wear the appropriate attire requested. If the host stands, you stand until he or she sits or asks you to be seated. Our gathering won't be quite that formal, so we will sit according to our arrangement, if any. The left-handed ones, you and Peter, will sit at the ends of the table. This is so arms don't bump together. He may toast or say a prayer or both. Always join in the toast and stand if he stands.

"Within the first minute, it is expected for you to place the napkin from its setting into your lap. Never remove it or use it to wipe your mouth, nose, or cutlery. If you need to get up to use the restroom, fold it loosely and lay it to the left of your plate. Never state you are leaving to use the restroom. Instead, you say 'Excuse me' or 'I'll be right back.' If a waiter or busboy clears the table, always say 'Thank you' and ask for services with a *please*.

"Now the layout of the silverware is really a simple concept. Just intimidating if you don't know the rules. American etiquette says you eat to your left and drink to your right. This means the food plates on the left are yours, and the drinks placed on the right are yours. Start with the silverware farthest from your center plate and work inward. On the left this will be the salad fork, then the dinner fork, then the dessert fork. On the right outermost, you will start with the soup spoon, the beverage spoon, and the salad/dinner knife. Food is served from the left and removed from the right.

Once you use your knife, the handle or blade never goes back on the table. Always have the blade facing inward and rest it on the four twenty position of a clock. In fact, all silverware when finished will be placed in this position to indicate you are completely done. When you cut your food, the blade of the knife is inward, and you stabilize the food with the opposite hand. Switch the fork in the hand you used to cut when eating and rest the other hand in your lap until you need it again. No arms or elbows on the table while eating.

"Only cut a few bites at a time, and make sure the tines of the fork are pointing downward in use. At the end, the tines will face upward when you are finished. Chew with your mouth closed and avoid making loud chewing noises or slurping. You never eat before everyone is served and eat slowly so as not to finish well before everyone. This is considered inconsiderate. If Mom gets up, we, all the men, will stand until she leaves and stands when she returns.

"If the food is too hot, never blow on it, just wait till it cools off and always scoop food away from you with the proper utensil. If you want butter for bread, place it on your plate first and then spread it on the bread. Also, when asking or giving salt or pepper, they should be passed together to avoid having orphaned holders.

"Always pass food from left to right. It is rude to intercept food in route to someone who asked for it. Always use serving utensils to serve yourself, not your silverware. Never throw your napkin in the plate or push dishes away from you when you are finished. Loosely fold the napkin and place it to the left of your plate.

"It's customary to have tea or coffee at the end, and it signifies that the formality of the dinner is over. You got all that? LOL."

"Damn! I'd rather take a calculus exam! Okay, shit, now I understand high society, right! And you say, *don't sweat it*? I have beads on my forehead just listening. I rather like my Mickey D's."

"Yeah, and I only do this when necessary. By the way, a calculus exam for anyone else, but you and Jerry Wong would be challenging. I'm just saying."

"Bro, I'm gonna have to download a GPS app for eating formally. Remind me to keep a low profile when I'm a doctor."

"I'm with you on that, and this whole medical science thing is beginning to fascinate me. If I were to plunge in any part, I think I would enjoy psychiatry. People and their behavior blow my mind. Right now I'm confused as to what I want to do."

"Hey, you and me, doctors. Hell yeah-ya!"

"Schollie, it's dark, and we should head back. Don't forget to make sure the suit is okay."

"Soy-lutions"—"Restaurantutions"

G dropped Scholls off, only to find Tina was gone and his father was about to leave. They connected the next day in biology, but Scholls was unable to get a ride to the game.

It was a difficult loss for Excalibur High, and Garrett was pissed off at himself for revealing he had a headache. Coach J placed Mark, the second string quarterback, in the second quarter and most of the third quarter because he felt obligated to take Garrett out. There were several errors made during this period, and he told Coach that his head was fine—when it wasn't—so he could go back in the game. Unfortunately, the Knights were unable to comeback from a 27–17 loss.

The season was over, and some of the pressure G felt was alleviated in what he had expressed to Scholls; only this time, it was his head that hung low in school. People tried to assure him it was okay, though it didn't make him feel any better about the situation. Mark was being treated unfairly by some students, and once again, Garrett stepped up and took care of the insults. He reminded everyone that even the top NFL teams don't win every game and Mark was a damn good quarterback. Garrett was proud to leave the team with him in charge.

Saturday morning, he woke up wondering why his head was hurting and figured stress was the cause. He texted Scholls he'd be coming around 3:00 p.m. Scholls packed a duffel bag and picked up Bandit to chat.

"Hey, lil' buds, gonna be gone tonight. Keep the house under control for me, will ya? And if Mom or Dad gets loud, you have my permission to hide under the bed so they don't throw you out. Okay, girl? I love you, bud. Oh, I need to figure out why Garrett is getting headaches again. You got any ideas?" Bandit purred. "What! Did he have some soy? Or did he have stress? Or is it another cause? I'll talk with you in a little while, Okay, Bandi? I need to go mow this old man's yard. He's not that old, but he is lazy and cheap. I had to insist he pay me $25 and almost lost the job. He reconsidered when I explained that removing weeds in the flower area would be extra for anyone else. Can you imagine that, Bandi? The nerve of some people. Well, off I go. See you in about one and a half hours."

Scholls carried on a conversation in his head. *What is going on with my friend? He looked fine in school, so what did he do to get such a headache? This whole soy thing has me troubled, and I forgot to talk with him about it. I am pretty sure he has eaten Chinese food before, and a high probability he has used soy sauce at some point in his life. I will find out this answer. It may be the source of his previous illness. However, I am not thoroughly convinced. I'm going to make my way down to the vitamin store and check out the entire contents of the protein mixes he drank. Oh boy, I'm here at Mr. Penny Pincher's estate. More thoughts later."*

Mr. Potts was outside and said, "Who are you, kid?"

"Uh…I'm Scholls, who lives in this trailer park and who you asked to mow your yard about ten days ago?"

"Really? 'Cuz you look totally different. All right, get this cleaned up and I'll pay you when you're finished."

"Oh, sorry, I got a makeover for something. I guess I do look different."

"Shit, you look like a totally different kid." He laughed out loud. "That old look was pitiful, but who's asking?"

"Yeah, ha ha. Who's asking anyway?" He faked a laughed.

Scholls wanted to smart off to him and say, *This is coming from a man who looks like he hasn't taken a bath in weeks—fifty-two to be exact."*

The yard at Mr. Cheap O's wasn't too large, but the grass was high and the weeds were thick. Scholls had a pretty good push mower that his uncle Randolph bought him last year. He borrowed some gloves from Mr. Potts—his temporary employer of the year—pulling weeds for over forty minutes. The flowers were barely any different from the weeds, so he spared some and finished the job. After collecting the money, he went home, cleaned up, and walked about three-fourth of a mile to the vitamin store. He envisioned Kipper and sent her a text to say hello, and she responded within a minute, asking him to call. Scholls decided to and made it quick.

"Hi, Kipper, you look great today."

"Huh, are you somewhere where you can see me?"

Scholls was so nervous he botched up his opening line.

"Oh, I'm sorry, I meant to say it was great to hear your voice."

"Ahhh, that was sweet of you to say. I like hearing yours as well."

"Really? I mean, that's nice. Umm…Garrett and I were talking the other day and thought maybe you and Tally might want to go to the beach and hang out one day. We can have a picnic if you like."

"Well, I need permission from my father, and this time, you will officially have to meet him in person. Good thing your voice was disguised on the phone, and by the way, we pulled it off. He didn't suspect a thing. When I get older, I will tell him what I did. When it's safe, that is. Ha!"

"Okay, yeah, I do feel a bit guilty about it. Anyway, Garrett said he would take me to your house if I needed permission. Tonight we are going with his stepdad to eat dinner and celebrate Garrett's homecoming and his movie, but how about next Saturday?"

"That sounds good. I also need to clear my work schedule. When can you meet my father? He is off on Sundays and Mondays."

"How about tomorrow, this Sunday? I'm sure Garrett wouldn't mind taking me by before he drops me off. I'm spending the night at his house."

"I'm pretty sure we can anytime after church. We usually go eat afterward and get home around two thirty. I will text you if this is good."

"Yes, ma'am, I'll do it. Bye, Kipper."

He arrived at the vitamin store and found the same protein mixture that his friend drank while weight training these past few months. "Let's see…There's GMOs, soy protein, maltodextrin, acesulfame potassium, antibiotics, artificial colors, fructose, and metals…particularly cadmium. Well, I will keep this in mind."

He walked back and saw his mother in the living room. She was watching TV, so he sat beside her, said hello, and attempted to have a conversation with her.

"Something wrong, Scholls?"

"No, ma'am, just wanted to sit here beside you and see how you are doing."

"For what?"

"Oh, maybe because you are my mother and I care about you in general. Am I bothering you?"

"Well, I guess you can sit here and watch the last part to my sitcom. So is your new look getting you any more attention at school?"

"A bit more, yes, but nothing I can't handle."

"Your friend—Jarod?—said you are most likely going to be the valedictorian this year. Is that true?"

"It's Garrett and actually—"

Tina cut him off. "Shhh, this part is funny."

He sheepishly finished, "I am."

His mother was so caught up in the show that her attention span was short and she forgot about the question. Scholls just walked off and went back in to find Bandit. "Hi, girl, I got my money from the old troll down the street, and now I have $197.00 saved. What do you think of me now, Bandi? You should have been my mother. I see you more and you like me." Bandit purred and laid on his chest to nuzzle his chin. "Life's strange, Bandi. We just have to make the best of it till we can change what we can. Wherever I go, you go. Oh, it's Garrett. Let's see what he says in his text."

"On my way, dude. Twenty."

"Roger that."

He continued to pet Bandit, and she fell asleep by his side. There's time to jot down a word or two in his diary. He added notes about Kipper and his attempt to bond with his mother.

"Another day, another dollar, well, $197 to be exact…out." He dated and put the time of entry.

Garrett pulled up, and Scholls let him in, but before they left, he walked back to the couch and leaned down to hug his mother. Her arms remained anchored to the remote and did not reciprocate the tenderness. She said, "Oh, hey, kid, good-bye." Poor Scholls. The persistent attempt for affection went flat, yet still he was obedient and as tolerant as a son can be. Will this woman ever wake up and smell the roses? She was undeniably self-absorbed and relentless. Doesn't her conscience bother her at all?

It was easy to see why he bonded so fast with Garrett. This kindred spirit took notice of his wit, intelligence, kindness, and humanity. Tina, bolstered by alcohol, had stripped away the parental-child relationship, and his dad was seemingly no better. Just because H. Parker earned a living doesn't mean he was fulfilling his paternal capacity. This man's anger was deep-seated from his youth and ill directed toward his wife and child. Harry and Tina swore they would not become their own parents—all those intentions played out like the quote from Thomas Edison: "A good intention with a bad approach often leads to a poor result."

The result equals poor parental skills and lack of recognition for a son. The only Parker in that household who was truly a loving individual was becoming a self-catalyst for breaking that circle of dishonor.

Garrett commented on what he witnessed, "Scholls, is that how your mom usually is, or was it because I was standing there?"

"Nah, man, she's usually like that. I asked her why she can't hug me, and her response was that she was raised like that. Here's the problem, I see her hug other people, and I have to admit, it hurts."

"Bro, it hurts me to see it. I can't imagine how it would feel."

Garrett pulled his friend toward him. "I'm not ashamed to hug you, man."

Scholls gulped. "Thanks, G."

"Tell you what, let's cruise on over to Schultz's Burgers and see if we can find Kipper."

"Really? Oh, hey, that reminds me of something. I spoke to her and planted the seed about going to the beach next weekend. I said it would be the four of us. Is that cool?"

"Of course, and I mentioned it to Tally. Let's just say I think we have a double date going on!"

"You were correct, dude, I will need to meet her father, and I was wondering if we could stop over there before you take me home. Her dad is off on Sundays. They go to church and then out to eat, so say around three?"

"Absolutely no problem. I'd actually like to meet him myself, 'cuz I feel a bit bad about it. Plus, he's a cop, and I like cops. There's some crappy ones, I get it, but most of them are good people and they *risk* their lives every day."

"Dude, here's ten dollars for gas."

"Are you crazy? Remember what I told you about my money from the movie?"

"No, I'm not crazy yet, officially, except about Kipper. Now remember what I told you? Take it or I'm jumping out, here I go.

I'm gonna open the door and jump, like, right now. Okay, here I go. Really…"

Garrett started laughing. "Shit, if it's gonna take $10 to save your life, give it to me."

"Dude! I thought you'd never take it. I can't jump. The ground is too hard That shit will hurt!"

They pulled into the burger joint and spotted Bianca. She could have been a contender for his homecoming date, but awkward due to the fact she works with Kipper. Nonetheless, Bianca was a pretty cool chick and very artsy. "Well, well, well, if it isn't the two boys from the coast." Bianca took a second look, acting confused. "Whoa! Garrett, who is that beside you? Hey there, handsome. What's your name?"

"Scholls."

"Bullshit, he has broken glasses and long hair. Okay, good try. Now who are you, really?"

"Bianca, really, it's me, Scholls. Remember last weekend?"

"Gotcha! Of course I remember you, dude. Please, I couldn't forget that night." They all started laughing, and Kipper finally came to the Hum.

"Hey, Garrett. Hi, Scholls. This is a nice surprise."

"Yeah, G went out of his way to accommodate me…as usual."

"We just wanted to give you a heads-up about coming over tomorrow around 3:00 p.m. so Scholls can meet your father. Is that a good time?"

"Yep, I asked him already, and he is looking forward to meeting you, Mr. Sexy."

Scholls's face turned red, and he said, "Mr. Sexy? Okay, I'll take that title for the first time in my life. That'll work."

⸺◦❖◦⸺

Kipper's dad had no clue about the boys except she told him they met a while back and that her mother, Kelly, met them at Schultz's. He predictably did a background check. No surprise, all was clear. Kipper mentioned Garrett as well because the transportation was provided by him, and her father would also want his info verified. Karl was stunned to find out G was the actor in *Constant Judgment*; Kelly and Kipper had to act equally startled and put on quite a performance.

When their brief visit with the girls was over, they headed to a gas station. Garrett looked in his rearview mirror to discover a van following closely behind and maneuvering each lane as if to make sure it didn't lose distance between them. He told Scholls to look back, and both of them were quite convinced they had a *razzi* on their heels. G warned his friend the ride was going to get a bit more turbulent, and he hit the accelerator and made a fast turn to the right. Scholls warned, "It turned. Shit. Okay, do what you need to. I'll hold on."

Garrett went a few more blocks and turned left. He gained momentum and so did a white convertible full of girls who see him pass by. They sped up trying to get their attention. Unfortunately for the brood of estrogen, he hit the brake, turning again to the right and leaving them no chance to follow.

"Any sign of the van?"

"Damn, G, I see it. Go for it, dude!"

Garrett sped up again and headed for the freeway. The van was a good football field behind them, and if only that genie of Randy's could change the Hum into the V12 Zagato, this matter would be solved in 4.2 seconds. He laughed and then yelled, "This reminds me of a future adventure. We're gonna take my dad's Aston Martin out for a spin, and unless a NASCAR racer is on our tail, we're gonna outrun everyone in Cali."

"I might have to get my license before I graduate from med school. Ha! Even though I'm scared as hell right now, it's ironically exciting. Okay, I don't see the van anymore."

Garrett exited the freeway cautiously, and they eventually found a gas station. He called his mom to let her know they were on their way, explaining they were at least thirty minutes out due to the fiasco. Barbara was upset and told the boys to call the police the next time they suspected someone was following them. With all the crimes committed, just assuming it was the *scabs for media* wasn't necessarily safe.

She began to understand some of Garrett's reservations about being famous, and this situation made her feel tremendous guilt for exposing him to the limelight. It all started randomly at a doctor's appointment. While awaiting their turn, a woman asked Barb if she had any children. The eager mother pulled out a picture of Garrett, instantly catching the lady's attention and desire to give a business card. She explained why he had "potential" assets for the camera. This woman recruited for So-Cal Talent Agency, and the rest was history.

"Look in the back. There are a few hats and sunglasses. I'm gonna have to remember I need to wear them every time I leave the house. It wasn't second nature yet, but this sure as hell fixed that."

In a few hours, the boys would be celebrating with Casey, Barb, and Dr. Berg at Le Palais Enchante, on a private terrace overlooking a beautiful view and anxiously awaiting the chance to tour the kitchen. Peter's friend, Feron, was the executive chef. The restaurant specialized in French cuisine and American food with an unexpected twist; plus, they had standardized meals as well.

Peter wasn't really happy for Garrett, nor did he want his best friend Scholls around; in short, the evening was staged for his lovely wife and devotedly arranged for Casey. Oddly enough, his little boy loved Garrett, and though there was despising contempt for that recently woven kinship, all in all, Dr. Berg's heart filled with joy to see his little boy smile. In his mind, their bond would be a short-lived connection, and it kept Peter from developing more futuristic separation anxiety. This neurologist had a cerebral fork in the road, and he could not journey down both until the timing was right. In spite of the pledge to detain subtle to moderate manipulations with G's health, temptation was too difficult, and that last episode gave him the secured feeling of power over his victim, *Garrett Errington Pierce*.

At some point in the condo, he researched the heritage behind the name *Pierce* and found it to be startling. It was derived from religious links to Saint Peter or Apostle Peter...commonly used for baptismal purposes, or citing, the "son of Peter." This angered him for several seconds, as he had no idea of the inadvertent connection.

"One little headache bout for the 'son of Peter' because there's only one son of Peter...Casey, and all I will ever want. You're the son of Thommason, the ol' love of Barbara's life, but not for long, my stepson. In the wise words spoken by Cassius in Shakespeare's *Julius Caesar*, 'The fault, dear Brutus, is not in our stars, But in ourselves, that we are underlings.'"

In other words, it simply meant that Garrett's fate was not in the stars but due to the feeling of disorderly ranking Peter felt with Barbara. This tertiary level *was not* acceptable—first, Thom; second, Garrett; and third, Peter.

<hr />

The route back to 11 Huntingdon Cove was longer than usual, and the boys found more time to talk about the holidays. General Randolph Parker would most likely breeze in at Thanksgiving or Christmas. On that information, they needed to coordinate the best schedule which would accommodate their families. Scholls and Garrett had been tinkering with the idea of a "redneck weekend" with Garrett's cousins. G knew if he did not keep in touch, the relationships would dwindle, and with Thom gone, he felt especially eager to salvage *Pierce* relatives. His best friend had never been anywhere except Arizona and California, making this adventure an *ad hoc* solution for enterprises in Texas.

"Before I forget, do you eat Chinese food?"

"Uh huh, I can remember eating it when I was about nine. Why?"

"Well, you are allergic to soy, and it's a high probability you have had it before, especially now that I know you *have* eaten Chinese food. How often did, or do, you eat it?"

"Probably four or five times a year, I guess. Come to think of it, I do use soy sauce on my rice."

"So in any of the times you've used it, do you ever recall getting a headache or nausea?"

"Let me think…The last time I had it was about four months ago when Randy and I went to hang out. I really can't recall if I did or not."

"Okay, we will just assume you are really allergic to it."

"What's going through that MD brainwave of yours?"

"I just want to make sure nothing else is the cause of your illness. I have to look out for my homey 'cuz we have decades to clown around. One other quick question, do you still feel leery of your stepdad?"

"Hmmm? I guess not much. He doesn't stare at me like he used to, and he's been very helpful. You ask because?"

"That's cool. Inquiring minds gotta to know. I'm just glad you feel better."

"I'm always amazed at your thinking process. I promise, if I have any episodes with soy, I will let you know."

"Whoa! Wait just a minute, dude. You can't eat *any* soy. It could literally be fatal. If you want Chinese food, we'll make it ourselves. I'll buy a wok and entertain you like the hibachi guys and wear a hat. I can't promise I will catch the egg, but I can promise I can make the onion volcano. LOL."

"Sweet. And you'll twirl the spatula?"

"Hell yeah-ya, like a majorette…or thereabouts. Ha ha."

"Thereabouts?"

"More like *whereabouts* 'cuz it will probably fly out of my hand and jack someone upside the head, which will be you or Tally or

Kipper, or God knows who else might be there, and my samurai skills will be compromised, especially the katana, aka spatula. My chances of getting on the Food Network shows will be harder than me trying to get on *Dancing with the Stars*."

"I need to see this. What's a katana?"

"The famous samurai sword. So you wanna see that? Wait 'til we have mastered our first double date with picnic supplies, which in my opinion will be much easier, as long as we don't have any American picnic rules of etiquette! Ha!"

"No, bro, we can eat with our hands! Speaking of that, are we good for next weekend?"

"It's all up to Mr. Manning. We'll find out tomorrow."

They ran inside to change clothes for dinner but not before confronting Barbara, who hugged them both on their safe arrival. Scholls finished timely, though he made sure his *golden* hair was on target. He cannot forget Randy's face, and it's like a ghost behind him in the mirror saying, "Uh huh, 100-24-7." The other *golden* child took his usual leisurely time. There was absolutely no jealousy when he thought of Garrett in this fashion, as G definitely was the boy everyone liked—and deservingly so. While waiting, he stepped out on the patio to think.

In the beginning, Garrett was skeptical of his stepdad, and Scholls tucked a personal inclination under his belt so as not to vocally address it either way, but rather be inquisitive of his friend's feelings, as this was most important. He was a lot like Sherlock Holmes in that he compartmentalized all facts relevant and suspiciously irrelevant before conclusions were made. He liked Peter, yet Garrett's initial instinct of "something different" set into his hippocampus, the section of the brain that is associated with memory function. While Garrett's uncomfortable initiations with his stepdad had diminished, S. Parker's had increased.

Most people have a gut feeling which is mainly known as *intuition*. Steve Jobs, cofounder and former CEO of Apple, Inc., once stated it was "more powerful than intellect." He found the

2005 commencement address to Stanford, by Mr. Jobs, very influential and powerful.

There was only one other person on earth who he would ever reveal his most intrinsic feelings to, and that was his uncle Randolph. Every minute he spent with this man was recorded in his journal, validating that regardless how much saturated loneliness he experienced from his immediate family, a ray of light beamed continuously on the Parker crest.

He called the general to coordinate the holidays but found he'd be unable to come either Thanksgiving or Christmas due to six months of conflicting FBI assignments in Houston, Dallas, and Chicago. A lightbulb went off in Scholls head, and he would run it by Garrett after dinner. Just maybe, they could align the honeymoon and Texas in the same time frame. He remembered the cousins were just under two hours outside of Houston, and depending on the day, his uncle might be available to see them, if only for a brief period. General Parker was especially apologetic and quite upset he had to give Scholls the bad news; however, he promised to fund the airline tickets if they could come to Houston in November during Thanksgiving.

Garrett finally emerged from "beautification" of his already striking looks. He chose to wear a suit similar to the one he gave Scholls, possibly making this choice not to upstage his dear friend but rather reflect even more of a brotherly connection in public. This time he need not disguise himself, as the restaurant was aware of their arrival time and routinely hosted many famous people which they aptly accommodated.

There was a separate small driveway that wound aside and behind the entrance, with a private entry and elevator that avoided the mainstream dining area, leading directly to the terrace. As expected, Peter and Casey sat close together, Barbara and Garrett sat across from them, and Scholls was placed at the other end of the table. He remembered the long list of rules, and when Dr.

Berg stood to make the toast, he got up in stride and executed his manners well.

One nice curveball was Casey making a toast of his own. This little boy was precocious and equally bundled with unaffected simplicity. What did that mean? It meant he was very mature beyond his years of intelligence with a cloak of childlike playfulness that would keep you from believing he was older than eight—and a half, that is. It was so cute; he stood up and made quick bows toward the guys and walked over and took Barbara's hand, gently kissing the top of it. He looked sophisticatedly confident and cracked them up when he placed his left hand behind his back in a horizontal fashion as they do in a gentleman's lounge. He began his toast and tapped on his glass of ginger ale: "Here, here...I'd like to pay honor to the greatest brother I could ever have...with the greatest mother I could ever have...and the greatest father of all. Of course, let's not forget the greatest friend at this table. I myself am the greatest kid, so we have the greatest group of people in the entire restaurant...but not the 'orld, *b* the three of us are gonna grow up and create a few more lil' greatnesess. Get it? LOL." Scholls thinks, "*quite the alliteration*".

He could not say the word *world* so the *w* was silent, and he also said *b* instead of the word *because*. These little imperfections stamped his unique language; no worries, the good doctor knew it would eventually be right. Besides, it was so adorable to hear. All in all, he was a youngster at heart. His words made whimsical sense, but the theatrical display of his hoopla made everyone laugh. He'd concluded the speech with his eyebrows up, arms folded, and one downward motion of his chin. It certainly set the mode for a more informal conversation among the group.

Peter was touched by his son's toast, even though Casey ascribed his own adorations about Garrett and Scholls. The rest of Dr. Berg's evening was completely relaxed, and for the first time since he set eyes on Garrett, he felt lackadaisical. Even his alter personality got a break; there was nothing to challenge about goodness.

Feron happily toured all three of the boys through the kitchen, allowing them to observe the sous chefs in action and pick out the dessert of their choice. Inside the walk-in freezers were sculptures of ice and butter for special engagements that the chefs designed by hand. The boys had no idea of the craftsmanship that went into the meals and centerpieces. One of the most beautiful ice sculptures was an American Indian in full headdress. It had infused colored sand, ornamental pieces frozen into the ice prior to carving, and LED lighting, which took a total of fourteen hours to complete. Scholls asked Feron if he would take a pic of them standing around the magnificent display. He was in marvel of the masterpiece and vowed one day to place an order when he graduated from medical school.

It was 10:30 p.m. when they left Le Palais Enchante, raking in over three hours of drama-free fun. Sherlock Parker was tossing several ideas in his head and concluded that Peter was not at all like his usual self, almost as if he had reverted back to a day when life was youthful—most likely how he acted when Paul was alive. He spoke heavily about that friendship. Scholls wanted to know what his parents were like, what kinds of hobbies Peter had, what kind of DNA he inherited, especially since he had a dual degree, MD and PhD, which is difficult to accomplish. Why did his biological father leave and was he still alive? Unfortunately, none of this was revealed. Scholls studied Dr. Berg's expressions and tones over the entire evening and perceived he definitely had two different personalities. But was this wrong? Everyone can have two personalities, or maybe three or four, or?

One can't possibly stay the same given any number of reasons or circumstances. One may be assertive at work but passive at home. One might have to limit their happiness in public with just a smile or belt out mounds of laughter where it is permissible. One might be coy with one person and off the charts with another—all reasonably feasible. In spite of this, it was the comparison of tonight versus the evening they had dinner at Garrett's house. What stood out clear as a bell was the *pitch*. He normally has a medium pitch. The night he talked about his parent's catastrophic ending, Peter had a low, very low, monotone pitch.

One's pitch is essentially the physical instrumentation of how one manipulates intonation, the pattern or melody of changes of our voice. That might be normal for what Peter revealed. The trouble is, a few weeks ago, he never transitioned from low, back to medium, and soon after he finished his story, instantaneously left the table. It was inherently different and precisely the opposite of this eve, where his pitch started medium, then changed quite a bit higher after he dwelt on Paul, and never lowered. Undeniably, it remained more escalated and personified a childlike attitude, which also caused Barbara to take heed with oblivious reciprocation. He showed more signs of public affection with her and was even over-the-top polite with G and Scholls. He had become someone else that night and was rather lively. Scholls kept his opinion to himself and factored in the consumption of alcohol Peter drank. He reflected on the eve.

Scholls said, "Bro, that was an incredible place, and Peter was actually lettin' loose. You see that?"

"It was hard not to notice, and Casey was hysterical tonight. Effing hilarious!"

"Garrett, one day I'm gonna be the one hosting and paying for an incredible evening. Mark my words. I can't thank you enough for this, and well, all of it man."

"I'm looking forward to it. Hopefully by then, I will be gainfully employed at something steady."

"Damn, dude, you're done with acting?"

"Man, I don't know. You might think this is crazy, but I really am fascinated by psychiatry. It's a real possibility."

"Crazy? That's a good play on words. LOL. I'm cool with that. Dr. Pierce and Dr. Parker!"

They busted out a video game and played for the next two hours. This time, they were actually tired, willing to sleep, and a bit anxious to meet Mr. Manning, Kipper's dad. If he approved, then the double date was on for next Saturday. Scholls decided to text Kipper and said goodnight to confirm 3:00 p.m. It was one thirty in the morning and not likely he'd get a text back, but she surprised him with a response. Overloaded with infatuation, his brain clouded the fact she worked until midnight on Saturdays and tossed around ideas of why she was still awake. Maybe she was thinking about the date, like he had been all week, or maybe she needed to do laundry, or maybe she was not tired and watching TV, or maybe he just got lucky. His heart raced when it lit up with her name: "Perfect. See you then, Mr. Sexy." This girl actually thought he was sexy—even before he was Randy's genesis. Priscilla continuously spun her *web du desir*, and lots of other girls were chatting with him frequently, but still Schollie's new look was a perpetual self-awareness issue.

Earlier at the restaurant, he was in the lavatory washing his hands. Looking hard into the mirror at his image, he said aloud, "You're still a nerd. You know that, right?" He looked over his left shoulder, and a man was standing there watching. The man crinkled his nose and shook his head, and then turned around and left the restroom. Scholls felt embarrassed and quickly dried his hands and headed back to the table. He didn't notice that man's attire, but when they were receiving their dessert, the same gentleman placed his Bananas Foster down, looked at him with a smirk, and rolled his eyes before leaving the table. Garrett witnessed the visual flak, and Scholls told him, "I'll explain later."

Just before G hit the remote to turn off the lights for bedtime, the waiter incident popped into his mind, so he invoked an explanation about the whole story. To Scholls's chagrin, the bathroom bringdown prompted him to admit if he hadn't spotted the waiter, it would have been more ghastly because Scholls was about to answer his reflection and say, "I know that, Mr. Sunshine!"

Garrett couldn't stop laughing, even with the lights off. He finally stopped, but there was a short period of silence and then another burst of laughter. S. Parker even started laughing. A little while later, Scholls said, "We good?" and G said, "We good, sunny boy."

CHAPTER 17

Double Daze

THE MANNING HOUSEHOLD was an example of hardworking middle-class people who pretty much lead a normal life. Kipper was a brown belt in karate, liked most sports, played chess, and also a straight-A student. Her approach was confident and direct with a sense of humor to boot. She was a member of the National Speech and Debate Association; in addition, she also placed as a national finalist in Humorous Interpretation. They had seen a bit of dry wit with her from Schultz's and during the entire homecoming "sneak-out."

Among all her talents, she was very likable and pleasant to be around, and she seemed to bond with Tally immediately, as their personalities enmeshed. She told Scholls her intentions were to keep in touch with Garrett's girl, and this made the double date even more interesting because there was nothing worse than two girls who don't get along—something he has heard from guys his whole life. He'd also analyzed women comprehensively and once asked his mother at age six, "Momma, does everybody have to get married?"

She replied, "Well, no, not everybody. Why?"

"Good, 'cuz I wanna do whatever I wanna do when I get older."

This hit her funny bone, and she reached over to squeeze her son's hand gently in admiration. I guess most women tend to dominate the outcome of family activities, and his little brain was at work depicting the future to the inevitable problems that seemed derogatory in nature. It was a pivotal moment for Scholls as he mostly remembered her laughing at him instead of laughing with him, something he recorded as a touching moment.

Mr. Manning had just settled in to watch the Sunday NFL game on TV when the two boys arrived. Kelly greeted them at the door and escorted them to the den for introductions. Karl had a beer in his hand and was sitting in his realm, while two amicable friends chanted from the couch. If this had been Scholls' dad, an outright war would have started by the mere interruption of the game. They did have to wait until the first commercial, and Kelly made the kids a soda before running upstairs to fetch Kipper, who was rehearsing a speech.

"Babe, your cutie pie is here, and Mr. Garrett Pierce."

"Okay, be down in a bit."

Karl and his friends agreed to pause the game on TV and made small side bets as to which team would have possession of the ball when they fast forwarded it. With Garrett's history of football, the entire group was able to smoothly chatter about the present game. This was a *manly* environment, and all these men had participated in football at some point. The testosterone was oozing from wall to wall. Karl asked Scholls if he played football, but Garrett immediately jumped in with a diversion of why he could not play, so as not to embarrass his friend. He explained that Scholls had household obligations, and it did not allow time for sports. G quickly changed the tempo, directing a conversation about his friend's intelligence and highlighting the valedictorian payoff, which caused Karl, and friends, to shake their heads in respect.

He'd grown to love his best friend and would not be able to stand seeing anyone dispraise him. Scholls looked at G with the utmost appreciation. How grateful he was for that biology experiment that rejuvenated his life. They were in the midst of broaching Garrett's fame when Kipper jaunted down the stairs in half the time she normally took.

Her heart wasn't the only one racing. Before coming down, she brushed her hair, put on a bit of makeup, and changed into a pair of shorts. Scholls's face reddened as he spotted the gorgeous, long-legged heir of his desire hurriedly declining from the stairwell. A few minutes passed and she asked her dad if they could excuse themselves to talk in private, leaving Garrett to continue entertaining the group of men. He reminded them cameras were everywhere and that he could run fast. Kipper and Scholls both laughed…hers, at her father's protective style, and his, at how nervous Karl made him feel.

In the backyard was a cozy gazebo similar to one he'd seen as a child. Mrs. Manning had excellent taste when it came to ornamental landscaping, and there was also a beautiful pond with flowing water that created an atmosphere of calm elements. Out of the blue, they heard, "Hello, hello, what's up?"

It came from the bird cage which held their African grey parrot, Caesar, who was nearly ten years old. The bird was in a feisty mood and seemed a bit raveled that it had competition for Kipper's attention, walking back and forth, swaying side to side. "It's a pretty day, pretty day. Caesar wants nuts…loves nuts." Scholls was in awe of the clarity and capability of the bird's voice to project soundly and inquisitively. He started telling her about Irene Pepperberg, an animal psychologist who created the Alex Foundation, which raises money to support research of parrots with focus on their cognitive and communication abilities. Dr. Pepperberg had an African grey parrot named Alex, who lived to be thirty-one years old. He died at least half the species known survival period but was able to distinguish colors, numbers, shapes, words, and also the first and only nonhuman to ever ask an existential question by asking what color he was. His legacy and accomplishments were to be attributed to Irene and her undying devotion; moreover, an incredible staff who also made her works possible.

They had quite a bit of fun with Caesar, and it was evident from Kipper's gestures she treasured her bird. He wanted to impress her, so he asked, "Did you mention you had a cat as well?"

"Scholls, you do pay attention. Yes, his name is Spanky."

"Cool, my cat is named Bandit, and it's a girl. I love dogs as well. It's just that my parents won't let me have one because…"

He kind of hung his head lower in shame, but she halted his letdown and lifted his chin up. She was not fully aware of his homelife or relationship with his parents but accustomed to making people feel better; her candy striping days at the hospital was proof of this. She did contemplate a career as a nurse like her mother or doctor like her uncle but realized her passion has been, and always will be, toward animals. Not only did she have a bird and cat, she had a turtle, a rabbit, and a fish tank with several different kinds of fish. On this subject alone, the two conversed for the next twenty minutes until Kelly came outside to check on them.

Garrett handled his own with the guys and even wagered on the paused interlude. He got so absorbed with excitement; he hadn't noticed how long his friend was gone. Celebrity status wasn't an issue—just a bunch of sports fiends hooting and hollering at the TV.

Whenever Kipper and Scholls appeared, it was time to wrap things up and say their good-byes. Karl gave his approval for the double date, and the kids would get together next Saturday at noon and be able to stay at the beach until 7:00 p.m. He did not want her, or them, out near the water after dark and suggested they continue the rest of the date at a restaurant or movie. Twelve thirty was the absolute latest she could stay out. He could not help the overprotective attitude because he'd seen the homicide of a young girl. Were it his way, she would never leave, but at some point, he would have to relinquish the thought of her *never leaving*. Their safety was important, and he warned more parents to take the high road rather than the low road when it comes to their children's whereabouts.

Garrett took Scholls home and called Tally as soon as he headed out. She was excited and would be calling Kipper to plan the picnic part. G didn't want her to go to any trouble or spend any money, yet she insisted that the girls provide the food for the day and the boys provide the food for the night. It was agreed that everyone liked turkey sandwiches and potato chips. They would bring bottles of water and sodas in an ice chest, along with blankets, towels, disposable utensils, napkins, and sunscreen. Garrett even had a portable sun canopy he would bring. As far as music, they all liked top 40, and Scholls also like some rap music which he could imitate pretty well. He had a wireless speaker General Randolph gave him for Christmas last year, and G had downloaded music on his phone, so they would provide the tunes.

<hr />

On 222 Cloverleaf unit 5 was a distraught doctor who could not balance the evening of Le Palais Enchante. It happened, and he was now solemn. Meaning, he knew it was pleasing for his family but displeasing for his ultimate plan. Betraying himself and letting his guard down caused him to be even more demented. As he paced around the living room, he became more agitated and began talking.

"What the hell am I doing? There's no room for him in our lives. I can't let him live. He's got to go."

Another voice challenged him. "Please let him stay!"

"*Stop it*! His existence is a barrier between Barbara and me, and my real son likes him too much. On top of all this nonsense, he has a best friend, and I could not have Paul in my life, so Scholls or Schollie, or whatever in the hell he is called, surely won't have Garrett. There's no changing my mind! I slipped up… That's all. He's going—period!"

"Honor Paul. He loved you. Stay as you were when he died. If not, what's left after that? Will you be content?"

"You'll find out. Just wait and see."

His phone rang, and Barbara was on the line asking when he would be home. She decided to make spaghetti, but he answered her with a fierce no. She was shocked by his answer and more so by his voice.

"Honey, are you all right? Everything okay at the hospital?"

"Oh, sweetie, I am truly sorry for my outburst. I am stressed with a case. I am just not in the mood for that. Can we have something else?"

"Of course. Any suggestions?"

"Why don't I pick up some take out Chinese food and bring it home? You won't have to cook. That's what we have Juanita for, but you insist on cooking every Sunday eve."

"Babe, I love cooking Sunday dinner. It's traditional for me. I enjoy it. I really do. By the way, please make sure there is no soy added in any of the food. Remember Garrett's allergy to it."

"Yes, my love, I am conscious of this, darling. See you at six."

Peter hung up the phone in pure frustration. The mere mention of spaghetti took him back to the night he cooked his parents their last meal. In fact, he had not eaten it since then. Secondly, her words *"It's traditional for me"* stirred his jealousy zone. He knew she had done this for her entire first marriage, and it did not make him happy at all. Even if he did allow soy in the food, nothing would happen, but they believed his word as a doctor, so he had to pretend the allergy was real. Fact of the matter was, he needed to wait a bit before giving Garrett another side effect—but hard to wield. The honeymoon was not going to happen for a several more weeks, and his plan to weaken him in an irreversible state was on hold.

He swung by Shanghai Hanna's and picked up dinner. Garrett was a little nervous about eating it and wondered if they added any soy to the brown sauces. Dr. Berg made sure he had shrimp with broccoli and white sauce. He also had soup and an eggroll that was soy-free. When everybody finished their dinner, Casey insisted on reading the fortune cookies.

Barbara's read, "You will live a long and prosperous life."

Peter's was, "There is yet time enough for you to take a different path."

Garrett's was, "Your heart is a place to draw true happiness."

Casey's was, "You will be getting a new bicycle real soon."

It took everyone a few seconds to realize his prank, and they all started laughing aloud.

It was also time for Garrett to receive another vitamin B12 shot, so Peter administered it about an hour after they ate dinner. His foot was so much better, and he only needed two more injections for the initial stage. It wasn't determined how long he would receive them, and no discussion was made. Dr. Berg anticipated his absence for good, which would rule out future treatments altogether, so why stir the pot? He chuckled at the fortune cookie message he received, "time enough to take a different path," and thought, *No different path for me.* He intended to do him in, and that was that. His delusional self could not spare any room for additional people as he believed Garrett was the enemy and Scholls was Paul's archrival.

Barbara set out to talk to Garrett about his double date and his cousins in Texas. However, that phone call was still bothering her, so she mentioned that Peter seemed to be under some stress tonight and wanted to know if Garrett noticed. Nope, he was still happy by the whole dinner on the terrace, which convinced him Peter was not a threat anymore. He asked her why she felt this, and her answer was simple; she had not ever experienced a sharp, stern mode from him before. Garrett comforted her and told her not to worry. "Even Daddy had stressful moments from work, remember?"

He changed the subject and told his mother about Karl's rules and what the double date would entail. She was actually glad Kipper's parents were so proactive about their daughter's safety, and it made her feel at ease with the outing. They wouldn't be far anyway, as the coast they were going to was within a mile from home.

The subject about the Texas adventure was not so pleasing to Barb. Garrett had never flown or travelled without an adult present, even when he filmed the movie. He addressed her concerns and explained that he and Scholls were old enough to travel alone; plus, they were meeting his uncle who was with the FBI. The tickets were a gift from Randolph Parker, and he wanted Scholls to experience a totally different environment. Keeping in touch with his dad's family was important to him, and backing down from the trip was not an option. Barbara really could not deny Thom's family and knew it was narrow to keep her son from his other relatives. She gave her approval but requested all the destinations be known, along with phone numbers and addresses. Barb had never gone to east Texas before, and she had no idea of their lifestyles. All Thom said was these relatives were simple and laid-back, with unpretentious ways.

Garrett decided to omit describing their trailer as he knew this would make her unsettled. Bubba had suggested they stay one night down at the deer lease, and if one of the nights were with General Parker, then not much could happen. Quite frankly, he couldn't wait to be around people who most likely would not know him from Adam.

The entire week seemed like it had lasted a month as the boys awaited the date with the girls. Finally, the sun came up, and Garrett went into the kitchen to make a bowl of cereal for breakfast. Casey was already eating, and Barb and Peter were still in their room.

Casey asked, "What cha doin' today, big brother?"

"Going to the beach."

"Oooh, can I go?

"Sorry, little bro, Scholls and I are taking dates. How 'bout you and I plan on going another day. Sound good?"

"Darn. Okay, but are you guys gonna kiss? 'Cuz I could look away and you wouldn't notice me at all."

"Lil' bro, we might, but we need to spend some time alone with them so we can—"

"Get married?"

"That's a bit premature. Meaning way too early for that."

"*Whew,* 'cuz I barely got to have you as my brother, and I don't want some ol' girl to take you away right now."

Peter was approaching the kitchen when he heard his son saying this. He came up behind Casey and put his hands over his eyes and said, "Guess who?"

"Daddy!"

"Right, and yes, Garrett will not be getting married anytime soon. He will be leaving the house one day, but you will always know him as your big brother. Let me see if Mom and I are able to take you to the water today…for an hour or two."

"Yes, you're the best dad in the whole 'orld!"

Garrett finished his bowl of cereal so he could leave to pick up Scholls. When they returned to the house, they gathered the stuff for the beach and called both girls to let them know when the Hum will arrive. Barb, Peter, and Casey must have left for the day, and on the table were two plates of goodies for the boys to take on their beach bang. Teenage boys have an incredible appetite, and they both ate the brownies right away. Since Kipper was the farthest out, they got her first and then drove to Tally's house.

G wanted to go to the Leo Carrillo Beach because it had tide pools, reefs, caves, and about 1.5 miles of sand. He was always supportive of cultural places, and this beach was named in honor of the actor, preservationist, and conservationist named Leo Carrillo, known most for his role as Pancho in the 1950s television show *Cisco Kid*. He did many other forms of performing throughout his career. Leo was born in 1881 and died in 1961; he served eighteen years on the California Beach, Parks, and Recreation Commission.

G respected his mother's wish for them to remain within a mile from home, but this made them unable to go to that location, so he regardfully called his mother to get permission. When he was a child, his father took him there. Once, Thom was reading a book and looked over to discover that Garrett was playing with another family in the water. It was moving and made him realize his son was a people person and not at all worried about that families' ethnicity. He watched as they laughed and played with him until coming ashore for drinks. G waved to his father, and Mr. Pierce captured that moment in time by taking a picture for their family albums. When Garrett saw the pic, he got emotional. Thom and Garrett made it a *rite of passage* to return to the beach every year and volunteer at the recreational center.

"Hi, Mother, it's your super obedient son, Garrett."

"Yes, sweetie, what do you want to schmooze me about?"

"I was wondering if we could go a bit farther…to the Leo Carrillo Beach. You know, where Dad and I use to hang out. Please?"

"Well, honey, I guess I will make the exception, as long as I know where you kids are, and promise me, you will stay there and only there until it's time to leave."

"Yes, ma'am."

"I appreciate you calling and asking me. You guys have fun."

"Thanks, Mom, I love you. We will. I'll call you when we leave, Okay?"

"Bye, sweetheart, see you late tonight."

The kids set up the canopy and decided to wait a bit before they ate their food. They checked out some of the tide pools and then walked around to see the caves. Scholls felt a little nauseous, and he thought he was going to vomit. Mutually, Garrett was experiencing the same thing, but neither one of them wanted to admit to the queasiness and kept it under wraps for the rest of the date; they did not want to damper the day. What were they experiencing?

Sherlock Parker knew he felt absolutely fine when he woke up and deduced that the brownie was the probable cause, but why?

Garrett secretly concluded that this was yet another symptom of his weakened immune system and was not convinced it was the brownie, though he briefly considered it.

Scholls waited it out, and within a couple hours, he was much better. He assumed it was Barbara who made the brownies, or Juanita, so there would be no reason for tampering. Oddly, he started to question something out of the blue. Had Peter made them or placed anything in them that would cause this? And if so, why didn't his friend have any symptoms?

Scholls chalked up his illness as an isolated case, except he did not dismiss it. He knew from anatomy and physiology that emotional stress, fear in particular, can cause nausea. He certainly had a lot of fear today; this was his first date ever, and he might have to kiss Kipper this evening, with intensity, and not like he was kissing his grandma good-bye. He would not abolish this suspicion because he already made several mental notes on the good doctor by piecing together each precedent of disorder. Right now, he feared that first kiss.

It was a great day at the beach—perfect weather, water, and company. They swam and played chicken in the water. The girls decided to compete against the boys in a sand castle contest, except the designs did not have to be a castle. Tally and Kipper made an elephant, which was incredible, while the boys made a spaceship. Whenever someone would walk by and make a comment, the boys would ask who had the best work of art, and unanimously, the girls won, even though it was only seven votes.

At 6:30 p.m., they packed up the gear and changed their clothes. The walk to the Hum was not a straight shot, as Garrett had to park way down the beach to deter any *razzi*. With his sunglasses and visor, he was able to keep his face under raps. The entire gang had a different look so they could remain inconspicuous. He had Tally and Kipper fetch the SUV while they lay low. The license plate had been covered by a paper one that was placed on a vehicle which was newly purchased. Scholls was the mastermind behind this divergence, and it worked so far. He knew it would get worse because the movie had now been out for several weeks, and more and more people would recognize this up-and-coming thespian actor. G called his mom and let her know they were leaving the beach and going to get some food at Donavan's Reef, a seafood restaurant that had booths which were positioned in different areas making privacy attainable. They also went bowling for two hours. Garrett had already reserved the section for private parties, and it had two lanes and a door that closed and divided them from the open lanes.

"Oh crap, she's looking at me like she is going to want a kiss."

Kipper walked over and placed her hand on his shoulder and surprised Scholls. All she wanted was to challenge him one-on-one, instead of the teams they had been playing. He let out a sigh of relief when she walked away to go get her ball. Tally whispered something in her ear, and the girls started laughing out loud. He was nervous now. Did they know he had never been out with anyone on a date? Did he look like he'd seen a ghost when she walked up? Was his bowling pathetic? It was.

Garrett asked them, "What's so funny?"

Tally replied, "It's girl stuff."

That really made Scholls nervous. He walked over to G and said, "What's girl stuff usually about?"

"It could be about anything, literally anything, but probably about us."

Kipper knew he had no experience with girls, and yes, they were laughing about that, just not mocking him, but rather shining on how innocent he seemed. She saw his face get more and more flustered as she approached him for the challenge.

At 11:45 p.m., they stopped bowling and put their shoes on. Garrett brought cash to pay for everything to prevent a paper trail, and once again, the girls completed the checkout while the boys quickly got into the back of the vehicle. Kipper decided to refrain from the closing smooch that would put her crush into anxiety overload; however, Scholls indubitably knew it was now or never, and when they pulled up in her driveway, he wanted to kiss her all week, and by God, he was going to do it, regardless.

She went to the back of the vehicle to gather her things, and he jumped out to help her. He leaned in and said, "I had so much fun today." When she turned to repay the compliment, he gently put his hand behind her neck, pulled her close, and kissed her lips. She was in absolute utopia. They made out for almost a minute, and that inspired Tally to climb in the back and kiss Garrett. All was blissful until they saw the lights come on, and precipitously, all locked lips ended. Scholls walked her to the door and greeted Mr. Manning. He invited him in for a bit and kept the door open. "Did you kids have fun?" Kipper was still lusting after that romantic session, and Scholls answered for the both of them.

"Yes, sir, we had a wonderful time, and I appreciate you letting Kipper go out on a date with me."

"Well, son, I am strict, but I do realize teenagers need to have fun, and I expect my daughter to have a boyfriend. I'm not that rigid."

Scholls winked at Kipper before Karl could see it, and he said his good-byes. Karl escorted him out on the porch and said, "Oh, good night, Mr. Henry, and thanks for making sure she had her shoes on this time."

Scholls felt a rush of panic, and his eyes widened; Karl had figured out that he was acting as her boss on the phone the night of homecoming and he'd spotted his daughter without her foot attire; his detective background put it together. Mr. Manning just wanted them to know he had figured it out without directly busting them. Their wide eyes looked at each other and said, "Nite." He shut the door, and S. Parker went back to the Hum in a funk and got in without saying a word. Garrett said, "Is everything cool?"

"He's *slyboots*."

"Huh?"

"Tell you later, dude. Let's get this young lady home on time."

As soon as they dropped her off, G asked Scholls, "What the hell does *slyboots* mean?"

"It's a phrase used to call someone who is very sly."

"Okay...and?"

"Dude, he put two and two together and figured out I was the voice behind the conversation he had with me, aka Kipper's boss, on homecoming night. Not to mention, I told her not to forget to put her other shoes back on, and I guess she forgot. Anyway, he figured it out."

"Shit, I hope it didn't hurt our credibility with him."

"Dude, I don't believe it did, 'cuz he doesn't seem like the type to allow much to happen if he doesn't want it to. Kinda reminds me of the actor Jack Nicholson in *A Few Good Men*."

G laughed. "You can't handle the truth!"

"Something like that."

CHAPTER 18

Brown E-mail

WHEN THEY GOT back to Garrett's house, Scholls excused himself to get a drink of water. Barbara had always told him from day one he did not need permission to go into the kitchen and get food or drinks. In the same direction, he noticed a light from the study and curiously walked over to see why it was on. He stopped tout de suite at once when he heard Dr. Berg.

"I'm the protagonist, and you are the antagonist. Let's keep our roles straight."

Scholls decided to look and see who he was talking to. There was no one in the room—just Peter standing with his hands on his hips and pacing back and forth. Maybe he was practicing a speech or he needed to discuss something with a colleague. He seemed erratic and angry. Scholls deciphered what each word means.

Huh, protagonist *refers to one who is the leading person in a movement or cause. An* antagonist *is one who opposes.*

It did seem rather weird he would be up this late and practicing a speech. He must have come home from a late night at the hospital, seemed reasonable. What didn't was the pitch. It was low again. Scholls was now edging up on the fact that Peter's voice would be either one or the other when he spoke about his past, yet consistently medium pitched when he seemed to be in the present. He was studying his mannerisms with a fine-toothed comb. It would be counterintuitive if he did not scrutinize his friend's initial sense of uneasiness when Peter entered the picture. Garrett meant everything to Scholls, and now it was time to make sure the neurologist had no hidden agendas. Uncle Randolph was the perfect analyst about behavioral science, since he specialized in this area for the Federal Bureau of Investigation. He gave his uncle a call the next morning.

"General Parker."

"Hi, Uncle Randolph, it's me, Scholls."

"Hey, son, it's great to hear from you. Have you boys decided to take my offer and use the airline tickets to visit Texas for Thanksgiving?"

"Well, actually, we haven't got all the fine details ironed out yet, but it seems highly probable we will, because we can kill two birds with one stone and visit Garrett's family as well."

"Great, when you work it out, let me know and it's a done deal."

"So, Unc, what I am calling about is kinda strange, but my inner gut tells me I need to check out something, and you are my best bet when it comes to what I need."

"Okay, what's bothering you?"

"My best friend, Garrett, has a stepdad that is very likable... but also very...let me think of a good word to describe it..."

"Complex?"

"Yeah, that's a good start. Anyway, he's almost seems crazy at times. When I first met my friend, he felt uncomfortable around his stepfather. Since then, he has changed his mind and feels fine. I, on the other hand, can't quite put a grip on it but have my suspicions my friend was spot on. I have been observing him now for several weeks in an ulterior fashion and want your opinion on a few things. I don't want Garrett to know anything, so can I e-mail you some facts and see if there is any concern for my suspicions?"

"Absolutely, find out as much as you can about him and what kinds of things he does that makes you feel the way you do. I need his age, race, family history, profession, likes and dislikes, if known, and anything else you can dig up."

"Perfect, I'll send you what I can. By the way, thank you for being such a cool uncle!"

"My dear nephew, I love you as a son. Talk with you soon."

Garrett took Scholls home around eleven at his request. He explained he had an assignment to do and needed to go home a bit earlier. G decided he would take Casey to the beach for a couple hours, as promised, if Peter doesn't object, since he had taken the lil' tike on Saturday.

Westward Trailer Park awaited his arrival, and Scholls picked up Bandit immediately and laid on the bed to formulate a list of all the things he saw, heard, or suspected in the time frame he knew Dr. Berg. Hours later, he shot a text to Garrett explaining that his uncle needed to arrange the flights.

Barb and Peter had planned a two-week venture to Europe, and Casey would spend the holiday with his aunt on Barb's side. He would return to school the following week, and both Juanita and Garrett would be his caretakers. He already had carpooling for school and after-school activities, so the hardest part was done.

"Mom and I have talked. No conclusions yet. Will confirm ASAP. Later."

"Okay, Texas needs a touch of class. Cross your fingers, dude. Out"

E-list for General Randolph:

1. Initial meeting was pleasant enough. Loaned G a scalpel for project.

2. Garrett mentions his uneasiness due to leery stares.

3. Garrett has nausea...dizziness, off and on, as well as blurriness at times.

4. He's tested for allergies and confirmed to be soy though G has eaten it from childhood.

5. Peter talks little of his immediate family or childhood.

6. He talks nothing about his previous wife.

7. He's brilliant and has an MD and PhD in neurological medicine.

8. His previous wife abandoned the marriage and parental rights. He is a great father to Casey, his only child (son) very protective.

9. He seems devoted to Barbara, Garrett's mom, and is adoring of her.

10. From the beginning, he has always had a very even medium pitch/tone in his voice. When he is talking about his childhood friend who died from leukemia, he has a high pitch, and very low pitch when mentioning any other past history, which is limited and trancelike at times.

11. He's probably around forty-five years old. Not sure. Caucasian.

12. Fluent in French.

13. Has few close friends. Mostly colleagues or other doctors.

14. Has mentioned he likes travelling.

15. Listens to classical music.

16. Has a specialty with autistic children. In fact, Barb has an autistic brother, about thirty-four years old.

17. Caught him talking to himself once, not definite if he was though, and only once, but vey late at night and he was pacing oddly-erratically.

18. meticulous grooming/OCD like habits

Fill in more as I learn more. Don't know exactly where he lived. I think Baltimore, but after his parents died tragically in a house fire, he was sent to DC area to live with his aunt and uncle.

Scholls e-mailed the list to Randolph on the phone and finished the laundry. He kicked off a few words for the acceptance speech; there was still months to go, yet unpretentiously knew he would be valedictorian. His incredible memory was the key. He wondered why he had been blessed and what it would have been like without it. Was he really that intelligent or just extremely lucky to be gifted?

An urgent need for prayers overcame the moment. This was not necessarily something he did routinely and found himself prompted by concern. He had a style of praying that was informal and not traditional in the form with hands together. He talked aloud and preferred to say "Father" because it seemed respectful. The scientific elements of his brain warranted researching the validity of biblical stories from the Old Testament, but the internal feeling he had was undeniably spiritual. He felt the celestial enigmas. Scholls traced several blessings he'd received over the years, which were evident of a greater force.

His conscience yearned to know why some suffer great pain and torture prior to death. He concluded that the *innocent* recipient was not due misfortune but received the misfortune from pure accidental timing or the unfortunate force of a situation that was initiated by at least one person of satanic evil. God is omnificent, and he preferred to believe in his goodness, making humans accountable for their actions through the free will he granted.

Scholls prayed for his family and now Garrett. There were so many relatives he wanted to know and pledged to seek them out when he could afford it. Unapproachable subjects stay dormant at this time. He had immediate concerns, which warranted protection for his benevolent friend.

"So, Bandit, I expect you to be a good girl when I leave to Texas for a couple of days. Well, not confirmed yet, but I believe it will happen. I met this cool bird the other day and another kitty you might like named Spanky. *Unfortunately*, you can't hang with him until you are spayed. I'm just a bit short on living space and money to have your little children running around. Now, your goal is to stay clear of Mom and Dad. I think you have a better chance with

Dad, so do what you can, and I have bought you this cool dish of food that has a timing device. It will open in sections for each day, and the water dish will be under my bed. I'm gonna tie the door handle to my room so it won't close. Hell, they never come this way much, and my room is your room. I know you prefer going outside instead of this litter box, but just in case they forget to do their humane responsibilities, it will be here for you. Oh, one more thing, I have some food outside in another dish under the trailer. It will open only once, in case they forget to bring you in. You just might have to catch a mouse or two if they do. Okay, sweets, gotta do some more stuff." He kissed her head and rubbed her fur.

It's late, so he finished his homework and checked the phone to see if Garrett had answered. *Huh? Nothing yet. Well, I will see him tomorrow.* He received a confirmation from his uncle about the list.

The next day in class, Garrett told Scholls he felt extremely tired yesterday and went to bed around 6:00 p.m. Just by mere coincidence, they both looked at each other and reflected back on the brownies. Garrett brought up that it needed to remain a secret to keep from ruining there hopes of Southern hospitality. Immediately, S. Parker began comparing their symptoms, and it was a match. Both boys had nausea and some pain in the stomach region. Who made the brownies? Did Casey have any? He wanted to know the answers to these questions, so the next time he goes over there, he would ask the appropriate people, less Dr. Berg.

By Tuesday, Scholls got impatient and began to read about these symptoms and what can make them occur. The most important detail he needed was how many people ate them. On a whim after school, he decided to catch the bus and walk the rest of the way to his best friend's house. Garrett was gone at a media event for his movie—but he already knew this—and he rang the impressive doorbell that resounded classical music Dr. Berg had customized for Barbara. Juanita answered the door and invited him inside. With no time to spare, he thanked her for making the brownies—hoping to get the response he needed. She said, "Thank you. I appreciate it."

That threw a monkey wrench in his theory. She did mention there were two plates. One plate had five brownies and the other had six. The boys ate two a piece on the same plate.

He asked, "Do you have any left? Oh no, Mr. Scholls, *porque* Dr. Berg took some to his patients. Casey was sort of mad at me because Dr. Berg had placed all of them in a sealed container for Sunday's hospital rounds. He did tell me to make sure you two got at least one each." He told her he left something in Garrett's room. Juanita nodded her head, and Scholls made his way down the hall.

He processed the information he got. *Okay, now we're getting somewhere. He definitely wanted us to have one. Next tier of information, are there any traces of the brownies?*

He sneaked into the same den, and a black leather bag sat off to the side. No sign of any container. There was a receipt for some kind of medical supply—paid in cash. He decided to take a pic of it with his phone. Other than that, there was nothing out of order. The bag held several documents from work. He made his way back to say thank you and was politely escorted to the door. The picture of the receipt was forwarded to Randolph with a message.

On Wednesday, Garrett finally confirmed he would be allowed to go to Texas with Scholls and must get General Randolph to call his mother. Next week was Thanksgiving, and the Bergs would leave to Europe on Monday morning. Garrett and Scholls would leave on Wednesday morning and return on Sunday eve. General Randolph and the boys had been invited to another officer's home for Thanksgiving, so the first two nights would be with him. On Friday, the boys would go to Bubba's, Thadeus Pierce's nickname. He wanted them to go to the deer lease, spend the weekend camping, and hunt.

Both boys were already seventeen and would need to take an Online Hunter Education Certification Exam and buy a permit to hunt.

The days couldn't go by fast enough. Their only downer was not seeing the girls over the holiday, but they would certainly keep in touch.

Randolph called Barbara on Saturday when Scholls arrived at his friend's estate. During the call, Dr. Berg stood close by and seemed a bit jealous of her conversation. He motioned her to hand him the phone. Garrett was impressed how Peter commanded the responsibility of their trip and in awe of the intelligent interactions between the two. Scholls was listening to any change in pitch. Yes, there was. Dr. Berg lowered his pitch, though not as low as before, after the initial greeting. They spoke for nearly two minutes.

After he hung up, he talked with the boys about his own personal hunting experiences in the medium pitch. Peter excused himself and went into the den, presumably. This large area had several books like a library and a smaller section that veered to the right where two windows would illuminate only that section of the room. This was where the family dog used to sleep. Mr. Speckles was a pedigreed English Setter and died at age fourteen.

Peter began pacing around. His general anxiety disorder sustained anxiety from the stimulation of the brain's BNST and amygdala, which he had studied. It almost seemed logical there would be two personalities. He was his own study. Like a dog chasing his tail. He understood the science of the disease; unfortunately, his narcissism would not heed to the acknowledgment. He was godlike to the patients, and being on their level of subjectivity was not going to happen. He paralleled the segment in *Paradis Lost*, book 1, John Milton:

> Farewell, happy fields,
> Where joy for ever dwells! Hail, horrors! Hail,
> Infernal world! And thou, profoundest Hell,
> Receive thy new possessor—one who brings
> A mind not to be changed by place or time.

225

The mind is its own place, and in itself
can make a Heaven of Hell, a Hell of Heaven.
What matter where, if I be still the same,
And what I should be, all but less than he
Whom thunder hath made greater?

It seemed Lucifer was reasoning his fall from heaven in a psychological interpretation of how he justified it. Peter could do the same.

Scholls excused himself to use the restroom. He was not surprised to see the doors of the den pulled together. Quietly, he opened it enough to see the good doctor talking again, which appeared to be to someone else, yet there was no one else.

"I have time."

Peter repeated the inner voice in a mocking tone. *"Please reconsider. You need not feel threatened."*

"Can't you see what I see? Favoritism for Charles is back in a different form. I'll be nothing again."

"My friend, you are loved now."

"Stop your pleading. Leave me alone!"

It conveyed the impression he was unleashing his sadness to a mental or invisible apparition. Maybe it was part of his therapy from what happened. Scholls wavered a bit but depended more on his gut. Will he tell Garrett or Barbara? Not at this time. He needed more. Besides, he would never ruin their honeymoon or his trip with Garrett. Unless, perhaps, Dr. Berg was dangerous, which had not manifested in any fashion he knew of.

Scholls had ears like an owl, eyes like a hawk, and craftiness like a fox. He reentered the living room to ask G for a ride home. The boys would take their exams online the next day. He sent this observation to his uncle. It would not be fair to assume that Dr. Berg was crazy; however, it was comprehensible.

"Hit me up when you get ready to take the exam."

"No prob, G. I'm gonna read a bunch of stuff before I do."

"Ya think? Of course you are, man. Ha!"

"Dude, call me if you have any questions. I'll be doin' housework and other crap."

"Later, bro."

"Later, G."

CHAPTER 19

Four Travel, One Trips

CASEY WAS TAKEN to his aunt's house on Sunday night. It was Barb's oldest sister, Marie. He cried when they said good-bye, and Peter was markedly upset. This was the first they had ever been separated for more than a day. You could have used a crow bar to pull them apart. A good old dose of bribery was in order, so they told Casey he would get to go to Disney World for spring break. Aunt Marie was able to get him inside before he relapsed.

Garrett got up early to put on his hat and glasses for the trip to the airport. He drove Peter's Bentley Flying Spur. It was a gorgeous car with soundproofing throughout. The *razzi* would not know he was in this car. It had the newest technology that allowed the driver to change the color of paint by adjusting the voltage sent throughout the body. It could literally be five colors but stayed silver most of the time. It was badass. Dr. Berg had been a car enthusiast and often went to car shows. G's dad had the same enthusiasm, but when he mentioned it to Peter, a gust of silence occurred. Dr. Berg apologized and said he was preoccupied. He kept driving and started to feel a bit of sorrow that Barb would be gone. Yes, this mama's boy had to come to grips that he was getting older and she was in a different world now. For the most part, G had changed his mind and opened up room in his heart for stepfather love. Garrett was naturally an example of *altruistic* love. Sadly, this would be the opposite ground plan of Dr. Peter Weston Berg.

Back at Westward Trailer Park, his best friend's parents were fine with the leave of absence. They never questioned who he was going to be with in Texas; presumably Garrett was trustworthy; after all, she knew the "Hollywood brat" would have ultimate provisions. Tina did ask him about Bandit. "What about your little four-legged piece of work? Have you arranged for her care? 'Cuz I distinctly don't recall you asking us if it was okay."

"Well, Mother, I have taken great strides in her preparation to be alone. I was hoping you could let her out on occasion. The food is all taken care of. It's okay if she sleeps in my room at night, isn't it?"

"Shit, I just don't want to have to worry about her, Scholls. I'm busy, and well, it annoys me you didn't ask."

"Actually, I was going to the other day when we were talking, and you got up and never came back, remember?"

"Don't turn thus shit around on me. I'll do my best. Next time, get a confirmed answer from me or your father."

"Yes, ma'am. I know she won't be much trouble. I appreciate this, Mom."

Tina stared at him and left the room. She returned with $20.00 and told him this was for spending money. In an attempt to be affectionate, she put one hand on his shoulders and said, "Call us and leave a message on my phone when you arrive." Scholls decided to take it upon himself, again, and hugged her. She was motionless and almost seemed afraid. A few seconds went by, and she said, "Okay, that's good, son." He let her go, and his heart felt that sad feeling everyone experienced when they were very hurt. He watched her walk off, and she turned around with what appeared to be a wetness in her eyes and said, "Be careful. Have fun with Jarod, and just don't do anything stupid. I know how teenagers can be. Bye, hun."

Damn it. It's Garrett, *Mom.*

Was she about to cry? He saw emotion from her and called him hun. Scholls sat down and fell back onto his bed. He saw her crack. She was affected by him leaving. Sometimes, people who really care for you act mean as a diversion to their true feelings. They don't want other people to know how they really feel, so acting mean or rude helps them to avoid this. What they seek is what they don't have and this frustrates them. No one is going to know they care. It's easier being mean, especially when other people are around.

He pondered the moment and said a prayer for her and his father.

It's time to pack, but that wouldn't take long. He had two pairs of shoes—the ones he had and the ones Garrett gave him. The duffel bag was stuffed with a few shirts—one nice one for the Thanksgiving dinner, two pairs of jeans, and two pairs of shorts, underwear, socks, and the cologne he got from Randolph, his razor, toothbrush, floss, and comb. *Oh yeah! Damn, I almost forgot the hair gel Randy gave me—100-24-7!"*

Some of the items would have to go inside Garrett's suitcase. This was his first flight ever. The anxiety of flying had set in, and fear was creeping up in slow increments. He called G to go over the plans. Barb arranged for a private driver to and from the airport. They would leave at 3:45 a.m. The flight was nonstop to Houston, and departure was just after 6:00 a.m. General Randolph would be there waiting. He would take them to Bubba's on Friday. At noon on Sunday, the boys would be picked up from east of Houston to have a final meal with Randolph. Their flight would return to California by six thirty. Scholls would get dropped off that eve, as they had school the following Monday.

"Okay, remember, dude, we have to keep a low profile. Act like geeks or something. I think I will wear a wig this time."

"Geeks?"

"Sorry, bro, I didn't mean to use it like that."

"No offense, 'cuz I'm known as a geek, and this geek is gonna make a difference in medicine, so, dude, what color are you gonna wear?"

"Hell, I don't know, anything but dark. How 'bout red?"

"Let's see…a redheaded geek. Never seen that. How original."

"Dude, I know, let's both wear red wigs. We can be geek brothers!"

"Sounds like you need to call Randy."

"You got it, bro. I'll borrow some from props. If he doesn't answer, I can go get them anyway."

"Hell yeah-ya!"

Garrett's friend Randy did answer. "What you got, G man?"

"I need a favor *again* and fast."

"Let me guess…You and Schollie are gonna need some disguises for the Texas Prairie."

"How'd you know, man?"

"'Cuz I have GSP."

"What's GSP?"

"Garrett sensory perception."

"That's funny. I guess you know me well."

"That I do, my friend, that I do. So how can I gladly help?"

"I was thinking that we, Schollie and I, could go as redheads."

"That's hysterical and brilliant! I even have Bubba teeth in stock."

"Let's skip the Bubba teeth for now. Maybe another adventure. Ha! But do you have any T-shirts for gamers?"

"Yep, I'll pick two out. See you in an hour. Ciao, baby."

It was lucky for Garrett that Randy lived about half mile from the studio. As promised, he had picked out some really nerdy shirts.

The first one said "Nerd? That's intellectual badass to you!"

And the second one said "Gamers rule! Mom says so!"

He knew the second one was his and the first was Scholls. He talked more with Randy about the interviews for the movie and then politely hurried along. He headed over to pick up Scholls. Bandit was sleeping, and his master gently stroked her fur and said, "See ya soon, girl."

In less than twelve hours, the boys would set foot on Texas soil. All the excitement made them unable to sleep right away, and they play the racing video before falling asleep. Both of them send the girls a text and promise to stay in touch. Tally and Kipper had their own family gatherings to attend.

"G, wake up, man. It's 3:20. We overslept, dude!"

"Shit, good thing we packed. Get the wigs."

"Okay, I'll wear the shorter one and my old glasses. I know which shirt I have, but which hat is mine?"

"The solid yellow one."

"Really? 'Cuz I'm the chicken getting on the plane. Yeah, yellow's my color. It ought to blend in just fine with this carrot-red hair."

"Dude, it's you, man."

"Okay, let's grab a bowl of cereal and make sure we have everything."

Juanita was already up making pancakes and bacon.

"Thanks, Juanita, you're the bomb!" They ate and then took turns brushing and flossing. She handed them some snacks for their bag, and minutes later, the driver pulled around to the back side of the estate and tended to their luggage. Off they go. Nerds again.

At the airport, people could not stop staring. They laughed at their shirts. In fact, it was the overall appearance causing the reactions. If only they knew these two redheaded nerds were gold boys. Having the star of a movie and his handsome sidekick would create a flock of fans similar to a shark-feeding frenzy. It was nice to meander around without hassle. Scholls relied on Garrett to walk him through the whole process.

Finally, they sit in their first-class seats. Uncle Randolph was a generous man and classy at that. One of the airline attendants became very inquisitive. She kept asking questions and looking at their hats and hair the whole time, as if she might wonder about how real it was.

"You have distinctive green eyes. They look familiar. I just can't put my finger on who you look like. Oh well, both you boys have great eyes. Enjoy the flight."

Garrett and Scholls looked at each other for a few seconds with fear and then smiled and enlarged their eyes at full potential. They couldn't help laughing under their breath, so to speak.

Along with their outward exhibition, the boys changed their voices. They had so many things to keep track of, but the only thing that went down bumpy was Scholls's first visit to the restroom. The plane went through some unexpected turbulence soon after he closed the door. He heard the pilot announce for everyone to return to their seat and buckle up—definitely a scary moment for the amateur traveler. The rest of the flight was fine. Texas touchdown. They headed to baggage claim receiving the same astounding glances from the airport cattle.

Scholls sent the general a text about their attire, and he was ready and waiting near the baggage claim. He shot back, "I might need you two one day…for spy missions."

Shortly after, he saw them and grabbed his nephew for a big hug. He shook G's hand, and they headed to his vehicle. The first thing the boys wanted to eat was good ol' barbecue and *wolfing* down those ribs.

During the ride to his uncle's corporate housing provided by the FBI, both boys sent a text to their parents. Europe was seven hours ahead of Texas time, and California was two hours behind. Harry Parker responded to Scholls and said, "Son, glad to know you made it safe. You boys have fun like I did when I was young. Well, maybe not that much fun. I'll tell Mom you texted." Barbara texted Garrett and asked him to call if possible. Once again, this made Peter irritated. They were on their honeymoon. Still, her little boy had flown into an area she was not familiar with and his voice was all that could soothe her motherly uneasiness. While Randolph and Scholls talked family business, he dialed his mother. Peter answered and acted like he was happy to hear from his stepson. It couldn't have been more the opposite.

"Garrett, it's nice to hear from you, son. How was your flight?"

"Hi, Peter, pretty interesting, but we landed safely and on our way to General Randolph's place. Thank you for asking. Is Mom handy?"

Peter's face shook with anger, and he tried to say she was busy, but Barb walked up as he was about to deter the call. Dr. Berg's psychotic behavior was spurned. He fumbled the phone, and it fell as he turned to her. She noticed his face and picked it up slowly with confusion. She cupped the phone and whispered, "You okay, babe?" just before putting it to her ear.

He told her, "Yes, darling, I was startled. No worries. I'm fine." He pointed to the phone and then kissed the side of her head. He retreated to the restroom and sat on the commode, clasping his temples, and professed in a low voice, "You spoiled brat, can't a text suffice? *No*, absolutely not! Just like I told my mother. This will be your last time for fun. I won't have you enter into the New Year. And I won't ruin my Casey's Christmas, but after that, your life expires!"

He heard his inner voice aloud. "Please, no. This isn't you. You need help. Please."

He responded as if he could see his opponent, "I need help? Stop it! People who need to be eliminated go. All your requests are denied! Can't you see what he's doing to me? Smiles of evil exude from his face."

Dr. Berg's psychosis was boiling like an erupting volcano. Poor Barb, she was so smitten with her new man, and foreshadowed by losing her first true love, the opportunity to see the vital signs of his mental degradation were minimal.

People have been studied as to why they snap. It is believed by many psychiatric specialists that the pathways of violence against others begins with thinking and fantasizing about a plan in a persecutory type—delusional disorder. Psychotic depression is an underlying layer of this delusion that triggers the feeling of pain or fear which propels such action. They have to *stop* this enemy, if you will; it usually occurs a few hours or a few days within the peak.

Peter had an unusually elongated planning phase, perhaps because of his patient ability to help others, as seen by the extensive work with autism. Up until his first wife abandoned the marriage and motherhood, the good doctor had not been triggered further with inoperable madness, though it seemed. Barbara had taken the place on Paul's level, and no one would ever come between them. That's why he drew up legal guardianship for Barb if he should die before his son was an adult. Casey was their child. Garrett was not. He was Thom's child. Garrett would go—end of story.

These psychotic geniuses are equally clever at covering their tracks. They are also capable of such acts through disassociation. They don't see the other person with feelings. Dr. Berg did not have voices telling him to kill; he had the need to eliminate the embodiment in his path that regenerated his torment.

Barbara was concerned about her husband and suggested they eat dinner and stay in for the evening. Surely his deadline for a grant was causing him extraneous pressure. She cradled Peter, "I love you, honey." That evening, they made intensive love. He felt nurtured in her arms. Albeit, the maternal black hole of her child's doom was just around the corner. She gave him the love his mother never did. This made her twice as valuable to Peter. His divergence from sanity to insanity was viably undetectable.

CHAPTER 20

Political AF-FectiBIlity

BACK IN TEXAS, the boys settled in and rested a bit before their meal. Scholls excused himself from Garrett and spoke to his uncle in private. "What's your overall opinion of the things I gave you?"

"My inclination is that he does have something to hide. I have an investigation going with his early background in Baltimore. I want you to have a great time while you are here, so let's put this on the back burner and relax."

"Yes, sir, will do."

They headed to Cow Head Bar-B-Q and ordered up a herd of food. The interior of the place had a definite Southern atmosphere and the tables had Lazy Susan spinners shaped like wagon wheels. The booths looked like stage coach wagons, and Scholls threw his yellow cap on one of them so it was not taken before they got the food. They ordered the Posse platter, which had several types of meat, four sides, plus plenty of rolls and two types of dessert. The food was incredible. But teenage boys were like garbage disposals, and by 6:00 p.m., they would be ready for another meal.

General Robinson was expecting to meet the kids Saturday afternoon; he would be hosting the Thanksgiving feast. Two other families from the military would join them. Everyone was in awe of Garrett, as expected, and impressed with Scholls. The hats and wigs could take a break—and so could the fake accents. The shirts still commanded attention. Garrett and Scholls described the first incident at the theater, where Garrett saw his movie in disguise. At that time, Scholls was a hot mess, and he needed nothing to ward off people.

Their selfies said it all. In fact, they were collecting quite an album for future laughs.

Uncle Randolph got the biggest kick out of his nephew's makeover. He pulled G to the side and began thanking him for his generosity and friendship with Scholls. In person, it was clear to see how kind he really was and why his favorite nephew had praised the friendship on multiple levels. Humbly, G reverted back to the greeting in biology, which effortlessly drew him to Scholls. Their connection was natural, in short, because psychology deals with thinking how it is and logic deals with thinking how it should be. He simply used logical thinking when it came to his friend. Normal aversion would have been expected due to the obvious outer characteristics that divided Scholls from most kids at that school; however, this natural assumption did not interest the logician, in that he looked for ideal connections that were exceptional and not realized without course of thought. Schollie was a dry-wit intellect with humanitarian undertones. Garrett sensed this from the get-go. He told the general it took only five minutes to grasp the special traits. He had never met a person of his age and gender that sent a signal so rapidly.

As they drove away, Randolph asked the boys if they wanted to go shopping for souvenirs, so they stopped at the mall and found items to take back. First, they bought a cowboy hat for Casey. Barb and Peter would receive Western shirts, and Harry and Tina got special sauces that were made in Texas. The boys ended up buying some more T-shirts for the flight home, along with a hats, boots, and belt buckles. Uncle Randolph gave Scholls plenty of cash so he could have a great time, and G already brought plenty of bills to keep his identity hidden. Speaking of hidden, they ended up buying some camouflage wear for the deer lease and decided to ditch the wigs for hunting only. It would be a long shot for Garrett to be discovered, and that's a chance he decided to take. I mean, how many of those old-timers even left the lease in hunting season? Yes, he might run into some younger folk, and this might pose a problem, but he felt like the odds were in his favor.

⊷⊷⊷◈⊶⊶⊶

Thanksgiving Day

"Our Heavenly Father, we are thankful on many accounts. Today symbolizes the recognition of your blessings for each and every person here. The food is a reminder of how appreciative we are for lack of hunger. Let us pray for those who are not as fortunate and remind ourselves to be mindful always. Lord, bless those souls who don't recognize a creator and challenge Your existence and may we continue to seek Your guidance. Amen."

It was a well-colonized and meaningful set of words, yet Scholls could not help remembering how the real story of Thanksgiving was. There were many types of Thanksgivings. Read the history of the Wampanoag Indians and other tribes. What we were taught in school represented what it should have been like. It was far more complicated and impoverished. Scholls had experienced that same cruelty of the indian people who were looked down upon for their appearance. He found everyone was subjected to uneasiness, but what they do with it was the deciding factor of their character. The key to recognition was *not* succumbing to the act of hurting someone verbally or physically because we saw them in a different light.

Most people would joke among themselves or friends—in a private setting. And it should be kept that way. Unfortunately, there are people who act on all their feelings, despite the pain it would cause. These people need to stop this practice. He thought, *How boring the world would be if everyone acted and looked the same.* No one is perfect, but striving to better one's mistakes is always available.

238

At 6:30 p.m., the guys thanked everyone and said good-bye. All that food made them sleepy, and they decided to stay in with Randolph and talk about whatever moved them. How fascinating is the FBI? Just exactly what do the letters mean?

Randolph explained, "Federal Bureau of Investigation...and their motto is Fidelity, Bravery, Integrity."

The current version of the seal was designed in 1940 by former FBI special agent Leo Gauthier and has been used since 1941. The images in the seal represent different meanings. The colors and symbols equate the values and standards of both the department and the United States.

First, the center depicts a shield bracketed by *two laurel branches* within a scroll inscribed with the motto above.

Second, the *gold-outlined strips* occupy the circumference of the field which has the words *Department of Justice* on top and *Federal Bureau of Investigation* at the bottom.

Third, the *thirteen gold stars* represent the unity of purpose for the original thirteen founding states of the USA.

Fourth, the *laurel branches* represent *distinction, academic honors, and fame.* Those two branches have a total of *forty-six* leaves that represent the number of states in the USA that were present when the FBI started in 1908.

Fifth, the *blue* field represents *justice,* as does the five vertically parallel red and white stripes. There's one more red stripe than white stripe, which echoes the American flag. *Red* stands for *valor, strength, and courage,* and the *white* stands for *light, cleanliness, and truth.*

Sixth, the *outer edge* of the seal consists of *gold* beveled peaks that represent the everyday challenges of the organization and alludes to their ruggedness.

Seventh, the *gold* represents the *richness and history* of the FBI.

Eighth, the *scales* in the shield also represent *justice.*

There is controversy as to who devised the words Fidelity, Bravery, and Integrity and the acronym itself. Originally it was

239

believed to be from one of the inspectors of the bureau named W. H. Drane Lester, 1935. This same year has also reflected credit to Edward Allen Tamm, a top aide to Edgar J. Hoover.

In 1908, the FBI was established and coordinated by attorney general Charles Bonaparte, under the presidency of Theodore "Teddy" Roosevelt. These two shared progressive idealism that efficiency and expertise should determine who could serve best in government—not political connections. Randolph advised the boys to read about the history of the bureau on fbi.gov, which really sheds light about the most prominent eras since the early 1920s.

Origins (1908–1910)
Early Days (1910–1921)
The "Lawless" Years (1921–1933)
The New Deal (1933–late 1930s)
World War II Period (Late 1930s–1945)
Postwar America (1945–1960s)
The Vietnam War Era (1960s–mid-1970s)
Aftermath of Watergate (1970s)
The Rise of International Crime (1980s)
The End of the Cold War (1989–1993)
Rise of a Wired World (1993–2001)
Change of Mandate (2001–present)

And the US Patriot Act, in 2001, signed by George W. Bush, after the 9/11 attack on America, which granted new provisions to address any future threats of terrorism.

"By the way, did you boys know that teddy bears were named after President Theodore Roosevelt?"

Scholls replied, "Uhhh, yes, I did, Unc."

G added, "Dude, of course you do. Why?"

"Well, he was invited to go on a hunting trip in Mississippi from their governor, Andrew Longino, in 1902. After three days of hunting, our president did not see any bears. In order to keep it from being a total failure for him, some of the guides tracked down an old black bear who was attacked by the dogs. They tied him to a willow tree so the president could shoot him. Our Roosevelt took one look at the old mauled bear and refused to shoot him, citing unfair sportsmanship. Since it was injured and suffering, he ordered the bear be put down to end its pain. When political cartoonist Clifford Berryman got word of this, he drew a cartoon showing President Roosevelt refusing to shoot the bear. It ran in the Washington Post on November 16, 1902, and was later revised showing a smaller bear shaking.

When Morris Michtom, a candy shop owner in Brooklyn, NY, saw the original cartoon, he had an idea to place two stuffed bears his wife made in the shop window. He got permission from the president to call them Teddy's bears, and the rapid popularity caused him to open a business and mass produce them. About the same time, Margarete Steiff of Germany made stuffed bears and an American ordered several, causing the international connection of popularity. They were eventually called teddy bears.

"You see why I like hangin' with your nephew? He's never boring!"

"Yes, he is a world of knowledge. You two get along well and quite funny together. What else would you two like to discuss?"

G voiced, "Actually, I'd like to know more about the Air Force. How long were you in the military…and when did you get to the rank you are?

"Wow. Okay, let me think back a bit. The first time I considered joining any military branch was age nineteen. As you may have heard, we came from a family with six boys, and my father worked in a factory. There was no money for college, so one day, I saw two recruiters eating at the local diner where I worked. After a few questions, they invited me to come for an interview. Now this was post-Vietnam. So in the early '80s, volunteering for the military was beginning to get back the morale it had lost from the "draft" era of the '60s and '70s. A few weeks later, I saw this poster with fighter planes going upward and large red letters at the top saying *Aim High*. It was so motivating I called and scheduled the interview. I had to complete a bachelor's degree through the United States Air Force and Academy and then Officer Training School. Then you go to UPT—undergraduate pilot training, which prepares you for specific types of aircraft. Eventually, I rose in rank to a one-star brigadier general.

"The Air Force only has 208 general officers allowed on active duty at one time, as with other branches that have limitations, which is explicitly mandated by the US Code of Law. To receive such honors, you are evaluated by a promotion board consisting of general officers of your branch in consideration for the permanent rank. A list is sent to the service secretary and the joints chief, and then the defense secretary sends it to the president. The president nominates candidates with the advice from the service secretary, secretary of defense, and sometimes the service's chief of staff or commandant. The Senate must confirm the nominee by a majority of vote. Once confirmed, they are promoted to that rank. The rank does not expire even after leaving the one-star position. They must retire after thirty years of service or five years in grade and serve at least one tour of duty. It can be extended, but due to the limitations of these honored rankings, we usually retire well in advance of the statutory limits of age and service so as not to impede upward career mobility of our juniors."

"Shit, excuse me, sir, that's damn impressive. I can really see why he respects you so much. Hell, he admires you. You're his idol."

"Sure is…always will be."

He smiled at his nephew.

"Thank you, Garrett. I wish our family was close. My other brothers are in different states. That's another story, another time."

CHAPTER 21

Podunk, Play, and Podspeak

IT WAS NEARLY 10:00 p.m., and after eating ice cream, they took showers, brushed and flossed their teeth, and prepared for a good night's rest. Both the boys had sent their previous dates a message or two, and the reciprocation was even. Tomorrow was time to take it down a notch and relax in the backwoods.

Garrett woke at 8:30 a.m. Scholls was already up and talking to his uncle in the kitchen area. After answering texts, he jumped in the shower and got ready. Randolph and Scholls briefly went over the pending information that was most disturbing—Peter's bouts of one-way discussions.

The general did point out how important it was to practice speaking before an event or even a conversation which would inquire debatable subjects. With his ranking, many situations required this, and Dr. Berg's position in medicine, research, and administrative duties would definitely heed continual probability. His nephew pointed out the *pitch* reference and shifts the seemingly obligatory work role to despisingly personal conversations, implicating psychiatric undercurrents.

Scholls greeted, "Good morning, Taylor."

For a few seconds, Garrett was confused. He finally caught on that his friend was referencing the movie he starred in. He had forgotten the hype already. They continued talking about his film and what led him to the acting field. General Randolph was just as eager and interested to know about G's past. Around 8:00 a.m., Bubba had sent a text to find out when his cousin would be coming, but it was a couple hours later before he noticed it. They gathered some overnight clothes and wore the new *camo* they bought. At noon, they met up with Garrett's cousin at a local gas/food mart. He's there and waiting in an old truck with water coolers in the back filled with beer and water. Instructions to the lease were difficult if you had never been in the area; plus, the rules of the lease required the guests to be limited and escorted by the person who leased their spot.

Bubba greeted, "Hey, cuz, we're fixin' to go to my pap's place first and see if we can borrow some guns. Y'all have your license's ready?"

Garrett answered, "Sure do, and by the way, this is my friend Scholls."

"What's your name, buddy? Skoals?"

"Actually, it's Scholls, with the *shhh* sound…no *k* sound."

"Fuck, that's too sissy-fied down here. I'm gonna call ya Skoals, like the dip I use."

He thought, *And Bubba is masculine? Oh well, I will appease this country boy. After all, we were in hiding. LOL.* "That'll work."

"And for my cuz, let's stick with G, and if they ask, your real name is George. Hopefully none of these hunters will recognize you, but you two are *high cotton*. Most of these folk won't. It's some of the younger girls that might have seen your movie. Hell, I need to go see it, in honor of my cousin! After huntin' season though."

Scholls grinned as he heard the reference of being included into the *high-cotton* status. He was low cotton. Even these country boys had more than he ever did.

They picked up the rifles and swung by Simon's place. The first thing they would do was shoot the guns in an area where his father Panhandle, aka Pervis, Thom's middle brother, built homemade shooting benches.

Bubba announced, "Hold on, city slickers!"

Where had they heard that before? Garrett and Scholls looked at each other and held their hats.

Bubba drove recklessly down some dirt roads that winded endlessly several miles away from the main highway hitting every bump and tree branch on the way. First, they had to get out and remove a large chain that looped from a pole to the gate. There was a sign on it that read "Only Authorized Members. Guests must be accompanied and recorded in the logbook." Once they got inside, Bubba blew right past the sign-in log. Bubba yelled to the backseat:

"What's that, Skoals?"

"You didn't sign us in."

"Fuck, no one does. That's for the uppity. We've lived around here for years, and everybody knows us. It's as useless as tits on a bull!"

Scholls looked at Garrett, and they both cracked up laughing. Once they got to the firing range, Simon offered the boys a beer.

Simon offered, "Grab a cold one."

G said, "Nah, we're good." Looking at Bubba, he added, "So which bench do you want us to shoot from?"

"Wait a minute, partner. Have either one of yas shot a rifle before?"

Garrett nodded his head yes. For nearly ten years, he had been shooting quail with his father on expeditions. Scholls was the least experienced because he had only been hunting once with his uncle from Tennessee. This was Harry Parker's second oldest brother, James. He worked in Nashville at the Grand Ole Opry House.

"Okay, G, you can use my grandfather's .243 Winchester. You probably were use to a 20-gauge for birds. For young guns, I'll start 'em with a .410."

Scholls asked, "Say, Bubba, what's the difference, if you don't mind me asking?"

"Listen, Skoals, caliber is the bore or inside diameter of the rifle barrel, measured in hundredths. Gauge is how many lead spheres equal to the bore that would weigh one pound. The smaller the gauge, the wider the barrel. The smaller the barrel, the less recoil, or kick, the shooter feels. That's why you are gettin' the .410."

"I think I get it. Okay, let's go for it."

Simon and Bubba went over all the necessary things for the boys to do. They had stacks of hay with targets and bottles on stands to shoot at. Garrett was very accurate and surprised his cousins. Scholls started poorly but within a half hour was able to hit the props. They practiced for several rounds before heading to the campsite area dubbed Crazy Joe's. There was a small travel trailer and an area that looked like an outdoor redneck kitchen. It had a large covering similar to a carport with a back wall and part of the sides enclosed. The front was wide open. Several pictures and country-type paraphernalia hung throughout the area. There was a stove and also a wood-burning fireplace, several different chairs and two old recliners. Piles of cut logs were handy. It pretty much contained everything a person would need for cooking and eating. The pictures were accumulated over several years by campers, hunters, visitors, and family. This was the place to be on Dover's Lease. Many early hours echoed stories and laughter from the multitudes of people accustomed to that lifestyle. They parked the truck, filled up a cooler with beer and water, and switched to their ATV. It was time to go wheelin' or muddin', but before they got to play, the deer feeders had to be checked.

Bubba instructed, "Hold on tight. I'm taking ya through some heavy brush, and we might have to bust through a couple banana spider webs."

G frowned. "What the hell do banana spiders look like... *Skoals?*"

"Hey, I might use Skoals. It's growing on me. Damn, *Nephila clavipes*...those effing things get huge. Sometimes people know them best as the giant wood spider. Their bodies range up to a couple inches, but the leg span can be several inches. In fact, they can adapt to their environment and grow bigger. *Nephila*, meaning loves to spin, are known to be the oldest genus of spiders. Their webs have separate smaller webs built around the main one to prevent birds from destroying the entire web when they fly into it. The webs are woven in a zigzag pattern and shine like gold in the sunlight. Don't worry. You'll see the web far before we hit it."

"What the fuck, we're gonna hit it? Why doesn't he just drive around them?"

"Dude, he's your cousin. I don't know, but he seems crazy enough to do it. I think it's gonna be a *redneck hazing.*"

On the way to the deer stand, they ran through one of the giant webs, and Bubba and Simon yelled, "Shit or get off the pot. Duck your heads!" Garrett went one step farther and buried his head in his knees. Scholls ducked and just missed the spider. They blasted right through the giant webbing. When they were completely through it, the ATV came to a sudden halt, and the cousins looked back, laughing their asses off at the hypertensive passengers.

"You fellas look more nervous than a cat with a ten-foot tail in a room full of rockin' chairs."

Neither one of them commented. It was all they could do to sit and endure the rest of the ride. They hit a couple of mud holes before making it to "holy territory"—the place Bubba shot up when he was grounded. Their heartbeats were lowering, and they helped Simon fill the feeder at the deer stand. They learned that after fall season, the vegetation dies and food sources are depleted, which causes the deer to look for food during peak hours from 4:00 to 10:00 p.m. and 4:00 to 8:00 a.m. The livestock searched the grove about half hour before sunset.

"We're gonna need a jacket for tonight and tomorrow. We've had some unusually cold weather this past month. *It's gonna be colder than a penguin's pecker.*"

Scholls thought, *He must have an expanded repertoire of slang sayings. I mean, everything is bigger in Texas, right?*

"Crap, Bubba, we didn't think about jackets. You guys have any extra ones we can borrow?"

Simon eagerly said, "I'll bet your right nut we have some."

Garrett and Scholls said quietly to themselves in rhythm, G first, "Okay, you give him your right one."

"And I'll give him my left one"

Both said, "And together he'll have a pair."

The cousins noticed the handshake and wanted to learn how to do it, so they spent several minutes teaching the country kids. They got the jackets and headed over to Crazy Joe's campsite. A hunter named Bo Dean was there cooking some burgers, steak, beans, corn on the cob, green beans, sweet potatoes, rolls, and misc store-bought desserts to be eaten. Garrett offered to pay them some money for the food but was declined; Bo explained everyone pitches in weekly on Thursday nights. His cousins had already given them enough for the anticipated meals they were going to eat. It sank in to Scholls that this must be part of the Southern hospitality he had always heard of. People started arriving around 3:00 p.m. Bo Dean introduces them to the crowd, starting with his wife.

"Hey, ya'll, we have special guests all the way from California. They're Bubba and Simon's cousins on their daddy's side. This here is G and Skoals." Everybody said hello simultaneously. He shifted the introductions back to the boys.

"This is my other half, Billie Jean. Then we have Muskrat over in the recliner…Fishbone on the stool…Cooter next to him… Earlene, Cooter's wife… Loribelle, their daughter…Hunter, their son… and Rusty, their other son. Now over on the other side we have…Tick, my best friend…his girl Peach…their friend Mark…and his girl, Beth. Don't you worry. There's gonna be more kinfolk. Now this grub is granny slappin' good. You may want to avoid the dippin' sauce 'cuz I make it hotter than a goat's butt in a pepper patch!"

It was obvious no one recognized Garrett. Cooter's daughter kept smiling at them, and she worked her way over to start a conversation. She stared at G for a second and then asked him, "What's your real name?"

"Oh, it's George."

She looked over, "And you? How did you get the name Skoals, living in California?"

"Actually, it's pronounced *Shhholls*."

Loribelle opined, "I like Skoals better. You are the cutest guys I've seen around here in my life. Well, 'cept for Jim Bob. He's my old boyfriend."

Both replied, "It's nice to meet you, Loribelle."

She left, and the boys chowed down on the food. According to the cousins, they needed to be at the deer stand by five fifteen to get things in order. Neither had given in to drinking a beer, and being sober for this adventure was needed. Scholls entertained the idea of trying a shot of moonshine the next evening, and his curiosity also stirred G's mind. After all, they wouldn't be driving and how much damage could a shot of moonshine be?

They finally got to the stand and settled in. One thing they discovered was just how quiet you had to be. Deer have a combination of techniques that make them able to detect danger. Although it is thought they don't have the ability to hear as well as a cat, they do have ways of determining sounds. For instance, deer move their ears separately, which allows them to hear from all directions. They live in the woods night and day, so they are keen to what should be normal sounds. Squirrels in trees, birds and their sounds, or animals in the brush are normal; whereas, a human talking, walking, or clicking the safety on their gun is abnormal. He will cup his ears. If they are moving separately, he is distinguishing the location and type of the sound. If a lone deer has both ears cupped back, you can bet another deer is following closely. When both ears are cupped forward, you have been seen by the deer and he is accessing information.

Secondly, deer have better vision than humans, and the peripheral range is broad. Their eyes can detect the slightest movement from several angles. That's why they bob their head up and down and move it side to side frequently.

Thirdly, those animals also have an incredible sense of smell. Not only can they detect scent, but they can determine how old a scent is. Their nostrils have olfactory receptors in each nose, and that nose is pretty long, and they have an organ in the roof of their mouth that also helps sort out smell. Hunters use scent killer sprays to help eliminate the smell of bacteria from human skin. It's fair to say deer are also crafty, especially an older deer, who can be quite ornery. They may know something is happening and send out a message to ward off other deer.

It's important for a hunter to know the wind directions in all locations, as it can be different on a hill than by water. If you can afford it, having more than one deer stand in structured places is best.

Scholls wrestled with the idea of hunting, and he was quite sure this would not be on his list to learn. In fact, his sensitivity level was high where animals were concerned, and he felt hunting them for sport was cruel. Garrett was less sensitive and enjoyed hunting, though he would rather stalk them for the hunt. Bubba and Simon were cultivated to be hunters. They geared up and prepared for the shoot. The deer stand could accommodate six people, and due to his lack of interest, Scholls forfeited his gun. He did think shooting at targets was fun.

There would be no more talking except extremely low whispers. Texting wasn't even allowed on silence because it lights up. It would be nearly one hour before they saw the first deer. Simon aimed and *boom* down went the creature. It was all Scholls could do to keep from shedding a tear. They called it a night and loaded up the carcass. Near Crazy Joe's campsite stood a homemade stand that looked similar to an old-fashioned hanging stand. Most hunters field or gut the deer by hanging it from the head with the legs dangling downward. It can be done the opposite way or on the ground. First they slit the belly and let the blood drain out. Garrett watched the completion, and Scholls had to throw up near the trees.

When it was flayed, the meat was removed and placed on ice in a large cooler and then later transferred to the freezer. At least they didn't just kill it for fun. It wasn't a large buck—only eight points, which was considered average. They weren't too far from the area that scored a nontypical net score of 258 4/8. This part of Texas is known for decent whitetail turf with typical scores of 124–144. The measuring system is quite detailed from the Boone and Crockett official scoring panel. Of course these guys tell hunting stories like fisherman do with one arm.

He wasn't joking; several more people were at the camp drinking and gossiping. The introductions played out again, and this time, they got to meet the girlfriends of G's cousins.

Bubba said, "G, Skoals, I'd like ya to meet my gal, Sweet Tater. And Simon's girl over there is Biscuit Butt."

G whispered to Scholls, "Dude, Biscuit *Butt*."

Being his usual intellectual self, Scholls must know how these people got their names. When Simon's girl jumped up out of the chair and walked to get another beer, he pretty much figured out why she was called Biscuit Butt. Her rump had more circumference than some celebs known for their round mound. Now Sweet Tater was not evident, so he asked Bubba about her nickname.

"I reckon she's called that 'cuz she is one sweet girl, nicest girl around, and pretty nice to look at. I'm lucky."

Simon belted out, "Okay, everybody, Skoals here wants to know how we all got our names. Who wants to be first? Hhmm, let's start with Bub?"

"Bubba got his name from his pap…'cuz he's just a Bubba. Look at him. Slick too. He could sell snow to an Eskimo."

"I myself am Simon, probably named after one of those famous chipmunks my momma always liked to watch."

"Now Fishbone is skinnier than most folks, and he fishes all day, every weekend, so when he was a youngin', they called him that."

"My friend Cooter is known for drinkin' too much. Should have called him *Cooler*. LOL.

"Earlene is an ol' Southern name.

"Loribelle was named from a book. She's a belle all right. Don't you boys thinks so?"

Both replied, "Uhhh, yes, sir. She sure is." Both boys nodded their heads.

Simon continued, "Hunter is his real and nickname. On account, he does like to hunt.

"Rusty, well, he stepped on an ol' rusty board when he was three and cried for ten minutes, so we called him Rusty Foot, but he hated the *foot* part, so we dropped it when he was twelve.

"Muskrat, this ol' boy has eyes close together and a little pointy-type nose, lots of fluffy hair and a big round gut, so one night, we put a sign on him when he was passed out that said "Muskrat, don't fuck with a muskrat." He woke up and said, 'Yeah, don't fuck with this Muskrat.' So it stuck. We need to find him a girl so we can sing 'Muskrat Love,' like the Carpenters did in the '70s.

"Now ol' Tick…this here is my best friend, known each other since we were knee-high to a grasshopper. He frequently got ticks stuck in his body, especially on his keister. I reckon he's as close to me as you two seem."

Both boys looked at each other and said, "Agreed."

Simon added, "Now that's some city talkin' there. Shit down here you best say, 'Hell yeah(-ya).'"

They definitely had this one down. "*Hell yeah-ya!*"

"All righty, then…now Peach is Tick's gal, and she's from Georgia, nuff said.

"Now *Mark* and *Beth*, those are downright biblical names and their families all work in the church. Beth's father is a preacher man. They're about the only two who don't drink. What about you two, ya'll drink?"

G said, "I've had some…a time or two."

"And what about you, son?" He was looking at Scholls.

"Well, my dad and mom drink all right. Mom a bit too much. She gave me some when I was a kid. I've had a beer or two and some wine…not much though."

"Tomorrow we're gonna let you try some *shine*…if your balls are big enough!" Everyone laughed.

The boys talked quietly and said, "We may need to get our balls back from Simon."

Approximately twelve more people in addition to the presented group sat around telling accounts of the day from their perspectives. This assemblage had a few guests of high cotton— Garrett's level. One family had two teenage girls who studied both boys with fierce intentions. If only they had the red wigs.

The boys got antsy and stepped out of the area a good forty feet away to look at the stars. The oldest daughter approached Garrett and asked him where he lived. The cat was out of the bag when "Californians" were announced earlier, so lying wasn't the ticket. She told G he looked like an actor she recently saw at the movies. He shrugged his shoulders and told her he couldn't act his way out of a paper bag. She laughed and then seemed relentless to know more about him. "So what city do you live in?"

Scholls began choking to stop the inquisition. The other girl raced to him and tended to his needs. When he stopped the phony choke, the younger daughter asked him, "Are you okay?"

He quickly answered, "I better go sit down somewhere that doesn't have any smoke." They all walked to the river bottom which was only sixty yards farther. It had a pier that people sat on to fish and an area where they could place their small boats in the water.

Scholls was fast on his feet and told the girls they were brothers and just recently moved to California, using a white lie to prevent chaos the rest of the trip. Instead, he told them about Arizona and where he, they, used to live. Moreover, he got them to talk about themselves. It worked; they forgot all about G's likeliness of such an actor. All four of them were sitting with their feet hanging off the pier, and Garrett leaned back and gave his friend the thumbs-up. It was time to eat, and they headed back to the campsite and found a place to settle down. The food smelled delicious. It felt nice to sit around and talk with people who were carefree. The boys sent the girls a text and a selfie of both their faces with big smiles. As they drove back to his cousin's campsite, Bubba reminded the boys that dawn would be approaching faster than "Simon can count two fingers."

Simon said, "Oh yeah, Bubba, you'd have to get smarter just to be stupid."

It was officially a battle of the cousin's colloquialisms.

"Well, Simon, you're ugly enough to make a train jump track and take a dirt road."

"Bub, you fell out of an ugly tree and hit every branch on the way down."

"Uh, Simon, you got picked before you were ripe."

"You're so short, Bubba, you have to stand on a shoebox to kick a duck in the ass."

Laughing, the boys say to each, "This shit is funny."

"Simon, you're just jealous 'cuz you couldn't whip half my ass if the other side was helping you."

"Bub, you're still short. So short you have to play handball off a curb."

"Oooh, Simon, that's your ass talkin' 'cuz your mouth knows better, so just butter a butt and call it a biscuit."

"Oh, you wanna go there, Bub? You're gal is so skinny, if she turned sideways holding a glass of tomato juice, she'd look like a thermometer."

Scholls and Garrett were laughing so hard they had to hold their ribs. Had the trash talkin' gone too far? They collected their emotions when his cousin stared them down. Seemed these country kids know how to play jokes just as well. Bubba quipped, "Don't worry, *dudes*. We do this all the time." Thank goodness for humor; it goes a long way.

Time was ticking as the previous downfall of rain created sedately sounds from crickets and bullfrogs. It was a reverberation of nature's mood music.

Scholls was not a fan of the extended hunting phase that would cause him to wake earlier than he wanted. This would be the last time they went to the deer stand, electing to spend Saturday night partying with the old-timers at Crazy Joe's stomping grounds.

It couldn't have gone any better; no one shot a thing during the morning hunt, so they called it a wrap and headed over to Leaky Swamp.

Talk about swamps. There was so much moss and decayed debris in the water that it was impossible to think you could actually swim here, let alone fish. Another hazing was about to occur.

Bubba said, "C'mon, you city-fied wussies. Go ahead, G, pick him up, if you can catch 'em."

"OMG. What the fuck is that? It looks like a huge rat! I'm not about to touch that thing!"

Simon answered, "It's just a lil' ol' rat. We call 'em nutria rats.

Bubba asked, "What about you, Skoals? You chicken?"

"Well, I prefer to be known as *sane*. You go ahead, Bubba. We'll watch."

They wouldn't get off that easy; Simon and Bubba cornered one, picked him up, and chased after them for several seconds.

G said, "Are you guys effing crazy? Get that thing away from us. He's got some big-ass teeth."

Garrett and Scholls ran pretty fast behind a bunch of wood. They negotiated a *test of courage* by saying they will definitely partake of the moonshine that evening. It put a stop to the chase, and they placed the varmint down. The cousins shook their heads and reveled they were born country people. G and Scholls adamantly agreed to themselves just the opposite.

Simon said, "All righty, let's head over to get some poles and go fishing. You two do know how to fish?"

Simultaneously, they answered yes.

It was much to their surprise how those banks of white sand beautifully lined the Trinity River. Who knew this desolate area could even compare after being habituated to seeing beach sands off the Pacific Coast. They couldn't really catch any rays because of the cool temperatures, but it was fantastically ideal for spending the afternoon enjoying the subtle moments of Redneckville.

Simon called Fishbone, and he showed up with Cooter and Tick. They brought drinks, food, and music. He pulled his ATV alongside the small fire they built and played several country songs. Even though the boys preferred top 40 and rock 'n' roll, they heard tunes which just might actually be added to their download. Several pictures were taken, along with random people just coming over and saying hi. Garrett purposely put glasses on and messed his hair up fairly well to disguise himself from potential onlookers who might have seen the movie. Thank goodness no one knew who he was.

Before dropping off the boys, Simon and Bubba took them to their camping spot so they could change clothes. All in all, the fishing trip was a success, and it would contribute to the nighttime festivities. Neither one of them wanted to cut up and carve the proverbial turkey, aka fish. These weren't just any fish. Tick and Fishbone caught these on trotlines out in the deeper parts of the river. Yellow ops are types of scavenger catfish that adapt to their surrounding and get fairly large. These monsters were all of 45 to 60 lbs. Interestingly told, the fishermen pleaded their case as to the divine flavor found deep past the thick layers of fat. It's time for the night hunt, and Crazy Joe's had two unexpected visitors that opted out of deer stand duty.

Early evening gave its time to the older generation of men who had been there and done that. Now, they would reap the benefits of forgoers who brought them the goods. It was pleasurable for these codgers to sit around and drink. Cooking was also something they took pleasure in doing. Tonight's menu was written on a chalkboard which hung slightly crooked. It read "Catfish, gumbo, french fries, green peas, rice, fried okra, and spinach casserole. Desserts: pecan pie, vanilla ice cream, and cupcakes (that the high-cotton girls made earlier that day)."

Who on earth could argue with those dishes? Old-timers had plenty of practice cooking savory food, and by the aroma, it was indeed.

Crazy Joe asked, "You boys gonna have a sip of some *shine?*"

Scholls answered in lieu of a verbal promissory earlier, "I think we may indulge just a bit. What can we expect in terms of the effect?"

"Ha ha ha ha ha," was all they could hear from the four guys. There was Joe, Mr. Not, Panhandle (Pervis), and Roy. Now you know young Mr. Parker had to inquire about the one name that stood out—Mr. Not. He asked G's uncle Pervis why they called him that.

Roy answered, "Son, he answers by saying, "Not gonna do that, not my liking, not up yet, not any of your business, not on my time, not my problem, not if I have any say, not able to go there, not under this roof, not my friend, not just that, not yours, not mine, et cetera. Get the picture?"

"Yes, not bad."

Mr. Not loved his answer. He picked up where they left off— the inquiry of moonshine effects. "Not for the weary…is my advice, boy."

Scholls thought, *Huh? Didn't expect that answer. Not!*

As the four men visited, he walked with Garrett down to the pier. They sat along the edge again and dangled their legs. He told G what he read about moonshine and what his father told him: "So in terms of how they brewed it, we want to make sure it is clear and not cloudy. If it's cloudy, then it wasn't filtered right or the still is dirty. So we aren't drinking it…We'll fake swallowing it and spit it out. Then, we need to shake it up. If there are large bubbles with a short duration, the alcohol content is higher. Small bubbles that disappear slowly mean a lower alcohol ratio to water. But if they give us a shot, we're screwed."

Garrett's curious about the name and history.

"Well, they made it in the dark to avoid being caught, and the moonlight shined on the brew. Alcohol was prohibited. It didn't become nationally legal until the Twenty-First Amendment was added on December 5, 1933. Most people associate it with Southern tradition, but it actually was traced back around Pennsylvania. Its heyday really came to life after the federal government started a distilled-spirits tax law in 1791. This pissed off the distillers, and they began tarring and feathering tax collectors. They even shot weapons at their homes. This sparked a whiskey rebellion that almost started the first civil war in America.

"Whoa!"

"So there were many states that brewed the alcohol in hidden areas—typically heavily wooded. Unbeknownst to most people, Brooklyn was a huge supplier and manufacturer by 1869. They had an area ran by the Irish immigrants, called Vinegar Hill, which was raided and publicized. Despite this, New York produced more than any other areas. Remember Al Capone? He ended up running the most successful illegal alcohol ring in history.

"Anyway, we typically hear a connection between NASCAR and moonshine. One prolific reason was due to a fourteen-year-old kid named Junior Johnson, who started hauling the shine and outrunning revenue agents by skillfully maneuvering his vehicle. He later entered in NASCAR and did very well. Eventually, when he was older, he manufactured and distributed his father's recipe. Have you ever heard the connection with Louis Armstrong?"

"No."

"He was so popular the government appointed him to help educate the public about the poisoning and death of people who drank corn squeezins, tiger spit, happy sally, scorpion juice, hillbilly pop, rotgut, and many other slang names—for the backwoods booze—that was made improperly. They used stills contaminated from bacteria and car radiators that omitted lead and glycol from antifreeze, and lye to speed up the fermentation. This also led to blindness and other illnesses. Mr. Armstrong delivered a radio message to the public, 'That junk will blind, paralyze, and eventually kill you, friends.'"

"Damn, we're definitely gonna have to have the breakdown of their process and ingredients! I've had enough sickly moments in the past few months."

Scholls took heed of that statement and reflected on the fact his friend had not had one episode of blurriness, dizziness, nausea, headaches, cramping, etc., since the brownie escapade. He pocketed this information for his uncle. The campsite was starting to fill with driftless people, so they headed back.

The city boys were quite amused by the men and held their own when comments whisk past them with invisible ridicule. Like clockwork, a very distinguishable female of negative aura approached them. Roy warned the youngsters that she was known as Radio Station. Looking at each other in a muddled state, he further clarified that her given title is "On account, anyone can pick her up at night."

"Let's just say she is *naturally horizontal*."

"Dude, G, she's a lease lizard!"

G laughed. "Thank God we have Tally and Kipper. This reminds me. You got saved, bro."

"Put it on my tab, dude. I owe you a hell of a lot more."

"Shit, you owe me nothing…but years of friendship. Now that I'll expect."

"I've got your back…for life."

By 9:30 p.m., most of the campers were present, but only the youngsters had eaten any of the food. It baffled them, so they asked why. Apparently, if drinking was the main aspect of the night, eating would kill the buzz, so they waited until after midnight. It satisfied their confusion.

Before the trip, Garrett took it upon himself to enlighten Barb while he was getting permission to come to Texas. She was afraid he would be exposed to alcohol and her position about drinking underage was not favorable. G promised her that his uncle Pervis would be present. All he wanted to do was see what the moonshine was like. Alcohol had never been G's deciding factor for fun, since the only times he ever drank were with his father; he vowed to toast his dad on behalf of the family. He cherished his father. What could she say? Garrett was a responsible, normal teenager who would soon be leaving for college. That alone gave her the chills when she thought about fraternities and collegiate freedom. Barb had nothing to worry about as he assured her it would most likely be the one and only time he drank the stuff.

Scholls's parents drank and encouraged him to drink. Like he pointed out before, his mother was a great deterrent. He was mainly curious to try this liquid gold. Everything about his personality was thirsty for information and results. He was just as indifferent about drinking as he was about his parents. No driving and safe company, along with his best friend, made the encounter willful.

Crazy Joe announced, "Okay, boys, put your panties on and let's put some hair on your chest."

Huh? Scholls pondered on the sarcastic side of reasoning, *Oh yeah, it makes perfect since, right?*

"Now we're gonna play a little game called **Moonshine Madness**. Ever heard of it?"

Both said nope.

"It's kinda like redneck trivia. You gotta answer questions and get them right. If you don't, then you must down a shot each time you miss one."

"Crap, G, I need to know the ABV because these guys sure aren't gonna let us shake that bottle to find out."

Cooter jumped in, "Now, Skoals and G, in this game, everyone answers the first question on an index card. Earlene picks a number one to one hundred and writes it on her card. The closest number without going over will start. When it's your turn, you must tag someone, anyone in the group, to answer your question. If they get it right, you are safe—no shots…but if they get it wrong, you and your dumb-dumb have to stand up and get blindfolded. We'll place you in the middle of the group with a full shot glass and turn you around one time. You have to find and give the other person the shot of shine within ten seconds. Then, the other person has to give you the shot in the same amount of time. Got it? But that's not all. It must be downed completely. If you miss their mouth, or they miss your mouth, it's a penalty. What's the penalty? *You* will have to stand in the center blindfolded until you are through with your session. The tap-in dumb-dumb sits down to wait their primary turn. Do it right and you go to the winner's wall.

"The second question gets ten seconds. If you miss it or time runs out, you will have to pick up the shot glass with your teeth after we guide you to the area where it will be waiting. You can't use your hands, except to find the glass. If you are successful, then you can remove the blindfold and sit down. If not, then you will have to remain blindfolded. Down another shot of shine, and sing at least two lines from a song you know.

"You only have ten seconds for that. Successful lyrics will save you from another shot, but you will be in limbo. That means if it comes down to players and there are no true finalists who failed all the questions or tasks, you automatically lose. If you fail to produce some lyrics, it's over, and you will join everyone else for a picture on the loser's wall. You will have to down one more shot that comes from the host, Earlene. All losers *must* clean up the campsite at 6:00 a.m. the next morning…and that's a lot of shit to clean.

"There are other things you have to do when more questions are played, but Pervis only allowed three turns for you boys. So tonight, three's the limit for everyone. The game ends when all the players have finished their round."

Garrett looked over at his uncle and smiles. Pervis asked him if he still wanted to do it.

G replied, "Sure, let me say first off, I'm super proud of my father and wish he could have been here with us tonight. I love you, Dad." He rubbed his left shoulder.

Everyone with a drink raised their container and said, "Hell yeah!"

Both boys toasted with soft drinks because alcohol was soon on its way.

Scholls was nervous about the preparation of the moonshine and its percent of alcohol content. He knew the juice was at least 30 percent, but it can range up to 100 percent depending on the number of times it has been run back through a distillery.

Scholls asked, "Uh, Roy, how much alcohol is in this stuff?"

"Tell you what, youngin'. We will use the double XX."

"I'm guessing the X's have a meaning."

"You betcha, Skoals. Each time it's ran through the still, the bad flavors and other crap in the water, and fermentation are filtered out, which makes it have more of a kick. Each X stands for those runs."

"Huh, so, I'm going to say around 50 to 60 percent for this jug."

"Shit, it's not piddlin', but you're close. Let's just leave it at that."

"Excuse me, but may I ask how it was made…or better yet, was the still modern or…"

Mr. Not answered, "Not gonna tell you who, what, when, where, or why. Just trust us. Your uncle wouldn't let us harm you city boys with bad brew."

Pervis nodded, and the boys were relieved. The next concern on their agenda was the questions being asked for the game. It was likely Scholls would not miss a question as long as it did not come from the redneck rhythm roster. That's when the boys politely walked several feet away to discuss their strategy. Garrett returned directing his questions toward Joe and Pervis. "What subjects are the questions about?"

Pervis replied, "Well, son, there are different subjects, and we pick a topic by suggestions each person writes inside a bottle cap. Then we throw it into the basket Earlene made."

"Okay, so where are the caps?"

"Bo Dean and Roy will hand them to you, and each one of us will write no more than two words with a sharpie, like, movie star"—G cringed—"hunting equipment, past presidents, US states. Just about anything you want that isn't any of the porn-o-graphy stuff. Then the host, which is always Earlene, will pick a cap and make up questions for the game. It usually takes her about thirty minutes to come up with multiple questions. In the old days before computers, we only had a few subjects, and it still took longer. We just sit around and bullshit until she's finished. We can also use the caps from previous games if ya like."

Scholls felt like he had such an advantage the boys decided to do just that—use old caps. They purposely wanted to miss the answers so they could experience the shine. It wouldn't be much fun if they answered them correctly and went straight to the winner's wall.

Roy announced to the group of ten, "Is everyone ready?" The old caps were placed in the basket, and Earlene drew for the subject.

Cooter yelled, "Come on, gal, don't you draw anything these two city slickers know 'bout."

What the camp crowd didn't know was that the *city slickers* were purposely going to mess up. What the boys didn't know was just how potent that bush whiskey was.

Earlene announced, "All righty. we have a winner. Tonight's questions will be all about US history. We haven't seen this cap for a long time."

Scholls said under his breath, "*Really? Let me think of what comes to mind using one of their sayings. Ahhh, here it is. 'Now you're diggin' where there's taters.'*"

Earlene vanished into the dark air and wouldn't return for forty minutes. In the meantime, the high-cotton girls begin to flirt with their handsome newcomers. The oldest one was obsessed with G's face, and it was yet another time for his copartner to save the day—or night, that is. She asked Garrett if he had ever done any acting or modeling.

"You're Christine, right? Well, I did some school plays growing up. Nothing special."

"Huh, it's just that you look like an actor. I can't remember his name, but I mean, you *really* look like him. Are you sure you—"

Scholls immediately interjected his comedy, "Wow, I can't believe you guys thought he was an actor over me. I am the spokesperson for the group called Worms of Planaria. Ever heard of them?

G looked at S and lipped, "Worms of Planaria?" and then rolled his eyes with a smirk. Both of the girls looked perplexed and shook their heads no.

"It's a special project that gears information for biological encounters."

Garrett kept smirking. He fed into the convo and said, "Skoals, stop being so modest. Tell these girls *all* about your worm farm."

The younger girl, Emily, got more excited and pleaded with him to tell them all about it. Scholls looked at Garrett and turned back toward the sisters recounting as much of the project he can customize for their ears, without giving them detailed information they could use to find out who G really was. It worked. They also used finesse and informed the two about their girlfriends in California. This also helped to reduce any further convos that warranted deviation.

Approximately five minutes later, Earlene was nestled onto her director's chair that Cooter bought her from a garage sale in Houston. The back read "Butts off. Earlene only!"

"Okay, everyone, get your index cards ready. Does everyone have a pen?"

All heads nodded yes. Garrett and Scholls decided to tag each other so they could purposely miss it. Unfortunately, Earlene had determined that city would mix with country. The two high-cotton girls had to leave when their parents, Gail and Robert, made them go home. All the younger participants were at least seventeen years old, and that meant the gold boys and one son, Rusty.

Mark and Beth called it a night as they had church in the morning. Even though they did not mix well with the drinkin', cussin', and fussin', their hearts could discern right through all the non-Christian behavior, and every time they visited was another time they could talk about God. One could say they were campsite evangelists.

Bubba was nineteen and Simon was twenty-two. Their friends were older than twenty-one, and that included the rest of the game show finalists. Pervis used Garrett's phone to text Barb and confirmed he was there with the kids. The show was about to go on.

CHAPTER 22

Prélude Rapide à Paris

PETER ASKED, "WHO the hell is Pervis and why is he reassuring you about Garrett?"

Barb emerged from the bathroom and said, "Oh, did Garrett's uncle send a text?"

"Yes, and?"

"Darling, that's his uncle on Thom's side. He is just letting me know the boys are in his presence, and he will make sure they are okay."

"Okay, about what?"

"Well, it's nothing to worry about. I just wanted to make sure he was present when Garrett and Scholls stayed up late. That's all."

"Why didn't Garrett just text you? Is this guy married?"

"Now, Dr. Berg, do I detect a bit of jealousy in your tone?" She nuzzled her nose on his nose and then gave him a quick kiss.

Peter didn't answer her as she walked back into the bathroom to finish getting ready for their bike tour. The good doctor, bad doctor was restraining from vocal irritation. He still had another week with his beautiful bride, and soon after they returned, the scheme to eliminate "Thom's son" would go full throttle. He walked confidently into the bathroom, put his arms around her from the back, and playfully bit her neck. He turned her around abruptly, and they kissed passionately.

French was spoken to her: "Les vélos peuvent attendre." The bicycles can wait.

"What does that mean, darling?"

He put her on the bed and began to remove her towel. His sexuality was stirred by the morning interruption which he believed to be another threat in his marriage. "I'm going to show you what it means."

Shots in the Dark

"Okay, ready, pick a number between one and one hundred." She wrote down number 45. Each person revealed his number.

Tick—12

Pervis—60

Roy—19

Mr. Not—32

Cooter—99

Garrett—41

Scholls—78

Bo Dean—2

Joe—47

Bubba—23

Simon—68

Robert—34

All the wives and girlfriends stayed on the sidelines. They rarely participated unless someone couldn't make it. It's much more fun to watch them and avoid taking a chance of making the loser's wall. These gals were frequently accustomed to cleaning up messes, and it was actually a benefit to be excluded.

Earlene announced, "Okay, the number is…forty-five. Looks like our California kid is up first.

"The question is, 'When was the first national draft used in military history?'" Ten seconds went by. "Time's up!"

Crazy Joe said, "Okay, G, who you gonna pick to answer your question? It can't be the other coastal boy, so who's it gonna be?"

Both boys had agreed to miss the first question; however, the guidelines were altered. Garrett went for the obvious choice—Simon. Surely this cousin didn't know American history. He barely graduated and ditched so much they had to keep him back a grade in high school. Garrett wanted Simon.

"I'm tagging Simon."

All they could hear was, "Ha ha ha ha" and "Good luck, sucka."

Simon started thinking. "Hmmm…now let me see." Seven…six…five…four…three…two…"I got it. The Cold War."

Earlene hit the old metal bucket and said, "*Wrong*. The Cold War? What did you do in class, boy, sleep? LOL."

Everyone was cracking up.

Scholls lifted his chin upward to give G a nod. He knew it was the Civil War, 1862. Earlene confirmed his thought.

Pervis said, "Okay, G, you and Simon have to stand in the middle while we blindfold you."

They got them ready for the express shot delivery. Both got spun around one time, and it was clear they were not oriented. "Ready…go!"

Garrett reached out and found Simon. He stabilized his hand on his face and carefully got the shot glass to his lips. Now Simon, *he loved him some moonshine*, so this part was easy. He swallowed the brew, and they all clapped.

"Okay, your turn, Simon."

They spun them again, and Simon couldn't find G right away but managed to touch his shoulder and guide his hand up to G's mouth. It was making everyone laugh. Five…four…three…G opened his mouth and downed the juice. They completed the task right, and after coughing for several seconds, Garrett yelled out, "Damn, this stuff is strong…blah…ahh…ahh."

Everyone clapped, and they removed the blindfolds and took the photos. G sat back by Scholls, and they did their special handshake. Garrett was clearly still overwhelmed by the strength of this brew. He leaned over and said, "Dude, have I got any hair on my chest yet?"

Scholls laughed. "It looks like your hair is sprouting out your armpits. LOL."

Earlene announced, "You're up, Skoals. Who ya gonna pick?"

"Oh, okay, how about Mr. Not. This old-timer seemed to be street smart and not book smart. No offense, but you call it like it is. Most likely he will answer with the conspicuous *not*."

"All right, the question is, 'Which president quietly and consistently bought slaves in Washington, DC, and then set them free in Pennsylvania?'"

Everyone chanted, "Nine…eight…seven…six…" He drew a sad face on the index card.

Earlene shouted, "Time! Whatcha got, Mr. Not?"

Mr. Not replied, "*Not* even close to knowin' that. Sorry, Skoals."

Scholls recalled in his head—President James Buchanan.

Earlene said, "It was James Buchanan."

Roy said, "Okay, dumb-dumb, you and Skoals hit the center for your blindfolds."

Game on. G gave his buddy the same chin lift and nod. He felt woozy from the drink. It was strong.

Crazy Joe said, "Hold still while we wrap you two like cheap Christmas presents."

Roy was spinning him. "Okay, Mr. Not, go for it!"

He's shorter than Scholls by about a foot, so it took him almost the entire time to find his way and put the shot glass near his mouth. Scholls bent his knees, and Mr. Not tilted the glass so Scholls could gulp it down. It was potent. He didn't want to stop at one shot, so he purposely missed Mr. Not's mouth and let it spill. Earlene stopped the session and told Scholls to remain standing and his partner to sit down.

Crazy Joe said, "Okay, Skoals, you have a penalty. Remember what that means?"

Everyone chanted, "Penalty…penalty…penalty!" He stood there blindfolded and gave a thumbs-up for recognition as he downed the second shot. The shine was affecting him faster than he imagined. He wanted more.

Earlene voiced, "The next question is, 'Who organized the Seneca Falls Convention that generated the Woman's Rights Movement in the US?"

Ol' Schollie knew the answer but decided to be funny and said, "Some dumb-ass."

Everyone started laughing, and he was guided to the area where he would have to down another shot of *rotgut*. That stuff really made him quite funnier than before.

Earlene taunted, "I'm gonna pretend I didn't hear that. It was Elizabeth Cody Stanton, 1848."

There was an old alligator head that had been preserved with its mouth open and teeth present. They decided to place the shot glass on the gator's nose and guide him to this area. He had no idea what was under the shot glass. As he felt around, he was confused, and this made everyone laugh as he finally touched the teeth and jumped back a bit. He was allowed to use his hands to find the glass, but only his teeth and lips to pick it up and swallow the liquor. After a few seconds, he spilled the shot glass, and Earlene guided him back to the center and put the final shot to his lips. He drank the juice and shook his head. He felt a warm sensation in his esophagus and up his temples; he'd only imagined what the 50, 60, 70 proof would do to his coordination. But what he wanted to know was, one, how fast it worked; two, how sensitive he would be to hard liquor; and three, how his motor skills would be.

Its onset was remarkably fast, and he was *drunk* already.

Roy said, "All righty then, Skoals. Let's hear two lines from any song you know. You have ten seconds to start. We do allow you to finish the lyrics—you just have to start within the given seconds. Ready…go!"

Garrett could see his friend was feeling the effects of the shine by way of his slurring and stance. It *was* strong and powerful for anyone, let alone beginners. The one shot G had, took immediately to his brain; Scholls had three shots bathing his brain cells.

"Amer-ica...Amer-i-ca. God shed His *grace* on *me*...And *crown thy good with motherhood...from sea to shiny me!*"

Garrett laughed so hard he had to personally go up and take the blindfold off his friend. All the people in the group kept mimicking his warped, alcoholically induced song. There would be no more shots for his best friend. He was done. They put him in the old recliner and continued with everyone's turns. By 2:30 a.m., it was over, and the drinkers finally ate the grub that was prepared. Joe admitted to Garrett that they actually drank an XXX product/100 percent proof. He poured out the XX and put it in another jar.

Scholls had fallen asleep, but 6:00 a.m. would invade soon enough. All the guys helped load him into the four-wheeler that took him to Bubba's camp, and in less than four hours, he was awoken by the cock-a-doodle-doos, plus the alarm G had set. He slowly rose and checked his dry tongue. No need to change clothes, he was still in his gear.

Scholls said, "Dude, did I make the loser's wall? I need something for my head."

"Sure, did, bro, have fun. I'm gonna be here sleeping till you get back. Ibuprofen's in my bag."

"Shit, that was some powerful fluid! Did I mention I hate, hate, hate to lose?"

"You did it on purpose, Susie homemaker, and don't forget to dry the spots on the shot glasses."

"Real funny, G-tater."

Bubba and Simon were on kitchen duty as well, so they rode back there together. What a damn mess. His head was pounding, he had cottonmouth, he still felt a bit tipsy, and he was tired. Thank God Uncle Randolph would be back at the food mart around noon. Out Redneckville. He had quite a story for the journal—and Bandit.

The general greeted, "Hey, kiddos, how was your weekend? Did you learn anything new?"

"Well, Unc, we discovered several new things, and we even learned to like some of the music. It moved us. Garrett and I have a parody on our favorite country song we heard this weekend by Hank Williams Jr."

"Let's hear it."

"Ready, bro?"

Both boys started singing.

> We came from the west along the coastline
> With all the sandy beaches and the paved road skies
> We can spend a few bucks; we can game online
> But here…a city boy won't survive!
> A city boy won't survive!"

Randolph started chuckling. He was impressed they took away positive aspects from someplace they knew little about. Thommason Pierce had been a very successful attorney in a very affluent area, yet his brother Pervis found comfort in the simplicity of the outer city limits. He noted from conversations that Pervis was equally as intelligent in a *poles apart* way. College was not his desire. He just preferred a more laid-back environment—nothing wrong with that. Diversity channels difference, and difference creates change.

They ate at one of the top Mexican restaurants in Houston and returned to his uncle's residence to gather their things and reunite with the red wigs, T-shirts, and caps. Scholls and General Randolph talked more about the list, but he was a structured person and liked to get his ducks in a row before revealing details. He'd contact his nephew when the timing was right. "See you soon, *Skoals*."

G said, "We had a great time. Thank you so much for the tickets…and your hospitality."

"Thank you, Garrett, I appreciate it. You are quite welcome to visit anytime. I hope to see both of you soon. I'm impressed by your mannerisms and docile ego with acting. Scholls is lucky to have you as a friend."

Those words couldn't be more devout or truthful. They went through the necessary protocol for the return flight. Garrett and Scholls took time to call the girls individually and bought them a Texas trinket before boarding. G decided to text his mom when they landed in California. It was time to rouse and remain notable nerds until seeing those taillights on the Pacific Highway.

The driver was ready and waiting. This trip was totally, successfully ruckus-free, except for that kinsman hazing, which they emulated many times. The bond these two generated in just a few months was stronger than some people develop in years. Presumably it would last their lifetimes. Would something ever tear them apart or end the friendship? Only Father Time had that answer.

Scholls was dropped off at home, and before he went inside, Garrett reminisced with him by the foot of the stairs. He stepped in the trailer to thank Tina and Harry and handed out their gifts. Tina looked shocked.

"We got you guys some sauces and small nick knacks from Texas. I hope you like the flavors."

Harry spoke up, "Thanks, I'm sure we will. How was the trip overall?"

"Highly interesting…and quite different from the city," replied Garrett.

"What did you think, son?"

"I'm gonna second that motion."

Tina chided, "What did you two expect, carte blanche with those hillbillies? How much moonshine did they get you to drink?" Her demeanor was sour, and she had been drinking quite a while.

"Well, let's just put it this way, Mother. We had enough to make a difference."

"So, smarty-pants, you got drunk! Welcome to the club."

Garrett said his good-byes, and Scholls walked him back out front. He silently recapped his uncle's conversation and looked at his friend. "Dude, back to the grind. Later."

"Later, *Skoals*."

"Yeah, I would've had a hillbilly throw down if they tried to make me dip. Ain't gonna happen honky-tonk. Later, *high cotton.*"

When G entered his house, Casey ran and jumped up on his back.

The feeling was mutual; both of them were happy to be reunited.

"Wanna catch a ball or two in the back?"

"Yes, yes, Garrett, but don't laugh so hard when I miss it."

"Okay, give me a minute to put up my things."

He reached in his bag and passed the gifts out. The house was quiet, and his mom and stepdad would be gone for several more days. After he played with his little brother and visited with Juanita, he remembered to send a text he'd forgotten to do earlier. Europe was into the early hours, so he made it short and sweet.

School resumed the next day, and he would get to lay eyes on his potential full-time girlfriend. Yes, the girls at the lease were pretty and nice, but all his affections were linked to Tally. He sent her a sweet text as well. A few idle moments over the holiday gave the boys time to analyze relationships among themselves. He learned a lot about his friend's background and amazed at his progress in life. The dark summons G to another visit with his father.

"Guess you saw us this weekend. Pretty funny stuff. I'm glad you guided me to be a well-rounded person. I know Uncle Pervis really respected you. I might make it an annual gathering, including my buddy 'cuz I doubt it would be as much fun without him. Love you, Dad."

CHAPTER 23

Prologue Rapide à la Folie

THAT FLIGHT BACK from Europe took nearly thirteen hours, and Peter's mind wondered back in time to his childhood. The first memory of abuse was around the age of four when Charles purposely tripped the little tyke and caused him to hit the floor. Ursula thought he fell on his own and gently picked him up. A big knot popped up on the right side of his forehead, so she wrapped a small washcloth around ice and held it on his bobo, which she referenced each time an incident occurred.

Before he turned six, his little sister was delivered stillborn. In preparation for the unpredictable arrival, they had chosen the name Charlene. His mother probably suffered from postpartum depression, amidst other kinds. Her motherly *instincts* became *extinct*, and as he aged, there was sufficient evidence to see she knew what was going on. What kind of hold did he have on her? To Peter's knowledge, she was never hit by Charles, and he rarely screamed at her. Maybe he controlled her addiction that overshadowed her maternal responsibilities; regardless, Ursula was neglectful to her son.

One morning, the school nurse called concerning a burnt marking on his neck. Good old Charlie boy had dropped wax on him the night before. This fourth grader was concealing pain.

"You better not say one word, kid, or it's gonna be far worse than what you felt just now. You're kinda wimpy, and I'm gonna toughen you up."

Peter was terrified of his stepdad, and after the broken leg incident, those random bouts of basement segregation seemed pleasant. He learned to hide food in his shoes and underwear. For some odd reason, Charles only subjected him to one overnight stay in the cement prison; though, the all-day sessions were still traumatizing. Metaphorically, Peter's hands were tied.

Ursula rarely defended Peter. She was so heavily medicated on pain pills and muscle relaxers that her son's coexistence was limited. She would ask him about his "clumsiness" and yell at him for being what appeared to be rude to Charles. Her little boy's silence was an invisible sheath of anger. He matured well beyond his chronological age. Paul was his only refuge.

Those two spent multiple afternoons walking to the park, riding bicycles, listening to music, and talking about every subject they could. Paul's take on the abuse was like a sponge soaking up water. All the cruelty Peter experienced needed to be rectified, and he planned on helping him leave at seventeen. That never came to fruition, as his disease resisted all treatments and cancelled his hopeful capability.

The boys developed a secret code system to communicate things they wanted private. Colors represented situations, and numbers represented the urgency or importance of that color. Red-10 meant Charles had just inflicted some kind of pain on Peter. Blue-1 meant they were going to go to have fun. Green-5 meant they were hungry, and fast food was on its way. Purple-100 meant that Paul was feeling very bad, and it was time for him to rest. Yellow-10 meant his mother was out cold from her medications. The multitude of codes could be infiltrated at any given moment without people knowing what they meant. They had created a lingo of their own that bonded them even closer.

Dr. Berg's antipathy resuscitated facts which bolted his psychoanalysis for ending Garrett's life. He had the perfect solution. Now, the execution had to be definitive. There was just over four weeks to complete his mission. On December 27, just after Christmas and before New Year's Eve, "those eyes" would close forever.

Barbara and Peter had bonded quite well themselves. The honeymoon was extravagant, and they were able to visit Italy, France, and Germany. Upon arriving back to the states, Garrett picked them up in the Bentley, gold this time. Erroneously, Peter acted appreciative and even gifted his unaware victim with relics from Rome. As sadistic as it sounds, he knew they would end up with Casey; it was a clever way of being the good guy-bad guy, which he'd perfected all along.

CHAPTER 24

Bird Brain

OVER THE NEXT few weeks, time passed by slower than usual. School was enjoyable due to Tally and Scholls, but G also had several appearances to make for the movie and was even a guest on two talk shows, greatly increasing his anxiety level. He'd invited Scholls, but his buddy declined. There were too many things to do, and he didn't want his best friend to create another "catch" and make him pose for cameras.

Garrett's symptoms began reappearing, and Scholls documented each one. In fact, the second day stepdaddy returned, G felt nauseated, and his eyes blurred again. Garrett seemed vigorless even though Dr. Berg had given him another vitamin B12 injection. When G told Scholls he was feeling better, this seemed contingent but peculiar. He'd known his friend could play down symptoms to prevent losing out on an event. The planned party for Tally, Kipper, himself, G, and Casey would most likely be a tag in for another white lie. Because the girls would not be home for Christmas and their families were going out of town to visit relatives, this party was a way for the kids to celebrate before saying good-bye.

S. Parker stayed in constant contact with his uncle, and important information was building. Randolph knew he would need to get inside that condo.

"Tell you what, Unc, school is out and a group of us are going over to Garrett's for a small preholiday get-together. I'll work my magic then. You should hear from me soon. I'll keep you posted."

"Okay, I've got some important findings that need to be confirmed, and this may be very pertinent to your cause."

It was monumental; Scholls realized he would have to do something he would never do without permission—get inside that condo. Somehow he will need to get the key off Peter's key chain. He wasn't 100 percent positive Dr. Berg was harming his friend, but he was 100 percent positive something wasn't right. Nonetheless, Garrett's safety was all that mattered, and time was ticking away. If he was wrong, Garrett might understand, but Barbara and Dr. Berg would not. They would jeopardize his friendship and ban him from coming around.

A light went off in Scholls's head, and he asked Garrett to find out if Caesar can stay at Huntingdon Cove for a couple of days. Kipper's family was in need of someone caring for her African grey parrot while they were out of town. Of course he wanted to help his sweetheart. He would feed it and essentially take care of him. Thing is, Tina and Harry rejected his request. Garrett had no problem asking, and Casey would be ecstatic for the bird's stay because he recently asked to go see it.

Now Schollie had a way to snoop more and try to get the key. Thank goodness for those key duplication kiosks. It shouldn't take more than forty-five minutes in the most to replicate one, if all went well.

G said, "Hi, Mom, can you do your son a couple huge favors? Please, please, please?"

"Schmooze time again, is it? What do you need, honey?"

"Well, first, I was wondering if I could have a small get-together on the back patio. Remember Tally?"

"Could I forget her? You're quite smitten by her, and you say her name a lot."

"True that. Well, she is going out of town with her family for the holidays, and I had this great idea to celebrate Christmas with her, Scholls, Casey, and Kipper. You know, exchange gifts and all. Of course this would be on Wednesday afternoon, the twenty-third."

"It sounds reasonable. I'll run it by Peter. I'm sure he won't mind Casey joining your group."

"And the second favor I need is to babysit Kipper's parrot for a few days. They could put him in a bird kennel, but I thought it would be neat if Casey could get to know him. Oh, his name is Caesar. Anyway, he's been dying to see her bird. Scholls promised he would tend to it, which means he would be here as well."

"Shocker! Truth is, I enjoy the heck out of him. He's becoming another son to me. He will have a cage, right?"

"Yes, and he has a cover to place over him at night. We have that area off the study where Mr. Speckles use to be, remember?"

"I don't know. That's where Peter does a lot of his paperwork. Those birds can be very noisy."

"Come on, Mom. Please, Peter usually goes in there at night, and Caesar sleeps all night."

"I'm not familiar with a bird's routine. What did they tell you?"

"Scholls texted me. Okay, let me read it to you. 'Caesar has two cages we can bring. Obviously a lot smaller than his cages at home. Usually they get a bird sitter, but she would not be available this time. I practically begged her parents to let me keep him, but I knew my mom would say no. So if your mom says no, it's cool. I'll understand. This bird sleeps about fourteen hours, and they put his cover on around 9:00 p.m. They feed him a certain mixture of fruits, veggies, nuts, and grains, which she will give me in containers. He has a water dish that I will change daily, along with the lining of the cage. I can take him out in a closed area since he will not be comfortable to the new surroundings, but if that's not okay, he'll be fine being in his cages for a couple days. Shouldn't be too bad. He usually talks a bit, not too many fits that are uncontrollable. If worse comes to worst, I will take him back to my place and deal with my parents' wrath. Her family has a credit card on file with the Avian Veterinarian, which they use in case of emergencies. It's a lot to ask your, Mom, I know. Let me know ASAP. Thanks, later.'"

"Yeah, it is a lot to ask, but how can I say no to him. He's so responsible, and we have the accommodations for this bird. I'll just have to pick Peter's brain and get him on board. That area off to the side of his study should be fine. I doubt Peter will even be in there much. Okay, let him know it's fine."

CHAPTER 25

"In-sane-lin"

GARRETT HUGGED HIS mother tight and thanked her. He quickly texted Scholls that Caesar and all the *birdly* necessities will arrive the day of the party. Kipper's mom wanted to pay Barbara for his stay, but Barb rejected her offer in a kind way. It just reconfirmed Kelly's impression of Garrett and his family—very humble people dwelling at that colossal estate. She could modestly boast about her personal connections to this movie star.

As the twentieth of December approached, Garrett was sicklier. He was fatigued and irritable. Dr. Berg had taken control after the honeymoon and requested that everyone begin "juicing" with breakfast. He was adding just a touch of the same meds he used before to make his stepson have symptoms. But with the injections, a whole different additive was distributed in his veins.

He took Garrett to the hospital and got another blood test. This time, he would not switch them with his vials of blood. The hospital already logged in G's records—blood type A positive. He would switch vials of blood taken from a sixteen-year-old boy who was diagnosed with type 1 diabetes and the same blood type. It's unknown where he got them, but the neurologist had his ways. Weeks earlier, he had altered the supposed B12 injections with insulin a time or two for testing. The lab results had been tampered prior to his arrival. Peter was cunning and crazy.

The supplies he purchased were stored at his condo—a place of solitude and turpitude. Now his beloved stepson was suffering from a disease he could use to traffic his true weapon. So he was allergic to soy, and now he was supposedly no longer producing insulin. Barbara was beside herself to find out Garrett was ailing and his diagnosis was shortcoming from weeks before. Peter calmed her down and explained that it can be a sudden onset; it's not hers or anyone else's fault.

"But didn't the blood glucose level show anything before? His sports physical this past summer was normal."

"Darling, it was slightly elevated before. There's no way to predict this unless he was checking his blood weekly. It's considered an autoimmunity disease."

"What's that mean?" He took her hand.

"Honey, it means that his body has attacked its own cells. The pancreas has islet cells that produce insulin, and for unknown reasons, they are attacked and destroyed by autoantigens which see them as a foreign agent. Once they are destroyed, they cannot be reproduced. He just reached the point where his condition manifested definitively. Garrett needs to have insulin given to his body every day. I will start him out on injections to teach him how to do it, and then we'll get him a pump that does it automatically. His diet will have to change dramatically."

Barbara began to cry. "I feel awful. I'm scared. Can Garrett die?"

"Babe, with control of his insulin, he has no chance of dying this way. He could suffer other problems as a result of diabetes, but with proper care of himself and medication, he won't die from the diabetes."

"So he can. Oh my god, do something. I can't lose him *too*."

Poor Barbara, since losing Thom, she feared the worst in everything. She couldn't help it.

"Sweetheart, you're working yourself up. We brought him in before he went into a diabetic coma. Calm down, honey."

He paused a bit then said, "I need to check something. Please go in and stay with Garrett until I get back."

That comment spurred another round of his dissociative identity disorder. He headed to a small office that belonged to another doctor who was off that day and locked the door. He leaned his hands on the desk without saying a word for over five seconds before repeating Barb's statement. His pitch was low and whiny.

"I cant' lose him *too*? Well, you will, my little pretty, you will. In roughly 144 hours, your precious, darling, perfect, Pierce DNA will be DOA...if all goes well. Oh, he'll be very cautious administering the proper amount of insulin—right. It's just that he's going to have one big problem. He won't make it, babe. But you'll be okay. Casey loves you and I love you more."

He heard the antagonistic voice and looked around to find it.

His eyes played tricks on him, and he grabbed his ears to avoid the plea. Just then, someone started opening the door. It's Dr. Harper, the head transfusionist.

"Oh! Dr. Berg, I'm sorry if I barged in on you. I had no idea anyone was in here. Dr. Stappleton asked me to leave a report on his desk."

"That's quite all right. I stepped in here to make a private call. My stepson was admitted...DKA. I recently noticed his symptoms, and here we are."

"I'm sorry to hear that, Dr. Berg. Hey, you look flushed. Are you feeling okay?"

"I'm just under a lot of stress with issues. You'd think I'd be totally relaxed after my wonderful honeymoon."

"She's a great lady. Please give her my regards on her son's condition."

"Our son's condition."

"Right, my apologies. Let me get back to my work. I'd like to leave this place by 7:00 p.m. if possible."

Dr. Harper had not known him very long but doubted his colleague was *just stressed*. Peter's hair was disheveled, and his eyes appeared hazy, and he didn't use eye contact. This neurologist was considered to be fastidious about everything he did, including his appearance. There wasn't one time he could ever recall seeing

Peter's hair out of place, and it was a running joke with staff that Berg's hair alone could withstand a hurricane.

Peter's response to Dr. Harper needed to seem caring, but it was just for show. The endocrinologist, Peter's friend, assessed the amounts of insulin needed based on the blood tests and his size and weight. With G feeling better the next day, he was released that evening in his stepfather's care. One might expect Garrett would not give up the approaching party, especially for his friends.

G slept well with the sedative and woke up to whole new world of complexity with his unannounced illness seeping into the picture. "I'm a diabetic, wow!" Garrett decided to look on the Internet and read more about his illness, so he loaded up a site that discusses it in lay terms. "Let's see…Okay, this is a pretty easy article to understand. Maybe I can impress Scholls with my intellect. Ha!

"Hmmm…my body isn't producing insulin anymore. It's important because we need this hormone for energy. Okay, my pancreas stopped making it. So insulin works like a key. It opens the doors, so to speak, of cells to let glucose in. Without it, they don't get the energy they need…What? If levels of glucose aren't regulated daily, I could have eye damage, heart attacks, strokes, damages to my kidney and nerves, and my wounds won't heal well. Damn…Okay, let me find another article that tells how the body breaks down the glucose…Crap! Lysosome…cytosol… oxidative phosphorylation…glycolysis…Krebs cycle…yada, yada, yada…Never mind! Never mind! This is so technical. It's Scholls's forte. I hope med school just whisks right through all this for psychiatry."

He picked up the futuristic medical scientist and headed to the store to buy some party arrangements for tomorrow's gathering. They were nerds on a mission. The theme of the party was Redneck Santa because the boys wanted to reenact scenes from their vacation and entertain the girls. Casey was a given chuckle.

This time, they bought Bubba teeth for speech affects and instigated humor, without disgracing any of the river-bottom residents. It was purely for theatrics, and they were getting really good at live parodies. The boys would wear their camouflage and keep the red wigs on to heighten the amusement. They also bought cowboy-themed party supplies and downloaded several songs played at the campfire where they fished near the river.

"Hey, bro, any chance you and I can study molecular science together?"

"Yeah, Garrett, that is if we are near each other, *like, I totally don't have a clue* where I'm going yet. I think I'm going to get into Stanford by way of a new program that allows certain qualified individuals paid tuition, with no room and board charges, due to underprivileged incomes."

"Awesome, 'cuz I'm gonna be in California as well."

"Can I ask why you brought that up?"

"Oh, no reason...Just a thought." He smiled.

"Listen, Garrett, I've noticed you have lost some weight, dude. Any more symptoms than the ones you told me the other day?"

"Yeah, I've noticed a bit of weight loss myself. Course, we've all been juicing now in the morning."

"Your whole family?"

"Yep, Peter's on some new health kick, and now that I'm diabetic, I need more structure in my diet."

"You know what's messed up, dude? I was about to catch a bus to come see you in the hospital, and your stepdad thought it wasn't a good idea. I started to come up anyway, but it would have been disrespectful. What you need to know is, if there is any time I feel your life is in danger or the situation is life-threatening, I won't give a damn what anyone says."

"Bro, let's hope that never happens. But if it did, you have my permission right here and now. Hey, Scholls, you always ask me how I feel, and well, I've been a bit irritated and sometimes my heart seems to race, like beating faster, especially since we got back. I guess the diabetes was spinning out of control. It's a good thing my stepdad noticed the symptoms or I might have been toast."

"Yeah, it's a good thing." Scholls was wary.

This information disturbed his best friend. He shot these incidences to his uncle and waited for a response. Meanwhile, they arrived at the store and found everything they needed.

Randolph replied, "Have you obtained a way to access that condo?"

Scholls quickly sent "No, plan in action. Shortly though."

Garrett took his buddy home, and he went in to stay for a while. He really wanted to give the Parkers a gift for Christmas, and he came up with the idea to have a customized photograph for their wall. Just before they started the moonshine madness game, Crazy Joe took a pic of them that captured a moment in time they can never forget; hopefully, his parents will appreciate such a memento.

He also wanted to give them a new coffee table. That one they had in the living room was broken. Knowing Tina's personality, this needed to done in a fashion that did not cast a shadow of fault or pity. Tina was not one to be reckoned with, and her underlying low self-esteem would emancipate the room with caustic language if she caught wind, perceiving it as subterfuge. Therefore, he would buy it, tell Scholls it was an extra that the studio was getting rid of, and have it boxed and wrapped. G knew Scholls would try to rebuff the offer as usual.

Garrett plopped down on Scholls's bed and picked up Bandit and talked to the kitty while his friend tended to some dishes in the kitchen. "Hey, Bandit, you probably *would* like that big ol' bird in this house. Wouldn't ya? Your owner is just about the best person I've met in such a long time, including my friend Randy. He cherishes animals. You're lucky. Thanks for being his best furry friend. I'm gonna check on him now."

G walked into the kitchen and immediately grabbed the hand towel on the counter. He wanted to assist with the dishes, and it was a chore he never experienced, making the task even more adaptable.

"Dude, I'm good."

"Bro, just chill, I've got this."

"Are you sure you want to get those delicate hands of yours ruined?"

"Delicate, my ass, these hands were made for work. Didn't you see me at the campsite when I helped rearrange things?"

"Oh, yeah, you mean the cards in the card deck? Or was it the drinks in the cooler?"

"Okay, yeah, those, but I'm referring to the logs I had to stack and bring back and forth for the wood-burning stove. Plus, I helped move all that crap from one side so we could make a circle for the game."

"Yeah, let me check out your hands. Damn, look at those things. I think I see signs of a healed callus."

"Very funny…Okay, so I don't have any battle scars. But I did do some country boy scut work. You have to admit."

"Yeah, I have to admit, you did burn a couple country calories."

"Did your parents give you permission to stay all the way through Christmas?"

"Yep, they both have to work shifts on Christmas Eve, so they didn't object. I do wanna go over there on Christmas Day after my dad and mom have slept. I need to spend time with them and give gifts."

"By the way, the studio was giving away an extra coffee table prop, and I snagged it for your parents. I'd like to give it to them for Christmas…plus, I have another surprise."

"Dude, are you sure it was extra prop giveaway? Sounds fishy."

"Well, put it this way. I'm getting it! Ribbon and bow accessorized…for 1726 Barker St. #2."

"Of course you are. I'm sure they will appreciate it, man. Thank you." He realized that Garrett's answers were getting agitated.

"I'm having our *pic* taken by Crazy Joe made into a larger photo with a customized frame. I'm hoping they like it enough to display it."

"You're something else, G."

"I'll drop you off in the afternoon on Christmas Day so you can see your parents before they go back to work. I'll be back by 8:00 p.m. on the twenty-seventh. I'll take care of Caesar. I've got it all worked out. My mom is going with Casey to my aunt's on the twenty-sixth, and she will be back on the twenty-eighth?"

"That'll work. Oh, hey, I need to take Caesar home in the afternoon on the twenty-seventh. Kipper will be back, and she'll pick me up and take me to your house. Is that cool with you? Then I can come back when you get me that evening. My parents pretty much expect me to be at your house if I'm not home. Mom even said I could chill from chores over the holidays. Go figure. I'm taking advantage of that. Isn't Peter going with them?"

"Nah, he's trying to finish his grant application on something for autism research."

"He's a brilliant, man. I'll give him that." S. Parker sent this info to Randolph. The key *would* be duplicated by the twenty-seventh, when he returns for the bird.

"Let's get this stuff and set up the decorations in the theater room. I'm thinking we should watch a movie about Christmas. Hey, maybe you and I should star in one called *Constant Christmas.*" Usually, G laughed when he clowned.

Garrett reacted non-chalantly,"Great, dude, we'll just star in *Constant Everything.* Scholls replied normal but with confusion in his mind, "You're the only real actor. My fame might be in research if I'm lucky."

After they make the area, party happy, Garrett showed Scholls how he had to inject the insulin. Peter decided to start him with a rapid-acting mixed combo prior to every meal. Scholls listened eagerly as G began his initiatory delivery of iatric language.

1. Decide what area you want to inject. I've chosen my abdomen. It needs to be rotated in areas from right to left.

2. My injections are given fifteen minutes prior to eating with insulin mixed with NPH. I have to roll the NPH bottle about fifteen to twenty times in my palm to mix it. Shaking causes bubbles. Peter approved this mixture, but normally it is injected in separate syringes/vials. This helps me regulate my glycemic control better.

3. Insulin should be room temperature for injections, with stored vials in the refrigerator. So I can keep a vial or two out at a time. It's easier to hold vials upside down when drawing in liquids. (Aspirating)

4. Wash hands prior to handling syringe. I use a short needle. Wipe the vial top with 70% isopropyl alcohol and let dry.

5. Before the meds, you need to draw air in the amount equal to the insulin and inject it into the vial to avoid creating a vacuum.

6. Draw rapid acting solution first, then regulator (NPH) second.

7. Check for air bubbles and flick the upright syringe a couple of times to release bubbles before injecting so you will get the appropriate amount of solution each time.

8. Pinch a half inch of skin. Hold the needle between forty-five-and ninety-degree angles depending on length. So I will use the ninety-degree with the ultra short one I use. The insulin is injected into subcutaneous fat (just under the skin but not into the muscle). I need at least three meals a day and approximately 60 to 70 units of mixture each injection per Peter's math. Of course this can fluctuate depending on my variables.

9. You monitor your glucose level by SMBG, self-monitoring blood glucose. Things that make up variables include

my diet, exercise, absorption, stress, illness, etc. I have to check it four times a day for about a month to make sure it's adequate.

10. SMBG is done by pricking for blood, usually my fingertip with a lancet, putting it onto a reagent strip, and placing it into the reflectance photometer to determine my glucose level. I have to log it manually for now—per Peter. He said I need the basics for everything, especially if I'm considering the medical field.

"I'm impressed, Dr. Pierce. You'll make a cool doctor."

"Thank you, Dr. Parker. That's a compliment coming from you." No laughter.

CHAPTER 26

Seeing Purple and Red

THE SUN BEAMED into a small section of G's window that was left exposed to visibility, waking him from a full night's rest. He rose to check his level. It seemed the dosages had been effective for the past few days, but why wasn't he feeling in tip-top shape? He gave himself an injection and then woke Scholls for breakfast. Juanita had already prepared the juices and some items for them to eat.

Juanita greeted, "Good morning, Senor Garrett."

"Morning, Juanita."

"Good morning, Mr. Scholls. I made you a glass of juice too."

"Why, thank you, Juanita, that'll work."

He wanted to see if the flavor was different from his friend's, so he "accidentally" took a sip from the wrong glass.

"Oops, sorry, G man."

He drank from his glass. *Hmmm, no difference.*

After they finished breakfast, it's off to fetch the parrot. Originally, Kelly was going to bring the bird, but Garrett wanted to say hello to Mr. Manning and chat a while. It gave his best friend time to spend with the girl he was crazy about, thus giving G more time to develop a relationship with the sports-minded fanatic.

Tally's family was leaving on the twenty-fourth and wouldn't be back until the third of January, which bummed Garrett out; nonetheless, the two planned to chat on the webcam, and that would of soothed his compulsion until their next date.

The Mannings had all the instructions typed up and enclosed in a laminated format. The food was labeled in appropriate containers, and he had special drinking water that was not in a plastic jug because birds were sensitive to toxins from plastic. Garrett decided he wanted Caesar to have both traveling cages so he could enjoy the outdoors, and luckily, both were able to fit in the back of the Hum.

Finally, Scholls could work wonders and found a way to get Peter's key, return it before anything gave way, and hand the duplicate to his uncle. General Randolph would most likely fly in on the twenty-sixth. Thank God Dr. Berg wasn't leaving with Barb and Casey.

<hr/>

Kipper said, "Oh, sexy, I'll see you in a couple hours."

Scholls's face turned bright red, and he climbed in the backseat to talk with the bird. Caesar was a bit nervous and kept walking around the cage and squawking a little.

"Hey there, Caesar. Shhh, it's okay. We're gonna take real good care of you."

The bird seemed to like his voice and calmed down for the rest of the ride.

"You're gonna like this place. There's a whole lot of land and water you can look at. Don't worry, fella, its' gonna be okay."

Garrett respected his friend's tenderness about animals. That was a clear sign of just how dedicated he would be for research and how softhearted he was with anything involving zoological genes.

It was a bit of a project unloading the cage because Caesar sensed another change of environment, yet again, Scholls was able to calm him down, and they set up his inside and outside destinations. He kept in mind the proximity to Peter's choice area in the study. About thirty feet would separate the wavering MD from his feathered guest, and hopefully Dr. Berg would not object. They would find out soon enough when he returned from the hospital later that evening. Barbara cleared it with him; however, the doctor might have condoned his stay just to please his bride. Peter's flip-flop tendencies were beginning to make appearances, which did not escape the keen discernment of Detective Parker.

Garrett took the other cage and put it outside where Barb had the groundskeeper organize. Meanwhile, Scholls took the opportunity to look inside the drawers of Peter's desk. Inside the smaller drawer, he saw a piece of paper with Purple-100-Final on it. What the heck did that mean? The writing appeared to be written by someone who had shaky hands. Why was it here? Oh well, he would just have to be curious and took a picture of it anyway. Maybe it was something Casey wrote for his father.

He looked pretty much everywhere he could for the next few minutes and was unable to find much. He had hoped for a second loose key but to no avail.

Garrett and Barb entered the study to see how beautiful this bird really was. The gray feathering was shiny, his beak was solid black, and tail was completely bright red. Minutes later, Casey woke up from his nap and ran into the room as soon as Juanita told him about it. This was exactly what Scholls needed, for little Berg to be so enthralled with the animal that his father would not be able to make the bird leave.

Casey asked, "Can I hold him. Can I, can I?"

"No, lil' bro, he's scared right now. He doesn't know us, and he is in unfamiliar territory. Just hang out here and talk to him. Oh, don't put your fingers in the cage. He might bite you 'cause he doesn't know you."

"Sweetheart, I'll stay here with Casey so you two can get your party underway. We're going to leave soon and go get a few more Christmas gifts. When we get back, Casey can join you for the party."

"Thanks."

Decorating was another talent this all-American kid latched onto from the time he was small. His family was routinely accustomed to hosting business parties and personal gatherings, and Garrett enjoyed making the areas theme related. He delegated the finishing touches in the theater room to Scholls and made small signs to designate the seating order for the movie.

Kipper and Tally would be there by 2:00 p.m. He ordered plenty of Mexican food from Hombres so Juanita would not have to cook and even ordered enough for her to enjoy. She was a great friend as well, and he often relied on her opinions about conflicting matters of the heart.

Tally called Garrett. "Hi, Garrett, on my way. See you in about thirty minutes."

"Drive safe."

Scholls texted Kipper, and she had just left. The boys' hearts were equally racing, and thirty minutes seemed like an hour while they waited for the girls.

"Dude, you sure you're okay? You look a little pale."

"I'll be fine. I guess my body is adjusting from the episode I had when I was admitted with DKA—diabetic ketoacidosis."

His best friend was apprehensive about this finding because G had a normal blood glucose level last summer. It just didn't seem to be right, but he couldn't argue with the hospital's diagnosis because they had the documentation to prove its existence. There were nurses and other hospital staff around, so how could Peter get by with creating this discovery? He decided to let Kipper know a bit about his concerns with Garrett. His gut instincts always led to success, though this escapade might be offset by uncanny timing.

"Hi, Unc, getting closer, shouldn't be too long. You'll be here on the twenty-sixth, right?"

"Correct, I have a backup plan if you can't get the key."

Being in the FBI had its certain advantages, and he would take any that came his way for Garrett's well-being. That alleviated his mind, but he was not going to give up that easily and challenging circumstances were what he thrived upon.

G announced, "Oh yeah, baby. She's here! It looks like Kipper is pulling up too."

Everyone headed to the party area, and conversations about this and that filled the air. Soon both girls would receive a kiss from their dates. It wasn't a contest, just something the boys had anxiously awaited to initiate as they stated before. Garrett made his quick and tapped Scholls on his back so he would stop kissing Kipper.

He thought, *Looks like he mastered it after all.* "Dude, let's go check out Caesar."

"Oh, hey, sorry. Lead the way."

Scholls's face was redder than his wig on the table. The anxious parrot was happy to see his owner and made a comment out loud, "Kipper…Kipper…hello…hello."

She sang a little tune to the spectacular bird before they went back to the theater room. Her heart sank as they walked off, and Scholls consoled the teary-eyed girl by placing his arm around her neck and kissing her forehead.

"You have a nice voice," said Tally.

"Thanks, I get it from my mom's side of the family."

"Okay, girls," G said with little enthusiasm, "are you ready to play some redneck trivia?"

Kipper and Tally looked at each other and smiled. "Sure, bring it on," said Kipper.

Garrett and Scholls excused themselves for a couple of minutes and returned in full wardrobe dressed as they were for the flights to and from their Texas adventure.

Tally laughed. "That's hilarious. Did you really travel that way?"

"Yes, Tally, we certainly did, except for the teeth. You dig our shirts?"

Kipper responded, "My intellectual badass is sexy."

Tally said, "Yeah, gamers do rule. Mom *and* girlfriend say so."

Did Garrett just hear what he thought he heard? Tally referred to herself as his girlfriend. That made his day, but he wasn't feeling well enough to express what she deserved. He gave her a wink, and his best friend explained all the rules. This time, there would be no alcohol or blindfolds, just good ol' trivia and soda pop.

They bought this game in Texas and saved it for the party. Garrett began, "Okay, so in this pile are questions we get to ask each other pertaining to a noncity-type setting. It's all good. No answer is stupid 'cuz we're just having fun. Each one of us will have a turn at reading the question, and everyone but the cardholder will get to answer. At the end of the game, I have a prize for the winner. Let's get started. You're up, Tally."

"Hmmm, okay...What do you call a redneck wishbone?

No one knew the answer after several attempts to define the question.

"When there is a six-pack with two beers left, two people pull the plastic and the one with the plastic ring still attached is the winner!"

G said, "'Kay, Kipper, it's your turn."

"Let's see. Okay...What's a redneck's favorite upscale drink?"

Tally answered, "Whiskey."

"Nope."

"Go ahead, I'm clueless," said Scholls.

"It's 'cheapuccino'!"

The three looked confused.

Kipper explained, "Get it. Drinks from a convenient store."

They all said "Cheapuccino!" at the same time.

Scholls thought, *I do that all the time. Crap.*

G then said, "Okay, Schollio, your turn."

"All right, in which month do you take down your Christmas lights?"

Tally offered, "February."

"No."

Kipper answered, "June."

"No."

"Ya'll need to go back to Christmas lighting school. It's *never!*" They all laughed.

G said, "Okay, hotshots, I'll read the final question."

"What does a redneck call a deer with no eye?" They all gave up.

"No 'IDeer.' Just like you guys." They laughed hard, but he just let out a small giggle.

When Casey ran in to join them, the tempo idled down, and they directed all attention to G's little brother. He excitedly asked to play pin the tail on the donkey, so Garrett and Scholls put up the poster and got the pins ready. It was great to be kidlike again, and they laughed the entire time. Of course, little guy was way off, but Scholls took his pin and positioned it on the correct spot so he would win.

Before the movie played, S. Parker was eager to educate the participants on the true meaning of the term *redneck*. For sure, most people associate it with the poor Caucasian who does lay work in the sun, causing their necks to get red. But after bonding with the East Texas comrades, this financially limited kid decided to find out more about the development.

"We've had a lot of fun here today, and I'd like to thank everyone for coming. Now, in honor of our Southern sidekicks, everyone raise your drinks"—all nonalcoholic—"and make a toast to Garrett's cousins and my newfound friends."

Garrett made the toast and rubbed his left shoulder. They couldn't say "Hell yeah-ya" because eight-years-and-nine-months was part of the group, and he really wasn't up to it anyway.

"I'd like to dissect the term *redneck*, if you will. There were three noted historical facts that link to this term. First, it was associated with the Ulster Scots who fled to Northern Ireland after they were persecuted by the British Crown in the 1600s for not accepting the Church of England as the official state church. They became known as the Covenanters, in which many wore red cloths around their necks and signed documents in their own blood that signified Scotland desired the Presbyterian form of church government.

"Later Ulster Scot settlers moved to the new world and lived in the hills of the Appalachia. They brought music and traditions which reflected strong support of Prince William of Orange, who defeated England and Ireland's Catholic king James II in 1690. His supporters were often referred to as Billy Boys, and eventually, the North American counterparts were known as hillbillies."

Tally reflected, *Huh, I don't even remember studying this.*

"Second, in the early 1900s, the United Mine Workers of America, or UMW, and other miner unions of the coalfields bonded to build a multiracial group consisting of *all* races who were coal miners in the strike-ridden coalfields of North America. They each wore a *red* bandana tied around their neck to symbolize this movement. The strike asked for higher wages, shorter work hours, and recognition of their union. It seemed to become an enduring identification and was also adopted in Colorado, Pennsylvania, and the Virginia's. Pretty much anywhere, there was a strike with coal mining. In fact, coal operators, company guards, nonunion miners, and strikebreakers used the epithet to scornfully mock the *redneck*s. They were also known as communists, or Bolsheviks, which meant the more radical members of the Social Democratic Party in America. The Russian affiliation didn't come into play until about 1918."

Kipper listened in pure ecstasy as her heart's desire spoke and then said, "Wow, this is interesting. You're so dynamic when you speak."

Scholls might not have had a red neck at that moment, but his face was. Casey said, "So what's the third thing about these redneckers?" Even though most of it was over his head, he was mesmerized by the delivery, so his attention span was lengthened for the time being.

"Okay, that brings us to the political term which preceded the union strikers in the 1800s. This is the most common association to the meaning of redneck, though you can see it had others. In 1893, a citation was issued that defined them as *'poorer inhabitants of the rural districts…men who work in the field, as a matter of course, generally have their skin stained red and burnt by the sun, and especially is this true of the back of their necks.'*

"Now, by the 1900s, *rednecks* was used commonly to designate political factions inside the Democratic Party comprising poor white farmers in the South. Often, they were also called *wool-hat boys*, because they opposed the rich men who wore expensive silk hats. Check this out." He read more from his phone, "A newspaper notice in Mississippi, August 1891, called on them to rally at polls for the upcoming primary election.

> Primary on the 25th
> And the 'rednecks' will be there.
> And the 'Yaller-heels' will be there, also.
> And the 'hayseeds' and 'gray dillers,' they'll be there, too.
> And the 'subordinates' and 'subalterns' will be there to rebuke their slanderers and traducers.
> And the men who pay ten, twenty, thirty, etc., etc., percent on borrowed money will be on hand, and they'll remember it too.

"These poor farmers began to wear red neckerchiefs to political picnics and rallies. Not to bore you or anything, here's one little side relationship right up my alley. I'll simplify it for you."

He looked down and discovered Casey was asleep. The rednecker's info was just a bit too much. He continued to read.

"During 1906 to 1940, a disease known as pellagra was contracted by three million Americans, with one hundred thousand reported deaths. A great doctor named Joseph Goldberger was assigned to this menace in 1914 by the US Health Public Service. In short, he solved the cause of it. The disease spread among the individuals whose diets were malnourished, consisting of mostly meat—pork, molasses, meal, corn, and rice. He inspected orphanages, prisons, and mental institutions where the diet was limited from fruits, vegetables, and red meats, fish, poultry, and milk. Then the insightful doctor deduced it was not from germs as believed but rather from a diet deficiency. He injected himself, his wife, and other willing participants with the blood and body fluids of patients, and not one person developed this disease. He also solicited Mississippi prisoners to a study that deprived them of the appropriate nutrients, causing many of them to develop the disease within months. This was in exchange for a pardoned sentence. Unfortunately, he died before the nutrient was deemed niacin, or B3. It was discovered in 1937 at the University of Wisconsin. So the moral of this episode is? Any guesses?"

Kipper offered, "*Rednecks* is a term to define a solid stand on things."

"Very nice, honey. Ooops, sorry, I meant Kipper." He's embarrassed.

"Your subliminal outburst is right up *my* alley. I like *honey*."

Garrett added, "It represents a bond with many people who are not of *high cotton*." The girls weren't sure of that meaning.

"Good one, G!"

Tally said, "The color red is significant for honor and courage."

"Oooh, good point, and yes, that seems correct, given what we just learned."

Casey was snoring. "Well, he's dreaming about me with duct tape over my mouth." They all laughed and nudged him to wake up.

"And my conclusion. Well, let's just say I'm definitely the *redneck* at Excalibur High."

CHAPTER 27

"Snea-key" but Not Cheeky

Two hours blew by, and they scurried around to clean up before watching the movie *A Charlie Brown Christmas*, created from the *Peanuts* comic strip by Charles M. Schulz, produced by Lee Mendelson, and directed by Bill Melendez, which originally aired on CBS TV in 1965. This seemed to be the most cohesive show for everyone to watch.

At the end of the movie, they exchanged gifts before saying good-bye to the girls.

Kipper said, "Hey, Casey, you wanna see Caesar again?"

Casey replied, "Sure, Klipper, I love your bird!"

"Ahhh, how cute. He called me Klipper."

G added, "Yeah, he's a trip sometimes." Casey frowned at G.

Caesar was calm when they approached him but immediately started talking when he spotted his owner. She got him to say a few more things and then looked at her watch and realized it was getting late, so she wrapped up the fun-filled event and told everyone good-bye. Karl would ground her if she was out driving at night regardless of this party. This also reminded Tally to get back and pack for her family's trip. No making out this time; Casey was present.

There was so much energy floating around that the boys decide to go in the pool and even little one was allowed to stay up since school was out. It wasn't until 11:00 p.m. before they quit swimming and took the remainder of the twenty-third inside. Casey was so tired he passed out watching the boys play video games; it wouldn't be traditional if those two had not challenged each other for another animated race.

Scholls went to the bathroom to brush his teeth, creating an avenue for his plan and scrupulous ingenuity to find that key. He saw the study light under the door way and decided to mosey on down and check things out. Dr. Berg was asleep on the chaise lounge. He sneaked in very quietly to see what was on top of the desk, knowing if he was caught, he could easily use the excuse he was checking on the bird. He shuffled some items and saw Peter's key chain.

It was the break he needed. Scholls put the keys in his pocket without making a noise and headed toward the cage. The cover was draped completely over the wiring and that meant Caesar was asleep, but he strained not to wake either one of them. Garrett was waiting to play another video game, and he didn't have much time to remove the key.

How in the world did Scholls know which key was which? Plain logical sense served this intense moment well, and strategically, Scholls figured out what each key opened. The house and car keys are remote, so that was easy. His office key in the hospital was gold and solid with letters and numbers. He noticed it weeks ago when Dr. Berg was pointing it out to Barbara.

In conclusion, there were only six keys altogether. One belonged to a small box, like a postal box of some sort, and two keys that appeared to be special. One had a musical notes theme and the last one was silver with a number inscribed on it. That was it! The numbers were his condo unit. Just in case, he took both keys and slid them into his pocket, left the room and went back to Garrett. It was the only time Scholls ever did something this incriminating, which caused his heart to pound excessively.

Now he needed a way to leave the house without setting the alarm. It was a time to use one of those white lies of Garrett's. "Hey, dude, I need to go to the twenty-four-hour pharmacy for just a bit. I know it sounds crazy and it is, but my butt is on the line."

G kind of snapped a bit, "Bro, it's late. What's so urgent?"

"Man, it's just that I promised my parents I would make a copy of our new house key and bring it back tomorrow. I totally forgot to tell you, and now I'm worried my mom will be without her key. I have to either take it there tonight or around six in the morning. I checked yesterday, and they have a kiosk machine for this."

"All right, let's cruise, 'cuz I'd rather go tonight than 6:00 a.m. Of course, you kinda got use to that in Texas, didn't you?"

"You funny. Let's go, dude."

G sarcastically replied, "We're gonna work on getting your driver's license next."

"That's gonna be interesting." Scholls detected the sarcasm, and his feelings were hurt.

Garrett shut his door and left the music on in hopes his mom would still think they were up if she passed down the hall. It must have worked because Barbara walked by his door, paused a bit, and smiled before entering the study. Caesar's head remained tucked under his wing, and the doctor was asleep with a book in his hand.

"Honey, honey, you fell asleep. Come to bed, babe."

Dr. Berg was startled and woke up, saying, "Oh, I did, sorry."

He looked at the desk and noticed the paper was off to the side. It must have slid down because Scholls made sure to keep everything as it was. That embittered Peter, and when he walked by, his eyes glanced engagingly as if something was different, though he couldn't quite figure out just what it was because his lovely wife steamrolled the summons by clasping his elbow, walking him out, and shutting off the lights. Oh well, maybe she went to his desk first.

Over at the pharmacy, Scholls must make the *keys* without his friend present, so he sidebars a request and has G look in the analgesic section to find an item that no longer exists. The product was discontinued in 2005, so he had a chance that Garrett wouldn't be familiar with the privy medication, giving Detective Parker several minutes to complete his task.

"Hey, G, can you do me a favor. Will you snag me a bottle of Bextra? It should be on the aisle where the headache medicine is."

"Okay, you got a headache?"

"Something like that."

Being able to mill your keys with the handy machine was magnificently efficient. By the time Garrett returned, he was finished duplicating, and S. Parker could sigh a big relief.

"Bro, I looked everywhere and couldn't find it. I even asked the store clerk, and they seemed confused. Said they never heard of it."

He patted his buddy on the shoulder and said, "Thanks for looking. I don't need anything." On the way back to the Hum, Garrett mulled over the situation and stated, "What about your headache?"

"Dude, it's gone. I can't believe it."

With an even more confused face than the store clerk, G responded, "Shit, I wish mine would go away that fast. Oh well, we have plenty of meds at the house if it comes back." Scholls gave him the thumbs-up and a big smile from ear to ear. Garrett couldn't help but attempt a snicker at his friend's facial expressions.

On a no-nonsense approach, Scholls pressed G about his noticeable irritability that evening. Even Tally was spared the overt affection he normally displayed with her. He seemed sluggish and almost as if he had to "try" to convince the gang he enjoyed everything by laughter.

G's routine mannerisms were patterned, and being cranky or inactive was not one of them. Why? What's happening to Garrett?

Scholls thanked the Higher Power for allowing them to meet and asked God, in his heart, to help his friend cope with the newest afflictions. He also asked for guidance to solve any wrongdoings that might be in the making and forgiveness concerning anything he had to do that might be risky. This mental crisis stood on the edge of quick decisions with right and wrong overtones.

"How are you really feeling, Garrett?"

"Man, I told you, I'm fine!" Scholls gulped. "Hey, sorry, I don't understand what's making me irritated."

"Are you sure you are giving yourself the correct dosage of insulin. Let's check your blood glucose when we get back."

"Whatever. It's been reading normal ranges, and I'm following the endocrinologist's recommendations."

"Well, let's check again anyway."

"Yeah, I guess."

He pulled the Hum into the second garage on the left, where his father's cars are stored. Garrett's parking space was close to the Benz and Aston despite Peter's prehoneymoon suggestions to have a new garage built farther out on the property, in memory of Mr. Pierce. G shunned that intention right away, and Dr. Berg just smiled on the outside and boiled on the inside. He realized right then and there, early on, this all-American kid was a chip off the old block. Thommason Pierce was known to be humble and even-keeled while equally publicized as a stronghold esquire.

"Hey, G, I need to use the restroom real quick. Then I'm gonna help you check your level."

"I'm pretty tired. I could fall asleep in two seconds."

He crept back into the dark study and having no flashlight, reached into his pocket for the phone. The keys were exactly as Peter left them. Suddenly, there's a noise, and he went around the back side of the desk and ducks. He continued to put the keys back on the clip, in case it was his only chance. A small gust of air left S. Parker's lips as he managed to pull it off. The keys were placed back on the desk precisely, but he bumped the corner just a bit when the distinct audible sound was back.

"Kipper...Kipper...Hello...Hello...Scholls."

His sweetie's bird was awakened and very astute, or maybe even artful enough to have toyed with his words, by leading in with Kipper's name and ending it with Scholls. Caesar was fully aware of another scent. S. Parker worked his way to the cage and talked to him as if he would understand what was being said.

Scholls whispered, "Hey, Caesar, it's okay, boy. I'll be back in the daylight to feed you. Don't worry, fella. It's gonna be fine."

As he turned to leave, the parrot said, "Scholls," as if to confirm he knew who and what was said. This touched his heart, sending butterflies to his stomach. He just might have a bird like him one day; he just might have Caesar, one day.

Several minutes elapsed, and upon returning to the room, he found his friend asleep. No sense in waking him now because rest was what he needed. Typically, teenagers needed at least nine hours. Their biology class was currently touching base on the subject of the immune system, and this was what they learned so far:

An Ohio State University research team suggested that psychological stress disrupts the communication between three systems: the endocrine (hormone) system, the nervous system, and the immune system. A system is just that, a system, not a single component, so it needs to have balance and continuity to function well. They speculated after many studies that long-term stress releases mainly glucocorticoids (stress hormones) and that these inhibit (restrain or stop) cytokine and interleukins, which stimulate and coordinate white blood cell activity (for healing). Furthermore, those hormones affect the thymus, where T lymphocytes are produced. WBC only last from thirteen to twenty days, (RBC around an average of 120 days).

The *Harvard Health Publications* have reported some stress studies in mice showed decreased production of antibodies and suppressed activity of T cells. In one study, they differentiated two types of stresses and the effects it had on the mice. First, some mice were put into a cage with a highly aggressive mouse, two hours a day, six days a week, continually threatened but not injured. This was *social* stress.

Other mice were put into tiny cages without food and water for long periods of time. This was *physical* stress. Both groups were exposed to bacterial toxin, and the *socially stressed* mice were twice as likely to die.

He certainly didn't want his friend any more stressed than he already was. In the morning, he would check G's levels, and in the future, he might save more lives.

"Hey, bro, I guess I fell asleep last night. I gotta take my insulin, so let's check my level first."

"Yeah, I couldn't sleep much, and I've been reading stuff on my phone for hours."

He had sacrificed a few cytokines for his friend's safety. The levels appeared to be normal. Scholls excused himself to go feed Caesar, and Garrett administered his insulin. Looked like Dr. Berg also lost a few and then some, though it was highly probable his three systems didn't connect well.

Peter greeted, "Good morning, Scholls, I took the liberty of removing the bird's cover when I came in earlier. Looks like he adjusted fine."

"Thank you, Dr. Berg. I guess I'll just go over and feed him and probably change the lining and water."

"Scholls, were you kids in my study last night?" He had a lower pitch, motionless face, and intimidating stare.

"Sir, we were. I checked on the parrot. He was making noises."

"All right, I knew I wasn't crazy. My desktop was altered." His low pitch was back to medium.

Scholls thought, *I don't know about that. You might be crazy. For sure you are OCD.* "Yes sir, I accidently bumped it trying to use my phone to light up a path. I'm sorry about that. Next time I'll make sure everything is proper before I leave."

"Son, why would you need to use your phone? The light switch is handy."

Damn, he's clever.

"Yes, sir, I guess you're right. I just didn't want to scare the bird into a squawking frenzy."

"Appreciated. How much longer is he going to be here?"

"Well, sir, he is staying until the twenty-seventh."

"Won't you need to go home for Christmas?"

"Oh yes, I am going home on Christmas Day and will be back on the twenty-seventh or twenty-eighth. Not sure exactly."

"I feel the twenty-eighth would be better for my schedule since Barb will be gone. Who is going to care for this bird while you are gone?"

"Oh!" He laughed nervously. "Sir, Garrett will do it until I return."

"Hmmm, Barbara didn't tell me that part of this *désordre*."

Out of respect, Scholls didn't ask him what it meant, but it sounded a whole lot like the word *disorder*. He headed to the cage and was greeted with shuffling feet and grunts. Dr. Berg left the room.

"Hey, Caesar, you know who I am, don't you, bud?"

The cage was cleaned, and he replenished the food and water bowls. Around lunchtime, he would go outside in the other cage and hopefully would love the new view. He headed back to G's room, and his friend was not there. He wasn't in the bathroom, kitchen, living room, or anywhere he checked. Juanita pointed Scholls to his location after she saw Garrett on the monitor of the security cameras.

"Hey, G man, what's up?"

"Just looking at the V12 and missing my dad."

"It's a badass set of wheels, that's for sure. How much are one of those?"

"I think my dad paid in the neighborhood of 550,000."

"Damn!"

"But as far as I'm concerned, it's priceless." His face was sad. "Let's get through Christmas and on New Years Day. We'll take her for a spin."

"That'll work. How ya feeling today?"

"Better, I guess. My stomach is a bit queasy, so I'm gonna skip breakfast. Let's go see what Juanita has in store this morning. You need your energy, bro, 'cuz we're heading back to the mall, and it's a warzone the day before Christmas. I totally forgot to get Randy a gift. There's no way I would forget him."

"All right, bro, let's get it on, as they say in Cali."

"Uhhh, I think Marvin Gaye said it best, but that's a future issue and a whole different subject."

Scholls woofed down a bowl of cereal and ate two of the fresh blueberry muffins one Hispanic food connoisseur prepared from scratch. Garrett snagged one for the road. They converted into nerds and drove the Benz into the shopping abyss. A lady with two smaller children was parking next to them, and the kids kept making faces at the nerdy boys.

"Look at those little kids, dude. You see what they just did?"

"Yep."

Scholls folded his arms and looked right through them with a stare similar to Dr. Berg's in the study; the kids stopped right away and never looked back.

Yeah, it's affective, all right. "G, what are you going to get Randy?"

"Well, I already received one of his gifts in the mail last week. I thought I would get him a gadget he could use for fun, and that way, Vincent would be included."

Garrett was such a thoughtful individual, and the more Scholls was around him, the more he understood his generosity was truly heartfelt.

G told his friend, "I also want to go inside this one high-tech store and check out some of the stuff, so help me out, dude."

Their costumes were appropriate, and no one in that place even blinked an eye.

"Hey, G, I got you something, but my funds were limited. I'll make it up to you in the future."

"Nah, man, whatever you got me will be fine. Anyways, you shouldn't have spent money on me. I'm not joking, dude. A card is perfect. In fact, I want you to take it back and get the money and keep it."

"I'm good. That's why this financially challenged teen budgets. I'm not taking it back. Kinda like you insisted on me taking all those clothes."

"Okay, settled. Let's look around. Here's something cool…the new Skylanders SuperChargers."

"Oh yeah, I'd probably blow you away with these."

"We'll see."

"I could stay in here all day." Scholls sighed.

"Yeah, me too. There's so much stuff, since I don't know Vincent that well, I guess I'll

just get them a gift card. C'mon, Scholls. Let's roll."

CHAPTER 28

Everything's Coming up Roses

UNBEKNOWNST TO HIM, Garrett tricked his buddy into coming along so he could find out just what he liked. Randy's gift was already purchased weeks ago. He was sending him and Vincent on a paid vacation to Aruba.

Garrett pleaded with Scholls to go to the bookstore and turnabout fair play, had his friend look for a book that doesn't exist. Neither one of them had any idea of each other's fictitious routing. He made up a title, "Explanations, Cures, and Questions."

Scholls believed G was at another store purchasing the gift card, but he went back, bought the video game, and had it boxed up. Then he told his best friend he bought another gift for his mother, and they were able to wrap it fast. You better believe slipping a $50 bill to a youthful employee got immediate results.

And the coffee table, that wasn't all he "supposedly got" from the extra movie set props. He bought Scholls a TV, along with other gaming devices. In honor of his friend, he also donated money in their names to the Animal Charities of America and had the certificate framed, along with the picture for his parents.

It was time to head back for these two mischievous techies. That crowd nearly drove them out of their disguises. They decided to head over to Westward Trailer Park and play Santa before Scholls's place was unoccupied, but first, they'd need to go back and get the coffee table and picture, along with goodies Barbara made for the Parkers. He switched vehicles and loaded up the gifts.

Scholls reminded G that Caesar needed to be put in the cage outdoors, so they moved him before driving off. The view was grandiose and seemingly had the bird pleased.

"Talk to you soon, lil' buddy. Ten-four."

Caesar echoes in perfect rhythm, "Ten-four...ten-four."

Both boys said, "Awesome!"

Mr. Parker was up watching TV and showing no signs of hostility. Maybe Garrett's friendship made him less likely to be violent because since they met, Scholls had not been hit. It was likely the Parkers had one of their rare moments of affection because Tina was calm and they were sitting together. Normally, Harry would be asleep till at least 7:00 p.m. Tina began the conversation.

"Hey, son. Hey, Jarod." *It was a lost cause.*

"Merry Christmas, Mr. and Mrs. Parker."

"Yeah, Mom and Dad, Merry Christmas."

Harry responded, "Thanks, boys, you, too. I'm glad we at least get Christmas Day off. Wish we were Rockefellers, and then we'd be looking forward to holidays. I'm sorry your dad and mom have jobs that make us work like this."

Scholls responded, "Don't worry about it. It's not your fault. I understand that. I really do. One day you'll get a break. Just wait and see. Hey, we'll be back in a sec."

They unloaded the table, and this confused his parents. Garrett explained his little scenario, and Tina smirked. "I guess our table was a true eyesore."

Harry gave her a look and then said, "Thank you, young man. This is way too generous."

"Oh, hey, I almost forgot. Be right back." G ran to the Hum to fetch the picture and desserts.

Scholls looked at his mother and said, "You know something, Mom? It gets old. He's a great person. Just give him a chance."

She lighted up her cigarette and sat down again. It must have made her feel awful, and for once, she backed down. As soon as

Garrett walked in, she said, "Hey there, kiddo, I'm sorry. It was really thoughtful."

Scholls walked over and gave her a hug. Her arms raised halfway up but did not embrace him. Instead, she told her son, "Merry Christmas, Scholls. Love you."

Garrett took charge, walked over to shake Harry's hand, and then advanced to hug Tina, letting her know he accepted the apology. She didn't look up or hug back but said, "Merry Christmas to you and your family. Please thank your mother for the treats."

S. Parker's heart was touched again, and his journal would be starred on this day. Bandit would get a pointed ear full. His parents unwrapped the photo, placed it on the new coffee table, and vowed to put it on the wall soon.

Was this a breakthrough? Scholls processed what happened and wondered if tomorrow will be the same, while G processed what happened and made a mental note of her resistance. Garrett realized human behavior was quite a flux of coagulated responsiveness, and this moment increased his quest to decipher causative actions. The visitation ended, and both boys headed back to Huntingdon Cove.

It was traditional in the Pierce household for each person to exchange one small gift at 8:00 p.m., Christmas Eve. Barbara felt happy and sad within the same unsanctioned emotion. The star at the top of the tree was hand carved by an old Indonesian man, and they, Thom and Barbara, bought it on a trip while dating. Her current spouse need not know given his predisposition to jealously; although at this point, it appeared to be corralled with mote effects. Memories of her late husband put her into a funk, and she walked in the shrine and cried.

Close to 7:40 p.m., Peter noticed she was missing and anxiously observed the monitor for her whereabouts. He spotted the room dedicated to Thom, and there was his bride, wiping her eyes. He breathed in deep and fast as the covetousness for her affections was threatened by the quixotic memory. He headed back to the study and tried to get a grip on his feelings but needed to release a few words in an angered, and low, pitch. "She still loves him. This house represents everything about that bastard. As soon as I get rid of the wonder boy, she'll want *no* part of this place. He's the one thing that links her most to *Mr. Pierce*. I'm sick of people hurting me! Décès for Garrett…décès, décès!"

He refrained from entering that repulsive room where Barbara was and headed back to find his son talking away with the opponent and his sidekick. The other voice in his head made repetitive efforts to calm and untwist his demons. Dr. Berg was acting like a sleepwalker, not conscious of his surroundings but able to move about as if he was. Once he sat down on the sofa, he blurted out, "Shut up!" All three of the boys instantly stopped laughing and looked over in total wonderment.

Casey said, "Sorry, Daddy, are we too loud?"

Apparently, this made Peter snap back into reality, and he said, "Oh, no, son, forgive me. Daddy was thinking about one of the Asperger's kids who frets a lot. I guess I verbalized his habit. You kids carry on."

They carried on, but Scholls found this to be very odd and indicative of more than someone repeating what he had heard. It seemed too odd. His intuitive radar went full throttle, and he was now sure the signs of one flying over the cuckoo's nest was looming. Peter's face said more than his command. His eyes were flickering, and he appeared to be highly agitated. But this didn't make him a monster, did it? Still, S. Parker needed more evidence that his best friend was in harm's way. He continued to watch Dr. Berg's actions sub rosa and sent the General more info. Scholls always favored that saying because of its meaning.

The term *sub rosa* or "under the rose" was believed to be a misinterpretation of an Egyptian hieroglyphic adopting Horus as a god. It showed a boy suckling his finger, but the Greeks thought he had his finger to his lips showing signs of secrecy. Cupid is said to have given Horus, aka Harpocrates, a rose as a token of gratitude for not betraying the reputation of his amorous mother, Aphrodite, the Greek equivalent to Venus. As a result, any *secret* was symbolized by a rose and also linked to love, beauty, pleasure, and procreation.

Some customs hung a rose over the council table to indicate all talks were private and not to be shared elsewhere. In Rome, if ceilings were decorated or painted with roses, it meant whatever was spoken *sub vino*, under the influence of wine, was also *sub rosa*, or secret.

A master mason's apron, worn by a Freemason of that honor, bears three rosettes which represent an obligation of silence for, one, fidelity to craft—their trade or skilled occupation; two, sacred secrets; and three, silence to the proceedings of the Lodge.

Not too much later, Mrs. Berg returned after getting herself together. It was now her role to make it equally the Berg household. Peter approached his wife, commented on her visually reddened eyes, and acted unaware of their origin.

"Darling, you've been crying. What's wrong?"

Barbara was afraid to answer and simply responded, "Nothing for you to worry about, honey. I get sentimental this time of year."

She reached over to hug him; Dr. Berg hugged her back with good conscience, though he knew she had lied to spare him the truth. Nonetheless, her touch was a powerful antidote for his anger.

All the gifts had been placed in a symmetrical fashion under the tree, compliments of Dr. Berg. Casey, Scholls, and Garrett all helped decorate the branches weeks earlier with no goal in mind but to make it look nice. After they finished, Peter went back discreetly and reorganized the ornaments in sequence.

Our young detective was nobody's fool and just as adept, spotting the change right away with a glare. All the bulbs that Garrett had placed were on the bottom. He distinctly recalled those bulbs were the ones labeled "Items from the PGC Kidz

Camp" and had special markings. Dr. Berg saw Scholls rendering judgment about the change and cleared his throat to interrupt Scholl's proficient valuation.

"All right, gang, I thought we would each express an appreciation for the holiday. It can be spiritual, familial, or an observation of something endearing. Scholls, let's start with you please."

These two were a mirrored image of intelligence on different planes, and Dr. Berg just served the ball in his court again. The younger mastermind detained his thoughts and answered the good doctor's requests. In a bold move, he voiced an obvious statement; only they were able to unriddle its clairvoyant message. Scholls flipped the script in a lower pitch.

"I'd like to thank the Higher Power and my lucky stars to be sitting here tonight with the best friend a person could ever have. Garrett and his family can count on me to help them in any way, should they need it. I plan on being his friend for a long time…a *very* long time."

Garrett looked at Scholls and tried to figure out why his voice was different. Peter just smiled cocky and nodded his head in accordance to the underlying message. He responded by saying, "Yes, Garrett seems destined for a lot. You're definitely a great friend and hopeful admirer."

They locked eyes for a few seconds, and Dr. Berg looked away to control the situation and change the direction of delicate tension between them.

When the presents were exchanged and the evening hour vanished, Juanita sorted through Casey's gifts and identified what, and who, for thank-you notes. In the course of the night and after that cerebrum dual, there would be no more verbal exhibitions between Scholls and Peter. S. Parker was sure of more to come and could not remain heedless because at the bare minimum, Peter was showing signs of instability, but most importantly, all the encounters might be connected to Garrett's sickliness, and that took precedence. He'd rather be wrong than right "too late." Scholls left the room to use his phone, sending a text to avoid Peter's knowledge: "Hey, Unc, there's something brewing with Mr. Hyde. He's definitely acting unstable, but to what extent, I'm not sure. Looking forward to your arrival on the 26th. Merry Christmas. Talk to you tmrw."

Before calling it a night, G administered his glucose and told Scholls he was super tired and weak. He was pale, with almost a light-yellow hue. Maybe the levels weren't accurate. Maybe his body had not been able to adjust that fast. Maybe he was more sick than suspected. All these questions floated around in Schollie's mind, and throughout the night, he checked to make sure his friend was fine. Garrett's head was slightly heated, and he had been sweating. Scholls placed a cold washcloth on his forehead around 2:00 a.m. Christmas was second to Garrett's health. He'll talk with Barbara in the morning when the excitement was down because G hid his symptoms from his mother.

What frustrated Scholls the most, Peter was not the primary doctor and really had no direct involvement with the diabetes. The blood tests were conclusive, and he had seen the printouts himself when Garrett brought them home; plus, the vials were legitimate with no obvious tampering.

The specialist was in charge. It was not a conspiracy. The emergency visit was warranted. Whatever it took, Scholls vowed to tackle this mystery like JJ Watt defended the NFL Texans.

CHAPTER 29

Presents and Pre-Med

IN ABOUT TEN hours, Casey would discover a twice bitten cookie and note from Santa Claus. Scholls had no intentions on disrupting that moment—unless a life-threatening matter occurred.

Casey exclaimed, "Mommy, Daddy, Garrett, Scholls, Santa left me a note! He even ate some of the cookie." He went running through the house and repeated it several times until everyone was awake. They began the ritual of passing out gifts with Peter at the helm. Casey was a busy little guy receiving nearly forty gifts in total.

Barbara received a beautiful vintage necklace with matching earrings from Peter that comprised over 16 carats of diamonds and emeralds collectively. He went all out and wanted to overshadow his rival. Despite this extravagant gift, Mrs. Berg showed equal appreciation for anything she received that morning. Barb did whisper in Peter's ear as he placed it around her neck, and the neurologist kissed her face on the side of the cheek as he secured the clasp from behind. He looked over at Garrett and smiled braggingly but suddenly stopped when his peripheral vision spotted Scholls silently clapping his fingertips as a phony gesture of approval. Game on. What could possibly be the reason for his rivalry with Garrett? Berg began wearing insecurity like a heart on a sleeve.

Keeping his son in suspense, Peter asked Casey to go on the back patio to see if St. Nick forgot to bring anything in the house.

The little one didn't want to leave all his toys and moped as he got up.

"Can't Garrett or Scholls go check? I didn't think Santa Claus was that lazy to forget stuff. He's supposed to go down our chimney."

Everybody laughed under their breath with that youthful observation. Casey crossed his arms and wore a scowl on his face as he left the area. They began estimating his discovery time.

"One...two...three...four...five...six..."

Casey shouted, "Yes! He left me a bicycle. Daddy, Mommy, I have a new bike! Scholls, Garrett, come look at my new bike! I love you, Santa. I love you!"

They walked out and discovered he was already riding it around the back of the house. Casey told them in person, "Santa left me a bike! I love Santa. He isn't lazy after all. It was too big."

That hit a funny bone with the boys, but only Scholls started laughing. Peter allowed him to continue riding for a few minutes, and Casey begged his father to let him keep it in his room for the night, "Dad, I think I better keep it in my room. Just in case one of the elves accidently come back and try to take it to another kid's house. That way they know it's mine. Those elves aren't as smart as Santa, you know. *Please.*"

Another round of laughter stirred everyone but G, and he's allowed to bring it in the first night. Barbara and Peter stayed outside and drunk coffee while he rode back and forth. The gold boys politely thanked the adults for their gifts and shortly returned to Garrett's room for a private exchange among themselves.

Mrs. Berg bought each of the older boys a gift card they could use at most stores and had the title of the V12 ready for Garrett to take over. He was floored, promising to keep it in top-notch condition; the car was a keepsake for life. She also gave Scholls a paid receipt from the Western Coastal Driving School. He got emotional and hugged his second mother, which evoked Garrett to lean in saying, "It's a gift, not charity. Merry Christmas from the Pierces."

Scholls and Barbara stepped away to speak in private. Good ol' Dr. Berg was trying to keep an eye on them and his son at the same time. That comment from his stepson concerning the "Pierces" didn't put him in a good mood.

Garrett's mother needed to find out her son was feeling ill yesterday. Immediately she took Garrett by the arm and led him to their kitchen to check out his condition. "Sweetheart, are you okay, honey? Scholls said you looked pale yesterday, and I'm sorry I didn't notice with all the running around and stuff. You didn't tell me."

"Yeah, my body's taking a little longer to adjust, that's all."

"Now listen, sweetheart, I don't care if the holidays are upon us. If you feel bad, we need to have it checked, and that's all there is to that. Your eyes do look tired. I need to know exactly what's wrong."

"I've had an upset stomach and headaches, dizziness, and lately, I feel more tired than usual. My heart races at times."

Barbara checked his head. "Stay right here. I'm getting Peter."

She motioned for him to come inside and meet at the doorway. Berg yelled to Casey to come back up to the house; he can ride his bike later.

"What's happening, babe?"

"Peter, Garrett is ill. He looks tired, and I personally think he looks bad. His symptoms are nausea, headaches, and heart racing, and he does look pale. He had a fever last night, right, Scholls?"

Scholls answered, "I believe so. He felt warm when I checked on him."

Barbara was nervous. "I feel just awful. How could I have missed all this? Please look at him. We're going to the hospital if necessary."

Peter walked into the kitchen and had Garrett repeat all the occurrences. Juanita left and returned with his medical bag, and Dr. Berg started by taking his temperature, listening to his heart, looking in his eyes, which he almost couldn't stand to do, and throat, then prepared his blood sample. He knew exactly what was wrong but fabricates yet another medical mishap. The glucose level was low. There are a few reasons why this would occur with someone; however, Peter was the only one who knew the truth. Too much insulin can cause a decrease, and Dr. Berg had medical facts to back it.

"All right, I believe I know what the problem is. Garrett's developed hypoglycemia." Peter injected him with glucagon, which was never just readily available to anyone, except maybe a doctor. Or does he? Peter really injected him with a very small mixture of prochlorperazine mesylate, which will help with the nausea. The rest of the mixture was saline solution. He neither wanted him better or worse at the moment. All his pharmaceutical knowledge was sovereign; he was like a modern-day witch doctor. Those giant, long, hard to pronounce words went right over the present company's heads.

"Garrett's doses are too high, and this would certainly throw him off. Sometimes the initial recommended doses need to be reassessed and changed." He stepped to the side and acted as if he had dialed the other doctor.

Just in case, Scholls typed in the search and ran across information to support it. He's happily surprised to find out that this was a fact. It eased his mind but did *not* erase his suspicions about the psychologically challenged physician.

Peter vented, "Garrett, did you calculate the correct increase in rapid acting insulin for your carbohydrates, especially when you kids had all that Mexican food?"

G sighed. "I never really paid attention to what was told to me about the levels being too low. I should have looked at the chart. It's my fault. I even have the app downloaded for conversions."

Peter pressed him more. "Why not? You have to compensate for your diet. No one expects you to eat perfectly. That's why the calculations allow for offsets. You need rest now."

"Listen, Mom, I need to go drop Scholls off at his house. I'll be back soon, and then I'll lie down and watch a movie in my room. I promise."

Barbara wasn't thrilled and said, "I will take him home. Peter wants you to lie down now."

Garrett was still irritable and responded snappy, "No, can do. I need to say Merry Christmas to his parents. I'm fine. When I get back, I will lay down like I stated earlier. We're gonna exchange gifts first. Let's go, Scholls."

She rarely heard her son disregard authority as a teen and allowed him to leave; unfortunately, her husband left out one fact, the drowsiness effect of the medicine. Peter didn't like his insubordination. "That was out of line. He was rude."

Barbara answered her spouse, "Yes, but this is not typical of him. I know he's not feeling well." Peter was aggravated yet showed no more interest. He knew Garrett's hours were ticking away. Even more unsettling was the medicine would cause Garrett to become a bit drowsy. He had a more opportune time to kill him, but what the heck, this might even be better for everyone. Garrett might fall asleep at the wheel. His thought rejuvenated a reminder for Charles.

The gold boys headed into G's room. In an attempt to buffer Scholls from spending too much, G limited the exchange to one gift. He pulled all his energy together and did his best to be happy.

"Sweet, OMG, the Skylanders. I can't believe it! Thank you so much, G. I guess when we were in that store, you probably saw my reaction to it. Thank God I didn't act like a jerk and say, 'Nah, it's not for me.' Your feelings would have been hurt since you already got it for me. This is rad!"

"Yeah, bro, good thing you liked it." Garrett wouldn't reveal his real mission that day.

Scholls reached to hand his friend a small package, and he felt terrible. "Your gift is so generous...and mine, well, one day I won't have this problem, and your gifts will be better."

G replied, "It's our friendship that counts. I have more than most kids will ever have monetarily. That's why gifts from the heart are so special, dude. I know whatever you got me is cool." He opened the small box and pulled out two things. One was a customized ball marker for divots on a golf course. It had a maroon capital G from the font Ravie, which he knew was one of Garrett's favorites, that was set into a gold-speckled background. The back had a small inscription: 2015-bio. Garrett loved it. The second item made him shake his head and give a thumbs-up to his country cohort. Scholls had kept the shot glass G used when he drank his moonshine during the game. "Thanks, man. I'll keep them for life. That's what I'm talking about. No one can change their meaning."

Garrett reached in his top drawer and pulled out the shot glass *Skoals* used for his penalties. It was time for their custom handshake, but he barely completed it. "Great minds think alike," said G. "Oh hey, Scholls, I forgot. There are a couple extra items that I snagged for you. C'mon."

"Really, dude? Typical G-style BS."

"That stands for *Bargain Stalker*, right?"

"I had other words in mind."

"C'mon, man. I thought, 'Hhmm? Why not give them to Scholls.'"

"You're runnin' out of white lies, dude."

Garrett led him into the garage where the items lay, and his best friend was stunned to find a large TV monitor, all kinds of gaming devices, and a chair. "Garrett, stop doing this, dude. I know you mean well. It's just that…Damn, it's way too much."

G looked around. "Is someone talking?"

"You sound like me now. I can't win with you, dude."

They loaded up and headed to Scholl's place. It would be two days before seeing each other, and by then, Garrett would presumably feel better. So how was Dr. Berg, Mr. Hyde, going to pull it off? This was truly a caveat.

His pseudo parental fellowship was shrouded by old scars that plotted against the acquired child. Berg's mind was contorted, and he was losing battle against good with evil. Could Scholls cope with his best friend's death and not seek revenge?

CHAPTER 30

Lil' Food for Thought, and What's Not

Study the past if you would define the future.

—Confucius, 551–479 BC

"HEY, MAN, I'M feeling pretty sleepy, so I better just drop you off. I'll be here by six, Sunday eve. You and Kipper stop by any time to get the bird. I have another event to attend that day, but I will come get you that evening. Later, bro. Merry Christmas. Sorry I'm so cranky, dude."

"G, no prob, you're sick. It's not you, man. I know that. Get some rest! Later, bro. See you soon. Merry Christmas!"

Early in his drive home, he chatted very limited with his father's spirit, "Dad, I miss ya so much. Merry Christmas from me and Mom. Wish you were here."

Several cars swerved past Garrett as he worked his way back to the cove. The medicine made him sluggish, and he drove slower than usual, causing motorists to take notice. Fortunately, it was dark and not even a *razzi* was around because Christmas phased their schedule. Besides, he took the Benz with the fake license plate—for protection. When Mr. Manning talked with him about his tactics for privacy, G told him the trick, and he said, "I'm not in your jurisdiction."

Barbara hurried to her son and made sure he was completely settled in for the night. Her plans to go to Aunt Donna's were cancelled, but Peter ensured his bride things would be perfectly fine and Garrett's health was in his hands; this calmed her anxiety about travelling. Contentment ran idle, and her thoughts would be to let him rest, per the doctor's orders, and return earlier if he showed any relapse. She had no idea her home wasn't a safe haven, and Dr. Berg's persuasion was another trait of functional psychotics, *charismatic charm*. Peter was a father, doctor, researcher, educator, and head of the household now.

Garrett hugged his mother and passed out. Instead of leaving the room right away, she sat with her baby and watched him sleep. The years had flown by, and it was only yesterday when he was Casey's age. There was a family picture sitting on his desk, and her eyes strained not to look, but the temptation pulled at her heart and she picked it up. Life was unpredictable. She prayed a small prayer and placed it back on the desk as she wiped away a small teardrop. One last look at her son and she kissed his head and lowered the lights. "Je t'aime." I love you. Peter whispered this to her every day at some point, so she ceased the opportunity to use it with Garrett.

In her jovial fashion, Juanita woke Casey for the trip to his adopted side of the family. He's not a happy camper when he woke up and fell back asleep before she returned to dress him.

Juanita insisted, "Mr. Caaasey, Mr. Caaasey, you have to get up, *mi hijo. Porque,* you are going to leave *un momento.*"

"No! *No un momentos*...mucho sleepy."

Juanita was tickled. "Now, Mr. Casey, you must get up now. *Porque tu madre* is ready to go."

"Uhhh..." was all he said. She finished getting him dressed and helped Barbara pack the smaller SUV with gifts. Off they went to celebrate with his extended family, which included two other children just a bit older than him. There would be plenty to do when he got there.

Barb said, "Your cousins can't wait to see you, Casey. If you want, honey, you can put a pillow to the side and go back to sleep. I will wake you when we get there. It's about forty-five mins to an hour."

"Okay, can I still call you Mom when I'm over there?"

"Sweetie, of course, you can. I will always be your mother from now on, no matter what."

"Well, my first mom left us, and I hate her!"

"Casey, for whatever reason she decided to go, I know in her heart she thinks about you and probably regrets what she has done. I hope one day you two can bond again."

"Well, I hate her! I don't ever want to see her again! My father looked sad when she took off. My teacher told me I was being bad. I don't want to see her again! What's *bond* mean?"

Barbara was saddened. "It means something that is held together…like two people who are very close."

"Well, forget it. She hates me, and now I hate her. My friend says mommies aren't supposed to leave."

"Casey, your teacher said you were bad? What grade were you in, do you remember?"

Little one snapped, "First grade! I was a good kid, I think, before she left…but I'm not sure. I was kinda bad 'cuz I snuck in my little frog a lot and he started making noises. Well, he was hungry. So I guess I got in trouble."

"Darling, that doesn't mean you are a bad kiddo. You do need to follow rules, okay? We all have to follow rules. It's part of life. I think we can forgive your frog incident. Did you know…that when Garrett was young, he got in trouble too?"

Casey responded eagerly. "Nope, what did he do?"

"There was one time when we punished him for cutting all the flowers off their stems, in front of the house. He wanted to give them to a little girl and didn't like the thorns. We made him go to his room with no TV or video or anything fun for the rest of the day. All he could do was read the books we gave him."

"What kinda books did you give him?"

"Well, *Bambi*, *The Hobbit*, and *Charlotte's Web*, to name a few. Every time he misbehaved, he had to read more."

Casey asked, "Can I read those books too? Of course, I'm not gonna be *that* bad like Garrett. I just want to read them."

Barb giggled and agreed to get them when they got back. Her thoughts reverted to an earlier statement he said about being in the first grade. Peter had poured his heart out about his ex-wife leaving, and she recalled a much younger age. It's gonna be on the back burner for now. Garrett would receive a text from his mother some time after ten that morning, in case he slept in.

And that he would do. Dr. Berg had gone into the night and gave him another injection of the Parkinson med—a quite hefty one. He would be bedridden for most of the day. His spleen was swelling, and his body would get weaker as the hours fade. Garrett was in the passage of a severe condition.

Shrewd and discerning techniques marked the distinct making of this neurologist, and he anticipated communication between mother and son. He took Garrett's phone because this teen wouldn't awaken for hours, and when he did, mostly likely would not want to do much. Berg had given him a little sedative as well. Like clockwork, she texted her son around 10:15 a.m. Peter answers her questions so well that Barb does not respond with any suspicion.

He did have one problem brewing because she mentioned speaking to Garrett that evening, and Berg had confirmed her wish. He thought quickly and came up with a plan. G—Berg— will text his mother to let her know he felt too tired and that he needed to go to bed early. Then, Peter will call by proxy and explain the situation, along with his recommendation. He fabricated again in layers and extended it to the next day knowing Garrett's whereabouts were in concealment. She asked Peter to call his agent and canceled the media event due to his illness and Peter fictitiously did just that.

Across town, Scholls anticipated the arrival of his uncle. Tina and Harry had not remained all that pleasant, and he heard them bickering when he went to get a bowl of cereal. It solved his thoughts on any consistent change for the two. He took the bowl back to the room and shut the door and then scooped a couple spoonfuls of milk and put it in Bandit's bowl. He placed the bowl on his bed and pets his furry friend. His uncle Randolph was arriving at the airport late that morning and renting a car so he wouldn't need to be picked up. Scholls heard a knock on his bedroom door, and his mother opened it swiftly and said, "So what time is your uncle getting here?"

Scholls replied, "I think he should be here by one thirty. He just landed and needs to get his car."

"Is he eating first or should we fix something?"

"I'm not sure, Mom. Let me text him and find out. I'll let you know, Okay?"

"Scholls, you know I don't like that cat on the furniture. Put her bowl back on the floor." She left, shutting the door.

In a wisecracking tone, he whispered, "Well, I don't like *not* having a driver's license either, so we're good." Then he talked with his kitty. "Isn't that right, Bandit? She's the mean ol' wicked witch. But if she returns for any reason, you'll have to hit the deck, Okay, girl?"

Finally Uncle Randolph was on his way, and the problem about eating was solved; he was taking everyone out for a late lunch. His beloved mother wasn't that thrilled because she wanted to lounge around in her robe and watch TV, while Harry was on a different wavelength; he was looking forward to seeing his brother, whom he always looked up to as a child. A horn honked twice, and General Randolph pulls up in a rented car that looked inconspicuous enough to be in any situation. He wanted very little attention drawn to him while investigating that condo.

His nephew was the first to go outside and greet him. Randolph hugged him for several seconds and then shook his brother's hand. Tina remained at the door, smoking her cigarette and blowing smoke outward and then raised her arm to wave a simple hello. He intimidated her in many ways, perhaps from his success and productivity in society. As a matter of truth, she had many reasons to blame other people and few to blame on herself;

this allowed her to refrain from owning up to the lack of attempts she made for bettering her education. Her partial efforts didn't reflect obstacles; they reflected random energy.

The general said, "I thought I would take everyone out for seafood, any suggestions?"

Scholls quickly answered, "I know, Mom, Dad, how 'bout Stingrays?" It was an all-you-can-eat buffet with sushi."

Harry said, "Sounds fine with me. C'mon, Tina, get your purse." She finished her cigarette and removed the clip from her hair. The last time they ate at the pricey eatery was two years ago when Harry got a small bonus from work.

Randolph mentioned to Harry that he was staying in a hotel on "official" business, and this in turn was the lead in for Scholls to naturally invite himself to stay with his uncle, executing their secretive plans. After they finished gorging, everyone returned to Westward Trailer Park. He stayed a couple more hours and reminisced with his younger brother about their experiences growing up. Randolph was just about the only sibling who knew where the other family members were and what they were doing in life. Graciously, he wrapped up the conversation and had Scholls retrieve his overnight items. All good-byes were said, and the two of them left to begin the quest.

A few hours before ending up at their overnight destination, Scholls mapped the route on his phone for 222 Cloverleaf, and they drove by to see if Peter was there. Perfect. He wasn't. Now Scholls would need to contact his friend to get reference of the bad doctor's location. He sent G a text, unaware of his Rip Van Winkle-like condition. In the meantime, they decided to check the hospital, and Randolph went in pretending to be an old colleague of Peter's, but it didn't take the nurse long to let him know Dr. Berg was at the autism school; in turn, he called a friend connected with local FBI and gave a heads-up on the ordeal.

If things were right, Peter would return sometime tonight or tomorrow morning. He had the place under surveillance, just seizing the opportunity to go inside as the condo's inspector for "remodeling purposes." Randolph already had an identity card made for this, after he discovered there was real need for concern. Circumstantial evidence can be powerful, and they had plenty of it; moreover, he had factual evidence as well.

Over the last few weeks, Randolph Parker's underground workload would reveal detailed information about Dr. Peter Berg. His parents were most definitely killed in a fire that was ruled accidental, but out of the blue, Peter became a whole new character just a couple years afterward, and he shared details with Scholls as they drove to the autism school, confirming Berg's location. There it was, the Bentley, in his favorite blue color. They parked a few rows away and waited.

"I've got some interesting news for you, son. After his parents died in that fire, he went to live with his aunt and uncle. Thing is, he took off at age seventeen and created a whole new identity."

Scholls gasped, "Really? He ran away? What identity did he create?"

"Peter Berg…Then he left on a bus."

Scholls was confused. "Huh? I don't understand."

The general explained, "His birth name is Scott Farrington."

"So he changed his name from Scott to Peter? How did he get his new name?"

"That's still unknown at this point. He managed to get a new social security number and also a driver's license after that."

Scholls said, "How is that possible?"

"Son, thirty years ago, things weren't linked by computers, and we didn't have the sophistication known today. Most home computers were used for playing games. It wasn't a common household item then, and unfortunately, Social Security fraud *still* exists today."

Scholls had more questions. "I wonder why he ditched his name. When he spoke about his aunt and uncle, it was pleasant.

It was kinda eerie when he described his parent's death, and like I told you, his pitch changed almost in mid-sentence…and his eyes changed direction when he spoke. Where did he go when he left?"

Randolph pulled up some information from his laptop. "Let's see, he went to stay with someone in California because when we spoke to people as if we were a close friend, they indicated he had family there. Best we can determine is he needed a new environment and fresh start. He actually graduated at seventeen, so he finished high school with a diploma. He started gambling extensively…and illegally.

"Back then, it wasn't that easy for a kid to move and just start college on his own, but that doesn't dismiss his illegal affairs. One thing is for sure, he excelled and was accepted into medical school after earning a BS in molecular biology."

Scholls thought, *Crap, we have a lot in common…except I'm not crazy or a criminal, but quirky, yes.* "Okay, we know he is brilliant. Barbara told me he had a dual medical degree, MD and PhD, which says it all. I'm just curious when he married Casey's mother. Did you find out much about that?"

"Yes, we did. They met in school, and she studied marine biology."

Scholls was amazed again and thought, *Damn, this guy's gal is similar to Kipper. Now I'm freaking out. We're too much alike.* "What was he like? Did anyone comment on his personality?"

Randolph read further, "Well, he was quite the ladies' man, and he dated routinely. Didn't like to be alone. He married his first wife by justice of the peace."

"What! He told everyone he had a big wedding. Garrett's mother did for sure. That's why they decided on a small private ceremony, with limited guests." *Well, we're not exactly alike. I'm not even close to being a ladies' man. Ha.*

Randolph read more, "It would appear he got her pregnant, assumingly with Casey, and married her. We have no records of any miscarriages or abortions. So he owned up to being a father, and there is evidence he did care for this woman from other friends' perspectives."

"Wow!" replied Scholls, "I hope Casey never finds out he wasn't planned, and not because it's a bad thing, that's how I came around technically, and well, look at me, I'm just saying. LOL. Oh, sorry, back to a serious note…because she also abandoned him. That would be a double whammy."

Randolph commented, "*Allegedly*, she left him. We haven't confirmed this yet."

"Allegedly? Whoa, what's her name?"

"Her name is Pamela Bauer."

Scholls shook his head. "Logic has it. His past is secretive for a reason. He's hiding something big. I just feel it in my bones… something very disturbing. Garrett's initial sense of uneasiness was merited, but he's so caring and kind. Peter, I mean Scott's, surreptitious mannerisms won him over. Thank God he's resting today with Juanita there, and I'm gonna see him tomorrow. At least we have time to find out more."

Regrettably, he wasn't right. Garrett was not with Juanita, and he would never get to speak to him on the phone like he anticipated. Dr. Berg gave her a monetary bonus and sent her off to return late afternoon the next day. Garrett would be sleeping like Romeo Montague in Shakespeare's *Romeo and Juliet* if Peter was successful. His friend was doomed. Scholls soon realized Garrett had not responded in any fashion for quite some time, so he sent another message. "Dude, you okay? I needed to ask you something important, but if you're still sick, let me know. I can wait. Hope you are feelin' better. Just text SS if so."

Dr. Berg's mental illness was in overdrive, with no chance of subsiding. He was inside the school passing out gifts to the children and suddenly felt Garrett's phone vibrate. "Uh huh, uh huh, well, you noisy brat. He can't talk." Peter was anxious, and he left the kids and went to the bathroom.

"I can't stand that kid. He's *so* smart. At least he thinks he is. He's dealing with a higher intellect now, and I'm out of his league."

Facing the mirror in a deadlock, low pitch, he said, "You and your friendship have come to an end. Barbara's golden child is pyrite...better known as iron sulfide"—using his fingers for quotation marks—"or should we say in G's case, fool's gold! And his best friend Scholls...what the hell kind of name is that anyway for a kid? Tells you right there *his* mother is warped. That noticeably nerdy transformed golden-headed valedictorian will just have to experience life on his own without being able to share all his...itty-bitty little secrets and deep-felt woes with Mr. Hollywood. Hah. *Constant Judgment*, my ass! You're a one-time wonder kid, and Scholliosis is gonna miss you, like I have for Paul. Ahhh, darn, he's gonna have a sideways curve all right."

Out of a stall walked one of the male patients from the autism school named Joshua. This lad rarely spoke, and when he did, it was fragmented. Dr. Berg was interrupted, and the boy just looked at him and made a sad face, pulled out some germ-killing solution gel from his pants pocket, and rubbed his hands. He said nothing, and Mr. Hyde was silently idle. The kid walked out, and the voice of another school caretaker was heard outside the restroom; that employee came back to check on Joshua. Peter turned on the water and splashed his face and smoothed his hair to make sure it was spot on and then left after rapping up the social event. It would be socially unacceptable if he did not respond to Paul's archrival on G's behalf, so he sent "SS" as instructed to appease the brat. Fifteen minutes later, Scholls saw him, and they followed his every move.

"Unc, there he is. Let's follow him. I hope he's goin' back to the condo."

"Already got the car started, and yes, he will go there. I'll bank on it."

Scholls replied, "I'm not gonna doubt ya. That's why you're a successful agent."

As predicted, Berg pulled into the condo gates and parked in his driveway; Randolph went in right behind him before the gate closed. Operation Inside Condo was about to start. "All right, Scholls, stay here until I return. I'm guessing twenty minutes or so."

While waiting, he turned on the radio and hummed to a song he liked by the Rolling Stones. His face lighted up as he saw a text from Garrett, but it didn't stay happy as he read the response "SS."

General Randolph's technique gave forth reasons to confirm why he received the Attorney General's Award for Exceptional Service, granted after his team was responsible for *exceptional* implementation on a federal case. He put on a hat and simulated badge that identified him as the property inspector. He already had the Condo Owner's Association shoot Dr. Berg an e-mail for approval of his interior structural change of unit 5, with inspection and completion of documents. Lucky for Randolph, Peter had plans to convert his interior. The COA president was sworn to silence with prejudice under the FBI investigation. Nonetheless, the general had a backup plan for an exterior structural inspection if the doctor recanted his decision. Mr. Dunn, aka Randolph, rang the doorbell and waited.

Peter had just logged into his computer to view a special hidden folder, when he heard the summons. "Damn it, who's here?" He opened the door slowly after peering through the curtain. The condo had great security, and he recognized the emblem on the badge.

"Yes, and you would be and...be here for what reason?"

"Oh, hello, Mr. Berg. I'm Walter Dunn assigned by the condo association to inspect the interior regions of your place. I assume you received the e-mail last week?"

Berg answered, "Excuse me for being so quizzical. I am in the middle of a project. Is there another time we can take care of this matter?"

Quickly, Mr. Dunn rebutted, "Well, sir, the e-mail indicated a small window for this, and I really need to complete my obligations in a timely matter."

Hesitantly, Dr. Berg let him in. "Have you had the chance to get all your documents in order, sir?" While observing the doctor, he was keen to the surroundings and noticed scant furniture, mostly consisting of a desk, small sofa, and table to its side. His highly innovative spy gadgets covered every possible chance to record sounds and sights. He had spy glasses on, a voice-recording pen in his pocket, and a video camera watch.

Peter excused himself for a minute and left to the bedroom apparently retrieving the papers. He asks the inspector to begin measuring to keep him actively away from his desk. Walter walks to the common area and scanned the room from his eyewear, and then he stood next to the computer and angled the watch at the screen. It only took five seconds to complete, and he left the area and acted like he was measuring the wall space.

Peter returned and said, "This should be everything you need in regard to the required documents. I see you are measuring the hall area as well. How much longer do you expect to be here?"

"Sir, should be ten mins in the most."

"Okay, great, I'm in the middle of something important. Do you need any of the color schemes at this time?"

"No, sir, that stuff can be communicated via e-mail or in person. Most people end up changing things during the process."

"Carry on, I'm gonna be over here at my desk."

He carried on indeed and managed to place a bug into the clock on the wall; in addition, Mr. Dunn wanted to catch a glimpse of his bedroom and asked Peter if he could use the restroom. Down the hall and to the left was the master suite, so he went to the hall bathroom but did not enter, shutting the door from the outside. The keyboard was clicking away, and he hurried to scan the bedroom, which was immaculate. For some reason, it was the only room in the house fully decorated and livable. One could surmise that he and Barbara probably spent alone time here.

There was a beautiful statue of James Barrie's creation *Peter Pan* standing a foot tall or better. Though it was placed appropriately in the room, the reasons for its existence plagued curiosity in the general's mind, aka Dunn. If it were Casey's, then the other bedroom belonging to his son seemed to be a more suitable place for observation. Enough time had elapsed and pushing his luck was risky, so he returned to the restroom and acted out the exit.

"Mr. Berg, I'm just curious. Will you be expanding the two bedrooms into one, or combining the living space with the secondary bedroom?"

Peter was annoyed and answered, "It's all in the blueprints."

"Yes, of course, I'll just be finishing here in one minute while I write down some information and take a few pictures." That wasn't necessary as the spy equipment had it all, but for Peter's sake, it needed to take place.

"That'll do it. I thank you for your time and good luck on your new place."

"You're welcome. Mr. Dunn, was it?"

"Yes."

As soon as he left, Peter e-mailed the COA president about the inspection by Mr. Dunn. Randolph removed his gear when he got into the car and drove away.

Scholls was dying to know what happened and asked, "Well, how'd it go?"

"As suspected, fairly smooth. I can't wait to find out about the document he had on the computer. He guarded my vision like a dragon."

"Then how'd you get the picture?"

"He had to go get the documents from another room, so I glided near the screen and captured the image on my watch."

"Badass! If I wasn't so interested in stem cells, I would follow in your footsteps. My friend and I have had to go undercover a few times."

Randolph laughed and then remembered studying a famous ball player from the 1920s named Moe Berg. "Now here's a Berg that might be of positive interest for you. He graduated from Princeton with a degree in modern languages and spoke at least twelve of them. Moe played ball for the Brooklyn Dodgers and the Chicago White Sox, but he wasn't content on just baseball; he also got graduate degrees in French and philosophy. On top of that and while playing ball, he attended Columbia and obtained a law degree. Eventually, Mr. Berg did spy work for the US government several years in Japan and Germany. He was considered the brainiest man in baseball.

"That's 360! I'm gonna read all about him one day. For sure, he's a Berg I can respect."

"We're heading to the FBI office here. They will take this and get back with me soon. Most likely in the morning. Let's get to the hotel afterward and relax. Have you heard from Garrett?"

"Yes, and it's unusually out of character, but he's sick and needs a lot of rest. Maybe his phone was on silent. I'm going there in the morning, hopefully before he leaves to that event, and check on his condition. Kipper is picking me up, and we have to get the bird."

"All right, sounds good. I don't know what to expect. He broke the law years back and has to be accountable for it, plus other details are percolating. I just feel bad for Mrs. Berg."

Scholls said, "Me too. She's a really a great lady. You'd like her."

"I'm sure I would. Let's hope nothing brings us together in a worse situation."

"True that," said Scholls, shaking his head slowly.

There were no other messages from Garrett, and this increased his uneasiness and concern for G's well-being, so he attempted to call the house phone, but no one answered that either. He left a voice mail in case Juanita checked it. "Hi, it's Scholls. I haven't spoken to Garrett all day and was wondering how is doing. Please let him know I called. Thank you."

Dr. Berg would later mock his message that night as he listened unmercifully and erased the request. Peter called his sweetheart one more time to say *je t'aime* and keep her at bay with the much-needed rest of her beloved son.

Dr. Berg made his way into Garrett's room and checked his condition by using the blood pressure fingertip method and observing his breathing and appearance. Peter got a pretty good indication his victim was in the final stages. He'd inject G with glucose in the morning and administer probably one more injection of the Parkinson's med, followed by some glucose later, leaving the vials of combination and syringe near his body to make it look like he gave a disoriented amount of glucose. The pharmacologically genius puppet master had alternated the right dosages to draw an obvious conclusion when he died. After all, he was godlike, and surely, no one would do an autopsy to prove otherwise because Garrett was admitted with plenty of evidence to support the ubiquitous illness.

CHAPTER 31

AM, p.m.—Carpe Diem

ONLY HOURS AWAY from his last breath lay the 6'2″ model, athlete, actor, and extremely well-liked 3.8 GPA. The family, best friend, and multiple other acquaintances had no notion of his true location or present life-threatening condition. Juanita arrived refreshed and earlier at the house around 10:00 a.m. with no inclination of G's situation. Garrett was in his Hum slouched over; he attempted to leave and get help after Peter assisted him to the vehicle, fully knowing this young man had the strength of an infant at best. In a worthwhile effect, Dr. Berg staged his room to appear as if he was out attending the movie's media event. There was a text sent to Juanita from G's phone that explained he was picked up by his agent, who in reality had repeatedly called a few times before Peter called him back the day prior; his curiosity was curtailed by the same information that Mr. Hyde provided to Barbara. She went about her daily household duties and heard the doorbell.

"Oh, hello, Senor Parker and Miss Kipper, please come in. Mr. Garrett is gone at his event."

Scholls answered, "Damn, we missed him. How are you doing? I miss your cooking. Ha! We're here to pick up Caesar."

"Well, he's in the study area. I checked on him earlier, and he seemed a bit noisy. He kept walking back and forth and talking about something. *Porque*, I have no idea what he said."

Kipper intervened, "He's probably nervous because he's usually around people most of the day, even in the kennels. He'll be fine. C'mon Scholls, lets go get him."

As soon as the bird heard Kipper's voice, he squawked in a tizzy and called out her name. It appeared he had been fed, but the water bowl was dirty, and Sherlock Parker noticed Caesar had the exact same paper from the last time he cleaned and lined the bottom of the cage. Scholls didn't want to alarm his girl, so he told her that Garrett was ill and didn't get a chance to clean it. But who fed him? Garrett would most likely have changed his water too.

They loaded up the other cage outside, empty the old lining, and remove the food and water for travel. Scholls headed to G's bedroom and left him a note while she tended to the bird. He couldn't understand why his friend had not text him back that morning. Something seemed off, so he inspected Garrett's personal bathroom. The shower area was dry. That was odd. The toothbrush was dry, and that was really out of the ordinary due to G's fanatical routine with brushing and flossing. Another thought crossed his mind; Garrett could have spent the night at his agent's house to make it easier. Inside, Scholls felt hurt because they shared everything. He couldn't remember a time since their friendship began that G didn't respond. He decided to get the bird back without fuss and returned that day if he did not hear anything by 4:00 p.m., even though Garrett was due to pick him up by 5:30 to 6:00 p.m., and no later than 8:00p.m. Coincidently, he remembered that his phone had Barb's number from a couple months back when she confirmed the dental information. He called her phone.

"Hello."

"Hi, Mrs. Berg, it's me, Scholls."

Barbara didn't recognize the number and said, "Oh, it's you. I almost didn't answer because I don't have the number programmed, and I hate solicitors."

"That's cool. Well, now you can program your 'other son's' number. Ha. I was calling because I've only heard from Garrett once since Christmas Day, and I'm really worried about how he is doing."

"Well, don't you fret, Peter has been tending to him. I heard from Garrett yesterday, and my husband gave him a sedative to sleep because of the incident. He is doing fine, and I will be home around nine tonight. Garrett went with his agent to the event and should be back by five or so. He gets so nervous about these functions."

By all means, this should have settled the ongoing anxiety; however, Scholls knew Dr. Berg had been shady in the past, so it's not comforting to know he was "tending" to the situation. With all due respect, G always shared his "nervousness" with Scholls, so this threw him a curve. Kipper took her sweetie back to the hotel where General Randolph was on the phone corresponding with authority.

"See you later, sexy." Kipper kissed his lips for a couple seconds. Pure bliss was all Scholls could feel. "Bye, dear, I mean, babe."

"Oh, hey, I forgot. Tally and I keep in touch, and she hasn't heard from Garrett in two days."

This made Scholls feel a bit better, and not as rejected, so he shared the latest conversation he had with Barbara. "Okay, I'll let her know, bye, sweets." Scholls was experiencing bipolar emotions at that moment: Kipper's affections and G's deflections.

"Hey, Unc, when are you planning to go back inside the condo?"

"Around midnight. Why?"

"It's just that I checked Garrett's bedroom and bathroom, and it appeared to be suspicious. He always brushes his teeth, which I know for sure, and the bristles were dry. The shower floor was dry. Can you slip over there today in a bit? I'd feel better."

"I'm still waiting on some information about Berg's computer. I'll go about 2:00 p.m. when he isn't there. We've been monitoring his steps, and he's fairly regimented, though the holidays have changed his schedule some. I have the key right here."

"Thanks, I'm just wondering what's going on and it's eating me alive."

Randolph Parker was completely confident with his nephew's intuition and headed to the condo on another spy mission. This time, he would be able to move out and about scrutinizing the entire contents at 222 Cloverleaf, unit 5. "Mr. Dunn" was no stranger to being stealth and dynamic. He walked to the door and entered with no problems whatsoever; it is true, he had complete cooperation from the COA and the law. The first item he went to was the Peter Pan statue that aroused his interest from the second he laid eyes on it. Underneath was a small key that appeared to be for a fire safety box.

Next, he scoured the master bedroom for the closet and found three of those boxes toward the back. This doctor was so incredibly neat, the clothing was arranged by designers in alphabetical order, followed in each style of clothing, from light to dark, such as short sleeves, short sleeves with collars, long sleeves, vests, jackets, pants, shorts, ties, etc. His shoes were enclosed inside a custom-built rack that opened with a soft close fashion requiring no electricity or batteries. Each drawer had glass in the front which allowed you to see the actual pair inside. The tie rack was automatic and held each tie the same as his clothes, except that it dispensed the tie with the touch of a button. Every hanger was custom-made, and he had an area for each cufflink. and watches. Well, let's just say he was the Imelda Marcos for them. The socks were also in a custom-built automatic dispenser that hung them neatly avoiding wrinkles.

In behavioral profiling, these often are signs of extreme neuroticism via obsessive-compulsive disorder and perfectionism. They were characterized by anxiety, fear, moodiness, worry, envy, frustration, loneliness, and jealousy. People with dissociative personality disorder tend to have higher measures of neuroticism.

Randolph learned that a highly respected psychologist named Hans Eysenck, PhD, DSc, did several studies that revealed high levels of neuroticism greatly affect the sympathetic nervous system's primary function—to stimulate the body's "fight or flight" response. This is the physiological reaction that happens in a response to a perceived harmful event, attack, or survival threat.

Before Eysenck's death in 1997, he was the most frequently cited living psychologist in *peer-reviewed* scientific literature. Peer-reviewed information had the highest standards of quality and scientific validity. Dr. Berg was mostly definitely neurotic to the oomph degree.

The general's instincts were working. "Let's try this one. It's the farthest out and likely to belong to this key." He turned it. "Got it!" For several minutes, he left no stone unturned and pulled papers out in a systematic style. There was also a small box inside, and when he opened it to see the contents, he found labels that looked to be kinds found on vials for blood. He also had labels that looked like ones for bottles used with injecting solutions, and at the bottom of the safety box were several disposable syringes. He confiscated the contents and looked elsewhere. In his desk drawer was a picture of Garrett, Barbara, and Thommason Pierce at some kind of event. It appeared to be a celebration of some sort by the decor in the background. There was a *D* drawn into Garrett and Thom's forehead, so he wasn't sure of a conclusive meaning, but he was sure it wasn't the actions of a child. He immediately got a sick feeling that it signified the elimination of these two, since Thom was already deceased and Garrett had increasing issues with his health. The anxiety his nephew harbored for his friend's fate was forthcoming.

The most unusual thing he found was in the refrigerator. It had stored vials of blood in a container and they were marked A positive. Was Peter using this blood for something? Of course he was. Without freezing, it typically has a seven-day efficacy when testing for a complete blood count. This meant he had plans for its use within forty-eight hours because the information indicated the vials had been placed five days ago. Now, Randolph had reason to believe there was foul play in progress.

He desperately wanted to open his PC and try to get into anything he could find useful, so he attempted to log in with different passwords, but they all failed. Surely, tomorrow was a new day, and he could confiscate it for evidence should the agency need it. He carefully covered his trail of detection and took off. Peter was still at the faculty building working on his grant. Next, he would head to the hospital and make rounds, giving him more time to avoid direct contact with Garrett. No doubt, he knew this would be a great alibi if he ever needed it.

What baffled the agent most was Garrett's attendance at the movie event as evidenced by Barbara's confirmation with Scholls. If he was too sick, he would not be there. The neurologist was up to no good, but when would Peter execute his plan? The general had to save this kid's life no matter what. He headed back to the agency to corroborate all the findings between himself and the officials.

Antsy is, as antsy does, and Scholls could not sit around much more, so he called a taxi and returned to Parkerville. Simultaneously, he sent his uncle a message to hang tight as he prepared for Garrett's arrival. Before he could even start packing, Kipper called about her bird.

"Hi, Scholls, every since Caesar has been home, he keeps repeating something really strange, and I can't make it out. It's something like *duhsays* or *desays* or *de cees*. And then he says, 'Garrett.' He also said another odd thing, '*Green eyes gone…green eyes gone.*'"

"Really? I wonder what it means. Thanks, honey, I'll call ya later. I'm waiting on Garrett, but I'll try to figure it out."

"Good luck, it's driving us crazy. Talk to you then."

EPILOGUE

S HERLOCK PARKER PUT his thinking cap on and pondered for several minutes before realizing that most of the bird's last two days would have been more likely to hear Peter's voice due to Garrett's illness, Barb's and Juanita's absence, and his departure on Christmas Day. He conceived that the only "green eyes" around belong to his best friend. Sherlock Parker's brain was in high gear. *Was the bird noticing that G was gone? C'mon, that would be highly impractical.* Logic prevailed again, and the only obvious conclusion was that he mimicked what he heard. Why would Peter refer to "green eyes" and "gone"? Then there was the other word Caesar repeated. He checked his phone by entering every spelling he could possibly think of. Nothing made sense, unless perhaps *gone* meant permanently gone. "Oh crap, maybe it's a foreign word. That's it! Peter speaks French." Scholls quickly typed in several spellings with the two letters of *d* and *e* combined phonetically and finally hit on the word *disparu*. "Okay, let me see any French synonyms for this word." As he examined the list, his eye immediately froze on the word *extinct*. The pounding of his heart practically burst through the seams of his shirt, and the poor kid from Westward Trailer Park took a deep breath as he typed in the pronunciation for *death* in French—"décès."

He screamed, "Garrett, Garrett, oh my god! That bastard! You crazy, ruthless, son of a bitch!"

The Hum wasn't expected for another hour and a half, but there was no time to wait, and Scholls called a taxi to the cross section of Hollister and Lancaster. He grabbed his savings out from the metal box and hauled ass. His face was sad, and he started panicking over and over for his friend's life. How could a well-respected doctor with pretty much all that life has to offer be this evil? He couldn't bear to think of losing his friend, his best friend for life, and if by some fluke, he made it too late, God forbid, all hell would break loose and Dr. Berg's fate would literally be in Scholls's hands. He visioned the doctor's last breath from strangulation.

On the corner stood a golden-haired boy with more determination than anyone ever knew existed. The cab pulled up and was quick to leave the site, heading toward Huntingdon Cove. "I don't mean to sound rude, mister, but I need you to go as fast as possible. This is urgent. My friend is really sick."

"Oooh, okay, we put the metal to petal," says Ahmed. What normally took an average of twenty minutes was trimmed by five. Scholls had already asked for the estimation of cost, and the driver quoted him a ball park of thirty dollars. There's no time to make change, and he threw two twenty-dollar bills in the seat and jumped out of the taxi.

Originally, he was going to have the driver stay, but he remembered where G kept his spare key for the Hum and wasn't going to be deterred by not having his face on some laminated card. He rang the doorbell and persistently knocked in an effort to get someone's attention. Garrett's face would be a welcomed sight, and there would be no need for shame if his presumptions were wrong. He didn't get that lucky and saw what has become a good face at the door.

"Oh, hello, Mr. Scholls, come." Juanita barely got to talk when the distraught young man rushed in and demanded to know where Garrett was.

"I'm sorry for my tone. Please, Juanita, have you seen Garrett?"

"Oh, no, Mr. Scholls. He is at a special party for the movie. *Porque*, his agent picked him up."

Scholls was frantic and said, "Are you sure? I gotta check his room!"

Juanita replied, "Look, Senor Garrett's *vehiculo* in the garage." She pointed to the monitor. That caused him some relief, but he rallied through the house anyway.

"There must be an address somewhere." Juanita helped him look around, and their search was unsuccessful. In complete desperation, Scholls went to the bottom drawer and removed G's spare key so he could check the Hummer for any other clues. "Be right back!" He ran like an Olympian and opened the door, not expecting to see his friend in a lifeless manner.

"Garrett! Garrett! Can you hear me, buddy?"

Scholls checked his breathing after receiving no response and placed his finger on the carotid artery, which had very little pulsation. This meant his heart was still pumping, and resuscitation wasn't needed. Garrett was clammy, and he looked rigid; if it weren't for the fact he had been slouched in an awkward position, one might assume he was just sleeping. Scholls screamed for Juanita to call 911, but in a panic, he decided to take it to a whole new level and yelled for the caretaker to bring the V12 key. "What's happening, son?" Mr. Newhart saw Garrett's body and helped him try to revive G.

"Screw this! Get the key to the Zagato. I'm taking him to the hospital right now!" They loaded him in, and Mr. Newhart raised the garage so he could exit. The vehicle only had two seats, and he directed the caretaker to have Juanita call Barb.

"Hold on, G. All that driving we did on the video is about to become real! I know, shit, I don't have a license, but who the hell cares anyway at this point? Hold on, dude. This could be bumpy!" *Vrooom...eeerrrrkkk...vrooom...eeerrrrkkk* was pretty much all you could hear for the next few minutes until they arrived at the emergency area where the Zagato made a distinct impression. Scholls honked the horn repeatedly to get the attention of some resident doctors who were standing just outside the hospital. "Help me, man. He's really bad, really, really bad."

One of the residents ran inside to get the ball rolling and informed the emergency desk of its newest arrival. The other resident said, "A stretcher is on its way son."

This wasn't good enough for the future stem cell specialist, and he replied, "You don't understand. Seconds count!" Scholls grabbed G and put him across his shoulder and then ran into the hospital.

Uncle Randolph had already been in touch with the hospital administrator and a few of the staff to inform them of their neurologist whose code of ethics no longer mattered. The bug put in Berg's condo revealed more information that confirmed their suspicions he was going to kill Garrett. He'd sent his nephew the text, but in all the commotion, Scholls had no idea.

To avoid total confusion and lack of organizational strategy, the staff was instructed to act normal and not give any signs of Dr. Peter Berg's presence other than what they usually did. The general planned on arresting him in a very private area of the hospital to avoid pandemonium within the facility. Berg was being tailed and on his way soon. The guardian angels must have been working overtime because Garrett Errington Pierce was hustled to the ER operating room. Given his celebrity status, people would clear the floor anyway, but his head was downward and his face was not visible. Scholls must remain outside the area and wait.

Randolph had one of the nurses send Dr. Berg a text that "his older boy" had been admitted to the ER, and on the speakers, the hospital announced, "Code blue, code blue, ER," and the alarm went off.

Peter was livid. As he drove, the doctor said in a low-pitched, controlled voice, "Je ne crois pas que ce!" I don't believe this! "He made it here? Okay, calm down, you have the upper hand here. I don't keep potassium vials for nothing. Hopefully the little mommy's boy will die anyway. His organs are jeopardized. I can't believe this happened!"

Undercover agents were everywhere in civilian and staff mode. Now, Peter must make it look as if *he* was winning a movie award. Randolph was near by and instructed the agents not to react until he gave them the signal. Barbara was over an hour away and not likely to see her son's plausible death. Inside the op, everyone methodically responded to the situation.

"Seventeen years old…Berg's son…Give me a CBC and call Dr. Harper stat!" The nurse pulled up Garrett's information, and the ER doctor ordered type A positive blood from the bank. "We need emergency release of RBC. Get the form completed!" He has the anesthesiologist sign the form. "What are his vitals?"

A resident announced, "Hypertension…unstable 150/90…tachycardia, 136. He's jaundice."

A nurse said, "ECG up."

The ER doctor said, "Give me his Q waves stat! I need his CBC now. Hematocrit…globin…with direct Coombs…"

The resident yelled, "His spleen is enlarged!"

Fifteen minutes later, they received the RML report from the lab, and the resident announced, "MCV-reticulocytosis…27.6…Dr. Harper is here!"

Dr. Harper, the transfusionist, asked, "Have we got the blood yet?"

The nurse replied, "It's on its way."

The resident said, "His LDH is 520…decreased hapto…less than 15."

The ER doctor said, "We have DI hemolysis!"

Harper ordered, "Start the corticosteroids and 50,000 microL platelets. Hurry!"

The nurse informed, "It's here!"

They continued monitoring his vitals, and Harper transfused Garrett with the A positive that was on record. G showed no signs of improvement and in fact looked to be getting worse. Outside, Scholls begged forcefully, and a nurse shook her head. "Isn't stable."

SP raised his voice, "What's wrong?"

Randolph said, "He isn't responding to the transfusion, son."

Scholls pleaded, "Are you sure he has the right type?"

The nurse replied, "Son, we have it in the system. We're sure. I can't relay anything else."

Scholls pleaded, "Please, please, I'm begging you, ma'am. What is it…the type?" He remembered when Garrett showed him the sports physical report from last summer, and he positively saw type O on it. Scholls raised his voice, "Damn it, he's type O. Are you sure he is getting type O!"

The nurse replied, "Calm down. Dr. Berg has taken great measures to make sure everything is right. He's type A positive."

Randolph showed his badge and whispered in her ear. She rushed to the operatory, and the inop phone rang informing the surgeon of this new information. They called the blood bank and demanded type O be delivered ASAP. Scholls Marcel Parker's incredible attention to detail was like no other. Just as Scholls didn't question his uncle's ability as an agent, Randolph didn't question his nephew's memory.

"You're a hell of a friend to Garrett." Scholls walked the halls in a fast pace as he waited the fate of his best friend. His clearance to be near the area was granted by the feds. They needed him to be present when the bad doctor arrived. Randolph knew Scholls's presence would aggravate Peter, and he wanted him in a vulnerable position. It was apparent they had a very sick, psychotic individual on their hands.

As exaggerated as he was, Peter Berg could stay cool as a cucumber in traumatic situations. All eyes were secretly upon the neurologist as he walked in like a bat out of hell to "find out" about "his son."

He ran toward the ER and asked the nurse, who was strategically placed and aware of the catastrophe, "I'm scrubbing. Get my stuff." He saw Scholls and said, "What's he doing here? Get him out of here!" Peter's face was lit up, and his eyes began fluttering. Things were about to change dramatically when Randolph approached the twisted physician. He took Berg by the arm and guided him to a more private area, while Scholls and six agents followed them.

"It's over Scott."

Peter turned his head to the general and said, "What did you call me?"

Randolph replied, "Scott Farrington, you're under arrest." He carefully lowered his voice and informed him of his Miranda rights.

"You have the right to remain silent. Anything you say, can and will be used against you in a court of law. You have the right to an attorney. If you cannot afford an attorney, one will be appointed to represent you before any questioning if you wish. You can decide at any time to exercise these rights and not answer any questions or make any statements. Do you understand each of these rights as I have explained to you?"

Peter answered in a high pitch, "Yes, sir."

"Having these rights in mind, do you wish to talk with us now?"

Peter answered again in a youthful pitch, "No, sir, I think I need to talk with my aunt and uncle first. Can I talk to my friend before we go?"

Peter's pitch had reverted back to the high sound he made with what Scholls discovered he did while talking about his childhood friend. It seemed to substantiate a good feeling where Paul was concerned. Randolph signaled everyone by his eyes. One solid blink meant "no action." Two repeatedly meant "take action." He blinked once, and they watched as he instantly began to transform into a younger persona. Scott turned to Scholls and at first saw a silhouette without a face. No one was sure what he was doing, but no one was in harm so they let him continue.

The silhouette faded, and Peter smiled big as he believed he was seeing his friend Paul. "Hey, Paul, I'm so happy to see you! I thought you were dead. Remember when I was at your bedside? I didn't know they revived you. They took me away. It's all gonna be

fine now. I'm so happy again. You're my best friend. I missed you."
He reached forward and embraced Scholls for several seconds.

Talk about a chilling moment, all ears and eyes could not veer away from the doctor, now youthful, who resurrected his friend's life. The lawful spectators stayed motionless and heard him out. He started questioning something from his friend's perspective, exactly like he did in the times he spoke aloud in distraught; though, this time, the tone was pleasant. Scholls stayed completely still from the start as he witnessed the mental disease unfold. He would answer Scott's questions.

"Did you miss me, Paul?"

"Yes, I have."

"Did you send me any signs all this time?"

"I was always there when you were upset."

"Oh my god, I didn't know that was you talking to me. I thought it was someone else trying to sabotage my plan. It was you all along. Oh, please forgive me. I'm terribly sorry. I love you. You're always gonna be my friend."

There was complete silence. You *could* hear a pin drop. "Paul, why are they arresting me? Can you come with us?"

Scholls replied, "You've done something bad, and I can't help you at this time."

"You mean my parents?" Now it caught everybody's attention. The fire was an accident by ruling. What did he mean?

"Scott, you need rest. Go with these gentlemen and we will talk later. Okay?"

"Okay, Paul. When will I see you again?"

"Soon…very soon."

"Let's go ride our bikes when this is over."

"Good-bye, Scott."

Scholls was numb, and he watched as they escorted him from the hospital without hand cuffing his wrists to avoid the onlooker's reactions. He wasn't going anywhere with seven of them present. Outside was plenty of local enforcement.

Barbara had called Scholls's phone several times, and he stepped away to return the call as he nervously awaited word of Garrett's status. A black dark-tinted car was waiting outside to take Scott away. Mr. Manning came inside to console his daughter's boyfriend. He let them know Barbara was not far.

As the car drove off, Scott made one last request to the agents with a high-pitched tone. They looked at each other, and Randolph said, "Okay, Scott, what is it?"

He replied, "Can I ask a favor of you guys before we go to the station? I need to go get my duffel bag, and it's just a few miles from here, I believe. Would it be possible for me to get it?"

THE END

CPSIA information can be obtained
at www.ICGtesting.com
Printed in the USA
FFOW01n0645280916
28028FF